D1624126

MARGARET TRUMAN'S
EXPERIMENT IN MURDER

BY MARGARET TRUMAN

First Ladies
Bess W. Truman
Souvenir
Women of Courage
Harry S Truman
Letters from Father: The Truman Family's
Personal Correspondences
Where the Buck Stops
White House Pets
The President's House

IN THE CAPITAL CRIMES SERIES

Murder in Foggy Bottom
Murder at the Library of Congress
Murder at the Watergate
Murder in the House
Murder at the National Gallery
Murder on the Potomac
Murder at the Pentagon
Murder in the Smithsonian
Murder at the National Cathedral
Murder at the Kennedy Center
Murder in the CIA
Murder in Georgetown
Murder at the FBI
Murder on Embassy Row
Murder in the Supreme Court

MARGARET TRUMAN'S

EXPERIMENT IN MURDER

A CAPITAL CRIMES NOVEL

▶▶▶ DONALD BAIN ◀◀◀

Doubleday Large Print
Home Library Edition

A TOM DOHERTY ASSOCIATES BOOK · NEW YORK

MARGARET TRUMAN'S EXPERIMENT IN MURDER: A CAPITAL CRIMES NOVEL

A Forge Book
Published by Tom Doherty Associates, LLC
175 Fifth Avenue
New York, NY 10010

Forge® is a registered trademark of Tom Doherty Associates, LLC.

ISBN 978-1-62090-630-9

Printed in the United States of America

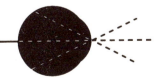

**This Large Print Book carries the
Seal of Approval of N.A.V.H.**

In the French poet Jean de la Fontaine's fable "The Monkey and the Cat," the cat, duped by the monkey, uses its paw to pull chestnuts from a hot fire, burning its paw in the process while the monkey happily gobbles up the chestnuts.

"A cat's paw" has come to mean one used unwittingly by another to accomplish his own purposes.

It happens in Washington, D.C., every day.

No assassination instructions should ever be written or recorded.

—FROM *A STUDY OF ASSASSINATION,*
A CIA TRAINING MANUAL, 1954

MARGARET TRUMAN'S

EXPERIMENT IN MURDER

CHAPTER 1

WASHINGTON, D.C.

He'd crossed Virginia Avenue a thousand times since taking an apartment across the street from his office three years ago. It meant jaywalking—one summons in the three years, a small price to pay for not having to trudge to a corner crossing, especially in the sweltering heat of summer in the nation's capital. His morning sprint across the broad avenue involved more than avoiding a ticket, however. Dodging speeding cars was a greater hurdle, with more dire consequences. He'd come to consider it a contest, a test of his agility and quickness of foot, a game he'd always won.

*   *   *

His move to the apartment followed the divorce from Jasmine, his wife of twenty-two years. Until the breakup he'd commuted from their home in Chevy Chase to his downtown office, where he spent the day listening to the trials and tribulations of his patients as they reclined on his couch, a box of tissues always within easy reach, and poured out their troubles to Dr. Mark Sedgwick.

"Dr. Mark," as his patients called him, at least those with enough tenure on his couch to be comfortable with it, graduated from the University of California Medical School in San Francisco in 1964. He'd aspired to become an orthopedic surgeon, but his manual dexterity was judged lacking by his professors. They suggested a medical specialty demanding less physical challenge. What could be less physical than psychiatry?

He wasn't disappointed at this shift in direction his medical studies had taken. He quickly discovered that he enjoyed delving into the human psyche more than peering into spinal columns or replacing arthritic knees and hips. *What* prompted people to do things became infinitely more interesting to him than *how* they did them.

He'd intended to do his residency in San Francisco, where he'd been born, and to establish a practice there. But an offer from the George Washington University Department of Psychiatry in Washington, D.C., lured him east. Fresh with an M.D. after his name—and now better able to secure restaurant reservations as Dr. Sedgwick—he would have followed through on his intention to return to San Francisco. But he met Jasmine, a nurse at the hospital.

Jasmine Smith—her parents chose the more exotic first name Jasmine to counterbalance her mundane last name—set her sights on the handsome resident Mark Sedgwick from the day he walked in. Her feminine charms were evident front and back, but it was her wide, ready smile that derailed his plan to return home. He accepted a staff position at the hospital, and they were married after a relatively short courtship. Two children later, a boy and a girl, they bought the house in Chevy Chase and settled into what was to be blissful domesticity. But the bliss soon came off the rose, to mix metaphors, and they grew increasingly apart, especially when Sedgwick resigned from the hospital to open a private practice on Virginia Avenue N.W. The pressure of getting an office up and running, coupled with a growing involvement with a psychiatric institute in San Francisco, meant little time at home for the good doctor and led to the eventual dissolution of the marriage, which Sedgwick choreographed in order to, as he told Jasmine, minimize the hurt to all. He was, after all, a psychiatrist.

Now, three years later, he began his day as he always did. Sedgwick was very much a creature of habit—routine was essential. His alarm went off at seven twenty, its backup buzzer sounding at seven thirty. Coffee had been ground and mixed the night before, and the coffeemaker was timed to begin brewing at seven fifteen. Because it was summer, Sedgwick took his coffee and a bowl of yogurt with mixed fruit and nuts to the balcony of his third-floor apartment, shady in the morning before the sun swung around to make it uncomfortably hot. He downloaded that day's *Washington Post* to his BlackBerry and read the news while eating.

At eight o'clock he was in the shower, dried off by eight fifteen, dressed by eight forty-five, and on his way downstairs at eight fifty-five. His first patient would arrive at nine twenty for her forty-minute session.

He prepared to cross the avenue the way he always did after having received his jaywalking ticket a year earlier, looking up and down the street for signs of the police. Seeing none, he stepped off the curb and took in the traffic. It wasn't unusually busy at that hour, men and women driving to work in the city's major industry, government and all its elements. He waited until a stream of cars had passed and there was a break in the traffic. The sun to his left blinded him as he looked in that direction, then he observed the situation to his right. It looked good, and he started across.

He was halfway to the other side when he became aware of a car bearing down on his right. He hadn't seen it, but he sensed it. He turned in that direction, and his mouth opened and a prolonged "Nooo" came from it. The vehicle, a white sedan, raced toward him, going at least sixty miles per hour, probably faster. Because he stood in the middle of the avenue, the driver could have opted to go either in front of him or behind. But the car straddled the median stripe, its engine revving loudly, no sound of brakes being applied, no sign of trying to stop. It struck Sedgwick head on with a thud that was heard up and down the street and sent him flying onto the hood, his head crashing into the windshield and creating a spiderweb of cracks on the driver's side. Sedgwick's body was propelled off. He hit the pavement and tumbled thirty feet before coming to rest, a pool of blood oozing from his crushed skull and creating a crimson circle around it.

CHAPTER 2

Shrieks were heard up and down Virginia Avenue. People turned from the scene and covered their eyes with their hands. Some cried. "Call for help" was a chorus. Cars came to a screeching halt to avoid the body.

The 911 calls poured in to police operators, some from the street, others from people who'd witnessed the scene through their office windows. Within what seemed like only a few seconds, uniformed officers in patrol cars arrived and took control of the swelling crowd. Other police vehicles joined them. Virginia Avenue was shut down in both directions. An occasional horn blew as though that would miraculously open the street. An officer walked up to one horn blower's car that was only a dozen feet from Sedgwick's body and said, "You blow that freakin' horn again, pal, and you're toast."

Some of the officers stood over the body. There was no need to press fingertips against the neck to seek a pulse. The victim's life was all over the pavement, bits of white brain matter, bones jutting through skin, and blood glistening in the morning sun. An ambulance with two EMTs joined the tragic scene, followed by an unmarked car. Two detectives got out.

"Hit-and-run?"

"Yeah."

"Driver just took off?"

"Seems so."

One of the detectives surveyed the crowd. "See if anybody can describe the car that hit the guy," he told an officer. "Whoever's car it was gotta be mangled, too."

"Got an ID on him?" asked the second detective.

None of the uniformed cops wanted to admit that they'd been reluctant to touch the grotesquely battered body. A detective bent down and fumbled for Sedgwick's wallet in his rear pants pocket. He stood and went through its contents. "He's a doc," he said to no one in particular. "Sedgwick. Mark Sedgwick." He consulted another card and looked across the street to a four-story office building. "He's got an office over there," he said, pointing. He turned. "Lives in that apartment building."

Sedgwick's body was photographed from every angle, as was the street in the direction from which the car had come. It had rained earlier, and close-up photos of tire tread marks were also taken. Measurements were made, although there wasn't much to measure aside from where the initial impact had occurred to where the body had come to rest. The area was searched for anything that might have fallen from the car, but nothing was found aside from a piece of clear plastic that presumably had come from part of a headlight. While one detective dictated into a small handheld tape recorder, the other went to the sidewalk where officers questioned bystanders.

"Anything?" he asked.

"A lot of people saw it but don't remember much about the vehicle. That woman over there, though, says that she saw the whole thing and can describe the car."

The detective went to her, introduced himself, and asked what she'd seen.

She spoke rapidly, and he asked her to slow down.

"You say you can describe the car?" he said.

"I think so."

He hated hearing "I think so."

"Go ahead," he said.

"It was white, a white car."

"What kind? A sedan? SUV?"

"I don't know much about cars. This one looked like any other car, normal, you could say, with four doors."

"A sedan," he said.

"Yes, a sedan. Like my parents drive. Just . . . just a normal white car."

"I don't suppose you caught a glimpse of the plate."

"It had the American flag on it, I know that much."

"D.C. plate," he said.

"Yes. I see them all the time in the city. I live in Virginia."

"What else did you notice?"

"Her."

"Her?"

"The driver."

"It was a woman? You're sure?"

"Oh, yes, very sure. It all happened fast, but it was a woman driving."

"Can you describe her?"

"Not very much. She was blond, though. I saw that much."

"Did she look like she was trying to avoid hitting the victim?"

A man interjected himself into the conversation. "Hell, no, she didn't try to miss him. Aimed right at him, was going like a bat out of hell. Looked like she wanted to hit the poor bastard. His head shattered the windshield. At that speed—"

The detective thanked them and went to his car, where he called in. Sedgwick's body was placed into the ambulance and driven away. Horns began blowing again.

"Get some cones on this mess," a detective ordered an officer. "Divert traffic around it until it's cleaned up."

The detectives moved their car to the curb in front of Sedgwick's office building, got out, and pushed through a knot of people.

"Hell of a way to die," one said as they waited for the elevator.

"Is there a good way?"

"You think what the witnesses said is true, that some blonde ran the doc over on purpose?"

"Maybe a patient. He was a shrink. Maybe he got too chummy with a blond patient, crossed over the line. They've got rules about that."

"About what?"

"Having sex with a patient."

"Do they? They should."

"Yeah, they do. Not that shrinks care about rules. I heard about a shrink who left his wife to marry a patient. Happens all the time, I hear."

"Well," his colleague said as the doors opened, "if that's the case here, maybe the blonde was his wife, not his patient. A woman scorned. Hell of a way to die."

CHAPTER

3

Betty Martinez had worked as Mark Sedg-wick's receptionist for seven years. There wasn't much to do as a psychiatrist's receptionist, so she assumed a variety of other roles, including insurance expert, bookkeeper, travel agent, and personal gofer. Sedgwick traveled a lot, often on the spur of the moment, which meant not only booking his flights, hotels, and rental cars but also salving patients who had to be canceled at the last minute. Most of his trips were to San Francisco, where he often met with others at the Lightpath Psychiatric Clinic, about which she knew little except that it demanded a great deal of his time.

Her dusky complexion and last name testified to her Hispanic American heritage, mother American, father Puerto Rican, no siblings, and half a degree in business administration. Lack of money had led to dropping out of school after her sophomore year. Her hair was so black and dense that it might have been mistaken for a high-priced wig. She was just a few sit-ups and fast-food meals away from sliding into overweight.

On this morning she'd arrived at the office at eight thirty, a little earlier than usual, and had settled at her desk in the reception room. It was a good job. Dr. Sedgwick was generous with pay and gifts. The office suite was at the rear of the building. She would have preferred an office at the front, where larger windows let in more light and afforded a view across Virginia Avenue. The few times she'd brought it up, Sedgwick had explained that the building's rear was quieter, a better setting for seeing patients. It wasn't her place to debate it, and so she didn't. Still, it would have been nice to be in the front.

Except for this morning.

The two detectives entered the area and one flashed his badge. "This is Dr. Sedgwick's office?" he asked.

"Yes." Having two detectives arrive unexpectedly unnerved Betty, and the quiver in her voice mirrored it. "Is something wrong?" she asked.

"I'm afraid so, ma'am. You work for Dr. Sedgwick?"

"Yes. I'm his receptionist."

"I'm afraid there's been an accident."

"To the doctor?"

"Yes, ma'am. Were you expecting him this morning?"

"Yes. I saw that he was running a little late but . . . is he ill?"

"He was struck by a car in front of the building, ma'am. He's dead."

She burst into tears as the door opened and the morning's first patient, a heavily made-up middle-aged woman wearing a tight beige pantsuit and huge gold hoop earrings that bounced off her shoulders entered. She looked at the sobbing Betty, then at the two men in suits. "What's happened?" she asked.

"There's been an accident, ma'am."

"I have an appointment with Dr. Sedgwick. Betty, what's going on?"

"Dr. Sedgwick is—" Her sobs muffled her words.

"I'm afraid you'll have to leave," said a detective. "The doctor won't be seeing patients today."

Confusion was written all over the woman's face. She started to ask more questions but took a hint from his stern expression and left. When she was gone, one of the detectives perched on the edge of Betty's desk. He placed a hand on her shoulder and said, "I know this is a shock to you, but do you think you can pull yourself together to answer some questions?"

"I . . . think . . . so."

A few tissues later, and a trip to the bathroom to splash cold water on her face, she returned.

"We'll need a list of the doctor's patients," said a detective.

"A list? I can't give you that."

"I know, I know, there's doctor-patient confidentiality involved. But it appears that what happened to the doctor might not have been an accident. The driver—she left the scene—might have deliberately struck him."

"Why would someone do that?"

"Can we have a list?"

"No. I mean, I'd get in trouble if I did that."

"We can get a warrant." He knew that few judges would issue a warrant for a doctor's patient list based upon the *assumption* that the doctor might have been a victim of a crime, but the threat sometimes worked. It didn't with Betty Martinez.

He shifted the conversation.

"Was the doctor married?"

"Divorced."

"Where's his ex-wife live? And kids."

She gave him the address and phone number in Chevy Chase.

"He have a girlfriend?"

She managed a smile. "A few."

"What about his patients? He get involved with any of them?"

"Involved? You mean romantically?"

He nodded.

"I don't think so."

He hated "I don't think so."

But she *did* know. She'd become aware over the years of working for him that he had become sexually involved with a few of his patients. It bothered her, but she wasn't in a position to challenge him about it.

The detective's cocked head invited her to answer again.

"No," she said, "I don't think so."

Nothing to be gained by pressing her.

"He have any enemies, you know, people who got mad at him for something he did or didn't do in his practice, somebody who held a grudge?"

"I don't think so. I mean, I don't know of anyone."

Their questioning of her lasted another fifteen minutes. Their final query was, "Do any of his patients have blond hair?"

This brought forth an incredulous, pained laugh from her. "Lots of them do," she said.

After suggesting that she call all the patients to alert them that the doctor wasn't available—and informing her that other officers would be back later that day to ask more questions and to examine the office—they left.

"He was screwing patients," one said as they drove back to headquarters.

"Looks that way."

"You figure that's the direction we go?"

The driver shrugged and swerved to avoid a bicyclist. "Idiot!" he muttered.

"The world's full of them."

"If the good doctor was playing kissy-face with his patients, the world has one less idiot."

"I'm hungry."

"Me, too. Dunkin' Donuts?"

CHAPTER

4

After jelly donuts and coffee, the detectives who'd been called to the accident scene contacted their superior and were instructed to go to Sedgwick's apartment, seal it off, and wait for Forensics to show up. They secured the cooperation of the building's superintendent and now sat in the living room, where they discussed their confusion over the order they'd been given.

"They're treating this like a crime scene," one said. "Doesn't make sense. The guy was just a shrink in private practice who got run over."

"Deliberately."

"Even so."

"Homicide is homicide," his partner said. "Doesn't matter *how* somebody kills somebody. Maybe there's something in here that'll point to the mysterious blonde with the heavy foot."

His colleague got up and perused a floor-to-ceiling bookcase, then went to the window and looked out over a pocket park. "Nice place the doc had."

"There's good money in treating head cases," said his partner, who'd left the living room and gone to a small second bedroom used by Sedgwick as an office. He slipped on a pair of latex gloves, sat at the desk and opened its drawers, fingered their contents, and closed them. A desk calendar contained handwritten dates and times of its owner's October schedule—lunch dates, a dental appointment, reminders of TV shows he'd wanted to watch, a Saturday notation "Day with kids," and other indications of his life slipping by. He looked up at the second detective, who stood in the doorway. "You figure they've notified the doc's ex-wife?"

"I hope we don't catch it," was the

response. "Petrewski enjoys catching next-of-kin notification. You know that about him? He's like a ghoul."

Their conversation was ended by the arrival of the Forensics unit. As the newcomers set about scouring the apartment, the two detectives who'd secured the place went to their car and called in. Ten minutes later, they sat with their superior at headquarters on Indiana Avenue.

Their boss listened to the results of their findings at the accident scene. When they'd finished, he said, "We ran a background check on the deceased. He had a top secret security clearance."

"I thought he was in private practice," a detective said.

"That's right. And he also had a top secret security clearance. Langley ran his clearance twelve years ago. It was updated last year."

One of the detectives laughed. "A shrink *and* a spook," he said.

His boss didn't laugh. "He was a consultant to the CIA's"—he looked at a note—"the CIA's Medical and Psychological Analysis Center. I want you to canvass people in his apartment and office buildings. Maybe someone picked up on a relationship with a blond woman, heard them argue, things like that. It's a long shot, but so is finding a white sedan with D.C. plates. I have people working on that now, checking MV records and repair shops. We're treating this as a homicide based upon what your eyewitnesses said. They seem to know what they were talking about?"

They nodded in unison.

"What about the ex-wife?" one asked as they prepared to leave. "She been notified yet?"

"As we speak."

"Maybe she's a blonde."

"Or a brunette wearing a blond wig," said their boss. "Get going. I have a feeling that this is going to heat up."

Jasmine Smith-Sedgwick wasn't a blonde, at least not that day. She wasn't a beautiful woman; handsome would be a more apt description. Her figure was nice, though, and she was tall, with reddish hair worn long. Her jeans and sweatshirt fitted her the way they should.

Two detectives pulled up behind a black

Mercedes in the driveway of her Chevy Chase home and rang the bell.

"Yes?" she said.

A badge was shown. "Your former husband was killed this morning by a hit-and-run driver," a detective said.

"Oh, my God," she said. "Hit by a car? Where?"

"Virginia Avenue, in front of his apartment building."

She looked back inside, concern etched on her face. "The children aren't here," she said. "They'll be devastated."

"Sorry to bring you bad news," one detective said. "Maybe it'd be better if we sat down inside. We have some questions to ask you."

"Questions? What kind of questions?"

"About your former husband. You see, it was a hit-and-run, and people who witnessed it said it appeared that the driver intended to hit him, deliberately aimed at him."

She gasped.

"If you don't mind, ma'am."

"Yes, of course, please come in." She looked past them and was relieved that they'd arrived in an unmarked car.

They went to a family room. It had a big flat-screen TV, a pool and game table on which a jigsaw puzzle was half completed, and plenty of comfortable furniture. She offered them a soft drink or coffee, which they declined. One detective remained standing while questioning her; the other sat on a couch next to her and took notes.

"Can you think of any enemies your husband had?"

She wrinkled her face in thought. "No. Of course I haven't been in his life for the past three years since the divorce. We see each other only occasionally, but he's inconsistent about spending time with the kids. Of course he's always traveled a great deal, which often gets in the way of visitation."

"Why does he travel that much?" Jasmine was asked.

She shrugged. "I never knew. It was always to some psychiatric convention or other. He's been involved for years with a clinic in San Francisco. I really don't know much about it and frankly never cared. I just knew that it took him away from home more than was healthy for the children."

"He ever talk about his patients with you?"

She shook her head. "That was strictly off-limits. I understood."

"A witness said the driver was a blond woman."

Her face was blank.

"He ever talk about girlfriends?"

"No, of course not. We've kept our private lives to ourselves since we separated and divorced."

"We're told that he had some sort of government connection."

"That's right. He had a security clearance and was a consultant to NIH, at least for a while. He also did work at GW, where he received his training."

"He was busy."

"Too busy. What will happen with . . . with his body?" She choked up, then allowed the tears to flow.

"That's up to the medical examiner, ma'am." He handed her his card. "Again, sorry to be the bearer of bad news. We'll leave you alone now. I'll see what the plans are for disposal of and—" He forced a smile. "Call me and I'll let you know."

She escorted them outside.

"Is that Mercedes your only car?" one asked.

"No. I have another in the garage."

"Mind if we see it?"

"No, of course not."

The taller of the two detectives peered through a row of small windows at the top of the garage doors and saw a white vehicle.

"Open the garage for us, please."

"All right but . . . you aren't thinking that—"

"Please open the door."

She did. The white car was another Mercedes. The detectives examined the front of the vehicle, which was perfectly intact.

"Many thanks, ma'am," they said as they got in their car and drove away.

"Nice lady," the driver's colleague said from the passenger seat.

"Must not be easy married to a shrink."

"The money's good, though. Two Mercedes Benzes. Not bad."

"My wife has a shrink friend, a psychologist. Whenever we're with her I think she's analyzing everything I say."

"She probably is."

"Makes me uncomfortable."

They drove in silence until the driver said, "There's more to this guy than meets the eye, huh? They send us to deliver the news instead of a Maryland cop. A Maryland cop would have been the one if it was routine."

"You never know about people."

"Especially shrinks. They're all weird. You ever see one? I mean for a problem?"

"No. You?"

"Once, to help me get off cigarettes."

"It worked. You don't smoke."

"I don't know whether the shrink helped or not. He tried hypnosis. That mumbo-jumbo didn't work. I kicked the habit on my own, cold turkey."

His partner nodded. "Hypnosis? Lotta mumbo-jumbo. Shrinks. They can really screw you up. Let's move, Harry. I'm taking the wife out to dinner tonight."

CHAPTER

5

The following day, Nicholas Tatum sipped cold tea from a Styrofoam cup that had rested on his desk since class commenced a little less than an hour ago. The classroom was filled to capacity, which it usually was when he taught his two-hour seminar on evaluating human behavior to aspiring attorneys enrolled in the George Washington Law School. He conducted the seminar only once each semester, and it had immediately become a favorite elective. Did students flock to it because they viewed the subject as important to their legal careers, or because it was a welcome respite from classes on torts and contracts and habeas corpus? It didn't matter to Dr. Tatum, or "Nic" to his friends. The behavioral sciences was a discipline about which he was passionate, and he enjoyed imparting what he knew to these young men and women no matter to what use they put it.

"Look," he told a student who questioned what benefit there was in knowing how hypnotizable someone was, "it doesn't have to do with hypnotizability. I'm not suggesting that you hypnotize a client to get to the truth. What I am saying is that if you pick up on the subtle clues about how that client processes life, you'll be in a better position to judge whether he or she is telling you the truth. The same holds true when questioning witnesses in a courtroom. Once you've discovered how a witness tends to react to various stimuli and then acts upon them, you know the best approach to breaking through whatever barriers he or she has put up.

"Let me go over the basic premise again. Each of us is born with a natural wired ability to be hypnotized, and it correlates directly with personality style and how we function. There are three basic types of people—Dionysians, Apollonians, and Odysseans, named after the mythical Greek gods Dionysius and Apollo, and the not so mythical Odysseus.

"Dionysus was the fun-loving god. He worshipped freely and with abandon, his approach to life based upon freeing one's natural self through madness, ecstasy, and wine."

Laughter erupted in the room and fingers were pointed.

Tatum waited until the merriment had ebbed before continuing. "People who are known as Dionysians tend to trust others. They're intuitive and make many decisions based upon feelings rather than cognitive thought. Apollo, on the other hand, was the god of logic, reason, and order. Apollonians tend to want to lead rather than follow. Put a Dionysian and an Apollonian in a car, and the Apollonian will want to drive while the Dionysian will be content to let him.

"Dionysians are prone to being influenced by others more readily than are Apollonians. And then there are the Odysseans. They form the middle ground between Dionysians and Apollonians. They tend to fluctuate between action and despair, between feeling and thinking. Most people are Odysseans. Now, which group do you assume is more hypnotizable?"

"The Dionysians," three students answered in unison.

"Correct," said Tatum. "Dionysians are more easily led than Apollonians or Odysseans, more open to suggestion. They often prefer to follow rather than to lead. Apollonians are the opposite."

Tatum checked his watch. "We'll take a fifteen-minute break. When we come back we'll get into how you can determine which category a client or witness falls into based upon some easily visible signs and traits. See you in fifteen."

Tatum exited the classroom and went to the faculty lounge, from which Mackensie Smith was just leaving.

"Are my best and brightest getting your message?" Smith asked, chuckling.

"Not sure, Mac, but it's easy to tell which ones are."

"The Dionysians," Smith said.

Tatum nodded. "Not hard to spot them. How's Annabel?"

"Fine, just fine. Available for dinner Saturday?"

"Saturday night? Sure. The weather forecast for Saturday is good so I thought I'd get in some flying time, but I should be finished by five."

Among Tatum's many hobbies was piloting a vintage aerobatic aircraft, a Micco SP26, which he housed at Potomac Airfield in Fort Washington, Maryland.

"Seven? Annabel is suddenly in the cooking mood. She's whipping up her signature veal martini. Bring a guest."

"Sounds great. Cindy and I had planned to get together for dinner."

"Looking forward to seeing the two of you. Fly safe, Nic. Do you ever worry that the wings on that aerobatic plane of yours might fall off one day?"

Tatum laughed. "Every time I go up."

"I have to run," said Smith. "Can't be late for my tennis match with Dean Molino."

Mackensie Smith had recruited Tatum to teach the law school course. Smith had been one of D.C.'s top criminal attorneys, the go-to lawyer when your life was at stake.

He was a ferocious advocate in the courtroom but a gentle, accepting man outside it. It was that lighter side that had attracted Annabel Lee to him. She'd been a successful matrimonial attorney until meeting the erudite Mac Smith, whose first wife and only child, a son, had been slaughtered on the Beltway by a drunken driver. When the drunk's attorney successfully mitigated his client's culpability before a jury of his peers and got him off with a minimal sentence, Smith reconsidered the use to which he'd put his extensive legal knowledge for all those years. He folded his private practice and accepted a teaching position at GW Law. Was teaching young attorneys to defend people any less unsavory than doing it himself? He sometimes wondered. But not often.

Recently Smith had succumbed to the lure of the courtroom and the give-and-take of negotiation, and had taken on a small select number of clients, mostly friends in whom he believed and whose legal needs weren't outside his comfort zone. Annabel wasn't especially happy with his reimmersion into the world of advocacy law but understood what was driving him.

While the classroom could be challenging at times, it paled in comparison with what her husband termed "the real world of the law."

After they'd married, Annabel, too, decided that she'd had enough of representing men and women whose need for revenge against a soon-to-be-former spouse trumped their common sense, especially when it came to the welfare of their children. She'd fostered a lifelong ambition of owning an art gallery devoted to pre-Columbian art, and with Mac's encouragement she took down her shingle, found the perfect space in Georgetown, and realized her dream.

While both were busy people, they found time to maintain relationships with a variety of Washingtonians, including some in high positions of government, a few cabinet members, the attorney general, congressmen and -women, and Senator George Mortinson, whose campaign to unseat the current president, Allan Swayze, had gained traction and placed him comfortably ahead in the latest polls. Smith had acted as counsel to a committee chaired by Mortinson, and they'd become good friends, their relationship embellished by their love of tennis. They often played when Mortinson was in the Senate and whenever Smith's bad knee wasn't acting up. Since Mortinson announced that he was running for the presidency, their tennis matches had become less frequent, although he occasionally took time out from campaigning to meet Smith on the court, much to the chagrin of his campaign staff and the Secret Service detail assigned to protect him while on the stump.

Tatum, in his midforties, had earned his Ph.D. in American University's behavior, cognition, and neuroscience graduate program. He'd been at the top of his class since high school and throughout college; his doctoral thesis that correlated a person's level of hypnotizability with the effectiveness of acupuncture was considered one of the best papers ever written by someone in the program, and he was recruited upon graduation by myriad universities, hospitals, and government agencies. To everyone's surprise, he opted to join the Washington MPD's small but growing Criminal Behavior Unit that had been established to better predict the actions of known criminals. Patterned after the FBI's criminal-profiling department, the CBU was soon emulated by other police departments across the country, and Nic Tatum was quickly recognized as a rising star in the division.

His resignation only three years after having joined the MPD didn't go over well with his superiors. They tried to persuade him to stay, but Tatum, whose decisions in life were carefully thought out and resolute, declined their vague promises of great things in his future and left to establish a private practice and to teach. Although he was no longer on MPD's payroll, he was often called in to help with a particularly baffling case in which his expertise in profiling criminal behavior was needed.

He sat alone in the faculty lounge and picked up that day's *Washington Post*. Dr. Mark Sedgwick's death received a surprising amount of column inches considering it had nothing to do with government or the presidential election a little more than a month away. Had Sedgwick died as a result of a vehicular accident, it wouldn't have commanded much space. But the reporter had cited an anonymous source within the MPD who'd told her that it was being considered a homicide and that the driver had, according to eyewitnesses, deliberately aimed for and struck the doctor. Being a diligent reporter, she tracked down those eyewitnesses and got their statements. The headline read: HIT-AND-RUN ON VIRGINIA AVENUE A DELIBERATE KILLING? The question mark had been inserted by her editor to cover for not having proof of the allegation.

Tatum dropped the paper on the table and drew a breath.

He'd known Mark Sedgwick. They weren't friends, but they had run across each other numerous times at NIH, where they were colleagues in federally funded experiments, and had sat together on various panels over the years. Tatum had always considered Sedgwick inaccessible, buttoned-up and defensive when it came to his personal life, and his professional life, too, for that matter. They'd socialized only a few times, including a dinner party at Sedgwick's home years ago. Tatum reflected on that night as he waited for his class to resume.

It had been a pleasant evening, although he'd soon tired of the conversation. The six male guests were all M.D.'s or Ph.D.'s, which limited the scope of topics, although politics did come up a few times. Based upon Sedgwick's comments, Tatum assumed that he leaned right on the political spectrum. Far right. He knew that Sedgwick had connections with the intelligence community, although he wasn't sure of the extent of them.

Deliberately run over?

He returned to the classroom, where his students had again gathered. "Okay," he said, "I know that you're wondering how this will benefit you with clients or in a courtroom." He proceeded to ask a series of questions of individual students, going to them and standing close while posing his questions. He also asked them to look straight at him and then to roll their eyes up as far as they could toward the top of their head. After twenty minutes of this, he resumed his place behind his desk and asked, "How many of you have ever been to a nightclub where the entertainment was a stage hypnotist?"

One hand went up.

"Stage hypnotists are very good at quickly

identifying the Dionysians in the audience. Their answers to the hypnotist's questions, as simple and silly as they may sound, provide him with clues to how suggestible certain audience members are. And he watches their eyes."

"Why their eyes?" a student asked.

Tatum went on to explain how the ability to roll one's eyes up and display a lot of white cornea indicates how suggestible and hypnotizable a person is.

"Obviously," he said, "what I'm telling you represents only the bare bones of the science behind the theory. Doctors who use hypnosis in their practices utilize what's called the Hypnotic Induction Profile. It was created by one of the giants in the field of medical hypnosis, Dr. Herbert Spiegel. I had the privilege of studying medical hypnosis with Dr. Spiegel at Columbia University in New York, and I based my Ph.D. thesis on a pioneering study he did at Columbia matching a patient's level of hypnotizability with that same patient's success when treated with acupuncture. Dionysians—the more hypnotizable—tended to do better with acupuncture, while Apollonians fared less well.

"What it boils down to for you as future lawyers is that if you know a client or witness is a Dionysian, your best approach is to appeal to his or her softer side, the more emotional, feeling side. The *heart* side. Apollonians will want a more factual approach, a more cognitive one to appeal to their *head* side. Knowing *who* you're questioning, truly knowing what makes that person tick, gives you a valuable leg up in the relationship."

"Sounds like it could be useful between the sexes," someone offered. "I think the girl I'm seeing is an Apollonian, always questioning me, always wanting to drive."

Tatum laughed and packed up his materials. "If I've managed to salvage a relationship this morning, it will all have been worthwhile. Have a good day, ladies and gentlemen."

CHAPTER

6

Four detectives augmented by a half dozen uniformed officers fanned out over the city in search of the white sedan with a broken headlight and smashed windshield. Motor Vehicle Bureau records contained lots of white four-door sedans, which led the force to first concentrate on repair facilities and known chop shops. They got lucky two days after launching their search. The car, a white Buick Regal, sat on the lot of a junkyard along with a hundred other damaged vehicles.

"Where'd you get this?" a detective asked

the yard's owner, a portly man whose clothing wasn't in better shape than his cars.

"I bought it."

"Yeah, but who'd you buy it from?"

"Some guy."

"Some guy?"

The man grinned. "Yeah."

"When did you buy it?"

"Two days ago."

"This guy drove it in?"

A nod.

"How much you pay for it?"

"Four hundred."

"He have a woman with him? A blond woman?"

"No. Just this guy. He says it was in an accident and didn't want to drive it no more. Says it was bad luck." His laugh was almost a giggle.

The detectives examined the front of the vehicle again. "Jesus," one muttered, "she didn't do much of a job of wiping off the blood." The car's owner had made an attempt but had succeeded only in smearing it over a larger surface.

"He," corrected his partner. "He says a guy brought it in."

"You saw the blood on the car?" the yard owner was asked.

"Yeah, sure, I saw it."

"It didn't raise any red flags with you?"

"Why should it? It's the fall. Lots of deer accidents."

"You think that's deer blood?"

"I wouldn't know. It could be."

"Who was the seller?" a detective asked through clenched teeth.

A shrug from the junkyard owner.

"Come on, he turned over the registration. Right?"

"No, no registration."

They opened the driver's door. The seats had already been removed, the radio, too.

"The seats were clean," the man said. "Good radio, too, CD and all."

"Where are the plates?"

"The guy took 'em with him."

"So you don't know who you bought this heap from."

"What does it matter? I paid him a fair price." He waved his hand in the direction of other vehicles in various stages of dismantling. "People crash their cars, they want to get rid of them. I don't blame 'em.

Once a car gets smashed, it ain't worth fixing."

"What did this guy look like?"

"Normal. Average. Wore glasses. I remember that. Had long hair, like a hippie."

"How long? What color?"

"Not too long." He used his hand to indicate a cutoff at the back of his neck. "Normal color. Brown, maybe a little gray. I can't be sure. I don't pay attention to people who dump their cars here."

"We're taking the car," one detective said while the other called for an MPD tow truck to be dispatched.

"Hey," said the yard owner, "I laid out four bills for it."

"You made a bad investment, pal. Where are the seats and radio?"

The yard owner swore under his breath as he led one of the cops to an area where dozens of automobile seats were piled on top of each other beneath an overhang that kept them dry. He pointed to a pair, gray with red trim.

"The radio."

"Yeah, the radio." It was inside the shack that served as his office along with a pile of other radios and GPS units. He picked one up. "This one. I'm out four bills. You gonna reimburse me, right?"

They ignored him as they took the radio from the shack. One stood with it by the seats while the other stationed himself next to the car. A half hour later, the Buick was on a flatbed along with the seats. The radio was tucked in an evidence bag and held by one of the detectives as they drove to MPD's vehicle inspection facility, where technicians went over it inside and out for prints and telltale scraps of anything left behind that might help identify the owner.

Later that afternoon, the vehicle's VIN was matched to a white Buick Regal that had been reported stolen six months earlier in Southeast. The same two detectives who'd discovered the car were dispatched to interview the owner, an older woman with blue hair who walked with the aid of a walker. "The car belonged to my deceased husband, bless his soul," she said. "He treated it like a baby, washed and waxed it every Saturday morning. I hope you caught the bastards who stole it."

The detectives smiled. They hadn't expected such language from this little old lady.

"We're working on it," one said.

"The insurance company gave us a hard time after it was stolen. Those insurance people are whores. They take your money until something happens and then they don't want to pay up when it's time. Bastards!"

As they drove away, one of the detectives said, "If some insurance agent gets whacked, we know who to go after."

CHAPTER

7

As police technicians combed the confiscated white Buick inch by inch, Dr. Nic Tatum was in his apartment in D.C.'s Capitol Hill district walking on the treadmill in the spare bedroom that he'd converted into a gym.

You wouldn't know from looking at him that Nicholas Tatum Ph.D. was one tough dude. Working out had been a sustaining part of his life since his teen years. As a skinny, nerdy kid with large glasses and lank, almost colorless hair, he was picked on by the usual cast of high school bullies, resulting in fights that had him retrieving the pieces of his broken spectacles, or returning home with a blood-spattered white handkerchief pressed against his nose. But his physical appearance wasn't the only reason he was picked on. He was clearly one of the brightest students in the school. While other academically superior students were sometimes reluctant to answer questions in class for fear of ridicule by their less intelligent classmates, Tatum never hesitated to shoot up his hand and give the correct response. Because of this, he was adored and respected by his teachers—and scorned by certain other students.

Like all teenage boys, Nic's life was filled with dreams of being something that he wasn't. He often imagined himself as invincible, a rough-and-tumble guy with bulging muscles, hair-trigger reflexes, and a granite chin, someone whom other male students avoided bumping into in the hallways. Of course his physical features changed, too, during these flights of fancy. He was movie-star handsome with a wide smile that displayed perfect white teeth, dark hair cropped close to his head, his complexion dusky, his eyes clear and filled

with understanding and wisdom beyond
his years. He'd never heard of Charles Atlas, but this skinny teenager was the epitome of Atlas's skinny kid on the beach
who was tired of having sand kicked in his
face—and did something about it. It was
all, of course, fantasy until . . .

"I think it's time that you fight back, Nicholas," his father said one night over dinner.
Nic had returned from school that afternoon with bruises and another pair of
glasses to be repaired.

The statement surprised Nic. Although
his father was a mild-mannered CPA who
never worked at a level beyond that of a
glorified bookkeeper, he stood firm in his
principles of justice and right. Had he been
born in an earlier era, he might have been
a Communist. His mother was a flighty
woman with a ready laugh, who worked
a variety of part-time jobs to help pay the
family's bills. They doted on their only child
and encouraged his academic efforts. And
it sickened them to see him return from a
day at school bloodied at the hands of
less gifted students.

"We're not suggesting, Nicholas, that
you become a fighter," explained his father.

"Far from it. But there's no reason for you to be at the mercy of these morons whose brains are smaller than yours and whose futures are dim. I want you to get in shape and give as much as you have been getting."

"And won't they be surprised when you fight back and *they* end up on the ground with a bloody nose?" his mother added with a gleeful smile that led Nic to believe that she looked forward to witnessing his next fight.

They signed him up at a local YMCA and purchased some rudimentary exercise equipment that was installed in their unfinished basement. Nic attacked his new workout regime with the same vigor as he tackled his studies, and the results soon became obvious. Not that he became muscle-bound; his basic skeletal structure wouldn't support that. But muscles did begin to define themselves, and his strength increased. At the same time his confidence grew, bolstered by the knowledge that should someone pick on him again, he'd be ready to offer resistance—to give as good as he'd been getting.

His social skills were bolstered also.

Until becoming a gym rat, he'd been awkward around girls in the school and was aware that some of them, especially those in cliques, made fun of him behind his back. That changed in his senior year, when a pretty blond classmate who belonged to one of the popular groups began to show interest in him. She'd grown to appreciate his academic achievements—she'd shucked off some of her previous silliness and had begun to embrace her studies with an eye toward college—and was open in her admiration of his intelligence. "You'll easily be our class valedictorian," she told him more than once while they studied together in the library after school, where he happily helped her with some of her more challenging science subjects.

Although they could hardly be considered boyfriend and girlfriend, they did catch an occasional movie together or end up in a local luncheonette enjoying ice cream sundaes. None of this went over well with a senior on the football team who had a crush on the girl and who took ribbing from teammates about how "that creep Tatum" was stealing her from him.

One night as Tatum returned home after a workout at the Y, his rival suitor, accompanied by three friends from the team, accosted him on a dark street. As the football player taunted Tatum and warned him to stay away from the girl, a sense of fury welled up in him that he'd never experienced before. The football player poked him in the chest, then shoved him harder, causing him to stumble back a few steps. The other players urged on their friend, who wasn't much taller than Tatum but was considerably beefier.

Tatum calmly removed his glasses, placed them in his shirt pocket, closed the gap between them, and smiled, which seemed to confuse his adversary, who looked over his shoulder at his buddies. Tatum didn't hesitate. He brought his right fist up from down near his knees, twisting his body to put every ounce of torque into the punch. It caught the football player flush on the side of his face and sent him sprawling into the arms of one of his friends. Before he could reset himself, Tatum swung again, this time his tightly clenched fist smashing into his opponent's nose and flattening it. Blood flowed, and the football player sank to his knees. Tatum grabbed the beefy student's hair, jerked his head up, and held his fist inches from his battered face. "More?" Tatum said. He took in the others. "You want some, too?"

They hauled their buddy to his feet and dragged him away, uttering empty curses and threats as they went. Tatum thought he might explode. He shook violently and his breath came in gulps. He couldn't believe what he had done, and back home in his room he swore to himself that he would never do it again. But he knew that he could if he had to, and that confidence carried forward throughout his college and adult life.

He'd dialed the treadmill to its maximum speed and was sprinting to keep up with it when the phone rang. He considered allowing the machine to answer but decided that he'd had enough exercise for the day. He reached the phone moments before the automated voice kicked in.

"Hey, Nic, Joe Owens. Hope I didn't take you away from some exotic scientific experiment."

"Not at all," Tatum said, wiping perspiration from his face with an already soggy towel and trying to get his breathing back to normal. "I was just seeing whether I could outrun my treadmill."

"And?"

"I was losing. What's up?"

"We've got a case here at MPD I thought you might lend a hand with."

"Mark Sedgwick?"

"You read the papers. Yeah, it's the Sedgwick case. You knew the guy?"

"Not well. We worked together on some projects. I read that it might not have been an accident."

"Looks like it wasn't. Got any time this afternoon?"

"Nothing but time today. Want me to swing by?"

"That'd be great. Three?"

"Three it is."

Joe Owens was a veteran homicide cop with whom Tatum had worked before. An affable African American with an infectious laugh, Owens had risen through the ranks to reach senior detective status.

Tatum arrived at MPD headquarters at three on the nose and was escorted into Owens's office. The detective eased himself up from behind the desk and greeted Tatum with a hug and a slap on the back. "Hey, man," he said, "you look great. Still pumping iron?"

Tatum nodded and took a seat in front of the desk.

"I love it," Owens said, "the way you hide behind that Ph.D. façade of yours, like a real milquetoast. Then, boom, you come out swinging. I'll never forget that night you beat up on Coleman in the tourney. Man, you really took him over the coals."

Tatum had entered the MPD's boxing tournament at 155 pounds and won his four matches before resigning from the force. He hadn't boxed since, although he occasionally worked out at the Downtown Boxing Club on F Street.

"He wasn't that good," Tatum said. "So, tell me about Mark Sedgwick's death."

"You know the basics from the papers. He got mowed down on Virginia Avenue on his way to his office. From what we've learned so far from eyewitnesses, the driver didn't try to avoid hitting him. According to them she aimed right for him."

"So the papers say. Any leads on the car and driver?"

"Yeah. We've found the car, or at least what we suspect was the car. In a junkyard. Stolen six months ago in Southeast. The owner of the place says a man brought in the car and sold it for four hundred dollars."

"A man? I thought eyewitnesses said it was a woman. Blond, as I recall."

"We're a little confused about that."

"Who was he?"

A shrug from the big detective. "He never said. According to the junkyard owner, he never gave his name, no registration, just removed the plates, pocketed the four hundred, and took off."

Tatum laughed. "All aboveboard."

"Forensics is going over the car as we speak. I just got a call from the garage. They've come up with something that might give us a lead."

"Oh?"

"A woman's shoe."

"Shoe? Just one?"

"We assume whoever had the car—the woman who was driving or this guy who delivered it to the junkyard—cleaned it out before dumping it. They missed the shoe in the trunk. Fancy woman's shoe, expensive one. Red, I'm told. Italian. We're running down exclusive stores that carry the brand."

"Any leads on the blonde?"

"Not yet. We're going on the assumption that it was a girlfriend."

"He's divorced."

"It wasn't his ex-wife. We've already questioned her. Wrong hair color, wrong car. Look, Nic, the reason I called you was to go over a list of Sedgwick's patients."

Tatum's raised eyebrows mirrored his surprise.

Owens smiled. "We went to the right judge to get a court order for the doc's patient files to be released to us. The judge balked at first, but we convinced him that homicide might be involved. The magic word, "homicide," works every time, at least for this particular judge. He slapped on some conditions, female patients only and no one who'd been a patient for less than six months."

"Why the prohibition on new patients?"

"Probably figured it takes a while for a patient to get mad enough at her shrink to run him down."

"I'm surprised he didn't restrict it to blond patients only," Tatum said.

"I guess he's heard of wigs and hair dye. Anyway, I thought you might pick up on something in one of the files that screams homicidal blond woman sleeping with her shrink who drives a white sedan. Up for it?"

"Sure, only don't expect much from me. I doubt whether the files will tell much, but I'll take a look."

"Can't ask for more than that."

"You have the files, Joe?"

"No. That's another restriction the judge added to the list. The files aren't to leave the doctor's office." He consulted a sheet of paper on his desk. "Dr. Sedgwick's receptionist and gal Friday is a Betty Martinez, worked for him for a number of years. I'll call and tell her that you'll be going over the records. She's already pulled the ones that match the judge's order. You call her and set up a time."

"Shall do," Tatum said. "The usual hourly fee?"

"It's in my budget."

As he prepared to leave, Tatum asked, "Why is Sedgwick's death—murder, if it is that—high on your priority list?"

Although they were alone and the door was closed, Owens looked around as though to ensure their privacy. "I don't have a good answer for that, Nic. Let's just say that some of the interested parties have clout—and don't work for the MPD."

CHAPTER

8

Despite the court order releasing certain of Mark Sedgwick's patient records to the MPD, Betty Martinez was still convinced that to do so would entangle her in some sort of bureaucratic imbroglio. She greeted Nic Tatum the following day with suspicion and overt reluctance to cooperate. But when he told her that he was a Ph.D. psychologist and a former friend of her boss, she softened her stance and settled him in Sedgwick's office. He declined her offer to get him coffee—he'd brought his own cup from Starbucks—and told her that he'd yell if he needed anything.

The folders that Betty had culled from the files were neatly piled on the desk, which Tatum ignored for a few minutes in order to take in his surroundings. The office was nondescript as psychiatrists' offices went. It looked to Tatum as though Sedgwick had ordered his furnishings from a company that provided sets to plays and motion pictures, nothing fancy but certainly utilitarian. There was the de rigueur leather couch with an attached matching leather pillow; a box of pop-up Kleenex sat on a small oval table next to it. The tan-and-white carpeting was industrial grade, the drapes a pale yellow with orange vertical stripes. In addition to Sedgwick's desk and desk chair, there was a second chair in leather that matched the couch and was situated close to where a patient's head would rest on the pillow. The setup interested Tatum. As far as he knew, Mark Sedgwick wasn't a Freudian therapist who practiced psychoanalysis, session after session in which the patient was encouraged to free-associate about the past while the therapist grunted, made notes, and tossed in an occasional comment to keep things going.

Tatum practiced short-term therapy. His patients sat in a chair—there was no couch in Tatum's office—and he focused on the here and now rather than indulging in archaeological digs into the patient's childhood. If a patient had a fear of flying, Tatum tried to get him over it as fast as possible. Discovering *why* he was fearful through months, even years, of dredging up his life history didn't seem to make sense. Getting him on a plane was Tatum's goal, and he was impressively successful at helping patients conquer their hang-ups in short order. Another difference between the way Tatum and Sedgwick practiced had to do with Sedgwick being a psychiatrist, a medical doctor with the privilege of prescribing medicines the way any M.D. could, something that psychologists like Tatum were prohibited from doing.

How many of Sedgwick's patients used that couch? Tatum wondered. The answer, at least for some of them, might be in the file folders, and he opened the first one.

He'd gone through half the files by noon without discovering anything useful. Betty knocked, entered, and asked whether he wanted her to get him some lunch.

"Thanks, no, Ms. Martinez. I think I'll run out for something. I need a break." He stood and stretched against a tightening in his back. He needed a workout.

"Dr. Sedgwick kept good notes," he commented.

"Lots of them," she agreed. "He dictated most of them after patients left, and I transcribed them. Sometimes, though, he wrote the notes himself."

"Any reason why he'd choose to do that for only certain patients?"

"I don't know. Sure I can't get you something?" She smiled for the first time since he'd arrived.

"Positive, but thanks anyway. By the way, did any of the female patients in these files wear red shoes when coming for their sessions?"

She looked puzzled.

"Red women's shoes," he said, "fancy red Italian shoes." He didn't know whether the police had asked her that question but decided to proceed as though they hadn't.

Her smile widened, but she still looked perplexed.

"Just a thought," he said.

"Sheila," she said.

"Pardon?"

"Sheila," she repeated. "She always wore red shoes. She used to say that Imelda Marcos had nothing on her."

Tatum laughed. "That's right, Mrs. Marcos was known for her shoe collection. What's Sheila's last name?"

"Klaus."

"I didn't see any file for her."

"It's there."

"Probably with the ones I haven't gotten to yet."

He shuffled through the remaining files and pulled the one for Sheila Klaus. He opened it, frowned, and looked up at Betty. "There's virtually nothing in it," he said.

"Dr. Sedgwick never dictated notes after their sessions. I suppose he wrote them by hand."

Tatum nodded and returned to the few pages contained in the folder. "He sure didn't write many for this patient," he muttered, turning the file on the desk for Betty to see. "There's a date on this sheet for when she started seeing him. It goes back to 2007."

"Sheila has been a patient for a long time," Betty said. "Not always steady. She sometimes stopped coming for months. I remember when she didn't have a session scheduled for six months."

Tatum continued to peruse what the folder held. On the bottom of the sheet on which her start date was mentioned were a series of notations written in what Tatum assumed was Sedgwick's handwriting: Up Gaze 4; Arm Levitation left 3–4; Squint 0; Amnesia to Cut Off 2; Float 2. The final entry was the numeral 5 with a box drawn around it.

"Dr. Sedgwick used hypnosis with her," Tatum said, more to himself than to Betty. "These notations are from the HIP test."

"He used hypnosis with a lot of his patients," she offered.

That wasn't surprising. Tatum and Sedgwick had worked together on a number of projects at NIH and at GW that involved medical hypnosis. Using trance to treat certain conditions, psychological as well as physical, was now firmly entrenched in a physician's bag of tricks. One trial involving the use of hypnosis as anesthesia for patients whose physical condition ruled out chemical anesthesia produced what Tatum considered remarkable results. Videotapes of patients undergoing major surgery using only hypno-anesthesia demonstrated dramatic proof of how the power of suggestion could be every bit as potent and effective as the chemical variety.

"Is Ms. Klaus a blond woman?" he asked.

"Yes."

"And she wore red shoes?"

"Yes."

He hesitated before asking, "Were Dr. Sedgwick and Ms. Klaus close?"

"How do you mean?" she asked, although he was certain she knew the answer.

"Close," he said. "Friends beyond therapy."

"I really don't like talking about things like that," Betty said.

"I can understand your reluctance," he said, "but I'm here as a representative of the police, Betty, and everything points to Dr. Sedgwick having been run over deliberately—by a blond woman who might have been a patient."

"They—" she started, biting her lip in the process. "They traveled together sometimes." She quickly added, "Just a few times."

Tatum nodded. He understood.

"When was the last time she saw Dr. Sedgwick as a patient?" he asked.

"Oh, it's been awhile," she replied. "Two months, maybe three. I can look it up."

"I'd appreciate that. There's no mention in the file of the last time he saw her."

She returned from the reception area. "Two months ago to the day," she reported.

"I appreciate your help, Betty. I think I'll run out for a sandwich. Get you anything?"

"No, thank you. I brought my lunch. It's cheaper."

"It certainly is. You have an address and phone number for Ms. Klaus?"

"Sure." She returned with it a minute later.

"Thanks," he said. "I'll be back in an hour to finish going through the files."

It had begun to rain while Tatum was in Sedgwick's office. He walked half a block before ducking into a luncheonette, where he settled in a booth, ordered a sandwich from the waitress, and dialed Joe Owens's number at MPD.

"How's it going?" Owens asked.

"It's going very well, Joe. I think I'm onto something, someone."

"Who?"

Tatum briefed the detective on the information he'd turned up on Sheila Klaus, including her address and phone number.

"Looks like you might have hit a home run, Nic."

"We'll see."

"I'll go have a talk with Ms. Klaus."

"Hold off until the end of the day, huh? Let me see what else I can come up with about her. And I'd like to be with you or whoever you send."

"Not a problem, Nic. Call me by four."

Tatum spent the next two hours finishing his examination of Sedgwick's patient files. Further questioning of Betty about Sheila Klaus was nonproductive, although he did learn that the receptionist considered the patient to be, as she reluctantly put it, "a little strange."

"How so?" he asked.

"Oh, I don't know. She's very nice, really sweet, but a little spacey, if you get what I mean."

"Not always here?" he suggested.

"Like she sometimes daydreamed."

"You've really been a big help, Betty. Thanks for coming in today."

"Dr. Sedgwick's lawyer wants me to

keep coming in to make sure that things stay in order, but I'm sure that won't last long. I'll have to find a new job."

"If I can be of any help in that, let me know. Thanks again."

He went directly to MPD headquarters and found Owens coming out of a meeting.

"You come up with anything else?" the detective asked.

"No."

"Let's swing by the address you have for her. Detective Breen is coming with us. If this pans out the way it looks like it could, Nic, I'll owe you big-time."

"Lunch at Ray's Hell Burger will do just fine."

CHAPTER

9

Billy Breen was a young detective whose enthusiasm for the job was still fresh. He talked fast and was quick to agree with everything that the veteran Joe Owens said. He reminded Tatum of a tall Mickey Rooney. His youthful verve was welcome; veteran cops tend to be dour individuals after spending years dealing with the dregs of society, although Joe Owens was a pleasant exception. Tatum gave Breen two more years before he became soured and cynical. It just happened, an occupational reality.

Sheila Klaus lived in a small one-story

white house in Rockville, Maryland. Owens had run a background check on her earlier that afternoon. She was forty-eight and a divorcée; her only marriage had lasted two years and ended fourteen years ago. She'd been employed in George Washington University's law school admissions office and had left a year earlier because of a disability, the specifics unstated. She had no arrest record, nor had she even received a traffic citation. Her credit score was high-average. A red Mazda was registered in her name.

As they pulled up in front of her house, they saw a blond woman gardening in the postage-stamp-size front yard. She wore jeans, a red sweatshirt, a floppy white hat, and low red sneakers. Even in her oversized gardening clothes it was obvious to her visitors that she was an attractive woman.

She looked up as they got out of the car but immediately returned to digging a hole for a potted plant that sat next to her.

"Ms. Klaus?" Owens said as they stood outside the low white picket fence that defined the yard.

She looked up and smiled. "Yes?"

"I'm Detective Owens. These are Detective Breen and Dr. Tatum."

She wiped perspiration from her brow with the back of her hand, stood, and approached, the smile still on her tanned face.

"Is something wrong?" she asked.

"We're investigating the death of Dr. Mark Sedgwick."

Her smile vanished. "Oh, yes, I heard about it. What a tragedy. He was a very kind and compassionate doctor. I read about it in the papers. "

"You did know him, then."

"Yes. I was a patient of his once."

"We're aware of that, ma'am," said Owens. "We have some questions we'd like to ask you."

Her expression turned to puzzlement. "Whatever for?"

"Mind if we come in?" Owens asked.

"I . . . I suppose that will be all right," she said, "It's just that—"

"Yes?"

"It's just that this is upsetting, having detectives come to my home concerning Dr. Sedgwick's death. What could I possibly know that would interest you?"

"We can determine that after we ask you a few questions," Breen said, hoping he wasn't treading on Owens's toes. He'd hardened his tone to sound the way he was sure a detective should sound.

"All right," she said, her smile returning. "You'll have to excuse the house. It's a bit of a mess."

She removed her hat as they followed her inside. She was blond. Tatum was struck by her demeanor. Aside from a natural curiosity about their visit, she was calm and pleasant, hardly the behavior of someone who had deliberately run someone down only a few days earlier.

The house was a lot neater than she'd promised. She invited them to sit in a glassed-in atrium at the rear in which dozens of plants sat on windowsills or on metal stands.

"Would you like something to drink?" she asked. "I made fresh iced tea this morning and—"

"No, thank you," Owens said. "Ms. Klaus, have you ever owned a white Buick Regal?"

She answered instantly. "No. Why do you ask?"

"Dr. Sedgwick was struck by a white Buick Regal," Breen said.

"How dreadful," she said. "I believe I read that some people who witnessed it said it appeared that the driver deliberately hit Dr. Sedgwick. Is that true?"

"Yes, ma'am, we think that's what happened," said Owens. "What kind of car do you drive?"

"A Mazda. It's in the garage. Do you wish to see it?"

"In a minute," Owens said. "You acknowledge that you were a patient of Dr. Sedgwick."

"Yes. Why shouldn't I? There's no crime in seeing a psychiatrist."

Owens smiled. "Of course there isn't," he said. "Did you and Dr. Sedgwick . . . well, were you friends aside from the doctor-patient relationship?"

She rolled her eyes up, blew out an exasperated stream of air, lowered her eyes, and fixed him in a hard stare. "Are you suggesting that—?"

Owens held up his hand. "I'm not suggesting anything, Ms. Klaus, but we've been informed that you and the doctor traveled together on a few occasions."

"That simply is not true!" she exclaimed. "Not true. Whatever gave you that idea? Who told you such a thing?"

"Please understand, Ms. Klaus, that it's our job to follow up on anything and everything we're told."

Tatum knew that Owens would ask Betty Martinez for more details about Sedgwick's travels as they might have involved Sheila Klaus and have someone dig into airline records. There was nothing to be gained by pressing her about it at this juncture.

Tatum had said nothing since they arrived. But he was keenly attuned to every word Sheila Klaus said, every gesture, the inflection in her voice, her posture, the vehemence with which she denied what Owens had suggested. It sounded to Tatum that she was being truthful, and he wondered whether the detective was barking up the wrong tree. He was aware, of course, that he was the one who'd initiated the interest in her as a possible suspect.

"Did you and the doctor ever have a falling out?" the senior detective asked.

She cocked her head and squinted.

"No, I can't say that we ever did. May I ask you a question, Detective?"

"Sure."

"Isn't this a violation of the doctor-patient privacy law?"

"Not in this case, ma'am. We have a court order that gives us access to Dr. Sedgwick's patient records. Because his death is being treated as a homicide, the judge—"

"Homicide?" she blurted.

"Yes, ma'am. As you read in the newspaper, it seems that whoever was driving the car deliberately struck the doctor. That's homicide." He hesitated before saying, "This may sound like a strange question to you, Ms. Klaus, but do you own a pair of expensive red Italian shoes?"

"As a matter of fact I do. More than one pair."

He pulled a note from his pocket and read from it. "Gucci shoes?" he asked.

"Yes."

"Would you mind if we had a look at them?"

"I don't understand."

"Only take a moment," Owens said. "We

could get a warrant, but I'm sure you won't put us to that bother."

"If you insist," she said through a laugh.

"Go with her," Owens told Breen.

The young detective followed her up the stairs.

"What do you think?" Owens asked Tatum in a low voice.

"She seems legit to me," Tatum said.

"To me, too," Owens agreed.

Sheila and Breen returned a few minutes later. Breen carried two and a half pairs of women's red shoes.

"Almost three pairs," Owens muttered as he examined them. "You're missing one."

Sheila laughed. "I can't imagine where it could be," she said. "This is so embarrassing. I have what I suppose you could call a passion for Italian shoes, particularly Gucci. And I'm fond of red. My friends sometimes kid me. They say I'm like Imelda Marcos. I hardly think that—"

Owens took note of the size of the shoes. Six. The shoe found in the Buick was also a six. He handed the shoes to her. "Have you driven a white Buick lately?" he asked. "Maybe a friend's car or a rental?"

"No. The only car I drive is my Mazda. It's red, too, like my shoes."

"Where were you the morning that Dr. Sedgwick was killed?"

"That was . . . let me see . . . I . . . I don't know. Here, I suppose."

"Anyone who can vouch for that?"

"No. I live here alone."

There was silence as Breen took notes and Owens formulated his next question. Tatum maintained his watchful silence.

"Is there anything else?" she asked.

"Not at the moment," Owens said. "Thanks for your time. We might have further questions for you at some later date."

"That will be fine. I know that you're doing your job and have to follow up on every little thing. I wish I could be of more help."

Before getting in the car, Owens checked the garage. The car in it was, as Ms. Klaus had said, a red Mazda. Owens also noticed tire tread marks in the driveway. "Get the camera," he told Breen, "and grab some shots of it."

They headed back to the District.

"I think she's lying," Breen offered.

"Oh?" said Owens. "What makes you think that?"

"Just a hunch."

"You think she's being truthful," Owens said to Tatum.

Breen quickly said, "Yeah, maybe she is."

"I don't know," said Tatum. "I do know one thing."

"What's that?"

"She's a classic Dionysian. Did you catch her eye roll?"

"What's that?" Breen asked.

"When she rolls her eyes up, her irises disappear. Nothing but white. That matches up with the HIP score in her file."

Breen's expression was pure confusion.

"That puts her at the very top of the scale," Tatum further explained. "Only a tiny percentage of people score that high. They're almost freakish in how suggestible and malleable they are. Of course there are other tests, but I'd be surprised if they didn't confirm the eye roll."

"She says she never traveled with the doctor," Breen offered. "You believe her?"

Owens answered, "Next stop Sedgwick's office to see if Ms. Martinez is still there. She says she arranged all of his trips. Let's see if she also bought tickets for Sheila Klaus."

As Tatum and Owens got out of the car, Tatum looked back and suppressed a smile. Breen was looking intently into the rearview mirror and rolling up his eyes.

CHAPTER

10

Betty Martinez was packing up to leave Sedgwick's office when Owens, Tatum, and Breen walked in.

"Don't want to keep you," Owens said, "but we need some information." He asked that she check the doctor's records to see when he and Sheila Klaus had traveled together.

"I don't know whether they did," Betty said.

Tatum said, "You told me when I was here going through his files that they had."

"I guess I shouldn't have said that," she said, eyes downcast.

"It's okay," Owens said. "You're not betraying any confidences. The court order doesn't exclude anything specific like travel records."

She drew a sustaining breath and said, "Okay. I guess it's all right." Then, without the need to consult the files, she said, "Sheila and Dr. Sedgwick traveled together to San Francisco a few times, only Ms. Klaus didn't use her real name."

"What name did she use?" Owens asked.

"Carla Rasmussen."

"How did she do that?" Tatum asked. "Didn't she need ID at the airport?"

"I asked Dr. Sedgwick about that the first time he told me to book the flights. I mean, I always reminded him of things that he and whoever he was traveling with needed for security. He told me that Carla Rasmussen was a medical colleague and had all the ID she needed."

"But you knew he was traveling with Ms. Klaus under that assumed name?"

"Yes."

"How did you know?"

"Little things. Sheila was the one who picked up the ticket for Carla Rasmussen from me for one of the trips. I remember because Dr. Sedgwick was angry that she had."

"Why was he mad?"

"I suppose because he didn't want me to know."

"What else led you to know that Ms. Klaus was this Carla Rasmussen?"

"Like I said, it was little things. I mean I didn't snoop or anything, but—"

"But you're sure that it was Ms. Klaus who traveled under the name Carla Rasmussen?"

"Yes."

"How many trips did they take together?" Owens asked.

"Four, I think."

"When did they take their first trip together?"

She went to a file cabinet and removed a folder. "Two thousand eight," she said after consulting a paper within the folder. "August sixteenth."

"Where did they go?" asked Breen.

"San Francisco. That's where they always went."

"I'd like a list of those trips," Owens said.

She used a photocopying machine to produce copies.

"And she always used that name when she traveled?" Tatum asked.

"Yes."

"Where did they stay when they were in San Francisco?" he asked.

"The Hyatt on the Embarcadero."

After a few more questions that produced nothing in the way of additional information, the men left and got into their car.

"Looks like the doc was cheating on his wife," Owens commented as they drove to headquarters. "According to the records, they were divorced three years ago. That first trip occurred a year before that."

"Why would she use a phony name?" Breen pondered aloud.

"Cover his tracks with his wife," was Owens's guess. "I know one thing. Ms. Klaus, or Ms. Rasmussen, has some explaining to do."

Annabel Lee-Smith had spent Saturday afternoon preparing veal martini for that evening's guests. She'd been toying with the recipe for months, never quite satisfied with the way it came out. Too many shallots or too few basil leaves? Needs more dry white wine or fewer sun-dried tomatoes? Her husband, Mackensie, thought that her previous attempts had tasted just fine, but Annabel disagreed and continued to tweak the recipe until she considered the dish perfect. That eureka moment had occurred two weeks earlier, and she now prepared the entrée brimming with confidence.

Tatum and the woman he'd been dating recently, Cindy Simmons, were the first guests to arrive at the Smiths' Watergate apartment. Cindy, a psychiatric nurse at Walter Reed Hospital, had met Tatum a few months ago when he'd joined a team of psychologists and psychiatrists studying new approaches to treating servicemen and -women who'd returned from Iraq and Afghanistan with post-traumatic stress disorder. Cindy was a short, solidly built thirty-year-old with a no-nonsense demeanor that Tatum found characteristic of most nurses, and to which he responded favorably. Drinks in hand, they stood with Mac Smith on the balcony and admired the view of the Potomac River and beyond.

They were joined by the evening's other guests, a couple who were friends of Annabel long before she'd met and fallen in love with Mac. The six of them fell into easy conversation as they enjoyed their drinks and hors d'oeuvres along with the setting sun over the spires of Georgetown University.

After dinner—Annabel's veal martini received unanimous praise—and back on the balcony with coffee and dessert, Mac asked whether there was anything new in the Mark Sedgwick incident. He knew of Tatum's past association with the dead psychiatrist and that he'd become involved in the police investigation.

After giving the other couple a thumbnail briefing of what Smith was referring to, Tatum said, "It's being treated as a homicide. They've narrowed in on a suspect, a woman who'd once been his patient."

"Obviously a mentally unbalanced woman," the wife said. "Only a crazy person would deliberately run someone down."

"And you knew him?" the husband asked.

"Not well," said Tatum. "I was involved in some research projects with him."

"This woman," the husband said, "you say she was his patient?"

"Yes," Tatum confirmed. Under ordinary circumstances he would not have revealed even that much to strangers. But he'd been tipped late Friday by Owens that a reporter from the *Post* was researching an in-depth story on the case, aided by a leak from

MPD concerning Sheila Klaus who, according to the leak, was considered a "person of interest."

The conversation drifted on to other subjects until the couple announced that they were calling it a night. "We're off at the crack of dawn," the husband explained. "Driving up to Maine to visit our daughter."

"Travel safe," Mac said as he and Annabel escorted them to the elevator.

They rejoined Tatum and Cindy on the terrace.

"If you're up to it, Mac," Tatum said, "I have something to discuss with you."

"The night is young," Smith said. "What's it about?"

"The Sedgwick killing."

Smith smiled. "I had a feeling that you knew more than you were willing to discuss earlier in the evening."

"There're issues involved," Tatum said. "I've already told Cindy about it. I've been working with the police on the case. They got a court order to release Sedgwick's patient records, at least those that involved females. You might recall that bystanders said the car that hit him was driven by a blond woman. Anyway, I went through

Sedgwick's records and came up with a possible suspect. I went to interview her with a couple of detectives. You might know her, Mac. She worked at GW's law school in admissions. Sheila Klaus."

Annabel drew in a deep breath. "Of course we remember her. Sheila and I became friends when she was at the university. We were in a book group together."

"And I remember her," Mac said. "A nice lady. I was sorry when she left GW."

"She left on a disability," Tatum said, "but I've never learned what that disability was."

"I don't know," Smith said.

"At any rate," Tatum continued, "the police have really focused in on her as a suspect in the Sedgwick murder." He looked at both Mac and Annabel before adding, "And it was murder no matter what weapon was used. In this case it was a white Buick Regal. The police have found the car and have gone over it. When I accompanied the detectives to talk with her, she lied about certain things regarding her relationship with Sedgwick. Those lies don't help her cause."

"I'm sorry to hear that," said Smith. "Do

you agree with the police that she's the one who drove the car?"

"Based upon the circumstantial evidence, yes. But there's something about her that bothers me."

"What's that?" Annabel asked.

"I almost get the feeling that she believes the lies she told. I mean, there's no doubt that she was involved with Sedgwick outside of the usual doctor-patient relationship. She denies it, but there are records that nail it down."

"Mind a question?" Smith said.

"Of course not."

"Why are you telling us this?"

Tatum broke into a wide grin. "Ah, the attorney's mind at work," he said. "Okay, here's why I bring it up. She needs legal advice, Mac. The police haven't formally charged her yet, but I think they're close to it. My hunch is that she doesn't realize the trouble she's in and will blunder into incriminating herself."

"Why do you feel that way?" Annabel asked.

Tatum held up his hands. "Let me explain," he said. "I don't want to come off as practicing some form of pop psychology, but I did spend time with her, not as a patient in any formal sense but enough to form some conclusions."

"You checked her eye roll," Smith said lightly.

Tatum nodded.

"He's always checking eye rolls," Cindy said lightly, too.

"And Sheila Klaus is a Dionysian," Annabel surmised.

Like Mac, she'd been educated by Tatum in the HIP developed by Tatum's one-time teacher, Herbert Spiegel. They'd spent an evening together at the apartment when Tatum had explained the theories behind Dr. Spiegel's groundbreaking work and its importance to medicine. It was determined that night that both Annabel and Mac were Odysseans—sort of in the middle—with Annabel leaning toward Dionysian (more pliable) and Mac more Apollonian in his hardwiring (more head oriented). It was a fascinating experience that Mac and Annabel often talked about.

Tatum continued. "There are notations in her file that indicate that Sedgwick had done a HIP on her. His findings go hand in hand with her extreme eye roll." He paused as his mind shifted gears. "You remember that panel I was on last year sponsored by Justice that looked into false confessions, people who confessed to crimes they hadn't committed?"

"Sure I do," said Mac. "I was asked to be on that panel but I couldn't clear the time."

"That's right," Tatum said. "I forgot that you'd been asked. Anyway, I have no doubt that those people who falsely confess are high on the HIP scale. They're suggestible and always want to please others even when it means being convicted of crimes of which they're innocent. I think that Sheila Klaus can easily fall into that trap."

"Which would be a terrible miscarriage of justice," Smith said as he refilled their coffee cups. "But why your interest in this particular case, Nic? I gather that you didn't know Sheila before Dr. Sedgwick's death and the MPD investigation into it."

Tatum shrugged and sipped his coffee. "I can't answer that, Mac, except that there's something about her that raises a red flag with me. She traveled to San Francisco with Sedgwick four times using an assumed name, Carla Rasmussen. It appears on the surface that Sedgwick arranged that to keep his affair with her from his wife. But that doesn't hold water for me. What difference did it make what name she used? If his wife discovered that he'd made those four trips with another woman, the name she'd traveled under is irrelevant. Airline records confirm those trips they took together. They also indicate that she made two additional trips to San Francisco in the past few months using the same assumed name Carla Rasmussen."

"With Sedgwick?" Annabel asked.

"No. She went alone."

"You say that she lied about her relationship with Sedgwick," Annabel said. "Isn't that consciousness of guilt, lying to authorities?"

"Usually it is," Tatum agreed, "but I'm convinced that she *believes* those lies. I'm hoping that if the police do formally charge her I'll have a chance to spend clinical time with her. I've already told the detectives that I want to do that."

Smith asked, "How likely is it that she'll be charged?"

"Very likely," Tatum responded, "according to what I've been told. They've questioned her twice more, and she sticks to her story about the relationship. What I was thinking is that because you and Annabel knew her from when she was at GW, you might . . . well, you might give her a call and see if there's some way you can help. I know that you're taking on some cases aside from teaching and—"

"I'd be uncomfortable calling her out of the blue," Smith said.

"I understand," Tatum said. "But if she's formally charged, she'll need an attorney, someone who understands the sort of personality she is."

"A Dionysian," Annabel said.

"If I'm not mistaken, a very *rare* Dionysian," Tatum said. "Just thought I'd raise the possibility."

As Tatum and Cindy were leaving, Smith asked how Tatum's flying had gone that afternoon.

"Great," Tatum said. "I've been trying to get Cindy to come up with me, but she refuses."

"You bet I do," she said. "You'll never find me in that stupid little plane."

Tatum laughed as the elevator arrived. As the doors started to close, Tatum looked at the Smiths and said, "Going up in that stupid little plane is a lot safer than crossing Virginia Avenue."

CHAPTER 12

SAN FRANCISCO

Dr. Sheldon Borger stood out among the dozen onlookers at the gym where sparring sessions were taking place in the ring. It wasn't that he was an imposing physical figure. The fifty-eight-year-old physician was of average height and weight. He was artificially tanned, which provided a contrasting scrim against which a set of gleaming white teeth shone. His gray hair was carefully trimmed and rested close to his pate and temples. Not a hair out of place.

It was his dress that set him apart. He wore an Italian white silk sport jacket, a designer shirt with vivid vertical stripes of blue, green, and yellow open at the collar, beige slacks with a razor crease, and tasseled brown loafers, five thousand dollars' worth of clothing, all of it meticulously tailored to his trim body. He was often mistaken for one of those former actors you've seen in movies but whose name escapes you.

Seated next to him was Peter Puhlman, whose sartorial approach was considerably less expensive. Puhlman's stout physique didn't support trendy, tailored clothing, and his drab gray suit testified to it. His gray pallor, perpetually furrowed brow, and pronounced jowls gave him a sad look, as though he'd just received bad news.

"That's him," Puhlman told Borger.

Their attention was not focused on the young fighters in the ring. They were more interested in another young man who held a heavy bag while an aspiring prizefighter peppered it with lefts and rights, his hands taped, perspiration flowing freely down his sculptured body.

"What does he do here?" Borger asked.

"Odd jobs," Puhlman answered. "He works to pay for gym time."

"He's a fighter?"

"He was, although he thinks he can still fight. Very paranoid, believes that managers and promoters have blackballed him."

"Have they?" Borger asked.

"For good reason. He took pretty severe beatings in his last few fights, left him with persistent headaches. Getting in the ring again would put him at risk."

Borger watched as the young man who'd been holding the heavy bag walked away and disappeared through a doorway.

"His name is Itani?" Borger said.

"That's right, Iskander Itani. His father was Lebanese, mother Italian. He tells me that his last name means that God gave him something special."

"You say he's paranoid."

"And angry. He believes that the Jews control the fight game and don't want an Arab winning fights."

Borger grunted and observed the two fighters finish their sparring session and leave the ring.

"Did he leave?" Borger asked.

His question was answered when Itani reappeared. Puhlman stood and motioned for him to join them.

"Iskander, say hello to Dr. Sheldon Borger."

Borger also stood and extended his hand, his smile wide and welcoming. "It's a pleasure to meet you."

Itani looked at Borger with dead eyes as he took his hand without enthusiasm.

"I understand that you're a fighter," Borger said.

Itani nodded.

"A good one, too," Puhlman said. "How are the headaches, Iskander?"

He grimaced as though the mention of a headache brought one on. "Not so good," the young man said, closing his eyes tightly and then opening them. "Sometimes it is worse than others."

Puhlman said, "I thought you'd want to meet Dr. Borger, Iskander. He's an expert in pain management and can help you get rid of those headaches—and possibly get you back in the ring."

Borger laughed away the compliment. "I've always thought I'd like to manage a fighter," he said. "I know it takes money to keep a fighter healthy and well trained."

"The promoters," Itani said to himself.

"Yes?" Borger said.

Puhlman interrupted. "How much longer will you be working today?"

Itani looked up at a large clock on the wall that read four o'clock. "I am finished now."

"I thought maybe the three of us could enjoy a drink together," Puhlman said.

Borger looked at Puhlman quizzically. Should he be suggesting a drink to an Arab? He wasn't aware that Itani's father was a Christian Arab and that Puhlman had had drinks with him before.

Itani seemed unsure whether to accept the offer, but Puhlman slapped him on the back and said, "A relaxing drink is good for headaches, huh?"

"Yes, I would like a drink," Itani said.

"Come, then," Borger said, "my treat at one of my favorite bars in the city, at the Huntington Hotel."

"I have to change my clothes," Itani said, looking down at his sweat-stained gray workout gear.

"Yes, you do that, Iskander," Puhlman said. "Take your time."

Borger used Itani's absence to further question Puhlman about the young man. "What's his family situation?" he asked.

"He lives with two brothers and his mother in a neighborhood just outside the city. There's no money. The brothers work at whatever jobs they can find. The mother isn't well, according to Iskander, cancer that's been treated but left her unable to work."

"The father?"

"He abandoned the family years ago. Iskander thought that he'd become a famous fighter and support the family, but it didn't work out that way."

"You told me when you called that he has strong political beliefs."

"He occasionally rants about politics and politicians. He's especially angry with George Mortinson."

Mortinson was the Democratic candidate for the presidency. With the election weeks away, the photogenic, charming Mortinson led the incumbent Republican president Allan Swayze in most polls by almost ten points. Swayze had been swept into office on a wave of protest against the previous Democratic administration. But the country fell into a deep recession during Swayze's tenure in the White House, and his chances for reelection were further reduced by attempts on the part of the Republican-controlled Congress to eviscerate funding for Social Security, Medicare, and Medicaid.

"He follows politics?" Borger asked.

"Not in any depth. He curses Mortinson for his pro-Israel policies and his hard stance on Iran. Typical Arab view."

Itani's return ended the discussion. He'd changed into a yellow-and-brown sport shirt, dark brown jeans, and sneakers.

"All set?" Borger asked.

"Yes," Itani replied.

They drove to the Huntington Hotel in Borger's silver Jaguar, which he'd parked just outside the gym. The uniformed doorman greeted Borger by name as they entered the opulent lobby and headed for the Big 4 Restaurant, the 4 referring to four industrial and financial giants of yesteryear who'd left their marks on the city's posh Nob Hill area. Once settled in the handsome wood-paneled bar with forest-green banquettes and lead-glass mirrors—and after Itani ordered a Tom Collins, Borger a Diet Coke, Puhlman white wine—Borger brought up the subject of Itani's headaches.

"How often do you have them, Iskander?"

"Often. Sometimes worse than other times."

Itani, drinking through a straw, drained his glass. He looked up at Borger and said sheepishly, "I was thirsty."

"Would you like another?"

"Yes . . . please."

"Tell me about when the headaches started," Borger probed.

"After my last fight. No, after the one before that."

"How many fights have you had?"

Itani looked to Puhlman.

"He's had fourteen professional bouts and a half dozen amateur fights."

"And you were beaten in your last fight?" Borger asked.

"Yes. He was a dirty fighter, an Irish fighter."

Borger sat back and smiled. "Do Irish fighters have a reputation for being dirty fighters?"

"Yes," was Itani's reply. "I was knocked out. I went to the hospital."

"You've seen doctors, I assume. I mean, aside from the ones you saw in the hospital."

"Yes."

"Well," said Borger, "I usually don't meet new patients in a gym or a bar, but I might be able to help you. I've helped many people cure their headaches. Let me see your eyes."

Borger brought his face within a foot of Itani's and looked into his eyes. "Do this for me," he said as he held his index finger above Itani's forehead. "Roll your eyes up and look at my finger."

Itani looked nervously around the bar.

"It's all right," Borger said. "Just look up at my finger without moving your head. That's it. Now, while you keep your eyes raised, slowly lower your eyelids. That's right, keep your eyes up and trained on my finger, and then slowly close them."

Itani's lids covered his eyes and stayed that way until Borger said, "That's fine, Iskander. I believe I can help you with your pain. That is, if you'd like me to."

"Yes, I would like that," Itani said.

He sat motionless, his eyes trained on something only he could see. Puhlman and Borger observed as the young man remained in that posture, not moving, physically present but mentally elsewhere. Then he abruptly stood and said, "I have to go to the bathroom."

"Interesting," Borger said to Puhlman.

"I'm glad you think so. It took awhile to find him."

"Can you get him to the house?"

"When?"

"Tomorrow night. I'll arrange a little get-together with people the young Mr. Itani will enjoy meeting. Tell him that there will be people who might be able to help resurrect his boxing career and that I'll work on his headaches. Ideally he'll agree to spend the night."

"I'll do what I can," Puhlman said.

When Itani returned, Borger told him how much he enjoyed meeting him but that he had to leave for an appointment. "I'm having some people to my home tomorrow night, a number of young people like yourself. I hope to see you there."

After Borger left, Puhlman said to Itani, "Dr. Borger is a wonderful man, Iskander, a brilliant physician who truly cares about people. Not only can he help with your headaches, he might have guests who can help launch your boxing career again. You'll come with me?"

"Yes."

Puhlman drove Itani home to the nondescript house he shared with his ailing mother and two brothers. After dropping him off, he went to his own home, where he called Borger. "What do you think?" he said.

"I think that all your work has paid off, Peter. I've just gone over the report on him you gave me. Coupled with my own evaluation today, I'd say he's perfect. Perfect! Did you notice the spontaneous trance states he lapses into?"

"He does it often. It's disconcerting."

"And so revealing. He'll be here tomorrow night?"

"Yes, he will."

"Good. He's ideal for the task. Well done, Peter. Well done indeed."

CHAPTER

13

Sheldon Borger's mansion on the crest of the highest hill in San Francisco's posh Nob Hill section of the city was once the home of a faded motion picture actress who'd left Hollywood to settle there. Borger bought it from her estate and expanded the gleaming white mansion on two sides, making it one of the largest residences in an area known for palatial homes. Long divorced, he alone reveled in the splendor of his fourteen-room home filled with expensive imported furnishings, especially ancient Chinese art, which he purchased through a dealer in Hong Kong who was always on the lookout for new pieces to add to his client's collection. Most of Borger's year was spent in his San Francisco home, although he maintained a condo in Washington, D.C., and occasionally escaped to a beachfront villa in Bermuda.

The only son of a wealthy Milwaukee family, he'd received his medical degree from the University of Wisconsin's School of Medicine and Public Health and became board-certified in OB-GYN. He practiced in Chicago until deciding one day that he was better suited to psychiatry. He obtained that certification at the University of Chicago's Pritzer School of Medicine and Neuroscience, abandoned his OB-GYN practice, left Chicago, and established a private psychiatric practice in Washington, where he reasoned that its residents probably suffered more mental problems than citizens of other cities.

It was in D.C. that he met Colin Landow.

Landow also was a psychiatrist, although he'd never practiced. He and Borger were introduced at a conference at the Omni Shoreham Hotel hosted by the mid-Atlantic chapter of the American Psychiatric

Association. It was during the closing night cocktail party that Landow suggested to Borger that he consider taking part in what Landow termed "a groundbreaking, and I might add lucrative, study with huge national security significance."

A phone call to Landow a few days later resulted in a series of meetings that revealed to Borger the nature of the study as well as its sponsor, the Central Intelligence Agency, where Landow headed a top secret division whose sole purpose was to stretch the limits of mind-control research.

"The Russians have been deeply involved in mind-control experimentation since World War One," Borger was told, "and the fear that they've moved ahead of us in this area is well-founded. We're taking steps to close the gap. We need men like you who are well schooled in medical hypnosis and the use of psychotropic drugs."

Borger often used hypnosis in his practice and had steeped himself in the literature. He was aware of the pioneering work of G. H. Estabrooks, who'd headed the psychology department at Colgate University, and had read Estabrooks's book

Hypnotism, in which a chapter was titled "Hypnotism in Warfare: The Super Spy." In that chapter Estabrooks focused on how a messenger could be programmed to securely carry secret information:

With hypnotism we can be sure of our private messenger. We hypnotize our man in, say, Washington. In hypnotism we give him the message. That message, may we add, can be both long and intricate. An intelligent individual can memorize a whole book under hypnosis if necessary. Then we start him out for Australia by plane with the instructions that no one can hypnotize him under any circumstances except Colonel Brown in Melbourne. By this device we overcome two difficulties. It is useless to intercept this messenger.

He has no documents and no amount of "third degreeing" can extract the information, for the information is not in the conscious mind to extract. We could also make him insensitive to pain so that even torture would be useless.

Also, with this hypnotic messenger we need have no worry about the double cross. In hypnotism we could build up his loyalty to the point that this would be unthinkable. Besides, he has nothing to tell. He is just a civilian with a business appointment in Australia, nothing more. He will give no information, for he has nothing to give.

Borger had also become intrigued with the phenomenon of multiple personalities and had treated two patients with this controversial affliction. He was particularly interested in Estabrooks's theory that creating the "super spy" was possible through the deliberate splitting of personalities within one person, which Estabrooks explained in *Hypnotism*:

We start with an excellent subject, and he must be just that, one of those rare individuals who accepts and who carries through every suggestion without hesitation. In addition, we need a man or a woman who is highly intelligent and physically tough. Then we start to develop a case of multiple personality through the use of hypnosis. In his normal waking state, which we will call Personality A, or PA, this individual will become a rabid communist. He will join the party, follow the party line and make himself as objectionable as possible to the authorities. Then we develop Personality B (PB), the secondary personality, the unconscious personality, if you wish, although this is somewhat a contradiction in terms. This personality is rabidly American and anti-communist. It has all the information possessed by PA, the normal personality, whereas PA does not have this advantage.

My super spy plays his role as a communist in his waking state, aggressively, consistently, fearlessly. But his PB is a loyal American, and PB has all the memories of PA. As a loyal American, he will not hesitate to divulge those memories.

Borger eagerly signed on with Landow and the CIA-funded project. Money wasn't a motivating factor. The deaths of his mother and father had left him with millions, so he didn't need income from his practice, with which he'd become bored anyway.

Participating in clandestine research was a heady experience, and he was devoted almost full time to the agency's mushrooming project. Funding was no object; he needed only to request money and it was there, delivered surreptitiously through myriad front groups. He eventually became the project's leader, traveling the country and the globe to confer with other physicians and to recruit those with the training and temperament necessary to fit in with the team. Unlike him, most of the doctors he recruited were enticed by the money being paid for their efforts. Psychiatry has never been as lucrative as orthopedic surgery or performing triple heart bypasses.

After a few years of working out of his Washington condo, he convinced his overseers at the CIA that it would be more secure to shift the center of research away from the capital and the continuing threat of congressional oversight. He lobbied for a front organization to be established in California, to which his superiors agreed. The plan made sense from the CIA's perspective. It also fit into Borger's personal agenda. Lately he'd been spending more time than he wanted to in Washington and yearned to get back to his beloved Nob Hill mansion and the California lifestyle that he much preferred to the cold, bureaucratic atmosphere of the nation's capital.

He'd spent the morning of the day after his introduction to Iskander Itani at the office he maintained at the Lightpath Psychiatric Clinic in Berkeley, across the bay from San Francisco. The one-story gray building on the northern end of Shattuck Avenue had once housed a small import firm that had gone belly-up. Using CIA funds, Borger had purchased the building and established the clinic in which he and a small handpicked group of psychiatrists and psychologists carried out the agency's mind-control experimentation.

On this particular morning, two of Borger's colleagues worked with a young man to regress him back to infancy using hypnosis. Borger observed through a one-way mirror that had been installed to allow visual access to the clinic's "session rooms." It wasn't going well. Previous attempts to bring about regression with other subjects had been successful, in one instance allowing a woman to regress to the suckling stage of her infancy. Other experiments in which hypnosis was used to anesthetize pain had been equally successful. But this particular young man surprisingly fought the trance state, which frustrated the two physicians working with him. They abruptly ended the session and escorted him from the room.

The subjects for these experiments had been chosen from a patient population provided by psychiatrists and psychologists on the CIA's clandestine payroll. Because only those with an extremely high capacity for entering into trance (4–5 on the HIP scale) were selected, the number of potential subjects was small. Most came from the San Francisco–Oakland area. But when a psychiatrist from another part of the country reported having a patient whose HIP score was a 5, travel arrangements were made to bring them to the clinic under the guise of participating in "clinical trials" that would provide advanced techniques to treat their problems, whether behavioral, addictions, or pain management. They were treated therapeutically, as promised. At the same time they were subjected to experimentation outside the therapeutic realm, their responses to myriad suggestions carefully evaluated and recorded.

After observing the failed session, Borger went to his office in the basement of the building, where Colin Landow, who'd flown in from Washington the previous day, sat with Peter Puhlman.

Puhlman, a clinical psychologist by training, had suffered a series of failures as a private practitioner. An inveterate gambler with a particular love of blackjack, and with two ex-wives, he was deeply in debt when he was approached by Borger to join the Lightpath Clinic project. CIA money funneled to him through Borger had bailed Puhlman out and provided him with a steady paycheck. He'd been fascinated with hypnosis early in his career and enthusiastically accepted the chance to work with a master who was willing to share his knowledge. He also enjoyed being close to Borger's lavish lifestyle and his friendship with celebrities.

Puhlman was a pragmatist, a man of few principles, which suited Borger, who'd learned from his involvement with the CIA that the only trustworthy motive for someone offering to spy against his country was money—not idealism, not anger, not misguided patriotism. As long as the money flowed, Borger knew that he could trust Puhlman. Should the funds stop . . . well, he would deal with that should the situation arise.

Landow was reviewing a file containing news reports of Dr. Mark Sedgwick's death when Borger arrived.

"Hello, Sheldon," Landow said, looking up from where he sat at a small round table.

Puhlman stood. "I'll be back in a few hours," he said.

"Good flight?" Borger asked as he joined Landow at the table.

"Is there such a thing anymore?" Landow replied through a small smile. He was a gaunt man with sandy hair that was longer than one might expect for a CIA employee. He wore half-glasses perched low on an aquiline patrician nose and was fond of Harris tweed sport jackets and solid-colored turtlenecks. On this day his shirt was navy.

"You flew coach?" Borger said.

"No, of course not. I'm referring to the poor souls in the back of the plane. I don't think I'd ever take a flight again if I was subjected to that nonsensical harassment that occurs at airports these days. I often think that I would like to be alone in a room with that moron, Reid, who tried to blow up the plane by lighting his sneaker. Because of him, millions of shoes are taken off every day around the world."

Borger laughed. "And if you were alone in that room with him?"

Landow made a pistol out of his hand and pointed it at Borger. "Bam!" he said.

"Sad what happened to Mark," Borger said, not sounding as though he meant it. "Anything new in the press coverage?"

"According to some articles, and information we've received through police channels, Ms. Klaus is still being considered a person of interest in the case."

"And?"

"Your work with her seems to have been highly successful. From what I'm told, she continues to profess her innocence and has no recollection of having done what they're accusing her of."

Borger adjusted himself in his chair and frowned.

"Something bothering you, Sheldon?"

"What? Oh, no, nothing is bothering me. I do wish they'd arranged a better way to dispose of the car. It never should have been found by the police."

"That's not posing a problem, Sheldon. It can't be traced back to her."

"Still—"

"Mark's unfortunate death is history," Landow said. "He was a foolish man. His increasingly negative reaction to the work we're doing couldn't be tolerated."

"But he *did* bring us Ms. Klaus," Borger said.

"Yes, he certainly did that. She's a remarkable subject. Your work with her was nothing short of brilliant."

"It's never difficult when you have a patient like that, just a matter of guiding her in the right direction while in trance. I believe I've found someone equally gifted. Of course, the stakes are considerably greater than silencing Mark Sedgwick."

Landow peered at Borger over his half-glasses. "Tell me more," he said.

"He's a young Arab American filled with anger, a prizefighter, although I gather he wasn't very successful. According to Puhlman, he took quite a beating in his last few fights, leaving him with headaches. I've offered to treat him. Peter is bringing him to the house tonight."

"You say he's angry. Angry at *what*?"

"The world. He's anti-Mortinson because of his liberal policies toward Israel." Borger laughed. "He even thinks that the Jews control professional boxing and are keeping him out of the ring."

"You've done a full evaluation of his trance capacity?"

"I will tonight, but from what I've observed already, he's an excellent subject."

Landow nodded and closed the file folder. "How fast can you program him?"

Borger shrugged. "Hard to tell, but I think I can do it fairly quickly."

"We need more than that," Landow said. "We're running out of time where Mortinson is concerned."

"I'm well aware of it, Colin. But as you know, finding the perfect assassin is never easy. I've evaluated every subject who's been brought here, and while some of them were potential candidates, none fully measured up. I'm hoping that this young man— whose name is Iskander Itani, by the way—will fill the bill."

"Let's hope," said Landow. "Our friends are getting antsy. The polls show that Mortinson will waltz into the White House unless drastic steps are taken. We all know how devastating that would be to our country."

"Speaking of our friends, Colin, I'm going to need a new infusion of money to pull this off, providing of course that this young man works out."

"How much?"

"A half million at least."

"That shouldn't be a problem. I'm flying to Texas tonight to meet with them. I'll bring up funding."

"Good. I think I'd better get home and prepare for tonight."

"Go ahead. The sooner this is done, the better it will be for everyone. The longer it drags out, the greater the likelihood that it can be traced back to the clinic—and even back to Langley, God forbid."

"I understand," Borger said, annoyed at being reminded of the obvious.

The project that he was about to undertake was, unlike previous projects, not funded by the CIA. The money behind the assassination of presidential candidate

George Mortinson came from a group of wealthy men, mostly from the South and Southwest, who considered themselves patriots of the first order. Through sympathetic rogue CIA employees like Colin Landow who shared their extreme right-wing beliefs, they'd turned to experts in mind control like Sheldon Borger to create the "perfect" assassin. Aside from Landow and a few others who were of like mind, the CIA itself was unaware of this criminal use of its Lightpath Psychiatric Clinic, nor was anyone connected with the agency's Medical and Psychological Analysis Center in Langley.

For Borger, seeking the perfect hypnotic subject to assassinate a presidential candidate reflected two things about him.

He shared the political views of the men behind the assassination.

But more important, he was enamored of being able to initiate direct action for everything he believed about the power of hypnosis and the use to which it could be put.

In a sense he considered what he was about to do a patriotic act unto itself, not simply because it would result in keeping a man like Mortinson out of power, but because it could be utilized by the government to rid the world of evil dictators and tyrants determined to bring down the United States of America. Too many half-cocked assassination attempts on such leaders as Fidel Castro (poisoning his cigars or putting depilatory powder in his shoes to cause his beard and hair to fall out); China's Zhou Enlai; the Ayatollah Khomeini; Rafael Trujillo of the Dominican Republic, and others had led him to believe that the government was woefully inept when it came to ridding the world of its despots and antidemocracy terrorists. The Joint Special Operations Command, an executive assassination ring reporting directly to then vice president Dick Cheney, had proved to be the government's gang that couldn't shoot straight.

The answer to Borger was simple. Only a perfectly chosen and trained assassin, programmed to kill but whose memory of the event was erased through hypnosis, could be trusted to do the job and do it right. And he, Dr. Sheldon Borger, knew how to make that a reality. He hung on to that belief whenever a twinge of guilt intruded. As a physician, he was expected to heal the sick, not create a human weapon of destruction. The oath he'd taken was to make people better, not be an instrument of their deaths. But what good was an oath when everyone around him routinely broke theirs? Politicians broke their oath to the Constitution the minute they lowered their right hand. Newlyweds promised to love and honor till death do they part, yet half of them ended up filing for divorce. Oaths were nothing more than empty words to be discarded for a greater good. His rationalization never failed to mitigate any guilt he might feel at odd moments.

"Keep me informed, Sheldon," Landow said as Borger got up to leave.

"Of course."

"And Sheldon."

"Yes?"

"Should this young man prove to not be the right subject and pose a possible threat to the project, you'll do what's necessary?"

Borger nodded and walked from the room.

"Do what's necessary" was a polite way of saying "kill him."

Borger had had to do that only once. The subject was a crusading California journalist whose columns persistently criticized the administration that was ensconced in the White House. The columnist was a known alcoholic subject to prolonged bouts of depression. His live-in girlfriend became concerned when he became suicidal and threatened to use a handgun he possessed to end his life. She'd been introduced to Borger a few months earlier and knew that he was a respected psychiatrist. She called, told Borger the problem, and he urged her to accompany the columnist to his house and to bring the gun with them. The girlfriend left her boyfriend with Borger and returned to the house they shared. Early that evening she received a call from Borger, who informed her that the columnist had agreed to spend the night there.

The next morning another call from Borger asked her to come to the house and take the columnist home. "I think you'll find him to be in a much more rational state of mind," Borger said.

He'd worked with the columnist well into the evening after persuading him to turn over the handgun, which Borger placed in a wall safe in his office. But when morning came, he returned the weapon to the columnist before sending him home with his paramour.

Later that afternoon, the columnist blew his brains out in the bathroom.

Naturally, the girlfriend questioned Borger about why he had returned the gun to the columnist.

"I had no legal right to keep it," was the psychiatrist's reply. "His depression was far deeper than I'd realized. You have my sincere condolences."

He was congratulated by Colin Landow for a job well done.

CHAPTER

14

Borger's household staff was busy preparing for the evening when he returned from the clinic. The menu had been decided in concert with his regular caterer and would include a few Middle Eastern dishes. Borger had made a mental note that Itani's favored drink was Tom Collins and reminded the caterer to include that drink's ingredients in the bar setup. He'd invited a dozen guests, including two young psychiatrists with whom he worked at the clinic. Also on the list of invitees was an attractive young prostitute whom Borger had used in previous situations, and her feminine charms had proved useful. His generosity with her (it was, after all, the CIA's money)— and with others—had been returned to him on occasion in the form of sexual favors. Music would be provided by a pianist-singer who worked the lounges at the city's better hotels, with regular bookings in Las Vegas. Borger's fat pocketbook ensured that the pianist would drop other gigs whenever the wealthy psychiatrist on Nob Hill beckoned.

Puhlman was scheduled to deliver Itani to the house at seven. Borger took a leisurely bath at five, carefully chose what he would wear that evening, took a half-hour nap, and was dressed and ready to greet his guests at six thirty.

Itani had dressed for the evening in what Borger assumed was his best clothing, a brown-and-black checked sport jacket, yellow shirt, tan chino pants, and black sneakers that were worn down at the heels. He'd tamed his unruly pitch-black hair with some sort of gel that smelled of eucalyptus. He followed Puhlman through the front door and was led by Borger to the living room, a huge expanse filled with items from his collection of Chinese art and artifacts. The pianist had already begun playing bouncy show tunes, and two waitresses from the caterer circulated among the guests carrying trays of hors d'oeuvres.

"How are you feeling?" Borger asked the young prizefighter. "Headaches any better?"

"It was not too bad today, but tonight I—"

"I think what you need to do is relax more," said Borger, nudging Itani in the direction of the bar. A drink or two and some pleasant conversation will do wonders for you. A Tom Collins?"

"Yes . . . please."

As the bartender made Itani's drink, he and Borger were joined by the prostitute, whose name was Elena, a vivacious brunette with dusky skin and wearing a tight white miniskirt and a low-cut teal blouse. Itani's eyes immediately went to her cleavage but shifted away out of embarrassment.

"Elena, I want you to meet Iskander Itani. Iskander, say hello to Elena Jones."

She flashed a wide smile and extended her hand, which he took tentatively.

"Sheldon has told me about you," she said. "You're a fighter? A prizefighter?"

"Yes."

"How exciting," she gushed. "My father was a big boxing fan, and he used to take me to the fights when I was a little girl."

"Oh, I . . . I think that's good," Itani said.

"It must take such courage to get into the ring," she said.

"No, it . . . it does not take courage if you are good, better than the other fighter."

"I suppose you're right," she said, touching his arm with long, painted fingertips.

Itani was handed his drink.

"I hope we have a chance to talk later," Elena said. "Will you be staying all night?"

Itani looked to Borger with a confused expression.

"You're welcome to," Borger said. "I have a guest suite with four bedrooms." He said to Elena, "You'll be staying, hon?"

"Yes."

"Good. You'll have plenty of time to chat with Iskander later in the evening."

Itani's eyes were trained on Elena's shapely rear end as she sashayed away in the direction of a knot of people.

"She's a sweetheart," Borger said to Itani. "A really nice girl." He smiled. "And pretty, too, huh?"

"Yes, very pretty, very pretty."

Borger pointed across the large room to where a man stood talking with Peter Puhlman. "I told you that there would be someone here who might be interested in backing you as a boxer, Iskander. He has plenty of money and has supported many young fighters."

"What is his name?" Itani asked.

"Jake Gibbons."

"I do not know that name."

"He works mostly on the East Coast. Come, I'll introduce you."

Gibbons looked like an ex-fighter, which he was. He'd also been a collector for one of the city's leading loan sharks and had had run-ins with the police on several occasions. His nose was broad and flattened, and there was scar tissue along the ridges of his prominent eyebrows.

But those days were in his past. He was now on Borger's payroll (by extension the CIA's payroll) as the psychiatrist's bodyguard, who could be called upon in the event muscle was needed. Unlike Puhlman,

Gibbons knew little about what Borger did and where his money came from aside from the occasional celebrity patient whom Borger treated.

Puhlman had arranged for Gibbons to be there that evening and had filled him in on Itani's boxing career and aspirations.

After they'd been introduced, Gibbons said, "You look like, what, a welterweight?"

"I was a super lightweight," Itani replied, "but I have gotten heavier. I can fight as a welterweight."

"I like it when a fighter moves up in class," Gibbons said, "puts on some added muscle. I hear that you haven't fought in a while."

"A year," said Itani, "but I am ready to fight again."

"You have management?"

"No. The—"

"I might be interested in taking you on," said Gibbons. "Of course, I'd want to see you in the ring. Maybe I can stop by the gym and watch you go a few rounds."

Itani's response was to shut his eyes against a sudden stabbing pain over his eyes. Borger noticed it and said, "Iskander has been suffering headaches lately. One of the reasons he's here tonight is to see how I can help him."

Gibbons said, "If anyone can get rid of your headaches, kid, it's the doc here. He's the best."

"You'll feel better after tonight," Borger assured Itani as he led him away from Gibbons and Puhlman. "I have a suggestion. It's hard for me to break away from my guests, but when the party is over we can spend a few hours together working on your headaches."

"That would be good," said Itani.

"I have a better suggestion. Is there any reason why you can't spend the night here? I always have a spare set of pajamas and a robe for my overnight guests. It would give me more time with you. We can work on those headaches tonight and again in the morning."

Itani thought of Elena, who'd said that she would also be staying.

"Okay?" Borger said.

"Yes, thank you."

"Good. I see that you've finished your drink. Go have another while I mingle with my guests. Make yourself at home, Iskander. It's a pleasure having you here."

While Borger chatted with other guests, he kept an eye on Itani from across the room. The young man had gotten a second drink from the bar and stood alone, surveying the room. Puhlman came to him.

"Enjoying yourself?" he asked.

"Oh, yes. This is a very nice house."

"The doctor has good tastes, Iskander, and the money to indulge them. Will you be spending the night here so that you and he can work on those headaches of yours?"

"Yes."

"A smart decision." He indicated Itani's empty glass. "You need a refill on that drink. Don't be bashful."

Puhlman motioned for Elena to spend time with Itani. She stood with him at the bar as he waited for his third drink and suggested that he take it outside to the expansive wraparound terrace that provided a glittering view of the city. As they stood at a low stone wall that rimmed the terrace, Elena leaned easily against his side. "It's beautiful, huh?"

Itani didn't answer. She glanced at him. He seemed to have slipped into a trance, vacant, not there, eyes focused on the horizon, breathing deeply.

"Are you all right?" she asked.

It took him a moment to return to the here and now. "Yes, I am fine. I was . . . thinking."

She smiled and said, "You seem like a very intelligent person, I mean for a boxer."

He turned and faced her. "Why do you think that?"

"Think that? I—"

"I am intelligent," he said into the air.

"I know. That's what I said."

He turned from her and retreated into his own world again.

Elena had become apprehensive. She'd had her share of weirdoes in the years that she'd been selling her body and wasn't eager to end up with another. She relaxed when he again turned to her and smiled. "I am sorry," he said. "I have these headaches that Dr. Borger will cure and they sometimes make me—" His smile turned into a laugh. "Make me a little crazy."

"I don't think you're crazy," she said, rubbing her hand on his back. "I like you."

"I like you, too," he said and sucked the rest of his Tom Collins through the straw.

"You need another drink," she said.

"Yes, I do."

She accompanied him back inside, where the bartender obliged.

"I'll see you later," she said. "You're staying over, too. We'll have plenty of time to talk and get to know each other better."

He spent the rest of the party in relative isolation, aside from the two psychiatrist colleagues of Borger's who made it a point to initiate conversation with him. As they did, they performed their own preliminary evaluation of his ability to enter trance. As the party broke up, they told Borger that it was their collective opinion that he could be a 5 on the HIP scale, a rare hypnotic subject. Of course, they pointed out that further testing would have to be done.

"I'll be doing that tonight after everyone leaves," Borger assured them. Neither of his colleagues was aware of the use to which Borger intended to put Itani. It was routine at the clinic to seek out good subjects for experimentation. That it was Borger's intention to turn Itani into an assassin was not on their need-to-know list.

Puhlman and Elena lingered after the others had left.

"You'll excuse us," Borger said. "Iskander and I have some work to do. I'm sure you'll have plenty of time to get better acquainted after we're done." He said it to Elena, who smiled provocatively at Itani.

Borger and Itani went to Borger's study. It was a large, thickly carpeted room dominated by heavy black leather furniture including two recliners that faced each other. The blinds were tightly drawn; the only light came from a lamp situated over one of the recliners.

"Sit there," Borger instructed, indicating the chair beneath the lamp.

Itani stumbled as he moved to sit. The drinks had affected him; he felt lightheaded.

"Comfortable?" Borger asked as he took the opposite chair.

"Yes."

"Good. I want you to be comfortable, Iskander. Now, I am going to ask you to do a few things for me so that I can determine how best to approach your headaches. Are you ready?"

"Yes."

Borger was concerned with the amount of alcohol that Itani had consumed. Despite the common belief that hypnosis puts you to sleep, the fact is that it results in intensely focused concentration on the part of the subject, and alcohol can interfere with that. But with a perfect subject—and Borger was convinced that Itani was exactly that—its effect should be minimal.

He picked up a gold coin from a nearby table and brought it to within inches of Itani's eyes. "Focus on the coin, Iskander, focus carefully. As you do, allow yourself to relax and to go to a peaceful place where there is no pain. I am going to count backward from ten. When I am finished, you'll be in that peaceful place and relaxed. Ten . . . nine . . . eight . . ."

Borger had reached only seven when Itani was in a deep trance. Borger smiled. This was going to be easier than he'd thought.

When he'd completed his countdown, he suggested that Itani's right arm was attached to a helium balloon and would rise into the air. Itani's arm floated up and remained outstretched.

"Good," Borger said. "Excellent." He proceeded to suggest to Itani that his head was covered by a special helmet that was very cold, and that Itani could put on the helmet whenever he felt a headache coming on. Itani's hand went to his head. "Do you feel the cold, Iskander?"

"Yes. It is very cold."

"Whenever you use the helmet, your headaches will go away. Do you understand?"

"Yes."

Borger next took a pad of paper and a pencil from the table and handed them to Itani. "I want you to start writing down everything that you're thinking, Iskander. Think of the evil in this world and the evil people who want to hurt you and others like you. Think of those who want to keep you from boxing again, the Jews who control your life."

Borger waited until Itani started to write. He formed the words on the paper carefully, writing with almost perfect penmanship. "Jews must die," he wrote. And then he wrote it again. And again. Over and over.

"That's right, Iskander," Borger said in his soothing, well-modulated voice. "Keep writing. Think of Israel and what it has done to you and your family, to all the families in your native country."

Itani continued writing, substituting "Israel" for "Jews" and saying that it must die. Borger waited silently as his subject continued his automatic writing. When Itani reached the bottom of the page, Borger took the notebook and pencil from him and said, "You're going deeper into trance Iskander. Deeper. Deeper. Deeper."

Itani's faced twisted into anger, and he clenched his fists on his lap. A low moan came from deep inside.

"That's it, Iskander," Borger continued. "Deeper. Deeper. People who want to help Israel must be stopped."

Itani's expression of sheer rage intensified.

"These people must be stopped," Borger said.

"Yes, yes," was Itani's response.

"They must be stopped. They must be killed to save you and your family."

Itani groaned.

The session continued for another fifteen minutes, with Borger reinforcing his hate messages. It was toward the end that he mentioned presidential candidate George Mortinson.

Itani lunged at Borger with his right fist, causing the doctor to increase the distance between them. "That's right," Borger said. "You must be angry at injustice. You must do something about it."

Borger decided to end Itani's trance. He gently told him that he would again count backward from ten to one. "When I reach one, you will come fully awake and feel wonderful. You will have no recollection of what has happened here over the past half hour. And when I tell you that it will rain tomorrow, you will go to the window and look out. You will feel that cold helmet on your head and it will feel good. There will be no headaches, but if there ever is, you will put on that cold helmet and the headache will go away. When I say that the forecast was wrong, the helmet will disappear and you will say, 'It was supposed to rain.'"

Borger slowly counted down to one. When he reached it, he snapped his fingers and said, "How do you feel, Iskander?"

Itani appeared to be startled. He looked around the room as though wondering where he was and why he was there.

"It will rain tomorrow," Borger said.

Itani slowly got up and went directly to

the window. He opened the blinds and peered into the darkness. His hands went to his head. "My head is cold," he said.

"The forecast was wrong," Borger said.

Itani dropped his hands to his sides. "It was supposed to rain," he said.

"Yes, it was," said Borger. "How do you feel?"

"I feel good."

"No headache?"

"No, no headache."

"Do you remember what has just happened here in my office?"

Itani looked puzzled. "No," he said. "We . . . we talked."

"Yes, we talked. Do you remember what we talked about?"

Itani shook his head.

"We talked about good things, worthwhile things. I hypnotized you."

Anger returned to Itani's face. "No. No you did not."

Borger had him take his seat again and handed him the notepad. "Do you recognize this?" he asked.

Itani squinted in the dim light as he looked at the page with his writings. "No," he said.

"You wrote that," Borger said.

"No, I did not," Itani said angrily.

Borger smiled and patted his knee, pleased that his subject now exhibited total amnesia of what had transpired. "The important thing, Iskander, is that you feel good and that your headaches are gone," he said. "But we must have more sessions together to be sure that your headaches will never return. Will you do that?"

"Yes, I will."

"Good. How about we go back to see Elena? The two of you will be my overnight guests, and I'm sure you have much to discuss."

Elena was waiting with Puhlman in the living room, which the caterer had cleaned up after the party and departed.

"Have a drink," Borger told Elena and Itani. "Relax. The night isn't over yet."

CHAPTER

15

Iskander Itani looked over at the naked Elena Jones, who slept peacefully, her mane of dark hair swirling about her pretty face. He looked down and realized that he, too, was still naked after their awkward lovemaking. He pulled the sheet up over him and thought back to what had led them there.

They'd had drinks together—one drink too many for him—and his memory of what had transpired was fuzzy. He knew it had happened, but it was as though it had involved someone else. The stripping off of clothes and tumbling into bed seemed to have occurred within seconds—the entire episode was compressed.

There was a slight, albeit constant, throbbing above and behind his eyes. Too many Tom Collinses? He remembered what Dr. Borger had said and the exercise he'd taught. Itani rolled his eyes up as far as he could, slowly lowered his eyelids, and drew deep breaths. He allowed one arm to slowly levitate and continued the rhythm of his breathing until he imagined that an ice-cold helmet had been slipped over his head. A smile came to his face. The pain in his head was gone. He remained that way for a few more minutes before opening his eyes and glancing over again at Elena. A recollection of last night's sweaty tryst now became evident to him as though barriers to memory had lifted along with his imaginary helmet. He rolled onto his side, the motion waking her.

"Good morning," he said.

"Good morning," she replied huskily, pushing her hair from her face. She sat up. Itani reached for a breast, but she pushed away his hand. "You're too strong for me," she said sweetly. "You tired me out last night."

"I am sorry."

"No, no, no, no need to be sorry. I loved it. Did you?"

"Yes, very much."

She bounded out of bed, grabbed her clothing from the chair on which she'd tossed it, and disappeared into the bathroom. Itani got up, stretched, and slipped on a pale blue terry cloth robe that was provided for guests. He went to the window and opened the drapes. It was sunny, with puffy blue clouds racing by. Two Hispanic men tended to flowers that bordered a flagstone patio.

He plopped in a chair and tried to remember everything that had occurred. He remembered the party, of course, the conversation with the man named Jake who said he could help resurrect his boxing career, and other people to whom he'd been introduced. He recalled sitting with Borger in his study after everyone had left, and the doctor's instructions about the cold helmet whenever he felt a headache coming on. But after that it was a blank—until having a drink with Elena and ending up in bed with her.

All in all, he felt better than he had for

weeks, months, even years. How fortunate to have met Peter Puhlman at the gym and to have been introduced to this amazing doctor who did in one session what other doctors had failed to do, and who did it with the caring gentleness of a father. Yes, that was it. Borger was like the father Iskander had never known, a good and decent man who knew so much, who knew everything.

Elena was dressed when she emerged from the bathroom.

"Have to run, love. I hope I see you again."

Itani stood and stepped toward her.

"Go back to bed, honey," she said. "Enjoy your stay. Bye."

He sat back in the chair and rubbed his eyes. American young women were so different from those he knew back in Lebanon, so carefree and full of life. He'd never been comfortable around pretty young women, cautious and afraid of being rebuffed. He laughed. She was the aggressor, and it was he who could have done the rebuffing had he wanted to. But of course he didn't.

He showered and made use of male toiletries provided in a pouch. He wished he had a change of clothing; the pajamas provided hadn't been necessary last night or useful in the light of day. He dressed, left the room, and wandered down to the main house where Borger sat in the dining room having breakfast.

"Well, good morning, Iskander," he said loudly. "Come, join me. What would you like, eggs, waffles? My cook whips up wonderful breakfasts."

"I, ah . . . whatever you have," Itani said.

Borger called for the cook and instructed her to prepare a hearty breakfast for his young guest. "He's a prizefighter," he told her. "He needs his nourishment."

Itani felt uncomfortable sitting alone with Borger and hoped that his host would not ask him about the night spent with Elena. To his relief, Borger immediately turned to the subject of boxing and further treatment of Itani's headaches.

"I have a proposal for you," Borger said as he patted his lips with his napkin. "But first I want to ask about your headaches. Have you had any since our session last night?"

"Yes, sir," Itani said. "This morning. But I put on the helmet and it was gone. Poof! Like that." He grinned.

"That's wonderful," said Borger. "But it's important that we continue working on the problem. I've found over the years that while a single session can be effective, it doesn't necessarily last long term. I want to continue working with you until we're assured that those headaches will be a permanent thing of the past."

"Yes, that's good," Itani said. He desperately wanted to please this man who'd entered his life so unexpectedly and who had his best interests at heart. "I would like that," he added.

"Good. I also want to follow up on resurrecting your boxing career. I've spoken with Jake Gibbons this morning, and he has agreed to consider managing you. He wants to see you work out."

"All right. I can go to the gym and—"

"No, not the gym, Iskander. He can come and watch you right here. I have a fully equipped gym of my own right here in the house, in the basement. If you agree, you can train here, live here. That will enable us to continue treating your headaches while at the same time you get in shape to resume your career. I realize that this is all new to you but, to be truthful, I've taken a sincere liking to you."

Itani squirmed in his chair and fumbled for an answer.

"There's no need to respond right now, Iskander. I'm not suggesting that you come and live here forever. I'm sure your family wouldn't take kindly to that. What I am suggesting is that you plan to spend two or three weeks here. That will give me the opportunity to rid you of those headaches forever while you put other aspects of your life together. I admit that I have a selfish motive behind my offer, Iskander. You see, it's important to me that my success in curing headaches be documented in a scientific way. I've done this with others. When I'm successful with a patient, it's necessary that I share with other physicians the techniques that I've developed over the years. I believe that you are one of those patients who will truly benefit from my treatments. In other words, you would be doing *me* a favor by accepting my offer to live here for a few weeks and to continue treatment."

He observed Itani for a reaction. The young man had suddenly drifted to another place known only to him. Borger waited patiently until Itani blinked his eyes and seemed almost startled that he was there at the table. He looked up as the cook delivered his breakfast—scrambled eggs, two pancakes, strips of bacon, and hash fries. Borger poured him orange juice from a cut-glass pitcher and coffee from a stainless-steel thermos. "Eat up, my boy," he said. "I'll be back in a few minutes."

When Borger returned, he patted Itani on the shoulder. "Looks like you were hungry," he said, motioning at the empty plate. "Come with me. I have something to show you."

He led Itani down to the basement gym that was equipped with the latest exercise equipment.

"It is so nice," Itani said. "So big and clean."

"And it will be even nicer this afternoon when they deliver the punching bags and the portable ring I've ordered."

Itani looked as though he might cry. Borger put his arm around his shoulders and said, "It's my pleasure to do this for a deserving young man."

"I don't think—"

"A problem?"

"I could never repay you, Dr. Borger. And my family. I don't know how they will be if I leave them."

"Don't be silly," Borger said. "You won't be leaving them. As I said it's only for a few weeks while we get rid of your headaches forever. I'll tell you what. I'll have Peter Puhlman drive you home, where you can explain to your family what you're doing. I'm told that your mother is ill. I can refer her to some of the top doctors in the area. She'll be delighted to see her son given this wonderful opportunity."

Itani started to say something, but Borger's raised hand stopped the words. "And let's not hear ever again of having to repay me. As you've probably noticed, life has been good, very good indeed, for me. But what good is money if you don't share it with others? I'll be happy to help you and your family during this difficult period. Neither you nor your family will have to worry about money while we work together. This country truly is the land of opportunity,

Iskander, and it can be for you. Frankly, that's why I'm very concerned with the presidential election that's coming up. Men like George Mortinson don't understand what makes this country great. If they have their way, they'll destroy it for everyone, you and me included."

Anger crossed Itani's swarthy, handsome face.

"In addition to my medical practice, I'm involved with influential men in our nation who share my views about Mortinson and enemies like him."

Mention of presidential candidate Mortinson sent Itani into an involuntary trance. Borger snapped him out of it and said, "Let's spend an hour together to reinforce ways to control your headaches. Then Peter will drive you home, where you can collect some clothing and tell your family that you'll be away for a few weeks. The new gym equipment will be here when you return, and you can start training again, free of headaches and with the whole world in front of you."

And so Iskander Itani moved into Dr. Sheldon Borger's palatial home on San

Francisco's Nob Hill. Naturally he faced questions about it when he went directly to the room he shared with one of his brothers and started shoving clothing into a battered backpack covered with faded, ripped boxing stickers and Lebanese flag decals.

"I have met a wonderful man," Iskander told his younger brother, "a medical doctor. He is an expert in managing pain like my headaches and has already helped me. He is *al-Mahdi,* truly a savior. He has many rich friends who want to help me with my boxing career. I will live with him for two weeks while he cures my headaches, *And* he has his own gymnasium in his own house and will have heavy and light bags and a ring set up for me."

His brother laughed along with Iskander. "What is he," the brother asked playfully, "a *shaz*?"

Iskander punched his brother in the chest. No, you idiot, he is not a queer." Iskander lowered his voice. "Listen. Last night I slept with one of the most beautiful women I have ever seen. Her name is Elena. She was at a party the doctor had, and she lured me into bed." He extended his fingers and moved them to indicate how she'd enticed him.

"I don't believe you."

"Don't believe me, then. It is true. Why would I lie to my brother? Look, the man who dropped me off—his name is Puhlman, a fat man—he will be back soon to take me to the doctor's house, and what a house it is, the biggest house in San Francisco."

His brother turned serious as he sat on the bed.

"Hey," Iskander said, "what's the matter?"

"I want to go with you."

"No. I mean the doctor would be mad if I bring someone else. I can't do that." He slapped his brother on the top of his head. "I'll be back in two weeks. This doctor he will make us rich. I know it. My headaches are gone. Good, huh? Listen, do not tell Mother where I've gone."

"What do I say?"

"You say that . . . you say that I went away to work for two weeks, that's all. Tell her I will be back with money. Okay?"

"Okay."

"Where is she and your brother?"

He shrugged.

Puhlman pulled up in front and blew the horn.

"It's the fat man. I have to go."

"Can I call you?"

"No. Two weeks." He kissed his brother on the cheek. "Two weeks and things will be good, better than they have ever been for us."

CHAPTER

16

Borger used Itani's absence to add to notes he'd made that would be included in his report once the exercise was completed. He was in the midst of that when he received a call from his CIA contact, the psychiatrist Colin Landow.

"How is it going?" Landow asked. He was calling from a Dallas hotel after having met with the project's moneymen.

"Very well. He's even more perfect than I'd hoped for. He'll be staying here at the house for a few weeks, plenty of time to prepare him."

"A few weeks is too long, Sheldon.

We've chosen a date eleven days from now, in D.C."

"Oh?"

Borger leaned back in his office chair and did a quick mental calculation. He'd assumed that the project's culmination would occur in San Francisco during a campaign stop there by George Mortinson. Shifting it to Washington would mean transporting Itani there and setting him up. That gave Borger nine days at the most to accomplish what he needed to.

"Is that a problem?" Landow asked in his New England–tinged voice.

"No, it's not a problem, Colin. Of course there's the logistics of getting him there and—"

"That will be taken care of. Your responsibility is to have him prepared."

Borger bristled at being told his responsibilities. He'd grown increasingly disenchanted with Landow over the past few years, resenting his imperious tone and need to remind Borger of the obvious.

"He'll be fully prepared," Borger said flatly.

"Good. I'm coming to San Francisco tomorrow, staying overnight. Do you have dinner plans?"

"I planned on working with him every possible moment."

"I'm sure you can spare a few hours for me."

"Yes, I'm free for dinner."

"Good. I'll call from the hotel. I'll be at the Hyatt on the Embarcadero."

Borger heard the click on Landow's end.

Borger went to the window and looked out over the grounds. He'd been contemplating bowing out of the program for a while now. Had the time come? It seemed to him that it probably had.

Although he had joined the program late in its history, the quest for creating the perfect spy or messenger had been under way since the mid-1950s when then CIA director Allen Dulles persuaded Harold Wolff, a friend and prominent Cornell neuropsychiatrist and an expert on stress, to examine returning American prisoners of war who had served in Korea. The goal was to uncover brainwashing that these POWs might have undergone. Working through a CIA-funded front, the Society for the Investigation of Human Ecology, later renamed the Human Ecology Fund,

Wolff and others delved deeply into brain-washing techniques used by the North Koreans.

While the original purpose of the research was defensive in nature, it soon became evident to those involved that many of the same techniques used by the North Koreans—and the Russians—could be utilized to program and manipulate Americans for, as the project's founders proclaimed, "the national good."

The research quickly escalated to include hundreds of scientists working at many of the nation's leading hospitals and universities, few of whom were aware that their financing came from the CIA. (Forty-four top universities around the country were eventually informed by the CIA in 1977 that scientific research conducted at their facilities had been, in fact, agency-funded.)

But that tip-of-the-hat demonstration of transparency in no way slowed the agency's ongoing and secretive investigations into means of controlling individuals. Large-scale programs with names such as ARTICHOKE, MK-ULTRA, and BLUE-BIRD heralded an expansion of research, with unwitting American citizens the human guinea pigs.

Did the clandestine, sometimes brutal, and even deadly nature of these experiments prick the consciences of the doctors and scientists involved? For some, the money justified everything and anything. For others, a perverted sense of patriotism salved their guilt.

In Sheldon Borger's case, on rare occasions he questioned whether using the power of hypnosis for other than legitimate treatment of needy patients was appropriate. He wondered if making nefarious use of the pioneering work of such giants in the field as Herbert Spiegel and his HIP test was justified. But such flashes of conscience didn't last long. As far as Borger was concerned, University of Illinois psychologist Charles Osgood summed up a defense of the practice: "If we had to do only things that would be safe when other people use them, there would be very little—damn little—we could do in science."

Borger often told colleagues who questioned the work they did, "Look, we invented atomic energy. It can be used to light a city or blow it up. It's not up to us to

question what use our research findings
are put to."

Borger never lost a night's sleep over it.
Nevertheless, he debated internally
whether the time was coming for him to
withdraw. The assassination of presidential candidate George Mortinson, using a
killer he'd personally programmed, would
be the touchstone of his long career. Not
only would he prove the potency of hypnosis, he would also make America a better
place by ridding it of the likes of Mortinson.
After that, his work would be done. He de-
served a nice long rest.

He returned to his desk and finished de-
termining the schedule for working with
Itani. He was cognizant, of course, that
things could go wrong. Although Itani appeared to be the perfect hypnotic subject,
Borger had seen others in that class fall
apart during programming. It was his thesis that those situations resulted from a
wrong move on the part of the hypnotist,
and he pledged to himself that he would
exercise the utmost caution in his approach.
He'd had great success with Sheila Klaus,
and from everything he'd heard and read,

the amnesia he'd programmed into her had held. She'd proved to be an excellent subject, but it was his judgment that Itani was even better. Shelia's misplaced and unrequited love for Mark Sedgwick had generated anger at him in her. It was important that the subject already be angry with the selected victim, and Borger had sensed Sheila's unhappiness with her therapist the first time Sedgwick had brought her to San Francisco and to the Lightpath Clinic.

Once the word came down that Sedgwick was to be eliminated, Borger wondered whether he would have to "change the visual" with Sheila to cause her to kill Sedgwick. Borger had lectured on that technique many times to young medical students who'd chosen psychiatry as their specialty. He'd explained to them that it was almost impossible to prompt someone under hypnosis to violate his or her core beliefs. He used as an example high school males who'd heard that they could use hypnosis to convince a pretty co-ed to remove her clothing. That was unlikely—unless the girl was already eager to undress for the school's football star. But it was possible under hypnosis to convince the young woman that she was alone in a very warm room and needed to undress to be comfortable.

Another example was telling a wife under hypnosis to shoot her husband when he came through the door. That wouldn't work with a loving wife. But she could be programmed to believe that when the door opened, it wasn't her husband coming through it. Instead it was a rabid bear intent upon killing her.

As it turned out, it wasn't necessary to apply that technique to Sheila Klaus. Her pique at having her sexual and romantic overtures to Sedgwick rebuffed was sufficient. The problem was that murdering someone, anyone, wasn't compatible with her basic beliefs. That's where her "second personality" came in handy.

During his sessions with Sheila, Sedgwick had uncovered another personality within her, an imaginary childhood friend she called Carla. Using hypnosis, he'd reinforced this alter ego to the extent that Carla could be easily summoned by him. While

Sheila was basically a passive person, she turned to Carla as the tough one, the person who would right the wrongs Sheila perceived as being perpetrated against her.

Sheila often demonstrated this second personality when Sedgwick brought her to San Francisco to participate in trials at Lightpath. Borger was delighted to see this imaginary person in her life and focused on further developing Carla. In doing so—and without Sedgwick's knowledge—he injected himself into Sheila's life as her second "control," someone whom she, and Carla, would obey without question. When Borger was told that it was necessary to get rid of Sedgwick, he instructed Sheila (and Carla) to stop seeing her therapist in Washington, which she did. She was then programmed to make two more trips to San Francisco without Sedgwick, during which Borger applied constant reinforcement of her negative feelings toward Sedgwick and the need for Carla to take revenge. Sheila had been given a code to which she would respond when back in Washington, a telephone call during which the caller would say, "It's a beautiful day for a cruise." That brought Carla to the fore, who did as instructed. Carla walked out of Sheila's house to a white Buick sedan that had been delivered and parked in the driveway. She got behind the wheel, drove to Virginia Avenue, waited for Sedgwick to cross the street, and ran him down. She then returned the car to Sheila's home, where the man who'd delivered it got behind the wheel and drove away. Once Borger had been informed that Sedgwick was dead, he called Sheila and said, "The cruise has been canceled." She instantly came out of her trance state and had no memory whatsoever of any aspect of what had happened, including her visits to Borger and Carla's violent act against Mark Sedgwick.

Borger knew, of course, that there would come a day when Sheila Klaus would have to be eliminated to ensure that her amnesia was truly permanent. There was always the threat that she'd end up with someone else who practiced hypnosis and have her programming undone.

But that was not his concern at that moment. Once his work with Iskander

Itani was completed, he would bow out of the program. Sheila Klaus would be *their* problem.

His only concern at the moment was to turn Itani into the perfect assassin, and he had nine days to do it.

CHAPTER
17

WASHINGTON, D.C.

Meg Whitson, chief of staff to George Mortinson, aspirant for the presidency of the United States, had arrived at the candidate's D.C. campaign office at six that morning and was in a meeting five minutes later with key members of her staff.

"I can't believe that he's taking the day off," a staffer said, throwing up his hands in desperation.

"Oh, come on, John," Whitson said. "I'm just surprised that it hasn't happened more times than this."

Mortinson often proved exasperating to his staff. He was brilliant. He was photogenic. He could deliver a stirring speech to rival Obama, Reagan, or Kennedy. He was also too nonchalant in the eyes of those who had guided him to this pinnacle in his political career.

"I've been working on that interview with Diane Sawyer that could have come off later today."

"Good thing you hadn't finalized it," was Whitson's terse reply. "Look," she said, "we all know that the guy needs his downtime. Remember what Gene McCarthy said when he was running?"

"Yeah, yeah, I remember. He said every president should take a day off a week to read poetry or listen to music. Look where *that* got him."

Whitson sighed and pushed away a lock of hair that had fallen over her forehead. "Can we shelve this?" she asked. "He's made up his mind to take a day off, and that's that."

She turned to another at the meeting, a Secret Service agent with a shaved head who was in charge of the detail assigned to protect the candidate. "Anything new on those latest threats?" she asked.

"Yeah, there is. We traced the latest one

to some loopy chicken farmer in Missouri who blames the senator for the price of eggs going down." He grinned. "The FBI has retained him for further questioning. If he hadn't talked about burying the senator underneath his chicken coop, he would have been ignored. We've gotten a lot more, though. Every time Senator Mortinson makes a speech, they come pouring in. That talk he gave yesterday about how you can only judge a society by the way it treats its less fortunate and vulnerable really opened the floodgates. But that's not the real problem. Can anybody here rein him in? Every time he works a crowd, he puts the pressure on us, especially with his spur-of-the-moment decisions."

The staffer who'd complained about losing a potential Sawyer interview laughed. "Lots of luck," he said. "Senator Mortinson really does march to his own drummer. Drives us nuts."

The Secret Service agent consulted a clipboard. "All we've been told about today is that he's playing tennis at eleven at the Sutton Racquet Club on New Mexico with a friend, a law professor at GW, Mackensie Smith, and lunch with him after the match at Chef Geoff's downtown. That jibe with what you have?"

Whitson nodded and said, "Chef Geoff's. He likes the burgers there."

The agent continued reading from his notes. "He and Mrs. Mortinson are having dinner at seven with this same friend and his wife, Mrs. Annabel Lee-Smith, and another couple from Wisconsin, a Mr. and Mrs. Morey, Jack and Maria. At least he's chosen the restaurant for dinner in advance, Bistro Bis in the Hotel George. He doesn't always. The Smiths were cleared long ago. We're checking out the Moreys now. The restaurants are being swept."

Whitson laughed. "Bistro Bis," she said, "where he'll have steak tartare, his favorite."

The agent laughed. "Eating raw meat will kill him faster than any terrorist."

"Not there," another staffer chimed in. "Best steak tartare in the city."

"He's got steel arteries," another staffer quipped.

"What's Mrs. Mortinson's schedule for today?" Whitson was asked.

"I haven't been told yet by her scheduler. I'll find out and let you know. Enjoy the holiday. There might not be another until he's in the White House."

Presidential candidate George Mortinson got off the stationary bike in the home he and his wife had shared in the District since his election to the Senate. It was six a.m. He'd gotten to bed at one after meeting with his campaign strategists.

Mortinson was one of those men who need little sleep to function, and he enjoyed late-night bull sessions with those closest to him, including his chief of staff, Meg Whitson, who'd been at his side since his days as a congressman from Wisconsin. He'd used that platform to run for, and win, a Senate seat and served almost two full terms in the senior congressional body. That he would one day run for the presidency was a foregone conclusion for pundits for whom politics was heroin.

Mortinson came from a Wisconsin political dynasty. His grandfather had served one term as governor, his father two terms in the same position. There was plenty of family money to support this third generation's foray into national politics. The grandfather had made his fortune in a chain of supermarkets that blanketed the country, followed by a fast-food franchise that grew to include outlets in every state. When he died, his financial interests were left to his son, who had little interest in following in the family's business footsteps. Instead of taking a hands-on role in running the companies, he hired the best managers and set his sights on emulating his father's fling with state politics. By the time his father retired due to ill health, he'd established himself as Wisconsin's most successful, forward-thinking governor; his son George's political future was ordained.

That wasn't to say that the path to the White House would be easy. George Mortinson's politics were decidedly left of center. Many on the right considered him the biggest threat to the nation since FDR, and attacks on his platform and policies were the nastiest since Barack Obama sat in the Oval Office. He was branded a Socialist; some even accused him of being a Commie lover, soft on national defense, too willing to cave to the demands of other governments, and too quick to wind down the country's military adventures and bring the troops home. A few years ago, his stance on such matters wouldn't have played well in a nation leaning far right. But the policies of the current administration led by President Allan Swayze had proved disastrous on many fronts, and the nation was desperate for change. Besides, Swayze's brooding, dour style and tendency to butcher the English language were magnified when compared to Mortinson's quick wit, wide smile, and good looks. Three television debates had highlighted the differences between the two men, with Swayze stumbling for answers while Mortinson smoothly laid out his vision for the country.

His wife, Trish, walked into the room as he toweled off.

"The voters should see you now," she said pleasantly, "all sweaty and with your hair a mess."

"It would add to my appeal," he countered, "especially with female voters. Male sweat is an aphrodisiac."

"Not for this female," she said. "Are you really taking the day off from campaigning? Is it true?"

"It sure is. I don't know why you didn't stop me from running for president. It seems like I don't have a minute to myself, every day planned like a military exercise."

"It'll be worse when you're president."

"Maybe I should concede defeat."

"They haven't voted yet."

"I could save them the trouble. If I didn't think that another four years of Swayze would doom the country, I might seriously consider it."

He snapped his towel at her as he passed on his way to the shower, stopped, gave her a quick kiss, and left.

George and Tricia Mortinson were referred to in the media as "the golden couple." She was as beautiful as he was handsome, her face a cameo framed by rich auburn hair. Like her husband, she came from money. She was a champion of the arts; a Mortinson presidency would benefit artistic institutions of every type— opera, ballet, theater, museums, public television and radio, and the music world. She was a fashion style setter, too, and it was expected that once she was first lady, the White House would be tastefully redecorated. Mrs. Swayze's heavy-handed decorative touch had been compared by one critic to a set from a 1920s Gothic motion picture.

Morrison emerged from the bathroom, a blue towel wrapped around his midsection.

"Did you clear your slate for today?" he asked.

"As best I could," Tricia said. "I'm tied up through lunch, but I'm free after that. What do you have planned?"

"Tennis and lunch with Mac Smith. We're on for dinner with them tonight. The Moreys, too. Bistro Bis."

Her expression mirrored her displeasure.

"Prefer another restaurant? If I change plans now, the Secret Service guys will rebel."

"No, it's okay. I just thought we might spend some time alone tonight. God, there never seems to be any time to relax, just the two of us."

He came up behind and wrapped his arms around her. "I know. Like I said, maybe running wasn't the greatest idea I've ever had."

She twisted so that she faced him, her face inches from his. "I'm just afraid that the country will end up owning you."

"Never happen," he said, kissing her lightly, then more firmly. "The country rents a president. *You* own me."

She pulled away. "Looks like we've developed hard feelings between us," she said, looking down at the towel.

He laughed. "We'll resolve our differences tonight when we get back from dinner. Wish me luck on the tennis court. Mac tells me that his knee is acting up again. I might even win this time."

She watched her husband leave the room and smiled. As far as she was concerned, he was the most unlikely politician she'd ever met, and she'd met plenty. It wasn't that he lacked ambition, or was unwilling to put his heart into campaigning. He thrived when shaking hands on the rope lines and when giving speeches. It was the political nitty-gritty that turned him off, the backroom deals, the wheeling and dealing, and the constant pleading for money from those who were willing to give it in return for later favors. As far as Mortinson was concerned, the nation's political system was terribly broken and wasn't about to be fixed by him—or by anyone else. It was beyond that. Congress voted

to please and appease its big-money con-
tributors whether it benefited the country
or not. The days when senators and congressmen from rival parties fiercely debated on the floor and then had a drink
together, played poker, and shared family
evenings were but a distant memory. The
best Mortinson hoped for was to use his
bully pulpit to rally enough of the citizenry
to undo the most toxic of Swayze's policies
and to build a consensus for new, more
progressive approaches to the nation's
myriad problems.

His dismay, even disgust with the political system was one of the reasons that he
sought out people like Mackensie and
Annabel Smith with whom to spend time.
He and Smith had a tacit understanding:
politics would never intrude into their conversations. They would talk about anything
else—sports, movies, music, gardening,
books, cars, vacation spots—anything but
the nasty business of politics. And, of
course, their performances on the tennis
court provided plenty of conversational
meat.

On this day, Mortinson arrived at the
Sutton Racquet Club, accompanied by

four Secret Service agents, where Mac
Smith awaited. They played two vigorous
sets, and to Mortinson's delight, he won
both, albeit by close scores.

"I'd like to blame my knee," Smith said,
"but it feels good today. Looks like you've
improved your backhand."

"Actually, I cheated. Some of your shots
that I called out were in."

"Don't let the press know."

"The hell with the press. Clinton cheated
at golf and he did okay."

Smith laughed and walked with Mortinson to the limo that had delivered the candidate to the tennis club. "I'll follow you,"
he said as Mortinson patted an agent on
the back and prepared to climb into the
limo.

Smith turned on the all-news station
WTOP as he drove to the restaurant. There
was breaking news: Virginia senator Marshall Holtz had been the victim of an assassination attempt while holding a town
meeting in his hometown of Fairfax. According to the reporter, the senator, who
was in his fourth term, had been attacked
by a man with an automatic weapon as he
greeted constituents following his speech.

The shooter, who was tackled by bystanders, had gotten off a dozen shots, one of them hitting the senator in the left shoulder and left side of his neck. Others were wounded in the attack and rushed to a hospital along with Holtz, their condition unknown.

Smith shook his head and rammed the heel of his hand against the steering wheel. "When the hell are we going to get smart about guns?" he said aloud.

By the time he arrived at Chef Geoff's, Mortinson had been made aware of the attack on Holtz. "You heard?" he asked Smith as they were escorted to a table with great fanfare.

"About Senator Holtz? Yeah, I heard."

"I had drinks with Marshall a couple of days ago. He told me that threats against him had been increasing."

"Did he beef up his security?" Smith asked. "I assume everyone did after the incident last week." He referred to an attack on a congresswoman in Mississippi that was thwarted by members of her security staff. The attacker, an older man with a history of mental illness, had arrived at a fund-raiser carrying a long curved sword and had rushed at her as she got out of her car. No one was hurt, and her assailant was immediately apprehended.

"He said he was working on it," Mortinson replied. "He had a briefing from the Capitol police and was in the process of deciding what to do."

"Looks like he didn't make his decision fast enough," Smith offered.

"I'm not sure there's a lot he could do. Hell, it's easy to knock off members of Congress. That's the new threat. The terrorists and crazies don't need to do something as spectacular as commandeering aircraft and knocking down buildings. They can go after us one by one, a senator here, a congresswoman there, kill a dozen people in a mall with a suicide bomber, toss a grenade into a town meeting."

Mortinson was right. Terrorist groups no longer needed to launch a sensational strike as they did on nine eleven. They could bankrupt the country with idle chatter on the Internet that sent the nation into a high level of alert with a cost of millions of dollars each time it happened. Shooting an elected official or killing a dozen people in a mall was enough to send the citizenry into a panic. How do you fight this and win? Billions of dollars to support the war effort in Afghanistan and Iraq had had little or no effect on preventing an assailant from walking up to a U.S. senator and pulling the trigger.

"What about you, George?" Smith asked as they bit into their burgers, with Secret Service agents looking on from different locations in the restaurant. "You're obviously a prime target."

Mortinson wiped ketchup from his mouth and shrugged. "I've got the best protection in the world," he said, nodding in the direction of the agents.

"Still . . ."

"I know, I know, if someone wants to kill me—*really* wants to kill me—they'll find a way."

Smith decided not to feed into this topic and said nothing as he concentrated on eating. When they were finished, Mortinson said, "I have to put out a statement about Marsh Holtz and get over to the hospital. "I'm not sure that I can make our dinner tonight."

"Let's cancel," Smith suggested. "We can do it another time."

"So much for my day off," Mortinson said as they walked outside, where a staffer waited.

"Senator Holtz survived the attack," she said. "A hospital spokesman just announced that his wounds are serious but not life-threatening."

"That's good to hear."

"She handed him a statement his PR staff had written. Mortinson glanced at it and handed it back. "Too contrived," he said. "I'll come up with something of my own."

Smith watched his friend climb into the limo. His attention then went to others in the vicinity, men, women, children, ordinary people going about their daily business. Some stopped to wave to the candidate. An elderly couple tried to approach but was kept by agents from getting close. A middle-aged man who looked to Smith as being of Arabic origins watched the goings-on. A young man wearing a hooded sweatshirt stood quietly, his face devoid of expression. Was one of them a potential assassin? Smith wondered.

He got into his car and called Annabel at her gallery to say that dinner with the

Mortinsons was off. "I talked to the Moreys, and they understood," he said. Annabel didn't seem unhappy about it, nor was he. If dinner had been planned at the Mortinsons' home, he might have felt different about it. But dinners out in public places proved to be unwieldy because of the protection for the candidate. Besides, Smith was due at police headquarters at four to meet with Nic Tatum and Sheila Klaus; she'd been brought in that morning to be questioned again in the murder of Dr. Mark Sedgwick.

CHAPTER 18

Sheila Klaus sat alone in an interrogation room when Mac Smith arrived. Nic Tatum had preceded him and stood with Detective Joe Owens on the opposite side of the two-way glass separating them from her.

"Mackensie Smith," Smith said, extending his hand to the senior detective.

"I remember you," Owens said pleasantly. "You grilled me more than once on the witness stand."

"And as I recall, you were a very good witness, well prepared and on top of things."

"You teach now," Owens said.

"Most of the time. I take an occasional case."

"*This* case?"

"For the time being." Smith glanced at Sheila through the glass. "Has she been questioned yet?"

Owens laughed. "Of course she hasn't," he said. "I know the rules. Nic told me that an attorney was coming, and that means no questions until you arrived. Of course we had interviewed her before, just part of the preliminary investigation."

"Have you come up with new evidence?" Smith asked.

"As a matter of fact, we have. Tire tracks in her driveway match the tread on the car used in the homicide."

Smith said nothing as he again looked at Sheila, who sat stoically in the blue plastic chair at the scarred table, arms wrapped tightly about herself as though trying to disappear into her surroundings.

"She looks distraught," Smith said.

"For good reason," said Owens. "Ready?"

Owens led them into the room. Their sudden appearance caused Sheila to gasp and to straighten in her chair. Owens took a seat at the head of the table. Smith and Tatum sat opposite Sheila.

"You know me," Owens said, "from when I spoke with you at your home. Dr. Tatum was with me."

"I remember," Sheila said, her voice quavering.

"Remember me?" Smith asked. "I'm Mackensie Smith. We knew each other when you were working at GW."

"Yes, of course. Why are you here, Professor Smith?"

"To act as your attorney during this questioning."

"Your wife is—"

"Annabel," Smith said. "You and she were in that book group together."

"How is she?"

"She's just fine. Sheila, you don't have to answer any of the detective's questions if you don't want to. You haven't been formally accused of anything."

She let out a prolonged sigh, sat back, and pressed the palms of her hands against her face. "Accused?" she said. "Why am I even being asked about what happened to Dr. Sedgwick? He was my psychiatrist, that's all. He was a good man and I'm sorry that he's dead. But I had nothing to do with it. This is all a nightmare, something out of a horror movie."

Owens leaned his elbows on the table and said, "Ms. Klaus, Mr. Smith is right. You have no obligation to answer my questions, but—"

"I've already answered your questions, Detective. You can continue to ask them and you'll receive the same answers. You don't seem to realize that—"

Smith and Tatum had closely observed Sheila as she conversed with Owens. Smith didn't notice the sudden change in her as quickly as Tatum did, but he wasn't far behind. Up until that moment her face had been an open book, an expression that pleaded for understanding and belief in what she was saying. Then that same face turned hard and angry, her mouth a defiant slash, eyes cold. But it was the change in her voice that was most shocking. It was deeper, and she spoke more slowly, each word heavy with sarcasm and challenge.

"You don't know what you're talking about," she said to Owens. "Go on, ask your stupid questions and then leave us alone."

"Us?" Owens said, as he, too, was aware of the change in her.

Sheila blinked her eyes and leaned toward him as though to bring him into focus.

"Are you all right, Ms. Klaus?" Owens asked.

"Yes, of course I am. I'm fine."

"I'd like to go over some things we've talked about before to see if there is anything that you can add to your answers."

She looked to Smith. "I've already told them everything I know, which isn't anything. Why do they have to keep asking the same things?"

Smith said to Owens, "She has a point, Detective. I haven't been privy to what you asked before, but unless there's something new to explore, or you're ready to charge her, I think this session is nonproductive and should end."

Owens knew that the attorney was right. He was unable to charge her in the Sedgwick murder because the United States attorney for the District of Columbia, whose office prosecutes all felony crimes in the District, had cautioned that the existing evidence against her was not sufficient to warrant an indictment.

Owens stood. "Thanks for your time, Ms. Klaus," he said. "You're free to go."

"Thank God," she said, drawing in deep breaths and wiping a tear that had run down her cheek. "I hope this is the last of it."

Tatum, who hadn't said a word since entering the room, said to Owens, "Mind if we stay here a few minutes?"

"Sure, stay as long as you like," Owens said as he left.

Smith looked quizzically at Tatum.

"I'd like to spend a few minutes with Ms. Klaus, Mac. That is, if she's willing."

"Why?" she asked.

"Let me put it this way," Tatum said. "I'm the one who asked Mac Smith to come and represent you. I'm not a cop, although I used to be. I'm a psychologist the MPD calls in on certain cases. I was the one who dug up your file at Dr. Sedgwick's office and suggested to Detective Owens that he speak with you."

"You did that?" she asked. "Isn't that a violation of doctor-patient rules?"

"Under normal circumstances, yes, but

where a homicide is involved, the courts will sometimes issue a search warrant even when it involves a doctor and his patient. That was the case here."

"Why did you choose me?" she asked.

"A couple of things captured my attention, Ms. Klaus. Look, maybe this isn't the place to continue this conversation." He looked around the spartan room and grinned. "Not nearly as pleasant as your lovely home. What say we—?"

The door opened and Owens reentered, accompanied by two uniformed officers.

"We're just about to leave," Smith said.

"I'm afraid Ms. Klaus won't be leaving with you," said Owens. "I've just received a call from the U.S. attorney's office." He turned to Sheila Klaus. "We're charging you with the murder of Dr. Mark Sedgwick. You have the right to remain silent—"

"Wait a minute," Smith said, interrupting the reciting of her Miranda rights. "Why the change?"

"New evidence, Counselor."

The officers came around behind Sheila and placed their hands on her shoulders. "Please come with us," one said.

Sheila stiffened but remained seated.

"Ma'am."

Sheila looked up at them and sneered. That hardened expression was back, and she said in her low, threatening voice, "Keep your hands off me." She then laughed, a laugh that sent a chill through Smith. "All right," she said, "just don't touch me."

CHAPTER

19

Tatum and Smith watched as the officers escorted Sheila from the room.

"I'd like to know what this new evidence is," Smith said to Owens.

"You'll have to talk to the U.S. attorney about that," was Owens's reply.

"I'll do that," Smith said.

After Owens departed, Tatum asked Smith, "Did you see the sudden change in her?"

"I certainly did."

"She talked about 'us.' That was a second personality who emerged."

"I've read about such phenomena but

have never seen someone with a second personality before."

"Chances are she's got more than one other personality, Mac. I've seen patients with as many as a dozen."

"She's schizophrenic?"

"No. Multiple personality disorder and schizophrenia are very different."

"Let me see if I have this right," Smith said. "Are you going down a path leading to a claim that this so-called second personality was the one who ran down Sedgwick?"

"I think it's a possibility."

Smith drummed his fingertips on the table as he gathered his thoughts.

"I'm not saying it's true," Tatum added, "but it has to be pursued."

"Let's say it *is* true," Smith mused. "Does that mean this other personality took over from Sheila and decided to kill Sedgwick on her own?"

"That's also possible," Tatum said, "but less likely. Multiple personalities are almost always found in people who've suffered severe physical or psychological abuse as children. The second personality emerges to protect the real person, to fight his or her battles and to right wrongs. But killing someone without being directed to do it by another party doesn't fit the pattern, at least based upon everything that I've learned and experienced—unless, of course, Sheila Klaus has murderous instincts, which obviously doesn't appear to be the case."

Smith exhaled and shook his head. "I'm still trying to get my arms around this," he said. "Let's say you're right, that Sheila, or whoever her second personality is, was programmed to run down Sedgwick. If that's the case, then who would want Sedgwick killed and would program Sheila, or her second personality, to do it?"

"That's worth finding out," Tatum said, "if it's even possible. Bear in mind, Mac, that many people who suffer from multiple personalities have more than just one. I had a patient who had sixteen distinct personalities that came out from time to time and for different reasons."

"Am I correct in assuming that you'll want to spend time with her?"

Tatum nodded.

"First things first," Smith said. "I'll visit with her to be sure that she knows her rights. This is an unusual situation, Nic, and it's going to take some serious legal thinking. Why don't you use your former connections with the PD and see what you can find out about this new evidence that Detective Owens mentioned. I'll head home after seeing her. Annabel and I had dinner plans that have been canceled. We can meet up at my apartment, say at six?"

"Okay."

When Tatum arrived at the Watergate, Annabel greeted him. "Mac is on the phone," she said. "He should be off soon."

Tatum settled in their living room and thumbed through the latest copy of *Washingtonian* until Smith emerged from his home office. "Find out anything about the new evidence?" Smith asked.

"Yes, I did. MPD had confirmed through airline records that Sheila Klaus did in fact make four trips to San Francisco with Sedgwick, traveling as Carla Rasmussen. They also checked records to see whether she'd traveled alone there under the name Carla Rasmussen. She did, twice. None of that's a surprise—I told you about it before—but her denials are working against her. What *is* new are the driver's licenses they've come up with. Sheila Klaus's license was in her possession, as would be expected. But they searched her house and came up with a second license, in the name of Carla Rasmussen. I got a look at it. The photo on it is of Sheila, only she's wearing a black wig. It's Sheila, all right, but she has the same expression in the picture as when she shifted into that second personality in the interrogation room. Same face, different person."

"She needed that second license to get through airport security," Smith said.

"Exactly," Tatum said.

"But the driver of the car was reported to be a blond woman."

"Just because it was this Carla personality driving the car doesn't mean that she put on a dark wig. Sheila might don that only when instructed to."

"Then who arranged for that second license?" Smith asked. "Sedgwick? That's a lot of bother to go through to keep his wife from knowing about his affair."

"A good question, Mac."

"Okay," Smith said, "she made four trips with Sedgwick under the name of Carla

Rasmussen, and then two more trips on her own. Where did she go when she was out there? What did she do?"

"I have the same question. I got back in touch with Sedgwick's receptionist, Betty Martinez. She paid all of Sedgwick's bills, part of her job. She went through the files again and gave me the name of a limo service in San Fran that Sedgwick always used when he was out there. I called from a phone at headquarters and told them that I was MPD working on a murder case that involved one of their regular customers, a slight exaggeration but close enough. They checked their records and told me that their drivers picked up Sedgwick and a female companion four times at the Hyatt on the Embarcadero and drove them to a clinic in Berkeley, the Lightpath Psychiatric Clinic. The dates match the airline records. The bill was paid by Sedgwick on his credit card."

"What about the two trips when she traveled alone?" Smith asked.

"No record of her on those dates from the limo company. She either took cabs or was picked up by someone. The fellow at the limo company also checked his records regarding trips that Sedgwick made on his own. There were dozens of them, and each time he was driven to Lightpath. The detectives who questioned Sedgwick's ex-wife reported that she said he was involved with some clinic in San Francisco. I'd say that he was *deeply* involved."

"I made a few inquiries myself after leaving her. This calls for full-time hands-on legal counsel, Nic. I want to bring in another attorney to handle it on a day-to-day basis. I'll oversee it."

"Whatever you say. Someone in mind?"

"Yes, a former teaching colleague of mine, Marie Darrow."

"Aptly named," Tatum quipped.

"She's a crackerjack. I'm meeting with her in the morning. She's agreed to work with me. We'll need your input, too."

"Sure."

"If what you say is true, the obvious defense for her is a plea of insanity using the multiple personality as its basis. Frankly, I don't hold out much hope for that with a jury, assuming it comes down to a trial. There have been cases in which multiple personality disorder was the basis for the defense, the accused claiming that it was his *other* self who actually committed the crime. Juries didn't buy it. But there was an Ohio case back in the seventies where a man was declared not guilty by reason of insanity in four rapes. And there was another case, this one in California, where some guy shot his common-law wife and claimed it was his second personality. He got off, too. Nevertheless, there are six or seven of those cases every year, and in most of them the jury dismisses the claim that there was a second personality involved."

"But it's a recognized mental illness," Tatum said. "The medical profession knows it even if juries are slow to accept the concept. There's another potential aspect to this that should be explored."

"Which is?"

"What we touched upon earlier, the possibility that she was controlled through this second personality."

"Mind control?"

"Exactly. I have nothing tangible to base it on, but I'm convinced that she has absolutely no recall of anything having to do with

Sedgwick's death. That sort of selective amnesia almost always involves someone else implanting it."

"Who?"

Tatum reinforced his shrug with, "I don't know, but I'd love to find out. If it's true, it would mean that the same person who created amnesia in her also programmed her to kill Sedgwick. Why else would he bother to wipe out her memory?"

"Whew," was all that Smith could muster.

"Yeah, I know, it sounds like a stretch, a big one, but unless you have a better theory, I'd like to pursue this one. It will mean spending more time with her."

"That shouldn't be a problem, especially with your credentials and connections with MPD. I could name you part of the defense team."

"No," Tatum said. "I'd rather keep it out of official channels. If I'm involved with her defense, I'll lose my inside track at MPD. I think a better way to go is to hire me to do an independent psychological evaluation of her."

"Consider it done. I have to admit that I'm having trouble accepting the concept of her being programmed to deliberately run down and kill her psychiatrist and have no recollection of it—the event *or* the programming. Oh, and on top of that, she has a second personality named Carla Rasmussen who actually did the deed."

"I can't imagine why," Tatum said through a small laugh. "But let me tell you this, Mac. I know that the media, the movie and TV people, love the subject of multiple personalities and mind control. *The Manchurian Candidate,* the Richard Gere film *Primal Fear, Sybil,* even more recently that dreadful Lindsay Lohan flick *I Know Who Killed Me*—they all make dramatic hay out of it. But it's more than a plot device. It's real for too many people, whether their childhood experiences helped develop other personalities inside them, or whether it's been induced by others. Look at the history of the CIA's experiments with innocent people as a good example of how someone can be manipulated to do someone else's bidding. It's not fiction, Mac. It's a medical reality."

Smith didn't challenge him. His own reading on the subject of hypnosis had educated him on its potential to control certain individuals, and the knowledge that the government—*his* government—had enlisted numerous doctors and scientists to conduct experiments on unwitting subjects going back many decades.

He'd seen some of the movies Tatum had mentioned and had read books about mind control. Once he and Annabel were introduced to Tatum's immersion in medical hypnosis, Mac had broadened his knowledge but never completely lost his skepticism. Nevertheless, its potential use to trial lawyers was what had prompted him to bring Tatum in to teach a seminar at GW on the subject.

But all the experiments involving the control of the mind that Smith had read about were conceived, funded, and conducted by the government. If Tatum's thesis was right, then someone with a grudge against Mark Sedgwick and who was skilled in the use of hypnosis used that knowledge to manipulate Sheila into killing him. As much as Smith bought into the notion that people could be brainwashed, applying it to Sheila Klaus was hard to accept.

"You stopped in to see her after I left?" Tatum asked.

"Yes."

"How was she?"

"Upset, as you can imagine. She continues to insist that she had nothing to do with Sedgwick's murder and that she never took a trip with Sedgwick, let alone four of them."

Tatum's expression mirrored what he was thinking. There was tangible proof that she'd taken those trips with Sedgwick, yet she adamantly denied having traveled with him despite being confronted with the evidence.

Annabel whipped up a quick dinner for them. Afterward, they sat on the balcony sipping single-barrel bourbon.

"You say that the limo company in San Francisco took Sedgwick and Sheila to a psychiatric clinic in Berkeley," Smith said.

"Right. The Lightpath Clinic."

"Do you know anything about that clinic?"

"Just scuttlebutt. Rumor has it that it's government funded."

"Government? What branch of government?"

"The CIA, other intelligence agencies, but that wouldn't be unusual. The CIA funds many such places, some within leading universities and hospitals. Lightpath, I'm told, is run by Sheldon Borger."

"He is . . . ?"

"A controversial psychiatrist in San Francisco, very rich, with lots of rich patients, handsome, very smooth, lots of white teeth. He was an OB-GYN before becoming a shrink. I met him once at a talk he gave here in D.C. hosted by a right-wing think tank."

"What did he talk about?"

"The threat to the country by other nations and how the medical profession, particularly psychiatry, could help in the fight."

"How could they help in the fight?" Smith asked.

"I don't recall much of what he said. I tuned out halfway through the lecture."

"Do you think that Sheila saw him when she went with Sedgwick to San Francisco? Your limo company contact told you that Sedgwick had a female companion with him during the four rides to Berkeley."

"I can't imagine why she would have accompanied him to that clinic. It's something I'd like to find out."

"Think you can?" Smith asked. "She denies even going to San Francisco."

"I'll give it my best shot. You'll have to

put in a formal request to MPD to have me examine her."

"First thing in the morning."

"Does Sheila have any children?" Tatum asked as he and Mac waited for the elevator.

"I don't think so. I know that she was divorced and worked at GW. Left with a disability."

"What disability?"

"I'll find out. She and Annabel were somewhat friendly. She might know, or I can check at the school."

The elevator arrived, but Tatum hesitated stepping in. Smith cocked his head.

"I've got a feeling, Mac, that we haven't even begun to scratch the surface with Sheila Klaus."

He entered the elevator and Smith watched the doors slowly slide shut, Tatum's words staying with him.

Mac Smith met with Marie Darrow the following morning and brought her up to speed. Darrow was a short, square, curly-haired woman who seldom dressed in anything other than black suits too tight for her frame. Smith respected her intellect and ability to cut to the chase. Anything other than a concise, on-the-topic response to her questions wasn't appreciated.

"A diminished capacity defense based upon multiple personalities?" she said after Smith had covered everything he'd written on a yellow legal pad.

"At this point, Marie, it's the only defense."

"It'll never play for a D.C. jury, not under the ALI standard."

She was referring to a standard of legal insanity designed by the American Law Institute and adopted by the District of Columbia in the 1960s, which basically decreed that defendants must have a substantial incapacity to appreciate the criminality of their conduct, or to conform their conduct to the law. It also demanded that the mental disease or defect be a medical diagnosis.

"Besides," she added, "the whole multiple personality thing is too science fiction. Mind control? There aren't a dozen people in the District who'll buy it, unless the defendant is a congressman. We all know that their minds are controlled by lobbyists."

Smith laughed. "You can use that in your opening statement."

Darrow played with an errant curl on her forehead. "Think she'll buy me as her counsel?"

"If she doesn't, it's not because of you. When I was with her yesterday, she kept saying she doesn't need a lawyer because she hasn't done anything."

"Despite the evidence?"

A nod from Smith. "I laid out for her what the evidence is so far. You're meeting her at two?"

"Right."

"Nic Tatum is with her now."

"Tell me more about this guy Tatum."

"As I said, he's a psychologist and friend. He was with MPD for a few years, now practices solo. He knows medical hypnosis inside and out."

"And he's the one who's come up with the multiple personality theory."

"Right."

"We'll need shrinks with bigger and better credentials than that."

"Never a problem finding shrinks who'll testify if the fee is high enough."

"Dueling shrinks on the witness stand," Darrow said scornfully. "I love it. There's plenty of them who'll debunk the whole multiple personality and mind control notion."

She was right, of course, but Smith didn't see anything to be gained by discussing it further. "Tatum will be contacting me once he's finished with Sheila," he said. "I'll let you know what he says before you meet with her this afternoon."

*   *   *

Smith had arranged for Tatum to spend an hour with Sheila Klaus. Tatum was in the interrogation room when she was brought in by a male officer and a matron. Tatum had requested and was given a room without two-way glass, or audio- and video-recording equipment. He'd also asked for two comfortable chairs which, after an initial denial, were removed from a reception area and delivered.

Sheila looked totally confused. Dressed in prison garb, she was frail, her eyes red from crying.

"Would you like me to stay?" the matron asked.

"That won't be necessary," Tatum said, "but thank you."

"We'll be right outside," the matron said ominously.

"Please, have a seat," Tatum told Sheila.

She hesitated, as though to take the chair would in some way render her vulnerable.

"There's nothing to fear," Tatum said. "I'm Dr. Tatum, Nicholas Tatum. We've met a few times."

"I know," she said as she perched on the edge of the seat.

"I'm working with Mac Smith. He spent time with you yesterday."

She didn't respond.

"The reason I'm with you today, Sheila, is to try and understand you and the situation you're facing."

She burst into tears. Tatum handed her a tissue and waited until her tears had subsided.

"The first time we met, I was with detectives who came to your house. I used to be with MPD, but I left years ago. I'm here now to help you."

"But why am I here?" she said, leaning forward. Tatum thought she might slip off the chair. "They keep saying I killed Dr. Sedgwick. That isn't true." She stood and shouted, "That isn't true!"

Tatum got up and placed a hand on her shoulder. "It's all right, Sheila. I believe you."

That simple statement caused her to look at him with wide-open eyes. "You do?" she said.

"Sit down, Sheila, and let me ask you a few questions that might help get to the bottom of this. One of the problems is that the police have evidence that you took trips with Dr. Sedgwick to San Francisco and—"

"No, I did not."

"You don't remember ever going there with him?"

She shook her head. "He was a nice man. He was my doctor. But they make it sound as though we were having an affair. That wasn't true. We never . . ."

She'd become agitated again, and Tatum gave her time to calm down before continuing.

"Have you ever been hypnotized, Sheila?" he asked.

She looked at him quizzically. "Of course not. I can't be."

"Why do you say that?"

"Because . . . because—"

"Hypnosis is a good thing," he said. "I use it in my practice to help people feel better, to remember things they sometimes forget. I know that you can't be hypnotized, but would you allow me to try?"

"Why are we doing this?" she asked.

"Can I try? It will help you relax."

He didn't wait for an answer. He took a small makeup mirror he'd had on his lap and held it up to her face.

"No," she said.

"I just want you to look in the mirror, Sheila, and concentrate. You're relaxed and calm and enjoying a pleasant place. I want you to take some deep breaths and picture yourself on a sunny beach, a peaceful place where everything is serene."

She did as instructed.

"That's it," Tatum said, bringing the mirror closer to her. "Relax, enjoy deep relaxation. I'm going to count from one to ten, and when I reach ten, you'll be completely relaxed. That's right. One . . . two . . . three . . ."

He didn't have to count further. A serene expression crossed her face and she closed her eyes.

Tatum reached out and touched her right arm. "Your arm is very light, Sheila, like it has a helium balloon attached to it. Let it float up. That's good."

Her arm slowly rose and remained suspended.

"Do you know where you are?" Tatum asked.

"I'm with . . ."

"Yes?"

She opened her eyes, and the change

was immediate and startling to Tatum. What had been a frightened expression turned hard. A cynical smile crossed her face.

"Sheila?" Tatum asked.

"Go ahead," a low voice challenged. "Try me."

"Try you?"

Sheila laughed. "She's so pathetic."

"Who's pathetic?"

"Little Miss Muffet. She's a wimp."

Tatum took a moment to collect his thoughts. When he had, he said, "Am I talking to Carla?"

Another laugh from her. "What do you care?" she said.

"I care because I care about Sheila. Where is Sheila?"

"Oh, she's right here, and you know it."

"I know that Sheila is right here, but now you've joined her. Why did you decide to come out, Carla?"

"Because she needs me." Her tone remained scornful and belittling.

"Needs you to do what?"

"To help her. She always needs help. She's such a weakling, always needing me."

Tatum shifted gears. "Were you with her

when she traveled to San Francisco with Dr. Sedgwick?"

"Of course I was."

"What did you do there?"

"I don't want to talk to you anymore. I don't like you."

"But I like you, Carla. What did you do when you and Sheila were in San Francisco? Did you go to the Lightpath Clinic with her?"

There was no response. Sheila twisted in her chair and her face scrunched up as though in pain.

"What's the matter, Sheila?" Tatum asked.

"Don't do it anymore," she whined. "Stop it! I don't want any vitamins. Stop it!"

"Who is giving you vitamins, Sheila?"

"Get away from me. It hurts when you use that needle. Stop it!"

She swung her fist in the air, shuddered, wrapped her arms about herself, and sank back into the chair, a series of moans coming from her until she was still.

Tatum watched with fascination as she went through these contortions. When she was quiet, he asked, "Am I speaking with Sheila now, or Carla?"

Sheila fumbled for an answer before saying, "Why are you doing this to me?"

"Doing what, Sheila?"

"It hurts."

Tatum changed characters and fell into the role of whomever Sheila had been talking with about the vitamin shots. He altered his voice and said, "The needle doesn't hurt. It's just vitamins. They're good for you. They make you stronger."

He sensed that she was slowly coming out of her trance state. He tried to deepen it: "Deeper, deeper, deeper."

She groaned and stretched her arms in front of her like someone waking up in the morning. She shook her head and looked around. "What am I doing here?" she asked.

"You're here in police headquarters with me," Tatum said. "How do you feel?"

"I feel . . . I feel all right. Oh, my God, you think I killed Mark."

"No, Sheila, I don't think that you did, but you have to help me prove that."

"How can I prove something I didn't do?"

"When you were a little girl, did you have imaginary playmates?"

"No. I mean, yes I did. Every child has imaginary friends. Didn't you?"

"Sure I did. Do you remember their names?"

She shook her head and smiled. "I don't think so."

"Do you remember having an imaginary playmate named Carla?"

The mention of Carla's name caused Sheila to stiffen, as though Tatum had poked her with a stick.

"Sheila? Do you remember Carla?"

She shook her head. "No, I don't. Why do you ask?"

"Just curious. I'd like to see you again, maybe this afternoon?"

"I just want to get out of here."

"I don't blame you. That's what Mac Smith and I are trying to do, help you get out of here and go home."

Tears rolled down her cheeks.

"I'll see if they'll let us meet again later this afternoon," Tatum said as he rose. He went to the door and summoned the matron and the uniformed officer who'd brought Sheila in. They came to Sheila's side and indicated that she was to stand. She did, and they flanked her as they left the room.

Tatum left the building, got into his car, and used his cell to call Mac Smith.

"I just left Sheila, Mac," he said. "I think I'm onto something."

"That's good to hear. What is it?"

"Not on the phone. I want to meet with Sheila again this afternoon. Will you put in a request?"

"Sure. Where are you now?"

"In my car. I just finished with her. I can come by if you're free."

"I'm here, Nic. Care to give me a hint as to what you've come up with?"

"Sure. I just met Carla Rasmussen. I'll be there in twenty minutes."

Smith was grading papers in his home office when Tatum arrived. A small TV on his desk had been tuned to CNN for most of the day. The assassination attempt on Virginia senator Marshall Holtz dominated the news, as might be expected. A hospital spokeswoman gave hourly updates on his condition, as well as for the others who'd been wounded. Everyone had survived, although one victim was listed in critical condition. Senator Holtz was listed as serious but stable.

Presidential candidate George Mortinson

gave a statement on the hospital steps that CNN aired over and over:

*"Marshall Holtz and I have been friends ever since I was elected to the Senate. He showed me the ropes and guided me through the committee maze and legislative roadblocks. I've never met a finer man than Marshall Holtz, and thank God the madman who attacked him wasn't successful in his mission to kill a leading voice in the battle to ensure fair play and a level playing field for every American. It is my hope that this incident, and too many others like it, will act as a wake-up call to curb the insanity of this nation where guns are concerned. My wife, Tricia, and I have met with the senator's family, and they're holding up well considering the circumstances. We've also met with the families of the other victims, and our hopes and prayers are with them."

Mortinson was interviewed by reporters following his statement.

"Do you think that the nasty political rhetoric continues to inflame people like today's shooter?"

"Of course it does," Mortinson responded,

his tone edgy. "Assaults on public officials have increased every year. The problem with those who deny that political hate speech contributes to it is that they hide behind the fact that no one speech or comment can be directly linked to an assassination attempt. But it's the general atmosphere that feeds it. Can you trace the aberrant behavior of one teenager to a specific violent video game or movie? Probably not. But the prevailing attitude that violence solves everything is there. You add that to the easy accessibility of assault weapons in the hands of the deranged and you end up with what has happened to Senator Holtz, and to Congresswoman Giffords in Arizona."

Smith turned off the TV as Tatum settled in a chair across from the desk. "If you intended to pique my curiosity, Nic, you succeeded. What's this about Carla Rasmussen?"

Tatum gave Smith a play-by-play of his session with Sheila as best as he could reconstruct it.

"She just appeared out of the blue?"

"Right."

"And now we're talking about needles and vitamins?"

"The government's experiments in mind control include pharmaceuticals as well as hypnosis. Maybe Sheila was being given shots in San Francisco along with being hypnotized."

"Slow down," Smith said. "We don't have any proof of what happened to Sheila when she was in California. No offense, but having a mention of shots come out while she was in a trance is hardly proof of anything. What about this Lightpath Clinic?"

"That's on my agenda," Tatum said, "along with spending another hour with her this afternoon. I have a friend who used to work in the psych division at the CIA and who might be willing to share with me what he knows about Lightpath."

Annabel arrived. She was in a bubbly mood because she'd just sold a pre-Columbian fourteen-inch-tall green serpentine drinking vessel to a New York City collector for her asking price. "He wanted to negotiate, but I held firm. It's a spectacular piece, very rare, one I've been holding for years, and I wasn't about to part with it for less than its actual worth."

"Good for you, Annie," Smith said. He said to Tatum, "Annabel often has trouble letting go of a piece once she has it in the gallery."

"Not good for the bottom line," Tatum said, laughing.

"But good for the soul," Annie countered. "Lunch, anyone?"

Attorney Marie Darrow had met with Sheila Klaus earlier that afternoon. Tatum arrived two hours after Darrow had left and settled in with Sheila in the same room in which they'd met earlier that day.

"How are you feeling?" he asked.

"Hollow," she replied, "as though every ounce of energy has been pulled out of me."

"I don't wonder," Tatum said. "Did you enjoy our session this morning?"

She shrugged.

"You said you couldn't be hypnotized, but you were."

"I was?"

"Yes. You're a very good subject."

"No, I'm not."

"Why do you keep saying that?"

"Because he told me I couldn't be."

"Who told you that?"

"Dr. Sedgwick."

"But he used hypnosis with you," Tatum said gently.

Sheila shook her head. "He tried, but he couldn't do it. He told me that I should never let anyone else try it, either."

"Why would he say that?"

"I don't know."

Tatum held up the small mirror. "Remember when you looked into the mirror this morning, Sheila?"

She didn't reply, but her eyes were focused on it.

"I'm going to count backward from ten, Sheila, and as I do you'll—"

She'd entered a trance state by the time he reached five.

He worked to deepen her trance until he felt she was where he wanted her to be. After a series of suggestions, which she followed, he asked how she enjoyed coming "out here" to California.

"I don't like it. You hurt me," she said in a singsong voice.

"I wouldn't hurt you, Sheila," he said.

"Yes, you do. You give me those shots, those vitamin B shots. I don't want to get them anymore."

"All right."

He paused as he watched her fidget, wringing her hands and emitting small whines and even an occasional growl.

"Do you know who I am, Sheila?" he asked.

The question brought about an abrupt change in her. He now sat with Carla Rasmussen, who fixed him in a threatening stare. A smile crossed her lips, a mocking, challenging smile.

"I know who you are," Carla said in her low, almost masculine voice. "You know I know."

"Then who am I?" he asked.

She snickered and shook her head. "You're the great doctor."

"Thank you for the compliment, Sheila. But you don't even know my name."

"Borger."

"Borger?" Her immediate stating of the name took him aback. "That's right, I'm the great doctor Borger."

"Mark says you're a great doctor." She guffawed. "What makes you so great?"

"I'm great because I know what's best for my patients. I know what's best for you."

"I want to leave."

"Go ahead, Carla," Tatum said. "Sheila doesn't need you to stay with her."

"She always needs me, Dr. Borger." She spit out his name as though referring to something vile.

"I'm not your enemy, Carla," Tatum said. "You do the things that Sheila cannot do. I'm proud of you."

"Oh, that's very nice," she said sarcastically.

"Do you remember when I arranged for you to go back to Washington and protect Sheila from Dr. Sedgwick?"

He'd pushed too far. Her mouth curled in anger and she gripped the arms of her chair so tightly that her knuckles turned white.

"You did a very good job," Tatum said.

"Great doctor," Carla said. "Good-bye, great doctor. We're going now."

"But you haven't had your vitamin B shot yet."

He'd lost her. Her body—Sheila's body— became smaller and sank back in her chair.

"Carla?"

Sheila said nothing, and Tatum decided the session should be ended. He brought her out of her trance and observed as she reacted to now being fully alert, eyes darting about the room, head swiveling.

"How do you feel, Sheila?" Tatum asked.

"Sleepy. I'd like to go to sleep."

"Fine," he said, and he called for the matron to take her back to her cell.

Tatum sat alone in the room for a while and pondered what had just taken place. He'd broken through, had regressed her back to being at the Lightpath Clinic, and he now knew who she was with, Dr. Sheldon Borger. It had happened faster than he'd anticipated. He'd foreseen having to devote dozens of sessions to reach this point. He didn't chalk it up to any special technique he'd used. He hadn't produced any magic. The truth was that Shelia Klaus was a remarkable subject, the best he'd ever encountered. The remaining question was what to do next.

"Mac," he said on his cell before leaving the room, "we have to talk."

CHAPTER

22

Tatum and Mac Smith spent an hour discussing what had come out of Tatum's latest session with Sheila Klaus. Toward the end of their meeting, Smith said, "I still can't make the connection between this Lightpath Clinic and Sheila being programmed—through her second personality, Carla Rasmussen—to kill Mark Sedgwick. You say the clinic is run by a Dr. Borger. Why would he—*if* he's the one who programmed her—want Sedgwick dead?"

"I can only speculate, Mac. I didn't know Sedgwick well, but I was aware that he was involved in some capacity with the intelligence community. Lightpath is government funded, just one of dozens of such facilities maintained and supported by the CIA and other intelligence agencies. I'm guessing, of course, but it's my assumption that once Sedgwick discovered that he had a perfect subject in Sheila, he brought her to Lightpath to become part of whatever research and experimentation they're doing out there. As to why someone at Lightpath—presumably Sheldon Borger—would want to get rid of Sedgwick, it's possible that Sedgwick started making waves, or was poised to become a whistle-blower. I also wouldn't be surprised that he and Sheila had entered into some sort of romantic relationship. If that hadn't gone well, it could have instilled in her a dislike for him, even hatred, which would fuel her acceptance of any suggestion to kill him."

Smith pondered what Tatum had said before asking, "Did Sheila admit under hypnosis that she'd been programmed to kill Sedgwick?"

"If she had, I would have yelled loud enough for you to hear me from MPD. No, she didn't, but when I mentioned Sedgwick's name, she shut down. The amnesia that's been implanted in her is powerful, Mac. So is the fear that's been instilled in her of allowing anyone else to hypnotize her. But I was close to breaking through, and I'm confident that I'll be able to if I can work with her long enough."

"All right," Smith said through an exasperated sigh. "What's next?"

"I mentioned a former CIA scientist I know pretty well. He left the agency because he was uncomfortable with the experiments he was being asked to undertake. I'm sure he knows plenty about Lightpath and Borger."

"But will he talk to you about it? Wouldn't that be spilling state secrets?"

Tatum shrugged. "Maybe he won't say anything directly, but he can at least affirm what I already suspect and the assumptions I've come up with. It's worth a try. How did it go with the attorney who saw Sheila this afternoon? I didn't ask Sheila about it because I didn't know how she'd taken to it."

"Marie told me that she had a good meeting with her, although she did characterize portions of it as strange."

"How so?"

"Sheila kept insisting that she was innocent. That's not unusual, of course, with people accused of a crime, but her adamant stance in the face of the evidence takes it to a new level. But Marie also said that there were times that Sheila seemed to slip into her own world, as Marie put it, to fade into a daydream."

"You've seen it happen yourself," Tatum said. "She goes into a trancelike state."

"I certainly have. Sheila is being arraigned tomorrow morning at the Moultrie Courthouse on Indiana. Marie will be with her at the presentment. We'll ask for her to be released on a bond, but the chances are slim to none that the judge will grant it in a felony homicide case. By the way, I made a few inquiries at the university why she left her job. They're naturally reluctant to give details, but from what I was told she was considered incapable of focusing on her job. A doctor offered some sort of medical diagnosis that led to the disability finding. Naturally I couldn't have access to the doctor's letter, although it might be possible to get a court-ordered release of it."

"I don't wonder that she couldn't focus," Tatum said. "She probably spent the

majority of her day going into spontaneous trances." He then said, absently, "She
hasn't worked and owns a home. What's
her source of income aside from the disability payments?"

Smith made a note to seek an answer
to that question.

"When can you talk with this ex-CIA
friend of yours?" Smith asked.

"Tonight. I called him before coming
here. We're having dinner together."

"That was fast."

"I suspect he's happy to have an invitation. He's a strange duck, Mac, very much
a loner, never married, teaches at a psychiatric postgraduate center here in D.C."

Smith stifled the temptation to link strange
ducks with the psychiatric profession.

Tatum left Smith's Watergate apartment
and drove to his apartment on Capitol Hill,
where he put in a half hour on the treadmill and lifted weights for fifteen minutes
before showering and dressing to meet his
friend David Considine at Montmartre on
Seventh Street, which Tatum knew was
one of Considine's favorite restaurants. His
friend was already at a pine table, a glass
of ginger ale in front of him, when Tatum

walked in. Tatum slapped him on the shoulder before sitting. "You got a head start," Tatum said.

"As long as you're the designated driver," Considine said dryly.

Tatum ordered a pinot grigio.

"Glad we could get together, Dave."

"It's been awhile."

David Considine, ten years older than Tatum, was a tall, thin man with a shaved head, a small clump of reddish hair beneath his lower lip, and active green eyes. For as long as Tatum had known him, his choice of clothing was a blue blazer, white button-down shirt, and tie. This evening was no exception.

"Steamed mussels?" Considine suggested. The moderately priced French restaurant was known for them.

"Sure."

After ten minutes of initial banter, most of which involved Considine's dissatisfaction with his teaching job, he asked Tatum what was on his mind.

"Do I have to have something on my mind?" Tatum said through a smile. "Just thought it would be fun to get together."

Considine grunted and drained his

ginger ale, then motioned to a waitress for a refill.

"Actually," Tatum said, "there is something that I wanted to discuss with you."

"I figured. Go ahead."

Their mussels arrived, which interfered with their conversation as they eagerly attacked the bowl. When only shells remained in the broth, Tatum said, "I was wondering what you know about the Lightpath Clinic in Berkeley."

"Lightpath? It's been around awhile."

"Run by Sheldon Borger."

Considine didn't react.

"You've worked with him," Tatum said.

"A long time ago. What's your interest in it, Nic?"

Tatum had pondered how much to tell Considine about Sheila Klaus and her involvement in the Mark Sedgwick murder. It wasn't that he was concerned that what he said would be repeated by Considine to someone who shouldn't know about it. Considine had bailed out of his involvement with the CIA's Medical and Psychological Analysis Center's experimental programs at least two years ago, and when he and Tatum met for dinner shortly after he'd given his notice, Considine was open about his reasons for leaving.

"You reach a point, Nic, when you question what you're doing with your life and education. To be honest, some of the experiments I've been involved in run counter to everything I've believed about medicine. *Primum non nocere.* First do no harm. That's the oath we took, but frankly, a lot of what the CIA is doing in the name of medical research does one hell of a lot of harm to the people involved. Don't get me wrong. Maybe some of it is necessary and justified, national security and the rest. I'm a psychiatrist. I don't know anything about intelligence agencies or military needs or war. But I *do* know when innocent people are being used as lab rats without ever understanding what's being done to them. I just wanted out."

Tatum had certainly understood what his friend was saying at dinner that night two years ago and admired him for having decided to distance himself from what was in all probability illegal and unquestionably immoral.

"You know about Mark Sedgwick's death," Tatum began.

"Of course."

"How well did you know Mark?"

"Not well at all."

"I didn't know him well either. They've arrested a woman in his death. She's charged with having deliberately run him over."

"So I've read. What's your interest in the case?"

"I was called in by MPD—I used to work for them, as you know—to help investigate Mark's death. I reviewed Sedgwick's records and came up with this woman, Sheila Klaus, as a possible suspect. It turns out that there's a lot of evidence to prove that she did, in fact, drive the car that killed him."

Considine took a sip of his refreshed soft drink. "What's this got to do with Lightpath and Borger?" he asked as he picked up a menu and began perusing the entrées.

"This woman went to Lightpath four times with Sedgwick, and two more times on her own."

"Why?"

"Sedgwick took her. She's a multiple."

Considine looked up from the menu. "How do you know?"

"I've been working with her in jail. Her attorney, Mackensie Smith, is a friend of mine. He's overseeing her defense, working with another lawyer. He arranged for me to do a psychological evaluation of her." Tatum leaned across the table. "I'm convinced, David, that she was programmed to kill Sedgwick."

Considine laid the menu on the table. "Tell me more," he said.

After they'd each had hanger steak and sautéed potatoes, for which Tatum paid, they left the restaurant. Considine lived only a block away, and Tatum walked him to his apartment building, continuing the story about Sheila Klaus and his theory that she'd been brainwashed at the Lightpath Clinic. Considine had done more listening than talking during dinner and continued to be a good listener all the way to his building.

"A fascinating story, Nic," he said as they shook hands.

"I appreciate your input," Tatum said.

"Let me know what happens, huh?"

"Of course."

Tatum walked back to where he'd parked his car near the restaurant. It was only after he'd gotten in, started the engine, and headed home that he realized that while he'd told his friend the entire story of Sheila Klaus, Considine had offered little more about the Lightpath Clinic and Sheldon Borger than he already knew. Considine had made some unflattering comments about Borger—"he's smarmy," "he's a money-grubbing guy"—but hadn't revealed the sort of inside information Tatum had hoped for. That didn't come as a complete surprise. It was common knowledge that once someone left the employ of the CIA or any of the other sixteen intelligence agencies, it was expected of him or her to maintain a silence about how the agencies operate, particularly top secret projects such as those involving mind-control experimentation. Considine had also reiterated his reasons for having left the CIA, branding as "barbaric" its widespread use of physicians, psychologists, and scientists to manipulate innocent men and women. But again, that was common knowledge within certain segments of the medical and scientific communities.

As Tatum settled in to watch a movie on TV, he decided that while it had been good to see his friend again and to share a meal with him, it had not been a productive evening. He soon dropped that line of thought as he became engrossed in the film.

Considine, too, intended to watch a movie before retiring. But he first placed a phone call.

"Colin, it's David Considine."

"Hello, David."

"Hope I'm not calling too late," he said to his former superior at the CIA.

"Not at all. I just finished reading a book and thought I'd turn in early. Your timing is good."

"Colin, I have information that you'll want to hear."

"Excellent. The usual place, say noon?"

"That will be fine."

CHAPTER
23

Psychiatrist David Considine had indeed severed his connection with the CIA two years earlier and was quick to tell friends and colleagues of his dissatisfaction with the work he'd been called upon to perform. Those in whom he confided were impressed with his sense of honor and his unwillingness to participate in some of the agency's more controversial medical and scientific endeavors. But he was never specific about the work he'd done for the CIA. He kept it vague, including just enough specificity to come off as credible.

What they didn't know was that Considine did so with the spy agency's blessing.

Leaving the CIA and the nation's other intelligence agencies was not easily accomplished, any more than walking away from the Mafia was. Certain conditions had to be met, among them an agreement to keep one's eyes and ears open for any sign of activity that might be considered potentially injurious to the agency and its goals. Countless former employees were kept on a sub rosa payroll in return for feeding damaging information back to their handlers. Some former employees were even encouraged to write books about their agency experiences, to adopt the public stance of being anti-CIA, and to include in their books what they claimed was "inside information" about the agency's operations. Of course, their books contained little more than what was already public knowledge. The books were vetted by the agency before the manuscripts were delivered to a small number of mainstream book publishers who were paid to publish them. By appearing to be anti-CIA, these "authors" tended to be trusted by those who possessed information potentially damaging to the CIA and who willingly shared that information with these "anti-agency" authors who were paid handsomely for their "literary" efforts.

Although Considine had not authored a book, he was one of many former contract workers who continued to be paid for acting as a conduit of information to the CIA even though no longer officially connected to the agency. In the two years since his contract with the agency expired, he'd had little to report, although he had provided the names of a few other physicians or scientists who'd trusted him and who had expressed their suspicions about the CIA's network of agency-funded underground experiments. They'd gone further in some cases: "The CIA ought to be brought to trial for what they've done to unwitting patients whose lives have been ruined as a result," one had told him over dinner, which he'd dutifully reported to Colin Landow. He'd felt good, useful, when adding those names to an already long list of "enemies." But he'd wished he could do more to justify the money that showed up each month in his savings account.

Now he could.

He and Landow met at noon at a prede-
termined bench in the Washington Harbour
area of Georgetown. Considine didn't waste
time relating to Landow every detail of what
Nic Tatum had told him about Sheila Klaus
and Tatum's hypnotic sessions with her.
Landow listened impassively, his eyes taking in his surroundings, his ears hearing
only what Considine had to say.

When the tall, bald psychiatrist, who
wore that day a gray running suit and white
sneakers, was finished, Landow patted his
arm and said, "This is all fascinating, David. Of course the part about this Ms.
Klaus having been programmed at Lightpath to kill Mark Sedgwick is pure science
fiction. As you know, Sheldon Borger and
his people aren't engaged in creating mur-
derers, or I suppose I should say murder-
esses."

"Yes."

"I'm also aware that Mark had brought
an excellent hypnotic subject, a woman, to
Lightpath. What's of concern is that the excellent work they did with her could be jeo-
pardized by Nicholas Tatum's probing.
Tatum is good at what he does."

Considine silently agreed. He'd worked

with Tatum and had observed how skillful his friend was in inducing trance in patients, particularly after returning from New York where he'd studied with Herbert Spiegel.

"Do you want me to spend time again with Tatum to see if I can find out more?" Considine asked.

"I think that's an excellent idea," Landow said. "Don't push him for information. We don't want to scare him off. But you're obviously good at gaining trust. I'm not sure what steps we'll take based upon what you've told me, but I assure you that we'll do what's necessary. Are things good where you're teaching?"

"It's boring," was Considine's response.

Landow laughed. "Maybe you should consider coming back to work for me."

"Is that an option?"

"Of course it is. As Uncle Sam says, we're always looking for good men. Thank you for bringing this to me." Landow stood and looked up into the sunny blue sky. "It's a lovely day, David. Enjoy it."

CHAPTER

24

Tatum was in the courtroom the next morning when Sheila, accompanied by her attorney, Marie Darrow, arrived for the arraignment. Darrow pleaded not guilty for her, and her request for bail was denied.

Tatum was shocked at Sheila's physical appearance. She looked as though she hadn't slept for days. She walked unsteadily and almost fell as she entered, the matron grabbing her and keeping her erect. Her hair needed washing; her makeup, what there as of it, was smudged, giving her an almost comical look, a poorly crafted marionette. The prison garb that she wore swam on her, adding to the impression of a woman on the edge.

Tatum and Darrow connected in the hallway after Sheila had been led away.

"We finally get to meet," the attorney said.

"Mac Smith thinks very highly of you," Tatum said.

"Which means a lot coming from him. The problem is that the best damn attorney in D.C. is going to have one hell of a job getting her off."

"Lots of circumstantial evidence to deal with," Tatum offered.

"Her lying about traveling with the victim hasn't done her any favors. I'm meeting with the U.S. attorney this afternoon to see if I can strike some sort of an agreement."

Tatum's expression mirrored his surprise. "Isn't that premature?" he asked.

"Premature?"

"It just seems to me that cutting a deal with the prosecution means she'll be found guilty, with some slack cut for her sentencing."

Darrow sounded annoyed as she said, "I wasn't referring to plea-bargaining. I've reviewed all the evidence and believe there's a possibility that I could get the charges dropped—at least for now."

"You really think that's possible?" Tatum said, his voice reflecting his pleasure at hearing it.

"A long shot," Darrow said, "but worth a shot. I've discussed it with Mac."

"What does he think?"

"He said to go ahead. If that doesn't work, we'll have to depend upon you and your pseudoscience."

"Pseudoscience?" Tatum said. "That's the way you view my theory about how and why she killed Dr. Sedgwick?"

Darrow realized that she'd offended him and manufactured a small smile to soften things. "I'll level with you," she said. "I've gone back and reviewed cases in which mind control and multiple personalities were offered as a defense. The results weren't what you'd call encouraging."

"Which doesn't mean it's not relevant in Sheila's case," he offered, trying to keep pique from his voice. "Look," he said, "I'm obviously not a lawyer. The way the courts work isn't something I know a lot about. But I *do* know that Sheila Klaus was programmed to run down Sedgwick."

"Prove it!"

"I . . . I can't, but I'm determined to break through the controls that were put on her and get to the truth."

"I wish you well, Mr. Tatum."

"*Doctor* Tatum."

"Doctor Tatum," she said. "You'll excuse me. I'm late for an appointment."

He watched her walk down the corridor and disappear around a corner. Her comments had nettled him, and he drew some calming breaths. Her negativity was unsettling. Still, he told himself, he couldn't blame her. She operated in a world far different from his. Her world was one of hard facts and a tightly prescribed system. He was dealing with the mind, trying to make a case that it was possible, even probable with certain subjects, to manipulate them to do the bidding of others, even to kill.

Their brief exchange had left him with the realization that if he were to succeed in proving his theory, he'd better do it fast.

He met with Sheila that afternoon. Smith had told him that the authorities were beginning to protest the frequency of Tatum's "psychological evaluations" of Sheila, but

he'd convinced them that it was necessary, and that to limit access would un-
fairly hinder his efforts to mount a credible
defense. They backed off.

Tatum wasn't eager to proceed with
Sheila, considering the shape that she
was in. Fatigued subjects were sometimes
difficult to work with; exhaustion got in the
way of being able to focus. But after some
initial expressions of concern for her, he
induced her trance state.

"Where are you now?" he asked after
ascertaining that her trance was deep.

"I don't feel good," she replied. "I want
to die."

"No you don't, Sheila," he said. "You have
Carla to help you."

"Carla," she said in a dreamy voice. "Yes,
she helps me."

"She goes wherever you go," he said.

"Yes." A little girl's laugh came from her.

"Do you remember when she made all
those trips with you to San Francisco?"

A look of concern crossed her face.

"You went to San Francisco with Dr.
Sedgwick."

"Oh, him," she said dismissively. "He was
a fool."

"He was?"

"A stupid fool."

"But he was your doctor, wasn't he? And he took you to see other doctors in San Francisco."

When she didn't respond, he added, "You saw Dr. Borger. He gave you vitamin B shots. Remember?"

Now anger replaced concern in her expression.

"Carla didn't like the shots, did she?"

"No, no, I didn't like them. They hurt."

Tatum thought for a moment before saying, "I'm going to give you a shot now, Sheila."

She straightened in her chair and waved her hands in front of her.

"Is Carla with you?" he asked. "Maybe she can convince me to not give you the shot."

"Carla is . . . of course she's with me."

"Are you there, Carla? Why haven't you said hello?"

The change in Sheila was slower and more gradual than it had been during previous sessions. Sheila's face tightened and her lips formed into a sneer. A low, guttural laugh erupted from deep inside.

"Hello, Carla," Tatum said.

She laughed.

"You are Carla, aren't you?"

"You didn't say the magic word," she said, elongating the final two words.

"Oh? What word was that?"

"You know."

"Maybe I forgot."

"You know, about taking a cruise."

"Did you take a cruise?"

"No," she snapped. "What are you, some sort of dumb bunny? You know what it means."

Tatum tried various questions to get her to elaborate but was unsuccessful. Realizing that he was losing her, he decided to be direct.

"You drove the car that killed Dr. Sedgwick, didn't you, Carla?"

She seemed confused for a moment before saying, "You know I did. You told me to do it."

"I told you? You mean Dr. Borger."

"You. That's you, isn't it?"

She shook her head and mumbled something about him being stupid. And she was gone, replaced by Sheila, whom Tatum quickly brought out of her trance.

"Are you all right?" he asked.

"I'm so tired."

"You should rest. I'll see you again tomorrow."

He quickly wrote on a pad the words he'd just heard:

> **I asked whether Carla had driven the car that killed Mark Sedgwick.**
> **She responded: "You know I did. You told me to do it."**
> **I said: "I told you? Dr. Borger?"**
> **She said: "You. That's you, isn't it?"**
> **She disappeared and I brought Sheila out of the trance.**

He was eager to report what had just transpired to Mac Smith and called him at his Watergate apartment. A machine informed him that Smith was away and would return the call as soon as possible. Tatum left his name and his cell phone number and drove home. He'd been there only fifteen minutes when his cell phone rang.

"It's Mac Smith."

"Hello, Mac. Thanks for getting back to me so soon. Listen to this." He read for Smith what he'd written on the pad.

"She said that?"

"Carla said it. She also mentioned some magic word that had to do with taking a cruise."

"Meaning?"

"I don't know. It might have been a word or words that Borger used to put her into trance."

"I don't suppose you had a tape recorder running."

"No, I didn't."

"It doesn't matter. She said it under hypnosis."

"Which doesn't make it less believable."

"Tell that to a judge and a jury. I don't mean to minimize the importance of it, Nic. Frankly, my mind has been spinning for the past hour."

"With what?

"The news that Marie Darrow just received. She met with the U.S. attorney earlier in the afternoon to see whether his office was secure in thinking they had probable cause with which to hold Sheila. It's Marie's opinion that the evidence simply doesn't rise to that level."

"You're not about to tell me that they agreed with her."

"That's exactly what I'm telling you. An hour after she met with the U.S. attorney, he called her to say that they've decided to drop formal charges against Sheila, at least until further evidence can be gathered."

"That's great news," Tatum said.

"Yes, it is," Smith agreed. "The real question is: why?"

"Lack of evidence, as you said. Not enough for probable cause."

"I'd like to think it's that simple, Nic, but something tells me there's more behind it."

25

The judge in Sheila Klaus's case had erupted in anger when informed by the U.S. attorney's office that it was dropping charges against her. He ripped into the attorneys for having proceeded with the case without having sufficient evidence to show probable cause.

"You've dragged this woman through the system without the goods to make the charges stick, and now you decide that you were premature. You rushed to judgment, and as a result a citizen has been subjected to incarceration and loss of dignity. I suggest that you get your act together and never—and I mean *never*—use this court again in such an unprofessional manner."

The attorneys who stood before the judge were not the ones who'd decided to drop the charges, but they took the tongue-lashing in stride. The order had come from the very top echelons of their office, a terse command that left little room for debate. One of the attorneys directly involved in the case had argued against the dictum but was rebuffed. The caveat that the case might be reopened was pure lip service. Sheila Klaus was to be freed, end of debate.

Marie Darrow was on hand at the jail to help Sheila process out and to drive her home. Sheila's personal possessions were returned to her, each item checked off a list. Nic Tatum had asked that he be allowed to join them, but Darrow nixed the idea, saying that it might be too traumatic for Sheila. Tatum didn't understand the rationale behind it but wasn't in a position to disagree.

Darrow stopped with Sheila at a supermarket on the way home and helped her pick up necessities. Sheila said little during the time they were together after leaving jail, and Darrow didn't press her for conversation. When they pulled into the driveway, Sheila said, "I can't believe I'm here."

"To be honest with you," said Darrow, "I can't either."

"It's because of you and Mac Smith," Sheila said. "How can I ever thank you?"

"No need. It's what we do for a living. I'll help you in with the groceries and your bag."

Darrow had been as surprised at the decision to drop the charges as Sheila had been. She'd entered her motion for dismissal more as a pro forma exercise than expecting it to prevail. When she'd asked one of the attorneys on the prosecution side for his reaction, he responded by shrugging, shaking his head, and extending his hands in a gesture of frustration. Darrow sensed that he wanted to say something but was holding back. It didn't matter. Her motion had prevailed. That was all that counted.

Being home rejuvenated Sheila. Her steps were light as she went room to room opening windows to air out the house. She went to the atrium at the rear and examined the multitude of plants there. "They need water," she lamented as she went to the kitchen, where she filled a large watering can, brought it to the atrium, and carefully poured the water into the pots. Darrow stood in the doorway and watched. She couldn't help but smile. It was seldom that her efforts on the part of an accused had such a happy ending. Sheila seemed suddenly aware of Darrow's presence and said, "Oh, I'm sorry. Here I am worrying about my plants and leaving you standing there. Would you like some tea or coffee? I have cinnamon rolls in the freezer. Cold cuts? We just bought some, didn't we?"

"Thank you, no, Sheila. I really should be going. I'm glad you're home."

Sheila fell into a chair and laughed. "Home," she said. "I never thought I'd see it again."

She closed her eyes, a serene smile on her face. Darrow was about to leave when she realized that Sheila had slipped into the sort of reverie she'd witnessed when first meeting her.

"Sheila?" she said.

Sheila opened her eyes and looked about, a startled expression on her face.

"Sheila?" Darrow repeated.

Sheila's stare was vacant as she looked at Darrow. A crooked sneer crossed her face and she said in a low voice, "You can go now."

Darrow was taken aback at the change. One minute Sheila had been happy at being home, watering her plants and offering refreshments. Now Darrow was faced with a different person.

"All right," Darrow said, "I'll go. Enjoy being home, Sheila."

This person who'd replaced Sheila said, "So long. We're fine now."

"We're?"

Sheila closed her eyes and leaned back. Darrow took a final look before leaving the house, getting in her car, and driving away, totally confused. The thought that kept running through her mind was, *Maybe Dr. Nicholas Tatum was right.*

Although this was a day that Tatum had set aside to see private patients, he'd canceled his morning appointments in the hope that he could accompany Darrow and Sheila from jail. When Darrow had rejected his offer, it was too late to reschedule, so Tatum used the morning to work out and to catch up on paperwork. Had he had a free afternoon, he would have gone out to Potomac Airfield and put in an hour's flight time in his Micco aerobatic plane. That would have cleared his mind of what dominated his thinking since awakening that morning—Sheila Klaus. Mac Smith had been right. There *was* more to her release than a decision by the U.S. attorney's office that they possessed insufficient evidence to hold her. What was most troubling was the thought that Sheila was now alone, on her own, and capable of being controlled and manipulated by those who had captured her mind in the first instance.

He and Cindy Simmons had made a date for dinner that night. Cindy was in a celebratory mood because she'd learned that afternoon that she would be receiving a promotion accompanied by a raise. Tatum wasn't in the mood for a fancy restaurant and suggested they order in from a local Chinese take-out place. Cindy's pout put an end to that plan, and they called and lucked into a last-minute reservation at her favorite restaurant, the Oval Room on Connecticut Avenue, across from the

White House. Although she denied it, Tatum knew that Cindy not only liked the food and service, she also enjoyed seeing members of D.C.'s political power elite at other tables, congressmen and congresswomen, cabinet members, and occasionally a Supreme Court justice. She was, as he playfully put it, a closet political junkie, and when she wasn't working at the hospital, her TV was perpetually tuned to C-SPAN.

It turned out to be a special night at the Oval Room. When they arrived, they were met at the door by Secret Service agents who had their names on a clipboard and who asked for picture IDs. Cindy's purse was examined, and Tatum received a cursory pat down, far less intrusive than being felt up at airports.

"What's going on? Tatum asked.

"A special guest," an agent replied tersely.

That special guest turned out to be presidential candidate George Mortinson, Tricia, and ranking members of the boards of the Washington Opera and the Washington Symphony and their spouses. True to form, Mortinson had chosen the Oval Room at the last minute, and the agents, as well as the restaurant's management and staff, had to scurry to prepare. Secret Service agents had visited the restaurant late that afternoon and given it a thorough going over. Mortinson disliked that his appearances inconvenienced people but accepted it as a necessary evil.

Tatum was glad that he'd worn a sport jacket that night.

"How exciting," Cindy said as they were seated at a table with crisp white linen and red leather armchairs. It was obvious from the way the room was set up that Mortinson and his party would be seated as far from other diners as possible.

"Do you think he'd give me an autograph?" Cindy asked after they had ordered drinks.

"Don't you dare," was Tatum's response.

"Why not? He wants every vote he can get. Anyway, you know I'm a fan and hope he wins in November."

Tatum shared her political views. The thought of Allan Swayze being returned for a second term was anathema to both of them.

Cindy ordered what she usually did when there—which wasn't often because of its prices—spice-salted free-range chicken. Tatum chose seared salmon. Salads for both. The bottle of white wine Tatum picked was uncorked and poured.

"Here's to you and your promotion," Tatum said, touching the rim of his glass to hers.

"Thank you, kind sir," she said. "And here's to your patient getting out of jail."

Tatum had told Cindy about Sheila's unexpected freedom while she dressed for their evening out. She, of course, thought it was good news.

"Yeah, it is," he'd agreed, "but I'm afraid of what will happen to her now that she's on her own."

Although he'd told Cindy every aspect of his theory about Sheila's brainwashing at the Lightpath Clinic, she didn't necessarily share his concerns. Manipulating someone to kill another person through mind control and hypnosis simply didn't play for her. That was science fiction, the stuff of Hollywood's imaginative screenwriters.

"What could happen to her now that she's free?" Cindy asked as their salads were served.

"I don't know," was Tatum's honest reply. "She's an incredibly malleable individual, Cindy, which puts her at risk if she falls into the wrong hands."

He continued to express his fears until Cindy said, "Can we talk about something else?"

"Sure," Tatum said, taking her hand in his. "Sorry. I get consumed by something and—"

The arrival of Mortinson and party brought all conversation in the room to a halt. Flanked by two agents, Mortinson led the way, stopping at tables to chat and to shake hands.

"He's so personable," Cindy said to Tatum.

"He's a politician," Tatum said.

"So is Swayze, but can you imagine him glad-handing people the way Mortinson does?"

Their table was situated away from the path Mortinson took, and Tatum sensed that Cindy was disappointed to not have been able to shake the candidate's hand. Like most people in the restaurant, they found themselves constantly looking over at Mortinson's table and trying to catch snippets of conversation. Over coffee and

a shared brioche soufflé with maple and
banana, Tatum mentioned that Mackensie
Smith was a friend of the Mortinsons.

"Think he'd mind if I used his name?"

Before Tatum could respond, Cindy got
up, adjusted her dress, and made her way
across the room in Mortinson's direction.
An agent stopped her just short of the table.
Cindy said something to him. He scowled,
turned, and relayed a message to Mortinson, who stood, smiled, and extended his
hand to Cindy. She'd taken the dessert
menu with her and handed it to the candidate. He turned and said something to his
wife, which resulted in her pulling something from a large envelope and handing it
to him. Mortinson signed it, shook Cindy's
hand again, and she returned to Tatum
carrying a signed 8-by-10 color photograph.
She beamed.

"A good day for you," Tatum said. "A promotion and raise, and now an autographed
picture."

"He's so nice," she said.

"He seems to be," Tatum replied.

The Mortinson party was still there when
Tatum and Cindy left. Tatum was staying
the night at her apartment; he kept a basic

set of clothes and toiletries there for such occasions. They were in pajamas and watching a taping of the House of Representatives on C-SPAN when Cindy said, "I could have killed him."

"Killed who?"

"Mortinson. I could have pulled out a gun and shot him."

"They frisked us when we arrived, Cindy. They went through your purse."

"But I could have carried a concealed weapon under my dress."

"I guess so."

"People like him are so vulnerable no matter how much security there is."

"I'm glad you didn't. Shoot him, that is."

They turned off the TV and got into bed.

"Thanks for a wonderful evening," she said, nuzzling his neck.

"Glad you enjoyed it," he said.

After making love, they turned off the light, and Cindy quickly fell asleep.

Tatum lay awake for a long time, two visions dominating his mind.

There was the vision of Cindy pointing a gun at Mortinson and pulling the trigger.

And there was the vision of Sheila Klaus behind the wheel of a white Buick and running down Mark Sedgwick. As concerned as he was about her, he was also keenly aware that she had, in fact, murdered someone.

It was that final realization, and the visual that accompanied it, that stayed with him until sleep reluctantly came.

CHAPTER
26
SAN FRANCISCO

Iskander Itani's fists flew so fast that they were a blur.

He pummeled the light punching bag that Sheldon Borger had had installed in his basement gym while Borger, Peter Puhlman, and Jake Gibbons looked on.

"He's fast," Gibbons said.

"He certainly is," agreed Borger.

"What about the headaches?" Gibbons asked.

"He hasn't had one since he's been staying here," said Borger.

"You still want me to sign him to a management contract?" Gibbons asked.

"Yes," Borger replied, knowing that it would be a worthless piece of paper from which Itani would never be able to benefit. "I want to keep him positive for the short time I have left with him."

Itani stopped assailing the bag.

"You're looking good," Gibbons said in his gruff, raspy voice.

"I feel good," Itani said, toweling perspiration from his face and neck.

"The doc here says that your headaches have been cured."

"I don't like the word 'cured,'" Borger said, "but they are under control, under *Iskander's* control. Isn't that right, Iskander?"

The young man nodded. "I will take a shower," he said.

Borger and Puhlman watched Itani and Gibbons leave the gym and head upstairs.

"How are the sessions going?" Puhlman asked.

"Extremely well," Borger said. "In all my years of practice, he's the best subject I've ever seen."

What he said was true, although there had been many others whose ability to enter trance and to be controlled through hypnosis came close. Sheila Klaus topped that list.

But there was a distinct difference between Sheila and Itani.

With Sheila it was necessary to enhance her second personality, Carla Rasmussen. As superb a hypnotic subject as Sheila was, she was not an individual who could easily be convinced to hurt another person. She wasn't filled with the sort of anger that consumed Itani.

But Carla, who'd emerged during Sheila's difficult childhood to fight her battles and right the wrongs done to her, was naturally combative.

Itani didn't need a second personality. His rage and his feelings of deprivation and betrayal were all-consuming, very much at his core. Without the necessity of dealing with an emerging second personality, Borger was free to work directly with Iskander to build upon what was already present, a young man with a murderous rage festering inside.

Borger excused himself and went to his study, where he'd lately been spending most of his time. He'd established a three-a-day schedule of sessions with Itani, some of which exhausted him. His subject harbored more inner rage than Borger had realized from their early times together, and on a few occasions he thought Itani might lash out at him physically. It hadn't happened, but those incidents only further convinced Borger that once the Itani project was completed, he would sever his relationship with the CIA.

He didn't regret the path he'd chosen to take with the agency. He had proved to himself and to his benefactors that the human mind could be controlled with the right subjects and when guided by a skilled physician. It would be nice if his successes could be heralded to the world, but he knew that was impossible. Perhaps one day when history was written.

He'd lived a rich, satisfying life. All you had to do was look at this magnificent home on Nob Hill, check out his fleet of expensive cars in the four-car garage, his wardrobe, homes in other places, and the beautiful women who'd shared his bed.

He was also buoyed by knowing that his work would be put to good, positive use. So much of medicine and research was theoretical, with little or no practical application. What good was coming up with a breakthrough if it wasn't applied? Although he wasn't particularly political—he considered all politicians to be weak-kneed and concerned only with hanging on to their bases of power—he did care about his country. He'd watched it disintegrate into what he considered a third-world Socialist shell of its former self, a welfare state in which the drive to succeed had been thwarted by a succession of presidents and Congresses that stood idly by and let it happen. He'd originally viewed Allan Swayze as someone who would put the brakes on the decline and was bitterly disappointed with the current president's inefficient bumbling. Still, this occupant of the White House was far better than George Mortinson. To Borger, Mortinson was the epitome of weakness, a handsome, glad-handing phony who would enable the continuing deterioration of what was once the world's superpower.

Something had to be done to stop him, and Sheldon Borger had proved that he was the one to do it.

A knock at the door interrupted his reverie.

"Come in."

Itani entered. He'd showered and dressed in stylish clothing Borger had purchased for him. The psychiatrist's barber had come to the house and given the young Arab a flattering haircut. Elena had visited again and spent the night with Iskander, and Borger had given him money to send to his mother and brothers using a post office box as the return address. Everything had gone smoothly, although Borger knew that he had to be careful to not do anything that might upset the volatile young man.

"Ready for a session?" Borger asked.

"Yes," Itani said, taking his usual chair across from Borger.

Borger handed him the notebook that had been part of the initial session, its many pages now filled with Itani's written rants against Jews, Israel, and the "Israel lover" and "Jew lover" George Mortinson.

"Did you see in the paper today, Iskander, that Mortinson is calling for increased military aid to Israel?"

"Bastard!"

"Money to buy weapons to kill your people."

Itani's fists clenched and his eyes opened wide.

Borger had reached a point with Itani that he no longer needed to hold the gold coin up to him to induce trance. He simply pointed to it on the small table between them. Itani's eyes rolled up into his head and he shuddered.

"You're in a nice place now, Iskander, a restful, peaceful place, with your family and your people, and with Elena."

Itani smiled.

"I want you to go deeper and deeper into your pleasant trance state. That's it, Iskander, deeper and deeper and deeper . . ."

The session lasted twenty minutes. During it Borger handed Itani an unloaded Glock 9mm and instructed him to go to the window. He was told that if he saw anyone outside, he was to shoot that person. Itani did precisely as ordered, taking aim at a Hispanic gardener. He was then told to resume his seat and to hand Borger the weapon, which he also did.

When he was brought out of his trance, he had no recollection of what had transpired despite Borger's questioning of him.

"I want to see my brothers," Itani said. The request came out of the blue.

"You will see them soon."

"I want them to come here," Itani said.

"That is not possible, Iskander. It would seriously interrupt the progress we've made with your headaches. Besides, Mr. Gibbons is ready to offer you a management contract as a fighter. We don't want to do anything to get in the way, do we?"

Itani glared at Borger.

"Is something bothering you?" Borger asked.

Itani shook his head and stood. He appeared to want to say something but left the room without another word.

This brief confrontation concerned Borger. He'd been aware of a growing restlessness in Itani over the past few days, a belligerence that was disconcerting. As he sat and pondered the situation, he came to the conclusion that he'd peaked with his subject. Itani would never be more ready to carry out his assignment than he was at that moment.

But that posed a potential problem.

There was always the possibility that something, someone, would enter the picture and undo the delicate control that Borger had over his subject. Itani wanting to see his brothers was troublesome, and he'd recently expressed a desire to visit the gym where he'd worked.

Borger made a decision.

He placed a call to Washington and reached Colin Landow at his home.

"I believe he's ready," Borger announced.

"I'm always nervous when someone says that he 'believes' something is ready," was Landow's reply. "It is or it isn't."

Borger masked his pique and said, "You mentioned eleven days, Colin. Why has that date been chosen?"

"We know what his campaign schedule is," Landow said.

Which meant that they had someone inside the Mortinson campaign feeding them information.

"He's at his peak," Borger said. "There's always the possibility of losing him. I'll have to keep reinforcing what I've accomplished, but I suggest that the schedule be moved up."

"That's impossible."

"What travel arrangements have been made?" Borger asked.

"I'm coming to San Francisco tomorrow. I'll give you all the details when I see you."

"It's my suggestion that he be moved to Washington in the next few days. He needs a change of scenery, Colin. We run a risk by keeping him here."

Borger gnashed his teeth as he heard Landow click off the connection. He'd grown to detest the man with his pinched speech and inflated sense of self. He had a fleeting vision of Itani killing not only George Mortinson but Colin Landow as well. It brought a smile to his lips. In the meantime he had to do what was needed to keep Itani under control. Some time with Elena might serve to calm him down. He reached her at her apartment and asked her to spend the night at the house.

"How is he?" she asked.

"Fine. Why do you ask?"

"I don't know. The last time we were together, he seemed angry. He scared me a little."

Borger forced a dismissive laugh. "He's a prizefighter, Elena, remember? He's really a pussycat, just a little tense."

"Pussycat? I wouldn't call him that," she said. "He can get rough."

"But nothing you can't handle. I remember enjoying rough sex with you. I really think he needs your charms to calm down. How does doubling your fee sound?"

She agreed to be there at six.

Borger greeted Elena when she arrived and summoned Itani, who'd been sleeping. Seeing her seemed to brighten Itani's spirits, and Borger was glad that he'd arranged for her to be there that evening. He'd instructed the cook to prepare what had become Iskander's favorite dinner, fried chicken and mashed potatoes, and made sure that the makings of a Tom Collins were present and plentiful.

He left the couple alone, got in his Jaguar, and drove to where he'd made a dinner date with Mica Sphere, a striking forty-five-year-old lesbian who owned a successful custom jewelry store on Pacific Avenue. Borger had discovered the shop a few years earlier and had become a steady, free-spending customer. He and Mica had struck it off from the beginning and fell into an easy friendship, one not marred by sexual expectations. Borger often turned to Mica when he was in the mood for good conversation, and she was always available when he called. Sheldon Borger was unfailingly entertaining. Besides, he enjoyed the finer things of life, which included the best restaurants and choice tickets to prime events. It wasn't that Borger didn't find Mica sexually alluring. She was a stunningly beautiful woman, tall and willowy, with a sexy come-hither smile, and Borger seldom left her company without being aroused. Mica was Borger's only female friend. He considered women sexual objects and tended to treat them that way. But Mica was different. He actually listened when she spoke.

They went to one of his favorite restaurants, Cafe Jacqueline in North Beach, where they enjoyed drinks followed by seafood soufflés for which the establishment was known. He considered inviting her back to the house for a nightcap but nixed that notion, not with Itani and Elena there. Ever since the young Iskander had moved in, Borger had been forced to keep everyone he knew away from the house and had grown tired of the restrictions on his lifestyle. Sending Itani on his mission couldn't come soon enough.

They topped off the evening with after-dinner drinks at the Top of the Mark, where they danced to a ten-piece orchestra. He dropped her at her apartment building a little before midnight.

Borger considered stopping in at one of the call girls on his list to address his passion but decided not to and drove directly home. It was twelve thirty when he walked through the front door and headed for his study to check his answering machine. He'd almost reached it, when something stopped him. It wasn't a noise. It was something less tangible, a feeling, a sense that all was not right. He cocked his head and stopped breathing to better hear. Nothing.

As far as he knew, only Itani and Elena were in the house. The cook had announced that she was leaving after dinner, and a handyman who'd been called in to repair a leak in the basement was gone by late afternoon. Borger's full-time housekeeper had taken the day off to spend with her daughter and grandson.

He didn't want to disturb Itani and Elena,

assuming that they were in bed together in Iskander's room. He almost ignored the feeling that nagged at him and continued on his way to the study. Instead, he went up a short set of carpeted steps leading to the guest wing and paused in the hallway. Itani's room was at the far end, a corner room with splendid views. Borger walked slowly and deliberately toward it, realizing after having taken only a few steps that the door was open. Strange, he thought, as he covered the rest of the distance. He stopped just short of the doorway and peered inside. What he saw shocked him.

Elena, who wore black silk pajamas, hung half off the bed, her head resting on the Oriental rug. A pool of blood formed a crimson circle around it; a few drops of it were on the hardwood floor.

"Jesus!" Borger said.

He looked across the room to a corner by the window where Itani sat in a chair, his face a blank. Borger wasn't sure what to do. He stood frozen in the doorway, his mouth open but saying nothing, his eyes darting back and forth between Elena's lifeless body and the passive Itani. He finally overcame his inertia and stepped into the room.

"What happened?" he asked Itani.

"She shouldn't have done it," Itani mumbled.

"Done *what*?"

"She insulted me."

"*Insulted* you? She . . . I can't believe this."

Itani continued to sit, his eyes focused beyond Borger.

Borger went to the body and pressed his fingertips against Elena's neck. "She's dead," he said. He turned to Itani. "You killed her."

"She shouldn't have said it to me," he repeated. "Whore."

Borger's first thought was that Elena had told Itani that Borger was paying her to sleep with him. Itani had made a few disparaging comments about American women over the days he'd been at the house, criticizing their provocative ways, their skimpy clothing, their loose morals. Of course it hadn't kept him from succumbing to Elena's sexual overtures.

"What did she say that made you angry?" Borger asked.

Itani didn't reply, and Borger knew that trying to elicit information from him at that moment was a waste of time. He went to where Itani sat, placed his hand on his shoulder, and said, "It's all right, Iskander. I'm sure she did something that made you angry. But we have to leave here immediately."

Itani slowly got to his feet and followed Borger to his study.

"I want you to stay here, Iskander," Borger said in a soothing voice. He picked up the gold coin and held it in front of Itani. "I want you to relax and think pleasant thoughts, of your family and pretty places. I want you to stay right here in this chair until I return."

Borger observed Itani. His trance was deep, and Borger assumed that he'd been in that state since before attacking Elena.

He left the study and called Peter Puhlman from a kitchen phone.

"I need you here right away," Borger said.

A sleepy Puhlman complained about being called at such a late hour.

"Damn it, Peter, there's been a dreadful accident here. I need you now. Call Jake and bring him with you."

Borger returned to the study, where Itani sat in the same rigid position as when Borger had left him. The psychiatrist's mind was flooded with thoughts and questions. One thing was certain, he knew. If there was ever a time for clear thinking, it was now. Confident that Itani would remain where he was, he went to the living room and awaited the arrival of Puhlman and Gibbons, who showed up a half hour later.

Borger took them to the guest room.

"What the hell happened?" Gibbons asked.

"Itani," Borger said. "He killed her."

"Why?" Puhlman asked.

"It doesn't matter why," Borger snapped. "We have to get her out of here."

"What'll we do with her?" Gibbons asked.

"Dump her somewhere," Borger said. "Get a boat and dump her out in the ocean."

"Just like that," Puhlman said.

"Yes, damn it, just like that," Borger said. "Wrap her in that rug and dump it with her."

Puhlman sighed and approached the body. He knelt and started to wrap the rug around her. He looked back at Gibbons and said, "Come on, for Christ's sake. I can't do this by myself."

Thirty minutes later, they'd secured Elena in the rug, tying it around her with duct tape that Borger brought from the garage. Gibbons worked on the small stain on the hardwood floor with a paper towel and a Brillo pad. "Careful," Borger instructed. "Don't take up the floor finish with the blood."

They'd stripped the bed and included the sheets and pillows in the duct-taped package. The few clothes that Itani had in the closet were moved to another bedroom.

Puhlman had driven there in his Mercedes. He and Gibbons carefully placed Elena's lifeless body in the trunk.

"Make sure she's never found," Borger instructed.

As they drove away, Borger, whose adrenaline had sustained him, now felt on the verge of collapse. He sat in the kitchen and conjured the possibilities.

Had Elena told anyone where she was going to be that night?

Did she keep records of her clients, including Borger? He hoped that she wasn't that indiscreet, but she was, after all, a whore who ran a business.

He knew that she lived alone because

he'd visited her at her apartment on a few occasions. But what about family? Did she have a boyfriend? A close girlfriend? Other hookers with whom she shared tales of her customers?

He decided that if he were contacted concerning her disappearance, he would simply deny that she'd been there that night. Whom would the authorities believe? A prostitute or an eminent psychiatrist?

What was self-evident was that he had to get Itani out of San Francisco, and do it fast. Landow was arriving the following day. Whatever travel plans Landow had for Itani would have to be changed. He had to leave for Washington immediately and bide his time there until it was time to strike.

He returned to the study to find that Itani was gone.

He raced from room to room, finally going downstairs to the gym, where he found Itani, now dressed in a sweat suit, pounding a heavy bag. Borger watched quietly until Itani grew arm weary and stopped.

"Iskander," Borger said.

Itani turned and faced Borger. He'd come out of the trance on his own. "I needed to work out," he said.

"Did you enjoy yourself with Elena?" Borger asked.

"Yes. Is she still here?"

"No," Borger said, "she had to go home. Why not come upstairs and get to bed?" Borger thought quickly. "I'm having your bedroom redecorated," he said. "You'll sleep in one of the other rooms. Is that okay with you?"

"Yes. That's okay."

"Fine. Let's both get a good night's rest. We have a busy day ahead of us tomorrow."

CHAPTER
27

Few events in his life had caused Dr. Sheldon Borger to have a sleepless night, but Itani's murder of Elena certainly did. He'd finally given up trying to sleep at five, showered, dressed, and made himself coffee and an English muffin. The cook wasn't due until seven. The housekeeper would be there at eight.

Puhlman called at six thirty.

"Well?" Borger said.

"We took care of it. We decided to—"

"Not on the phone. Come to the house."

"I have some errands to run. I'll be there at ten."

"*Errands?*" Borger hung up with force.

When the housekeeper arrived, Borger told her that he was having one of the guest bedrooms redecorated, including wall-to-wall carpeting, and was keeping the door locked until the decorator arrived. "Mr. Itani will be staying in one of the other rooms," he added.

"He's such a quiet young man," she said.

"Yes, he is. He'll be leaving soon to resume his career as a prizefighter."

She made a sour face. "Prizefighting," she said in a tone to match her expression. "So brutal."

Borger ignored her editorial comment and went to the kitchen, where Itani had just walked in.

"Good morning," the cook said.

Itani returned the greeting.

Borger didn't want to engage in a conversation with Itani in the presence of the cook and said to her, "Would you be good enough to bring breakfast for Mr. Itani to my study? We have work to do. I've already eaten."

Once in the study, Borger closed the door and sat across from Itani. "Did you sleep well in your new bedroom?" he asked.

"Yes. It was fine."

"Did you have a good time last night with Elena?"

Itani seemed puzzled at the question, and Borger wondered whether he was about to recall what had happened. His answer confirmed that he hadn't. "She went home," he said.

"Yes, she went home."

Itani nodded and looked up as the cook brought in a tray.

"Go ahead and eat," Borger said, relieved that his amnesia of the event had held.

When Itani was finished with breakfast, Borger said, "I have news for you."

"What?"

"Well, first of all, Jake Gibbons is preparing a management contract."

Itani exhibited a rare smile.

"Not only that, he's arranged for your first fight to take place in Washington, D.C."

Itani's creased brow wasn't what Borger had expected.

"You'll be going there soon, maybe even as early as tomorrow."

"Who am I fighting?" Itani asked.

"That's being discussed. We'll know in a few days. There are details to be worked out, papers to file to get you licensed, things like that."

"Will my brothers and mother be there?"

Borger had anticipated that question and had a ready answer. "As soon as you've had your first few fights in Washington, we'll arrange for your family to attend your next one. Right now, Iskander, it would be distracting to have them there your first time back in the ring. Do you understand?"

"Yes."

"Good. Now, let's do a session to make sure that those headaches don't come back."

Borger worked on reinforcing Itani's amnesia of what had occurred with Elena and was pleased with the result. It was as though last night had never happened.

Itani went to the gym to work out following the session.

Peter Puhlman arrived earlier than announced—he'd sensed Borger's pique on the phone—and Borger took him outside to a secluded corner of the garden where they sat on a black wrought-iron bench, a pretty setting for an ugly conversation.

"Tell me," Borger said.

"Jake rented a boat this morning, five o'clock. He told the man that we were going fishing. Jake knows boats. He said he used to own one. He wanted to try and rent one after we left the house, but I felt it would look suspicious to rent one at night so we waited until this morning and took her out into the bay, off the airport. Jake tied cement blocks and he dumped her. She went right down. He says she'll never be found."

Borger could only hope that Gibbons was right. One of many thoughts he'd had since discovering Elena's body was that he wished he was Mafia connected. The mob dealt with getting rid of bodies all the time and knew how to do it. How many years had Jimmy Hoffa been missing, along with countless others? But he didn't have mob connections, so he had to depend upon Puhlman and Gibbons. While their backgrounds were shady, he needed them to pick up people at the airport and drive them to the Lightpath Clinic, search out suitable subjects for the clinic's experiments, and deal with troublemakers who posed a threat to the program. They were jacks-of-all-trades, men for whom money was the prime motivator.

There were differences between them, of course. Gibbons knew little of Borger's *real* work, and Borger kept it that way.

Puhlman was another psychiatrist. He'd been brought into Borger's inner circle and was well aware of what went on at Lightpath and why Itani had been recruited. He professed his belief in what Borger intended to do with Itani from both a psychiatric point of view as well as for the good of the country, although his convictions didn't run nearly as deep as his boss's.

Both men were well paid for their services and presumably trustworthy. *Presumably!* **Was anyone totally trustworthy?**

"Why did the kid do it?" Puhlman asked.

"He snapped. She said something that set him off."

"What've we got on our hands, Sheldon, a psycho?"

"No, he's not a psycho," Borger said angrily.

Puhlman fell silent and stared straight ahead.

"I appreciate what you did last night and this morning," Borger said, slapping Puhlman on the shoulder.

"I don't like it," Puhlman said.

"Do you think I like it?" Borger responded.

"I've never been involved in anything like this before," Puhlman said, and Borger wondered whether he was about to tear up. "Jake didn't seem to mind. I almost think he enjoyed it. I suppose he's been exposed to things like this before. But I don't like being involved." He turned to Borger. "What if they trace her back to the house and start asking questions?"

"They won't, Peter. You have to trust me."

"Maybe it would have been better to call the authorities and tell them what happened, turn Iskander over to them and—"

"Peter," Borger said in the tone of a father correcting a wayward child, "you know how important it is to go through with our mission."

"But what if—"

"There is nothing to worry about. Look, Peter, we are about to do something for our country that is monumentally important. You've agreed with that since the beginning, when you set out to find the perfect subject. Well, you succeeded. Iskander is perfect, more perfect than I could ever have imagined. Everything will go forward without a hitch—*if* we keep our eye on the goal. It will be over soon. Colin is arriving here today. Because of what happened last night, I'm insisting that the schedule be moved up. I want Iskander away from here and in place in D.C. sooner than planned. He'll go through with his part of it, and then we'll be free to pack up and go our separate ways. I'll be receiving a large amount of money from those financing the project, and I intend to give much of it to you. You can take the money and leave San Francisco, settle wherever you like." When Puhlman didn't react, Borger added, "I'll tell Colin when I meet with him today that we need more money, a million. All you have to do is trust me, Peter. No one is going to miss a prostitute like Elena, and even if someone does, there's absolutely no reason to trace her back to us."

"To *us*?"

"To *me,*" Borger corrected, resisting the temptation to remind Puhlman that he was now an accomplice. Not that he had to. That reality had dominated Puhlman's thinking all morning.

"Now, here's what I want you to do," Borger said. "You'll be leaving with Iskander for Washington soon, sooner than expected. I'm sending Jake, too."

"Why? He doesn't know the plan."

"I want him there to deal with Iskander should he become difficult. Iskander thinks he's going to Washington to resume his boxing career. Jake can sustain that belief. You and Jake will come back to San Francisco the day of the event. Go on now, go home and prepare for your trip."

"You aren't coming with us?"

"No. I'll reinforce Iskander by phone. Colin has made all the arrangements. I'll find out more when I see him. Go on now, put last night and this morning out of your mind. We're about to do something that will turn the country on its head, Peter, and you and I will know that we did it, that we proved that it could be done."

Borger watched the beefy Puhlman walk into the house. For the first time since embarking on the project, he felt apprehension, even fear. What had occurred last night with Itani and Elena had created a complication that no one could have predicted, certainly not him. Yes, he'd seen growing anger in Itani and had even wondered on occasion whether the physically fit young man would strike out at him during one of their hypnotic sessions. But kill the girl? Preposterous!

Borger returned to the house and went to the gym, where Itani continued to work out. He watched as the young man battered both the heavy and light bags, skipped rope, and did a series of sit-ups, squats, and push-ups. When he took a break, Borger applauded. "You look splendid, Iskander," he said, "ready to fight."

"Yes, I am ready," Itani said. "I've never been more ready, thanks to you."

"I appreciate that, Iskander, but it's only because I believe in you. I want you to stay in the house today and speak to no one. Understand?"

Itani looked at him quizzically.

"I'll be out for a few hours. When I return, we'll do a session to make sure that those headaches of yours don't come back. It would be terrible if they spoiled your return to boxing."

He left Itani and went to his study, where he took a call from Landow, who'd taken an early flight from Washington and was now at his San Francisco hotel.

"We have to talk," Borger said.

"Yes, we certainly do, Sheldon. I'll come to the house."

"No. There's been an accident here. We'll take the ferry to Sausalito, from the ferry terminal. You know where it is. The one o'clock ferry."

"What sort of accident?"

"I'll fill you in when we meet."

"I'm not sure I like what I'm hearing."

"It's nothing that can't be worked out, Colin."

There was silence on the other end.

"Colin?"

"It would be terribly disappointing should anything cause this to fail, Sheldon."

"I told you the accident that happened here can be worked out. I've already done what's necessary to—"

"There's another problem," Landow said flatly.

"What other problem?"

"As you so discreetly suggested, not on the phone."

"The ferry leaves at one," Borger said. "Be there at twelve forty-five."

*   *   *

They arrived at the terminal simultaneously. Borger was dressed uncharacteris-
tically casually; Landow wore his usual
sport jacket and turtleneck, forest green
this day. He carried a manila envelope.

"What's this about an accident?" Landow
asked as they walked to the passenger
holding area with their tickets.

"I'll tell you when we're under way,"
Borger said.

The men said nothing to each other as
they waited to board. As they walked down
the gangplank toward the gleaming white
ferry whose idling engines churned the
green water of the slip and created a
constant gurgle, Borger smiled at Landow
and said, "It's a beautiful day to be on the
water."

Landow grunted.

Borger was fond of the ferry ride across
the bay to Sausalito and sometimes took
it on the spur of the moment, reveling in
the sunshine and salt air, the magnificent
orange Golden Gate Bridge coming in and
out of view as the ceaseless fog swirled
around and over it, its damp cold felt even
from a distance.

The ferry backed from its slip, turned, and headed for the picturesque town of Sausalito, once a busy lumber port, now an elite, touristy conclave of bohemians, many of whom lived on their "arks," houseboats, moored along the bay that formed one of the world's largest and most diverse houseboat communities. Borger and Landow found a spot on the upper deck away from the throng of day-trippers and helmet-clad locals with bikes but where it was hard to hear over the sound of the engine and the stiff wind.

"Here's the situation," Borger said, leaning close to Landow's ear. "Itani killed someone last night."

"What?" Landow responded.

"A prostitute I supplied for him," Borger said. "There was some sort of squabble, and he hit her hard enough to kill her."

Landow looked away from Borger and thrust his sizable chin into the wind.

Borger continued. "It's all been taken care of, but I thought you should know."

Landow returned his attention to Borger. "What do you mean it's been taken care of?"

Borger explained how the body had been

disposed of and that Itani had no memory of the event. "In a sense," Borger added, "as tragic as it was, it proves to me how complete his amnesia is. He's ready, Colin."

"Why didn't you exercise more control over him?" Landow asked.

"I wasn't at home when it happened," Borger explained.

"I'm surprised that you'd admit that."

"There was no need to be with him every waking moment. Let's not get sidetracked. He has to get out of San Francisco immediately."

"He's scheduled to leave four days from now."

"Make it sooner, tomorrow. Where will he be staying?"

"A safe house we own in Virginia, right across the river from the District. You'll be traveling with him."

It was a statement, not a question.

"No. I'm staying here in San Francisco. I've already told you that. Peter will accompany him. Jake Gibbons, too."

Landow's prolonged sigh said many things.

"Listen, Colin," Borger said, unable to keep annoyance from his voice, "I have worked long and hard to prepare Itani for this. He is under my control, not yours, and I'll make the decision about how to control him. There's no need for me to be in Washington. Let's put this to rest. I want him on a plane to Washington tomorrow."

Landow again faced the wind, a pose, a sailing ship's captain looking for land.

"I'll have Itani ready to leave tomorrow," Borger said. "He thinks he's traveling there to resume his boxing career. Jake Gibbons is giving him a phony management contract this afternoon, which should appease him for a few days. Peter is perfectly capable of handling him. I have the same level of control over Itani by telephone as I do in person. The relevant code words have been implanted and enforced many times."

When they reached Sausalito, they walked along the Bridgeway on their way to a bar. Landow said, "We'll do it your way, Sheldon. I can only say that a tremendous amount of thought, planning, and money have gone into this project. It had better work as planned."

They secured a table on the patio overlooking the bay. They ordered Bloody Marys.

"There's another problem," Landow said after the waiter had delivered their drinks, taken their lunch orders, and walked away.

"Yes, you indicated that when you called. What is it?"

"Sheila Klaus."

Borger had just started to sip his Bloody Mary. He returned the glass to the table and said, "What about her?"

"You know that we arranged for her to be released from prison."

"Yes, I'm aware of that. I'm also aware that she still claims her innocence. The programming obviously worked and continues to."

"So far. It was our belief that it was safer having her out of the hands of the authorities."

"And I agree. But either way, I see no reason for my control of her not to continue."

Landow asked, "Do you know a psychologist named Tatum, Sheldon? Nicholas Tatum?"

"No, I don't think that I do."

"He claims that he knows you."

"So?"

"He says that he met you at conferences."

"That's possible. I've attended many of them."

"He further claims that he's aware of Lightpath and your involvement with it."

Borger drank. "That's highly unlikely," he said.

"Sheldon, this Tatum has been working with Sheila Klaus."

"Working with her? How?"

"When she was incarcerated. He hypnotized her on more than one occasion. He's the reason we worked through channels at the highest levels to gain her release."

Borger's furrowed brow mirrored his sudden concern. "How do you know this?" he asked.

"A credible source." Landow leaned closer. "According to that same source, Tatum was able to summon Klaus's other personality, Carla Rasmussen."

"Nonsense! Whoever told you that?"

"That same source, who, I might add, heard it directly from Tatum. I'm also told that Carla Rasmussen identified *you* by name as the doctor she spent time with."

What had been concern now morphed into fear. Borger drank from his Bloody

Mary and summoned his thoughts. "This is very troubling, Colin," he said. "Something will have to be done about this Tatum character."

"That goes without saying," Landow said. "The question, Sheldon, is what do you intend to do about it?"

"I think that's your responsibility," Borger said.

"My responsibility?"

"You and your people back at Langley."

"Oh, no, Sheldon. I'm afraid that you have that wrong. The work you did with Ms. Klaus, and now with your latest find, is outside the realm of what the agency has approved."

"Now wait a minute, Colin," Borger said in a loud voice.

Landow raised his hand, leaned closer, and said, "Quietly, Sheldon. We're in a public place."

Borger was angry at being chided but lowered his voice. "Everything I did with Sheila Klaus and am doing with Itani has been with your blessing. How dare you lay it all on me? You're the contact with the money people in Oklahoma. You've approved my work at every stage."

"You're quite right," Landow said, "but my involvement has been outside of my usual channels at the Company. As far as they are concerned, you and the work you do at Lightpath is purely legitimate, government-approved science." He looked left and right before adding, "I'm afraid that if this Dr. Tatum manages to link you to Mark Sedgwick's murder, and to the up-coming event, you'll be quite alone in defending yourself. You knew from the very beginning that your work has gone far beyond the experiments that have been sanctioned by the Company. You also knew that should something go awry, there would be no link to the Company, which will deny anything and everything." Landow smiled. "But all is not lost, Sheldon. You have only Ms. Klaus and this new subject to worry about—unless there are others I haven't been made aware of."

Borger said nothing as he finished his drink and stared out over the bay.

"I get the feeling, Sheldon, that you might have lost interest in the work we've been doing."

Borger turned his attention back to Landow. "It isn't a matter of losing interest in the work," he said. "You know, Colin, when you recruited me, you had no idea that you'd recruited a genius."

Landow, who seldom laughed, laughed. It was a controlled laugh, as pinched as his voice.

"I'm serious," Borger said. "Do you realize what I've accomplished? Until I came aboard, you were dealing with theory. Was it possible to create the perfect spy, the perfect assassin? How many millions of taxpayer dollars have been spent in pursuit of that elusive goal? I'd like to have just a small percentage of what was spent. And what did those millions buy the CIA? Possibilities, that's all. But I've gone far beyond theories, Colin. I've proved that it can be done in the most tangible of ways. You know, they say that we use only a small portion of our brains. I've proved them wrong. I've tapped into the brain as no one has ever done before. All the surgery in the world can't produce what I have, the ability to totally control another human being, to lead that individual to do things that have only been speculated about. I did it, Colin, and no one can take that away from me. They ought to give you a huge bonus for having discovered me, build a monument to you on the Mall. Because of me, the nation will be safe from those who would harm it. Because of what we're about to achieve, the world will be a better place."

"I've never cared for monuments," Landow said sourly. He pushed his soup bowl and salad plate away and sat back. "So," he said, "I've told you of the threat this Tatum poses. I suggest you take some action." He slid the manila envelope across the table. "Here's background and a few photos of Dr. Tatum. I can't do more than provide you with information. What you elect to do with it is entirely up to you."

Borger picked up the envelope and weighed it in his hands as though he could read its contents without opening it. He motioned for the waiter, who delivered their check, which Borger paid with a credit card. A satisfied smile crossed his face. "My treat," he said, "to celebrate my retirement. Is that what you do when leaving behind this sort of work? *Retire?* It has a nice ring to it, doesn't it? What about you, Colin? Are you considering retirement?"

"I haven't thought about it."

"If you do, I insist upon being invited to your going-away party. Let's go, Colin. I have things to do."

They took the ferry back to San Francisco, where Landow caught a cab at the ferry terminal and Borger walked to the parking lot in which he'd parked. He was glad to be away from the overbearing Landow. What was he? he thought as he drove home. Nothing but a bureaucrat working for a dysfunctional spy agency.

But another series of unpleasant thoughts bombarded him as he neared his Nob Hill mansion. If Landow was right that this Nicholas Tatum had managed to break through Sheila Klaus's programmed barriers, he, Borger, was in jeopardy. This realization evoked a burst of anger in him, and he slammed his hand against the steering wheel. First Elena being killed, and now this.

As he pulled into his circular driveway, the first thing he noticed was a strange car parked by the front entrance. It took him a moment before he recognized it as belonging to Mica Sphere.

He opened the front door and saw her sitting in the living room with Itani, a plate of deviled eggs and crackers the cook had prepared between them, a Tom Collins in Itani's hand, a glass of white wine in hers.

"Sheldon," she said, standing. "Where have you been?"

"I was ah . . . I was at a meeting. What are you doing here?"

She crossed the room and kissed his cheek. "I wanted to thank you for a lovely evening last night and to give you this." She held out a small box. In it was a sterling silver cigar cutter.

"It's lovely, Mica, but I don't smoke cigars anymore."

"Then maybe it will prompt you to start again. You always looked so distinguished when you did. Oh, why didn't you tell me about your houseguest?" She turned and indicated Itani. "We've been having a wonderful conversation about his boxing career. You devil, you never told me that you were going to manage a fighter. He showed me the gym you installed and—"

"Thank you for the gift, Mica. I'll get myself a drink and—"

"Love to spend more time with you and your young friend, but I really must run." She said to him sotto voce, "He's adorable, the strong, quiet type. If I were into men, I might spend more time here with him." She called to Itani, "Good-bye, Iskander. I hope to see you again soon."

"Yes, that would be nice," Itani said.

"Bring your drink with you, Iskander," Borger said after Mica had left. "We need to do another session."

Nic Tatum taxied his Micco SP26 to the hangar, parked alongside three other aerobatic aircraft, shut down the engine, and drew a deep, satisfied breath. He'd put the slick craft through its paces that morning, performing loops and rolls, sheer vertical climbs, free-fall dives from a stall, Immelmanns, and sustained inverted flight. Spending an hour in the Micco was always exhilarating, but this morning was even more so.

It had been a tense couple of days. When Sheila Klaus had been freed from prison, the judge had emphatically denied the prosecution's request that she be confined to house arrest and be prohibited from leaving the area. "You either have a case against her," he'd proclaimed from the bench, "or you don't. You either bring formal charges and lock her up, or you let her go, no strings attached."

And so Sheila was free to live her life as she wished, unless the authorities came up with more concrete evidence to recharge her with Mark Sedgwick's murder. No one in the U.S. attorney's office would bet the farm on that.

Tatum had met with Mac Smith the day after her release and expressed his concern for her, talking about the ramifications of whether she'd been programmed to kill Sedgwick. "The fact is, Mac, she's a killer," he said, reluctant to use such a harsh term but deciding to not hold back. "And she's a killer because someone turned her into one."

"Let's say that's true," Smith said, "and I'm not questioning for a second that you're right. The question is, what can you or anyone else do about it?"

"Expose it," Tatum said with hesitation.

"How do you do that?" Smith asked."

"I'm not sure," Tatum replied. "I suppose the first step is to spend more time with her."

"Do you think that she'd agree to that?"

Tatum shrugged. "I can call and ask," he said.

"That'd sound like you're chasing business."

"Ambulance chasing."

"No, that's what it would be if *I* called her as an attorney. Maybe you should start with a call to this psychiatrist in San Francisco. What's his name?"

"Borger. Sheldon Borger. He's not likely to talk to me. Hell, I'm suggesting that he programmed a murderer."

Smith laughed. "Yes, I can't imagine that he'd open up to you about that. What about the friend of yours you spoke with?"

"Dave Considine. He confirmed just about everything I've thought."

Which wasn't entirely true. Considine had offered little in the way of new information. He'd spent their dinner listening and agreeing with what Tatum had said.

"Maybe you should talk with him again."

"I intend to."

"I don't think I mentioned what Marie

Darrow told me after she'd accompanied Sheila home from jail," Smith said. "According to her, as she was leaving, Sheila seemed to go into some sort of trance state and told Marie, in a very different voice, to leave. Sheila said to Marie, 'We're fine now.'"

"*We're.* Plural. Sheila and her second personality Carla Rasmussen."

"What are your plans for the rest of the day?" Smith asked.

"I don't have any patients today. I'll probably head home, work out, and call Dave Considine to set up another meeting. I suppose I'll spend most of the day trying to figure out what to do about Sheila Klaus."

Smith walked him to the elevator. "I wish there were some way that I could help you, Nic."

"You've already been a tremendous help, Mac. My love to Annabel."

On his way home, Tatum weighed his next move. While he'd decided to pursue what he'd learned about Sheila Klaus and her involvement with Sheldon Borger and the Lightpath Psychiatric Clinic, he had no idea how to proceed. He considered calling Sheila but was certain that she'd blow him off. After all, she had no reason to agree to see him again.

A few blocks from his apartment building, he made his decision. He turned off the street he was on and headed for Rockville, Maryland. He'd stop in unannounced and hope that his sudden appearance would prompt her to at least hear him out. It would be harder to get rid of him in person than on the phone.

Sheila's house was as he'd remembered it when he'd first visited her along with Detectives Owens and Breen. He parked in front and looked for signs that she was home. He remembered that she'd been working in her front garden during that previous visit and wondered whether she might be in the back tending to her plants and flowers. He got out of his car and approached the house. The front door was open, and he peered through the screen door. His hunch was correct. She was visible in the backyard through the atrium at the rear of the house, dressed in the same floppy white hat she'd worn earlier. Tatum debated ringing the bell or skirting the house and surprising her. He chose the latter.

She was kneeling over a flower bed when he arrived.

"Hi," he said.

Startled, she looked up.

"Nicholas Tatum, Ms. Klaus."

She got to her feet and wiped perspiration from her face with her sleeve.

"We spent some time together, if you'll recall," he said, smiling broadly.

"I remember," she said. "Why are you here?"

"I just wanted to . . . I just wanted to see how you were doing."

"I'm doing fine."

"I guess you are. The flower garden is beautiful. It must take a lot of work to keep it that way."

"Yes, it does. Are you a gardener?"

"Afraid not. I have the proverbial black thumb."

Her smile was small and transient.

"That's a beautiful flower," he said, pointing to an orange-and-white bloom that occupied much of the bed.

"It's a red sage Lantana," she said. "I'm especially fond of them."

"I can understand why," he said.

They looked at each other in awkward

silence before Tatum said, "Look, Ms. Klaus, I was wondering whether we could have a talk."

"About what?"

"About what you've been through—and why you had to go through it." She started to say something, but he continued. "I realize that you probably view me in the same light as you do the police, at least the ones who brought you in and accused you of having killed Dr. Sedgwick. I used to be a cop, but that was long ago. I'm now a licensed psychotherapist who just happened to get involved. What's really important is that I want to help you."

She turned her back on him and walked to another flower bed on the opposite side of the small, meticulously maintained yard. He followed.

"They are beautiful, aren't they?" she said absently as she looked down on a vivid mosaic of purples and yellows, reds and whites.

"Very. Have you heard from Dr. Borger since your release?"

She didn't respond.

"Sheila," Tatum said, coming closer and now standing directly behind her, "some people have done a terrible thing to you and you know it, only what you know is trapped inside. That's the way they want it to be, buried in your subconscious, beyond your conscious knowledge. Dr. Borger is one of those people."

Sheila slowly turned, cocked her head, and said, "I don't know what you're talking about. Please leave."

It occurred to Tatum that should he be successful in freeing her from the grip that Borger had on her, he was placing her in jeopardy. If he were able to drag the truth out of her, it would result in her being charged again with murder, and as both Mac Smith and Marie Darrow had said, a defense based upon having been programmed to drive the car that killed Sedgwick was flimsy at best. If he, Tatum, were to successfully expose Borger and the CIA-funded experiments in mind-control at places like the Lightpath Psychiatric Clinic, he'd be sacrificing her. It would be for a greater good, of course, but that would be scant comfort for her if she was again arrested, charged, and convicted.

But his awareness of the consequences didn't deter him. Some other innocent person could be turned into a killer by the psychiatrists and scientists working for the Central Intelligence Agency.

If he were successful in eliciting the truth from her, he would have to make a difficult decision. Under ordinary circumstances, he would be bound to turn over to the authorities whatever facts emerged, unless, of course, he chose to invoke the doctor-patient relationship and its inherent privacy rights.

He'd cross that bridge when and if it arose in his path.

"Sheila," he said, "as long as this knowledge remains inside of you, you'll never truly be free. All I'm asking is that you work with me to get to the truth. I promise to do everything in my power to use what we learn to hold those responsible accountable. I'm not out to hurt you. You've been hurt enough."

"Leave her alone!"

"Carla?" Tatum said.

Until that moment, Sheila's face had been relaxed and placid, her only expression one of sadness and perhaps confusion. Now it was hard, lips tautly stretched, eyes angry.

"Leave her alone," Carla repeated.

"Why do you have to fight her battles, Carla?" he asked.

"Because she's a wimp, that's why. She's pathetic. If I weren't here, she would have made a fool of herself when the press arrived, asking their stupid questions, wanting to know whether she did kill that bastard Sedgwick." Her laugh was cruel. "I told them to get lost and they listened. Go on, get out of here. She doesn't need you snooping around."

"Does Dr. Borger agree that you have to speak for Sheila?"

"That pathetic excuse for a man, the *great* Dr. Borger. He knows better than to mess with me."

Tatum thought before saying, "If you really want to help Sheila, you'll do everything you can to get rid of Borger's control over her—and over you."

Another wicked laugh.

Anger welled in Tatum. This nice middle-aged woman named Sheila Klaus, who loved flowers and plants and who kept an immaculate house, had been violated by Borger and his gang, as violated as any rape. Born with an innate susceptibility to entering trance, she had been manipulated by those who didn't give a damn about what happened to her, all in the name of science and the evils to which it could be put by those with a twisted sense of self-worth and patriotism. A fleeting vision of Sheldon Borger as Tatum remembered him from conferences flashed before his eyes, and he knew that if Borger were physically present he would strike out at him, just as he'd done to those bullies in high school.

"You think you're in control, Carla," Tatum said, "but you're not. I'll see to it that you aren't."

"Empty words," Carla said. "Go away. We don't want you here."

Tatum wanted to grab Sheila and shake her, as if by doing so he could shake Carla loose. But he knew there was nothing he could do at that moment. He turned and walked from the yard, Carla's ominous laughter following him until he slammed his car door shut and silenced her.

When he got home he put himself through a vigorous workout and called Considine, who agreed to meet for dinner that night.

* * *

In Rockville, Sheila Klaus microwaved a frozen chicken potpie and whipped up a salad. She'd just finished eating and was rinsing her plate in the sink when the phone rang.

"Hello?"

"Hello, Sheila. It's Dr. Borger."

"I don't want to talk to you."

"Don't say that, Sheila. I hear that the red sage Lantana are blooming."

Sheila's face toughened.

"Are you there, Carla?" Borger asked.

"What do you want?" Carla asked.

"You're needed, Carla. Sheila needs you."

"She always does."

"A Federal Express envelope will arrive tomorrow morning for you. It will contain everything you need."

"I can't wait," Carla said.

"And I can't wait to see you again. Sleep tight."

CHAPTER 29

Tatum and Considine met for dinner that night at Bourbon on Wisconsin Avenue.

Over mac and cheese and snifters of single-barrel bourbon, Tatum told his friend of his visit to Sheila Klaus's house and what had transpired there. He was revved up, his words spilling out in a tumble. Considine listened patiently, seldom interrupting while Tatum vented: "I tell you, Dave, I'm not going to just turn my back and walk away," he said. "Sheila Klaus has been raped by the CIA and its goddamned perverted sense of national security. It's an outrage and something has to be done about it. Sheldon Borger is behind it, damn it. Sheila's other personality, Carla Rasmussen, told me so, and I'm going to do everything that I can to see that he pays."

"Finished?" Considine asked.

Tatum broke into a laugh. "Yeah, I'm down off my soapbox."

"Look, Nic," Considine said, "I completely agree with you. If this woman has been manipulated the way you say, it means that the Company created a murderer. But you're dreaming if you think that the CIA will fess up to it. The only proof you have is that this woman says things while in a trance, or that her second personality comes out while you—and I stress *you*—are alone with her. Who else has seen it?"

"Mackensie Smith, for one," Tatum said. "I told you about him. And the lawyer who represented Sheila. Name's Marie Darrow. She witnessed the change in Sheila's personality and mentioned it to Smith."

"Big deal," Considine said. "So they observed a change in her. That's a long way from proving that Borger programmed her to kill Sedgwick. You simply don't have any proof."

"You sound like you don't believe me."

"It's not a question of believing you. You know how the agency functions. Or do you?"

"No, I don't. But you do. Educate me."

"Okay. The CIA creates lots of layers between projects like the ones you're talking about. Facilities like Lightpath are legitimate agency projects. The work they do there is legit and sanctioned by the government. Sure, maybe some of the results get misused and some people are impacted by it but—"

"*Misused?* You think turning Sheila Klaus into a homicidal zombie is being misused?"

"Hey, Nic, back off. I'm not your enemy. I'm just trying to look at this realistically."

"Sorry. It's just that—"

"It's just that you see an injustice and want to correct it. That's admirable. Tell me more about this Mackensie Smith and the other lawyer."

As they were leaving, Tatum said, "I'll tell you one thing, Dave. I'm going to get Sheila Klaus to sit with me if it means tying her down. I'm going to get to the truth about Mark Sedgwick's murder, her role in it, and how Borger programmed her to do it."

"I can't argue with that, Nic."

"Will you help me, Dave? At least you agree with me that these so-called medical and scientific projects have gotten out of hand. You still know people in the program. Maybe you could find out something about Borger and his operation from one of them."

"Sure. I'll make a couple of calls."

David Considine did make a call on Tatum's behalf.

"Hello?" Colin Landow answered on his cell phone.

"It's Considine. I have some more."

Landow called Borger.

"I suggest that whatever it is that you intend to do about Dr. Tatum, you do it fast. And here are two other names who have been brought into Tatum's fold, a Washington attorney named Mackensie Smith, and another D.C. lawyer named Marie Darrow."

"Thank you," Borger said, "but I have already put things into motion."

CHAPTER
30

The United Airlines flight from San Francisco to Washington Dulles International Airport departed on time. Seated three abreast in the coach section were Peter Puhlman, Jake Gibbons, and Iskander Itani, with Itani in the middle seat. The young Arab had been on a plane only once before, when he and his mother and brothers flew to the United States from Beirut. He hadn't liked flying as a boy, and his nervousness hadn't abated in adulthood.

"Relax," Puhlman told him as they roared down the runway and lifted into a gray sky. "It's safer on a plane than in a car."

Gibbons heard Puhlman's words, meant to comfort, but they did little to alleviate his own fear of flying. He gripped his armrests and breathed heavily.

Puhlman had tried to get them reservations in business class, but none were available. He felt cramped in his seat and muttered that it was built to accommodate midgets.

Itani visibly relaxed once the plane had reached cruise altitude. A flight attendant, who reminded Itani of Elena, asked whether they wanted to buy drinks. Itani asked for a Tom Collins.

"What's that?" she asked.

"It's a drink," Puhlman replied. "Bring him some gin and club soda, and one of those little sugar packets. I'll have a white wine. You, Jake?"

Gibbons, who sat ramrod straight as though to make himself part of the seat, mumbled, "A beer."

Puhlman, too, was on edge, but it had nothing to do with a fear of flying. Borger had given him last-minute instructions late the night before, and during that conversation Puhlman had expressed concern about Gibbons accompanying them. "He keeps asking me why he's coming with us," Puhlman told Borger. "Says he doesn't like planes."

"He'll get over it," was Borger's response.

"There's more to it," Puhlman pressed. "Jake doesn't know what's going to happen in D.C. He's been asking questions lately about what's going on with Itani, the management contract, all of it."

"He doesn't need to know anything more than he already does, Peter. As far as he's concerned, we're involved in a top secret government program. He's well-paid to do as he's told and not to ask questions. I want him there in D.C. with you and Iskander. You've seen what Itani is capable of doing. I've got him at the peak of my control now, but keeping him at that level is a delicate balancing act. He's volatile, as you well know. I'll stay in contact with him by phone, of course, but I want someone like Jake present in case Iskander gets out of hand physically."

"I still think that you should be with us."

"Out of the question. Once Iskander is in place to carry out the assassination, you and Jake will head back to San Francisco.

It wouldn't be prudent for any of us to be there when it happens."

"But now Jake is asking what this is all about, especially the mess with Elena."

Borger shook his head, leaned back in his red leather office chair, and took a sip of sherry. "Why do I get the feeling that you're having second thoughts about what we're about to do?"

"No, that's not true, Sheldon."

"You even considered turning Iskander over to the authorities."

"It was just a thought."

"A dangerous thought." Borger placed his glass back on the desk and came forward. "Peter," he said, "if the unfortunate incident with Elena hadn't occurred, Iskander would arrive in Washington the day before the event. But the incident with Elena *did* happen. That's reality, and I suggest that we keep reality uppermost in mind until this is over."

"Okay," Puhlman said, "but I still have reservations about Jake coming with us. Maybe it would have been better to fill him in on what we're doing and why we're doing it. He might say the wrong thing while we're waiting in D.C. You've told him that

Iskander is to be kept under wraps in Washington, but he doesn't know why."

Borger slapped his hand on the desk and stood. "Enough!" he said. "Stop second-guessing me. Go on now, get some sleep. I have things to do."

Puhlman left the house, and Borger poured himself another glass of sherry. The conversation had unsettled him, although he was already edgy when Puhlman arrived. Itani was asleep in the bedroom he now occupied. A carpet company would arrive in the morning to install a wall-to-wall black-and-white tweed carpet that Borger selected during the salesman's visit earlier in the day.

As he picked up his glass, he noticed that his hand shook, not much, just enough to be of concern. Strangely, his uneasiness had little to do with what was about to transpire in Washington.

As far as he was concerned, there was no way that Itani's action against presidential candidate George Mortinson could be traced back to him. Even if Itani's short residence at the house was revealed, it didn't translate into Borger having done anything illegal. Itani was a frightened young man who suffered from blinding headaches and who wished to resume his boxing career. Borger had often treated patients in his home, and some, including well-known show business figures, would attest to it.

Too, he reasoned, there was no way that anyone could know what had taken place between him and Itani. He'd treated him for headaches, pure and simple. Once Itani had accomplished his mission, arrangements had been put in place to dispose of him, ensuring that should his implanted amnesia falter, he wouldn't be alive to reveal anything about the true nature of their relationship.

No, it wasn't the Washington event that concerned Borger. It was what had happened to Elena, followed by the unexpected intrusion of Mica Sphere.

Borger had questioned Itani about his conversation with Mica immediately after she had left.

"What did you talk about?" Borger asked.

"Some things," was Itani's reply. "Boxing."

"She talked about boxing?"

He nodded. "She said that she likes boxing and has gone to the fights."

"Interesting," Borger said. "What else did you talk about? Did you mention Elena?"

Itani brightened at the mention of her name.

"You talked about Elena?" Borger pressed, attempting to keep concern from his voice.

Another nod. "I told her that I had a girl-friend named Elena."

"I see. Did you tell her that Elena was here at the house last night?"

"Yes. Where is Elena? Will I see her be-fore I leave for Washington?"

"No, Iskander. She had to go out of town for a few days. We'll arrange for her to come see you after you have a few bouts under your belt."

"Good," he said. "I would like to see my brothers before we go."

"That's impossible," Borger said, "but you'll see them soon. I promise you that."

He induced trance in Itani and worked at reinforcing his hatred of Jews and Israel, and particularly of George Mortinson. He ended the session after twenty minutes, and Itani went downstairs to work out.

*   *   *

Now alone in his study, Borger mentally revisited every aspect of the situation and its potential ramifications for him.

Things had been meticulously thought out well in advance.

Once Itani had been identified as Mortinson's assassin, there would be some people who could link him to Borger and the "treatment" he'd received, although that number had been kept to a minimum. The housekeeper and cook would be shocked that an assassin had been in the house. They'd cleaned his room and fed him his meals, and they would question their employer about it. He would simply say that he, too, was shocked and had no inkling that Itani was capable of killing anyone. He'd treated him for headaches in order to allow him to resume his boxing career. End of story. That this obviously deranged young man had gone to Washington to assassinate a presidential candidate was beyond his, Borger's, wildest imagination: "If only I had known, if only I had seen signs of his insanity." And, of course, he would offer to work closely with the authorities to unravel the illness that had driven Itani to take a public official's life.

The CIA would deny any involvement should some investigative reporter seek to link the agency with Mortinson's assassination. The agency's scientific and medical research projects were funded by the Congress and designed to enhance national security. Borger was an esteemed member of the medical community whose contributions to these valuable projects were well known. For anyone to think that someone of Borger's stature would be involved in a political assassination was absurd.

Puhlman and Gibbons would travel to Washington using phony IDs that were readily available through Landow. Itani would make the trip under his own name. Borger would enhance Itani's amnesia by phone, virtually wiping out everything leading up to the assassination, including his stay at the house, the flight to Washington from San Francisco, and the hours immediately preceding his attack on Mortinson.

Would Itani's amnesia hold up? He'd bet his professional reputation on it. But he also knew that the only fail-safe way to ensure that Itani could offer nothing to the authorities was his elimination.

Prior to Itani delivering the fatal shot to Mortinson, Puhlman and Gibbons would be on their way back to San Francisco, again flying under assumed names. There would be no record of their having been in Washington at the time of the assassination.

Every potential problem had been addressed and worked out.

Except there was a dead prostitute named Elena.

His friend Mica Sphere knew too much.

And now a meddling psychologist in Washington named Nicholas Tatum threatened to undo everything he had accomplished with Sheila Klaus, and by extension place him in jeopardy.

Something had to be done, and he had four days to do it.

CHAPTER

31

Meg Whitson sat with a dozen people in her office at the candidate's Washington headquarters. Everyone was aware that the campaign was coming down to the wire, and that every step leading up to Election Day had to focus on avoiding any major gaffes no matter how far ahead in the polls Mortinson was.

"Let's go over the schedule for the next week," Whitson said as everyone dutifully opened their notepads to the printed schedule that had been distributed earlier in the day.

"Wow, he's not taking a day off for a

whole week," someone quipped, accompanied by a chuckle.

"He wanted to," said Whitson, "but I laid down the law."

Those in the room knew that if anyone could lay down the law to Mortinson, it was Meg Whitson.

"I want to concentrate on the rally four days from now," she said.

It was billed as a meet the candidate event to be held in the Woodrow Wilson Plaza, a four-acre courtyard adjacent to and part of the Ronald Reagan Building and International Trade Center on Pennsylvania Avenue in downtown D.C., the largest building in this city of large buildings, 3.1 million square feet of multiuse space designed to bring together the best minds to forge a national forum for the advancement of trade. The building, owned by the General Services Administration, was the only federal building dedicated to both government and private use; many lavish weddings and political events had been held there, as well as numerous international trade conferences.

The thinking behind the rally reflected Mortinson's approach.

Some in his camp advised that it be a fund-raiser, a suggestion that Mortinson vetoed. The campaign was flush with cash, especially since the polls showed him to be far ahead. Fat cats seeking favors who would ordinarily finance the Republican Swayze's campaign saw the writing on the wall and had started writing large checks to fill Mortinson's coffers, as had major corporations that were now free to donate as much as they wished thanks to the recent Supreme Court decision that gave them that right. "The whores know which side their bread is buttered on," Mortinson quipped in private to close aides. In public he advocated taxpayer-supported elections with the big-money interests cut out, although he knew there was scant chance of that ever becoming law. "This is no longer a country by and for the people," he proclaimed in some of his speeches. "The corporations own the country, and it's time to give it back to the people." That message resonated with a majority of voters, who were fed up with the stranglehold lobbyists and corporate leaders had over elected officials and the resulting legislation that favored them.

Some of Mortinson's political advisers urged him to tone down those remarks for fear of losing the support of business, but Mortinson overrode their objections. "I want the voters to know who I am and what I stand for," he preached at staff meetings. End of discussion.

And so the rally four days hence would bring together chosen representatives of hundreds of civic organizations, unions, teachers, firefighters and police officers, charitable groups, government workers, community organizers from major cities, local athletic clubs, the clergy from every faith and some of their parishioners, senior citizens and schoolchildren, and Mortinson's cadre of friends who'd stood with him since his days as a family member of Wisconsin's preeminent political dynasty and as a U.S. senator. Music would be provided by one of the city's top Dixieland jazz bands, and booths would be set up for guests to enjoy soft drinks, popcorn, and other snacks.

Of course the choice of venue had generated some amused comments from political pundits. After all, the building was named for Ronald Reagan, a Republican, and Mortinson had uttered some critical words about the fortieth president during the campaign. But he'd always been quick to assure that he'd admired Reagan the man, which he did, and keep his criticisms to policy matters about which they differed. No sense in alienating Reagan lovers in the crowd.

"What happens if it rains?" someone asked.

"It shifts indoors," Meg said. "The space has been cleared."

The Secret Service agent charged with protecting the candidate, and who attended as many staff meetings as possible, took the floor. "We have concerns," he said. "It's my understanding that the senator will give a speech but then insist on personally greeting everyone in attendance."

"That's right," said Whitson. "After Governor Thomas gives his own talk as the VP candidate and introduces Mortinson, the senator will speak for twenty minutes. Following that, he, the VP, and their families will form a reception line, and those in the crowd will have an opportunity to shake their hands and have a photo taken with them."

"How long is the Reagan Building booked

for?" a staffer asked, not bothering to disguise the cynicism in his voice. "There's how many people on the invite list, five hundred?"

"Four hundred and forty," Meg Whitson replied. "The Wilson plaza can accommodate eight hundred."

"And he's going to shake hands with four hundred and forty people?" the aide asked, his cynicism even more pronounced. "And have pictures taken with them?"

Whitson laughed. "Senator Mortinson is the fastest handshaker in the business," she said. "Besides, he feels that because many of the invited guests will have come great distances, the least they can go home with is a photograph. Governor Thomas is good at photo ops and handshakes, too. The gathered will get to press the flesh of the next president of the United States and spend a few days in D.C. visiting the monuments and seeing how Congress runs."

Someone at the meeting laughed. "They take one look at how Congress runs and they'll renounce their citizenship and won't be able to vote anyway."

"Do I sense a skeptic in the room?" Whitson said.

No one answered, and she turned to the Secret Service agent who was indulging in a habit whenever he was dismayed at something—rubbing his shaved head. "I know this puts a strain on your people," Whitson said.

"That's a lot of people getting close to him," the agent replied.

"True," said Whitson, "but the guests have been carefully selected."

The agent was tempted to challenge that—he'd heard it too many times before and seen the results—but he didn't say what he was thinking. "We'll do our best," was what he settled for.

Everyone in the room knew that he and his people would. Anything less would be disastrous. Everyone also knew that the Secret Service was the best, the most efficient and loyal security detail in the world. Still, bad things could happen, and had. There was never a moment when Mortinson was on the campaign trail, out in public shaking hands and schmoozing with the voters, that concern about his safety wasn't on everyone's mind.

"Okay," Whitson said, eager to end the meeting and get on with other items on the agenda," the senator leaves three hours from now for San Francisco and the fund-raiser out there. He'll stay overnight and be back in D.C. tomorrow." She read off a list of names of those who would accompany the candidate, which included her. "Let's move," she said. "We're that close, so no mistakes."

Three hours later, as the charted jet carried Senator George Mortinson, members of his staff, and a cadre of reporters to San Francisco, another jet landed in Washington. Puhlman led Itani and Gibbons from the terminal to a black SUV with deeply tinted windows. The driver said nothing as they loaded their carry-on bags into the back and got in. There was no need for him to say anything. He knew what the plan called for.

He drove into the District and pulled up in front of the Allen Lee Hotel on F Street in Foggy Bottom, where two rooms had been reserved for Puhlman and Gibbons using their false identities. They checked in, went to their rooms, waited what they considered a decent amount of time, and walked out to the waiting SUV.

The next stop was the JW Marriott on Pennsylvania. Puhlman, carrying an overnight bag that had been in the SUV, accompanied Itani inside, where he checked in using a credit card bearing his name that had been provided by Colin Landow. They went to the room, and Puhlman emptied the bag of its contents—a few items of clothing that he put on hangers in the closet, underwear and socks that were placed in a dresser drawer, and a kit containing toiletries that was hung on the back of the bathroom door.

"This is my room?" Itani asked.

"Later," Puhlman replied. "We have to go someplace else for a while."

Itani looked puzzled but didn't press. Part of his conditioning by Borger involved doing whatever Puhlman instructed.

Back in the SUV, they headed for a nondescript house in a Virginia suburb that had been rented by Colin Landow through a front organization. The Central Intelligence Agency also had such safe houses, but Landow didn't dare use any of them for this mission.

Itani had grown visibly agitated during the flight despite being fed a series of

Puhlman's answer to a Tom Collins. He'd squirmed in his seat and uttered some almost unintelligible four-letter words; at one point Puhlman thought it might be necessary to physically restrain him. The in-flight movie was a silly comedy that did nothing to ease Itani's obvious discomfort at being strapped in a seat and wedged between two large men for more than six hours.

Now he huddled in the backseat of the SUV, again between the two men, as it headed for the safe house.

"You okay, Iskander?" Puhlman asked at one point during the drive.

"No, I am not okay."

"What's the matter?"

"I want to see my brothers and my mother." He'd expressed the same desire during the flight.

"Look, Iskander," Puhlman said, "Dr. Borger told you that once you had a few bouts under your belt, your brothers and mother would be brought to see you fight. Now isn't the time."

"When do I fight?"

"Soon." He leaned across Itani and said to Gibbons, "Isn't that right, Jake?"

"Yeah, that's right. I've got to get you licensed in D.C. before you can get in the ring."

"My opponent," Itani said. "Who is he?"

Borger had prepped Gibbons about how to answer such questions, and the former leg breaker for San Francisco's loan sharks grappled with remembering what Borger had said.

"There's a couple of possibilities," Gibbons said. "You might be filling in for a fighter who flunked his physical."

"Who is he?"

Gibbons wanted to smack Itani in the mouth. He was fed up with the questions and couldn't wait to reach their destination and get out of the car. Instead he patted Itani on the leg and said, "Hey, kid, just be patient. Doc Borger has invested a hell of a lot in you, so don't get antsy, okay?"

Itani looked angrily at Gibbons. He'd grown to dislike the gruff-talking man and his short temper. Puhlman, too, had gotten on his nerves. He wished Dr. Borger was with them. Borger was a wise and kindly gentleman who had his, Itani's, best interests at heart. And Elena was his friend—his girlfriend. He missed her as much as he missed Borger and wondered

how long it would be before he again saw
her, held her, breathed in her perfume, and
luxuriated in her soft skin.

As they drew closer to the house, Itani
wanted to call off the trip and return to San
Francisco. Why did they have to travel all
the way to Washington, D.C., for him to
fight? By the time they pulled into a driveway shielded from the street by a row of
high, thick hedges, he'd decided that he
wanted to talk with Borger and told Puhlman this.

"He's pretty busy," Puhlman said.

"I want to talk with him," Itani insisted.

Puhlman looked at Gibbons, whose expression reflected his displeasure.

"All right," Puhlman said. "We'll call him
once we're settled inside."

The three-bedroom house was a nondescript cape, white with black shutters. The
small patch of lawn in front was in need of
mowing, and flowers in a narrow bed now
competed with weeds.

"Who owns this place?" Gibbons asked
Puhlman as they carried their suitcases in
through the front door.

"It doesn't matter," was Puhlman's grumbled reply. The trip had tired him and he

wanted to nap. But that would have to be later. He looked into each of the bedrooms and assigned Itani the middle one; Puhlman and Gibbons would take the rooms on either side. Gibbons opened the refrigerator and saw that it was fairly well stocked. Nonperishable groceries in brown paper bags sat on the red-and-white Formica counter. Landow had done a good job of anticipating their needs for the few days that they'd be there.

Heavy maroon drapes covered all the windows. A small television set sat in a corner of the living room, whose furniture was worn and drab; a cushion on a tan love seat was torn. The only telephone, tethered to a landline, sat on a table next to the love seat.

A door from the kitchen led to a flight of crude wooden stairs leading down to the unfinished basement. Puhlman whispered to Gibbons, "I'll be right back," as he opened the door. Using a flashlight he'd retrieved off the kitchen counter, he slowly went down the stairs. He trained the flashlight's beam into a corner of the dirt floor where a table was covered with a bright blue plastic tarp. Puhlman removed the cover. Beneath it was a gray metal box with a padlock. He took a key from his pocket that Borger had given him and undid the lock. The hinged top opened easily, revealing the box's contents, a Smith & Wesson 638 Airweight revolver that held five rounds of .38 special ammunition, and a box of those bullets. The third item was an ID tag encased in plastic with a blue ribbon with which to hang it from the neck. The ID read ISKANDER ITANI—WESTSIDE BOXING CLUB, SAN MATEO, CA.

He returned everything to the box with the exception of the ID tag, but before rejoining the others he placed a call on a special cell phone he'd been supplied.

"The items are here," he told the man who answered.

"Good. Put them on the front step."

"Now?"

"Yes, now."

Puhlman carried the box up the stairs and deposited it on the front steps of the house. The man who'd taken his call was parked at the corner, lights off, his vantage point allowing him to see the house. After Puhlman had left the box and disappeared inside, the man drove to the front of the house, got out, retrieved the box, placed it in the backseat, and drove off.

When Puhlman walked into the kitchen, Itani and Gibbons were arguing.

"What's going on?" Puhlman asked.

"He wants to call the doc. That's all he keeps saying," Gibbons replied angrily.

Puhlman motioned for Itani to follow him into the living room. "I'll place the call for you," Puhlman said. Using the same cell phone he'd used in the basement, he dialed a number that connected to a separate cell phone carried by Borger.

"Sheldon, it's Peter. Iskander wants very much to speak with you. What? No, I think you should, Sheldon."

He handed the phone to Itani.

"Hello, Iskander," Borger said pleasantly. "Did you have a good flight?"

Itani ignored the question and said, "When can I talk to my brothers?"

"Very soon, Iskander," Borger said in a soothing voice. "Very soon."

"But I want to—"

"Iskander, the golden chalice will soon be yours," Borger said.

Puhlman, who sat on the love seat, observed the change in Itani. Up until that moment he'd been visibly angry, bordering on belligerent. But his face softened and he looked across the room, and seemingly beyond, as he held the phone to his ear.

Borger had used the phrase he'd implanted in Itani during their many sessions. *The golden chalice will soon be yours.* The moment Itani heard it, he entered a deep trance and would do whatever Borger told him to do.

Borger had used key phrases with Sheila Klaus and to bring out Carla Rasmussen: *The red sage Lantana are blooming* would induce a trance state in her. When he was readying her to kill Mark Sedgwick, he'd used the phrase *It's a beautiful day for a cruise* to prompt Carla to follow through on the instructions Sheila had received while under hypnosis, and the accompanying amnesia.

"I want you to go deeper and deeper into the pleasant thoughts you're having," Borger said to Itani over the phone. "Deeper and deeper. That's it. Where are you now?"

"In Washington."

"Who's with you?"

"Mr. Puhlman and Mr. Gibbons."

"They are your friends, Iskander. They

want only the best for you. You must listen to what they say and follow their instructions. Do you understand?"

"Yes."

"Tell me what it is that you understand."

Itani repeated what Borger had said.

"I'll be coming to see you in Washington in a few days," Borger said. "Until I do, Peter and Jake will take care of everything you need. Jake will be working on getting you licensed to fight in Washington and setting up your matches. That takes time and you must be patient. There are some events you'll be attending, large events that will give you the opportunity to right some wrongs. I'll tell you more about that later."

"Elena," Itani said.

"What?"

"Elena."

"Oh, yes, Elena is fine. She called to tell me that she misses you and is looking forward to seeing you fight. I'll make sure that she does."

"All right."

"Okay," Borger said. "I'm going to count backward from ten to one. When I reach one, you'll be out of your pleasant trance state and will forget we ever had this conversation. When I reach one, you'll hand the phone back to Peter. Do you understand?"

"Yes."

Borger started counting. He reached one, but Itani had snapped out of his trance by the count of six and had handed the phone to Puhlman.

"He should be fine," Borger said.

"I hope so," Puhlman said.

"Is everything going as planned?"

"Yes. The materials were here, including the ID tag."

"That's good. If everyone just stays calm and follows the plan, there won't be any problems. I'll be here at the house tonight and all day tomorrow. Call anytime. Use this phone. Good night, Peter."

Gibbons made dinner for them. To be more accurate, he heated frozen packages of chicken marsala and tossed a salad from a bag of prewashed lettuce. Itani's conversation with Borger had calmed him considerably. Although he ate in silence, he occasionally smiled, or even laughed, at something Puhlman or Gibbons had said. Puhlman had made him a Tom Collins (Borger had told Landow of Itani's preference for the drink, and arrangements had been made for the ingredients to be on hand.) Later, they sat in the living room. Gibbons, who'd consumed multiple cans of beer, nodded off in a chair. Puhlman and Itani sat on the love seat and watched television, one of the *Godfather* films. During a commercial break, Puhlman switched channels to CNN to see what was going on in the world. A report on the recovery of Virginia senator Marshall Holtz from his gunshot wounds—"The senator is making a good recovery and is expected to leave the hospital within days," a hospital spokesperson said into the camera—was immediately followed by a statement from presidential candidate George Mortinson: "Senator Holtz's recovery is heartening," said Mortinson. "I only hope that those who defend the rights of people like his assailant to easily purchase lethal weapons will face the reality that our gun laws desperately need to be changed."

Itani stiffened on the love seat. Puhlman glanced at him and saw that his handsome, dusky face had hardened. *Good,* Puhlman thought as he switched back to the movie. Borger's control over Itani was holding, and with Borger's ability to induce trance via the telephone, there was no reason to doubt that things would go smoothly until the big day in the Wilson Plaza at the Reagan Building.

When the movie ended, Puhlman suggested that they get some sleep. Gibbons told Itani that he'd be gone the following day arranging for his licensing and went to bed. Puhlman suggested to Itani that they spend the day watching TV and relaxing. "Once Jake sets things up for your first fight," he said, "things will be getting pretty hectic. You'd be smart to take advantage of a few days to rest up. That's what Dr. Borger has ordered. He doesn't want any stress for you because of the possibility of your headaches returning."

Itani didn't offer any resistance to the idea. He yawned, stretched, and disappeared into his assigned bedroom, leaving Puhlman alone in the darkened living room, the only light a flickering one from the TV set. It wasn't until that moment that the enormity of what they were about to do hit home.

CHAPTER 32

Cindy Simmons and Nic Tatum had dinner that night in Georgetown at Bistro Français on M Street, where they splurged on steak au poivre and a bottle of good red wine. After that they took in a movie, enjoyed a nightcap at the romantic Degrees bar in the Ritz-Carlton hotel, and headed back to his apartment, where she'd decided to spend the night. He poured them each two fingers of brandy in snifters, put on a Modern Jazz Quartet CD, and joined her on the couch. He raised his snifter. "To us," he said.

"To us," she repeated.

They sat in silence.

"Okay," she said, "what's wrong?"

"Wrong? Why do you think that something is wrong?"

She guffawed. "I think something is wrong because you're as edgy as a cat in heat and you've been that way all evening. Sometimes I think you're somewhere else."

"A cat in heat? Is that a seduction line?"

"No, it's not. Come on, Nic, share with me."

He exhaled a long, steady stream of breath, took a sip, and said, "Yeah, I suppose I am preoccupied. It's Sheila Klaus."

"Her again."

"Right. Her again."

He'd told Cindy about his futile visit to Sheila's house and how she'd morphed into her second personality, Carla Rasmussen. He started to retell the story when Cindy said, "Nic, you've become obsessed with her. I can understand that to a degree, but what is it you want to do about her? She's made it clear that she doesn't want to talk to you, let alone allow you to dig into her subconscious mind."

"I know that, Cindy. The problem is that

she's a murderer and she's out there on her own."

"Since when are you so concerned about someone who's a murderer?"

Tatum felt his frustration level rising and grappled to keep it under control. When he thought he had, he said, "She's a murderer, Cindy, because someone turned her into one. Someone got hold of her, recognized what a unique personality she is, a freak, actually, and used that knowledge to manipulate her into killing Mark Sedgwick."

"The CIA," Cindy said.

"That's right, the CIA, our bastion of patriotism, protector of our national security, the world's greatest spook organization." He turned and faced her, becoming more animated. "Look, I'm not saying that the CIA as an entity did it to her, although its damned psychological experiments sure as hell paved the way. You don't have any idea to what extent the agency—or the Company, as it's called—has turned medicine upside down, converted doctors, shrinks, and scientists into something out of a B movie. Dave Considine split from them because he was disgusted with what they were doing to unsuspecting citizens, playing with them, turning them into subjects, guinea pigs for the agency's selfish use. Do you think we're any safer because of their experiments? Do you think that everyone can sleep better at night because Dr. Frankenstein is twisting innocent people into pawns? I've told you about Dr. Borger in San Francisco. He's been involved in these experiments for years. When Sheila Klaus's second personality, Carla Rasmussen, emerged to me, she named him as the one she deals with. He's the guy who knows how to summon Carla whenever he wants Sheila to do something nasty—like killing Sedgwick."

He realized that he'd become strident and backed off.

"I understand everything that you're saying, Nic, but what can you do about it? You're talking about the Central Intelligence Agency, for God's sake. What are you going to do, put on a red cape and save the world?"

"That's the problem, Cindy. I don't know what to do. It was better when Sheila was in custody. I had access to her then through Mac Smith. That's another thing, her being let loose overnight, just like that, a complete about-face by the U.S. attorney's office. Why? Lack of evidence? They had plenty of circumstantial evidence to hold her. Somebody pulled strings in high places."

"The CIA?"

"Is that so far-fetched? They can do any damn thing they want and chalk it up to national security. Somebody very high up the chain of influence arranged for her release from prison. I can't prove that, but I just know it's true. The result? No one can get to her—except . . ."

Cindy cocked her head.

"Except guys like Sheldon Borger, who programmed her in the first place."

Cindy realized that her challenging of Nic was creating a hostile atmosphere, the last thing she wanted. She placed her hand on his arm, lowered her voice, and said, "Nic, do whatever you think you have to. But remember that people like Borger and an agency like the CIA won't take kindly to your trying to expose them. Have you thought of that?"

"It's crossed my mind."

"And I want to apologize."

"For what?"

"For trying to dissuade you from what's obviously important to you. One of the most attractive things about Nic Tatum is how passionate you are about your flying, working out, your patients, politics, movies, just about everything."

"You forgot to add Cindy Simmons to that list."

"How far up on the list?"

"At the top."

"Sure about that?"

"Well, near the top."

She playfully punched him in the chest and suggested they go to bed, which they did, although sleep came an hour later.

Cindy's support meant a lot to Tatum, and he got up in the morning filled with resolve.

"What's on your agenda today?" she asked after they'd showered and dressed, and were sitting at his small kitchen table enjoying breakfast.

"A couple of patients this morning," he said, "last one at eleven, a woman who wants to stop smoking. I'll use hypnosis with her. The trick is to teach her self-hypnosis to use whenever the urge strikes. Works better with smokers than with people trying to lose weight. Anyway, I thought I might swing by Sheila Klaus's house again and take another stab at getting her to talk to me. You?"

"Ah, freedom," she said breathlessly.

"Oh, that's right. You're off today. A woman of leisure."

"I thought I'd go back to my place and clean out my dresser drawers and closet."

"Good use of free time, but I have another suggestion."

She cocked her head.

"How about after I'm finished with my patients, and you've gotten your dresser and closet in shape, we go together to Sheila's house?"

This time a puzzled expression accompanied her cocked head.

"I was just thinking that she might be more amenable if a woman was with me. Besides, you should at least meet her. I talk enough about her."

"Are you sure it's a good idea, Nic?"

"Can't hurt."

"You'll call first?"

"No. Better to just show up. Game?"

The truth was that Cindy had been dying to meet this mysterious lady ever since

Tatum had begun talking about her. "Okay," she said.

"Great. I'll pick you up at twelve thirty."

Jake Gibbons's day was considerably less structured than Tatum's. He'd left the safe house at eight that morning, presumably to work on getting Itani licensed to fight in the District of Columbia and to arrange for the first bout on his comeback trail. It was all a sham, of course, and Gibbons knew it, but he wasn't in a position to argue.

What the hell is going on? he wondered as he tried to decide how to spend the day away from the house. He'd been to Washington a few times before and never liked the city. He considered the government to be a total waste of time and of his taxes, and his view of elected officials was no more benevolent.

Gibbons had been told from the outset of Borger's involvement with Itani that they were engaged in a top secret and vitally important government program. *What the hell did that mean?* What sort of secret government program would need a young Arab prizefighter with a lousy boxing record and a history of headaches? Gibbons had attempted to make sense of it but couldn't no matter how hard he tried. All he knew for certain was that Borger paid him well for doing very little, and he wasn't about to kill that golden goose by asking too many questions.

When he'd gotten up that morning, Itani was pacing the living room.

"You have a good sleep, kid?" Gibbons asked.

"No."

"Hell, you went to bed early."

"I couldn't sleep," Itani replied. "I've been up all night."

"Yeah? Well, maybe you need some sleeping pills. The doc ever give you sleeping pills?"

"No."

"Maybe we can get you some at a drugstore. There's gotta be a drugstore around here."

What Gibbons was really thinking was that he'd like to give the kid something to put him out for good.

Puhlman heard the conversation from the kitchen and joined them. "He's just nervous, that's all," he told Gibbons. "It's good for a fighter to be a little nervous before a bout. Right?"

"I want to talk to Dr. Borger," Itani said.

"Okay, Iskander," Puhlman said, "but there's a three-hour time difference between here and San Francisco. You wouldn't want to wake the doctor, would you?"

Itani said nothing.

"Why don't you take a nap?" Puhlman suggested. "You must be tired."

"Yeah, that's a good idea," Gibbons echoed.

"I'll put you through to Dr. Borger after you've rested," said Puhlman.

Itani left the living room and slammed the bedroom door.

"The kid is getting on my nerves," Gibbons said.

"Relax, Jake. This will be over soon and we'll be back in San Francisco."

"With him?" Gibbons asked, nodding in the direction of Itani's bedroom.

"No. He'll be staying here."

"So what's this all about, coming here and being locked up in this cruddy house?"

Puhlman's voice took on an edge. "Jake, will you please stop asking questions. Dr. Borger knows what he's doing. He's been working with Iskander on a special project. You know it's top secret, and that's all you have to know. That's all that *any* of us has to know. Now, you have to get out of here and spend the day somewhere else. Iskander thinks you're getting him licensed and setting up a bout. Let him think that. That's what Dr. Borger wants him to think. Go kill some time, take in the sights, have lunch and a beer someplace. Stay away until six. Okay?"

And so Gibbons left. He followed Puhlman's instructions to put a considerable distance between him and the house and walked six blocks before hailing a taxi. The cab driver was of Middle Eastern descent and wore a maroon turban.

"Take me to a monument," Gibbons said.

"Sir, what monument?"

"Any one. Washington. Lincoln. It don't matter."

The driver cursed under his breath in his native language and dropped Gibbons at the end of the Mall nearest the Lincoln Memorial.

It was a crystal-clear day in the nation's capital, which brought out its citizens in droves, Frisbee players, couples walking hand in hand, joggers, and tourists in their funny outfits, thousands of them, it seemed, cameras slung around their necks, silly hats to shield them from the sun, little kids screaming and running amok, their metallic voices grating on Gibbons. The more he walked, the more annoyed he became.

He'd been married to a woman who insisted on dragging him on sightseeing excursions. "We should expand our cultural horizons," she often said to Gibbons, who'd barely managed to graduate from high school and whose idea of culture was to get in the ring with somebody who wasn't a white, natural-born American and beat his brains out. After a year with her, he announced that he was leaving before they ended up with kids. "Take your culture and shove it," were his final words as he walked out of their cramped walk-up apartment in the Bronx and headed west to find his fortune the way gold speculators had years earlier. He'd read about those men who'd traveled to San Francisco during that area's gold rush and admired their courage. Of course, he'd arrived decades after the gold rush was long over, and if his fortune was to be made, it would be with his brawn and the pleasure he took in administering beatings.

He'd found a manager in San Francisco and had fought professionally for two years, amassing eleven bouts, most of which he'd won. It was the last fight against an up-and-coming black contender that ended Gibbons's career as a pugilist, at least one who plied his trade inside a ring. His opponent knocked him silly, and his manager dropped him. After that Gibbons bounced around the fabled City by the Bay doing odd jobs. He drove a truck, signed on as a bouncer at a couple of gay nightclubs in the Castro district, did construction, and worked as a mechanic at various gas stations. His last job before hooking up with Borger was with a limousine service. He'd liked that job the best because he got to wear a uniform and meet many of the city's big shots, one of whom was Dr. Sheldon Borger, psychiatrist to the rich and famous.

For Borger, Gibbons was just another driver who squired him around town when he didn't feel like driving. But one night two years ago had changed all that.

Borger had attended a charity dinner at the Mark Hopkins hotel. He'd decided to leave early and called for a car from the limo service. It arrived driven by Jake Gibbons, who'd driven the doctor in the past.

"You goin' home, Doc?" Gibbons asked as Borger slipped into the backseat.

"Too early," Borger responded. He scrolled through phone numbers in a small black book until deciding on one, a call girl with whom he'd spent time before. He gave Gibbons the address and instructed him to wait outside her apartment building. "I'll only be an hour," he said, handing Gibbons a twenty-dollar bill. "Go get yourself something to eat while you're waiting."

Gibbons stopped in a tavern a few blocks away and had a meatball sandwich and a beer at the bar. He returned to the apartment building forty-five minutes later but couldn't find a parking space directly in front. He made a U-turn and parked on the opposite side of the street, where he stood next to the black Lincoln Town Car and lighted a cigarette—smoking was prohibited in any of the company's vehicles—

and waited for Borger to appear. He was on his second cigarette when the doctor emerged through the front door and looked right and left for the car. As Gibbons was about to call out, a man carrying a knife stepped from the shadows behind Borger, wrapped an arm around Borger's neck, and pressed the knife against his throat.

Gibbons sprang into action. He bolted across the street, yelling as he went. Borger's attacker loosened his grip on him and turned to flee. Gibbons grabbed him and threw him to the pavement. He came down on top of him, his knee pressed into his chest, and brought his right fist against the man's cheek. He hit him repeatedly until Borger, who'd stepped away and cowered behind a tree, said, "Okay, that's enough."

Gibbons hauled the man to his feet and hit him again, this time in the stomach, causing him to double over. Gibbons's knee came up into his face, which straightened him.

"Let him go," Borger said.

Gibbons looked quizzically at Borger.

"Let him go," Borger repeated.

Gibbons took a step back as the man

stumbled away, vomiting and moaning, and disappeared around the corner.

"Are you all right?" Borger asked.

"Me? Yeah, I'm fine. How come you wanted me to let him go?"

"He's just a punk, not worth getting involved with the police. I owe you a big debt."

"Nah. Just a good thing I was around. How was—?"

"How was what?"

"The lady you visited."

"Oh, she's fine, just fine. I'd like you to come back to the house, where I can thank you properly."

"I have to drop off the limo."

"All right. Drive me home, get rid of the limo, and come back. I'll make it worth your while."

An hour later, Gibbons sat with Borger in the living room of the house on Nob Hill, a bottle of locally brewed Iron Springs beer in his hand. "This is some nice place you've got," he commented, taking in the expansive room filled with valuable Chinese art and antiques.

"It's comfortable," Borger said. "You

know, this incident tonight might prove to be serendipity."

Gibbons wasn't sure what that meant but nodded in agreement.

"Tell me something about yourself," Borger said.

Gibbons shrugged and finished his beer. "Not much to tell. I used to be a prizefighter, but that didn't work out, so I've been doing different things."

"Like driving a limo."

"Yeah."

"Another beer?"

"Wouldn't mind, thanks."

When Borger returned from the kitchen with a fresh brew, he asked whether Gibbons knew anything about cars.

"Matter of fact I do. My old man was handy with cars, anything mechanical, and he taught me what he knew."

Borger shifted in his chair and casually crossed his legs. "You saved my life tonight, Mr. Gibbons."

"Didn't take much. He was probably a druggie, a skinny little bastard."

"But you didn't hesitate to act. You came to my defense, and let's face it, you really don't know me. The reason I asked about your background is that I've been looking to hire someone like you."

"Like *me*?" Gibbons asked. "What do you know about me?"

"What I *do* know is that you're a man of action, and I assume you're loyal. Do you think you'd be interested in coming to work for me?"

"Doin' what?"

"Oh, I don't know, being available when I need you, do some driving for me, be a bodyguard of sorts, take care of my cars. I have some nice ones out in the garage. Want to see?"

Borger took him to the garage where his collection of four expensive automobiles was housed.

"You've got some beauties here," Gibbons said after whistling.

"Just a hobby of mine. I need someone to care for them."

"Don't look at me, Doc. The engines in these are all computers, nothing like the ones I worked on."

"I have two very fine mechanics who specialize in cars of this class. I need someone to keep them shining and ready to go."

As they returned to the house, Gibbons began to wonder whether the doctor was a strange-o, maybe even a homosexual. No, that couldn't be. He'd just been with a woman he'd called from the limo. He decided as they settled again in the living room, and Borger had fetched another beer, that he'd hear this doctor out. Nothing ventured, nothing gained was the way his father used to put it.

"Well?" Borger said. "Would you be interested in working for me? I should tell you that I lead a very busy life. I have a clinic across the bay in Berkeley, where I spend much of my time, and I have my private clients, some of them quite well known. I'd have to be assured that you're a man of discretion, someone who can keep secrets."

"No problem there," Gibbons replied.

"I should also tell you that I do some government work, highly secret work. Obviously, discretion is a must."

"What sort of secret work?"

Borger put up his hand and smiled. "If I told you, it wouldn't be secret any longer, would it?"

"No, I guess not. You serious about a job?"

"Yes, if you are."

"So what's it pay?"

"Would sixty thousand a year be sufficient?"

Gibbons was speechless. He started to respond, drank from his beer instead, and looked around the room.

"Well?" Borger said. "I have a partner who will have to approve, but he never disagrees with my decisions. Your pay will be off the books because of my government work. There will be no benefits, no health insurance or pension. But you will be paid on time. When can you start?"

Another swig of beer and a belch preceded, "How about right now?"

Gibbons wandered the Mall and eventually made his way into the Air and Space Museum, where he took in the World War II aviation display. But he soon became bored and left the building to continue walking down the Mall until reaching a tourist information kiosk.

"Hello," a woman in the kiosk said.

"Yeah, hello. I was wondering if there's a gym in this city, you know, where boxers train."

"Boxers?" she said. "I'm afraid I wouldn't know anything about that, but I can look it up for you."

"Yeah, that'd be good."

She consulted a thick phone directory. "Here, look," she said, turning the directory so he could see where her index finger was pointed. The listing was for the Downtown Boxing Club on M Street. "Are you a boxer?" she asked.

"I used to be," he said.

"I met Muhammad Ali once," she said.

"Oh, yeah?"

"He was the greatest."

"Yeah, he was pretty good. Thanks. Where's M Street?"

She tried to give him walking directions, but he became confused. "I'll take a cab," he said. "Thanks again."

His taxi driver dropped him in front of the address he'd been given, and he entered the gym in which a half dozen fighters went through their routines, one skipping rope, one hitting a heavy bag, some doing sit-ups, and two of them sparring in the ring. Gibbons felt immediately at home. He'd been in gyms where it seemed that only yuppies wearing pastel spandex workout clothing exercised to piped-in rock music, not a real boxer to be seen. But this was different. It was like a scene out of *Rocky*—the Rocky movies were Gibbons's favorites. There was no music playing, no women in fancy workout clothing, just the odor of sweat and a bunch of young men (and one woman) training to get in the ring.

Gibbons noticed two men standing at ringside watching the sparring contest going on. One looked to easily be in his seventies; the other was considerably younger. The older man, who wore a T-shirt that was too short on his bulky frame, his sizable belly protruding from beneath it, had a towel draped over his shoulders, and barked instructions at one of the fighters in the ring. Gibbons sidled up to them and took in the scene until the older man called out, "Time!" The boxers removed their protective headgear and left the ring laughing, their arms around each other.

"The kid in the blue shorts looked good," Gibbons commented.

The older man turned. "He's coming along."

"Nice gym," Gibbons said.

"You in the game?" the younger man asked.

"The fight game? Used to be," Gibbons replied. "I manage a couple of young fighters."

"That so? Anybody I know?" the older man asked.

"Probably not. I'm on the West Coast." He shook hands with them. "Jake Gibbons."

Another pair of fighters climbed into the ring, and Gibbons stayed to watch. He also stayed through a third sparring session. He felt very much at home in the gym, more at home than he was in the small house in Virginia with Puhlman and Itani. He checked a large clock on the wall; he'd been there for two hours.

"Nice meeting you," the older man, who'd been a trainer for most of his adult life, said.

"Same here," Gibbons said.

He stepped out onto the street and realized that he was hungry. He'd spotted a bar and restaurant a few blocks away while in the taxi and walked to it. The only people at the bar were two young bikers wearing black leather jackets, sporting multiple tattoos, and downing vodka kamikaze shooters followed by beer from bottles. Gibbons took a stool at the far end and ordered a beer. Seeking out the gym had been a smart move. He'd been in his element there and he wasn't looking forward to returning to the house. What would he say about how he'd spent his time? He was supposed to have arranged for Itani to be licensed to fight. What if the kid asked for specifics? What if the kid asked again who his opponent would be? What would he say, that the license was now arranged for and that the opponent was still unknown? He'd depend upon Puhlman to fill in the blanks. Puhlman was a good talker. Let him handle it. Gibbons wasn't paid to make up stories.

He downed the first beer that the barmaid, a pretty young thing with lots of cleavage showing, had served him and ordered a second. And a third. By this time the other two men at the bar were drunk and boisterous. One of them turned to Gibbons and said, "What do you think, old man?"

Gibbons looked at him and ignored the question.

"Yeah. Whatta ya think?"

Gibbons asked, "About what?"

"About that crud Mortinson."

Gibbons shrugged and ignored them again, drank from his bottle, and motioned for the barmaid to set up another.

"Hey," said one of the bikers, "we got a Mortinson lover here."

"That right?" his buddy said. "You like Mortinson? What are you, some Commie pinko, some nigger-lovin' do-gooder?"

Gibbons felt his temper rising but held himself in check.

"You don't say much, do you?" Gibbons was asked.

"Why don't you clowns cool it?" Gibbons said.

"What? What'd you say?"

"Just cool it. Don't ask for trouble, okay?"

"You call me a clown?" one said.

Gibbons drew a breath and tensed, waiting for the next verbal assault.

The two bikers got up and slowly approached him. Gibbons downed what was left in his beer bottle and gripped the bottle's neck.

"You got a problem with us?" Gibbons was asked.

"No, I don't have a problem," Gibbons said, increasing his grasp on the bottle.

One of the bikers moved closer, too close, and bumped into Gibbons. Gibbons pushed him away with his left hand while holding the bottle in his right. The biker pushed back. Gibbons motioned to the barmaid, who'd been taking in the budding confrontation from behind the bar, that he wanted a check. The biker grabbed Gibbons by the collar of his shirt and yanked. Gibbons didn't hesitate. He spun around on his barstool and raised the empty bottle. As the second biker lunged at Gibbons, he swung the bottle and hit the first biker in the temple, causing him to stumble back. Simultaneously Gibbons sprang off the stool and delivered the bottle to the second biker's face, splitting his lip and generating a string of four-letter words.

Gibbons was now on his feet, his heart pounding, sweat pouring down his broad face. "Come on, punk," he snarled, feet set apart, slightly crouched, ready for the attack. One of the bikers picked up a wooden chair from a nearby table and swung it at Gibbons. It missed its target and smashed against the bar. Gibbons grabbed a splintered piece of it and jabbed it into one biker's gut, causing him to double over. Gibbons's response was more than the bikers had bargained for. They stood side by side glaring at Gibbons and deciding whether to continue the battle or to leave. The decision was made for them when the door opened and two uniformed cops entered, having responded to the barmaid's call to 911. They ordered the bikers and Gibbons up against a wall.

"What the hell is going on?" a cop asked.

"Just a little argument," Gibbons said.

"That son of a bitch attacked us," said a biker.

"The hell I did," Gibbons said. He pointed to the barmaid. "Tell 'em who started it," he said.

"I didn't see," she answered.

"All right," one of the cops said to Gibbons, "name." He was poised to write in a pad he took from his uniform pocket.

"You don't need my name," Gibbons said. "These punks started a fight, that's all. It's over, no harm done."

"What about the chair?" the barmaid said.

"You want to press charges?" she was asked by a cop.

"My boss'll kill me if that chair isn't paid for."

"All right," Gibbons said. "I'll pay for your goddamn chair."

"You want to press charges?" a cop repeated.

"No, just get them to pay for the chair and their drinks and get out of here."

"I still need names," a cop said. "Gimme your licenses."

The bikers complied, and their names and addresses were noted.

"You," Gibbons was told.

While the cops took down the information from the bikers, Gibbons had time to process what was taking place. He carried two driver's licenses—his legitimate one from California and the phony license he'd been given to use to get through airport security in San Francisco—and didn't know which one to hand over.

"Come on," a cop said.

Gibbons pulled out his wallet, slid his legitimate license from its plastic sleeve, and gave it to the cop.

"How much for the chair?" his partner asked the barmaid.

She shrugged. "A hundred maybe."

Gibbons had plenty of cash on him and tossed bills on the table, which the barmaid scooped up and tucked in her cleavage.

"Okay," a cop said to the bikers, "why don't you jerks take a hike."

They started to leave, but the barmaid stopped them. "Your drinks," she said.

They combined what cash they had, paid the bill, and left, tossing a couple of curses at Gibbons over their shoulder.

"Thanks," Gibbons said.

"Stay out of trouble," a cop said. "San Francisco? Always wanted to visit there."

Gibbons remained behind after the cops had left and ordered another beer. It occurred to him as he drank that it might have been a mistake giving them his real driver's license. Too late now. He decided as he paid his tab, added a good tip, apologized to the barmaid for the fracas, and left the bar that he wouldn't mention what had happened to Puhlman. As long as he kept it to himself, no harm was done.

Nic Tatum's eleven o'clock client told him at the outset of their session that she couldn't be hypnotized. He conducted the Spiegel Hypnotic Induction Profile and determined that she was in the midrange, an Odyssean, and asked that he be allowed to at least try. She agreed, and after a few minutes she'd entered trance during which he went through a prescribed set of suggestions aimed at her smoking habit. When she came out of trance she laughed and said, "I told you I couldn't be hypnotized." Tatum didn't argue. He gave her a CD and suggested that she listen to it a few times each day, especially when she had the urge to smoke. She promised that she would and asked about another appointment.

"I don't think you'll need one," he said, "but if you do, just call."

He picked up Cindy at her apartment, and they headed for Sheila Klaus's home in Rockville.

"How did your morning go?" she asked as they drove out of the District.

"Good. I had another client who said she couldn't be hypnotized. She slipped into trance easily."

Cindy laughed. "Do you ever worry that a female patient will accuse you of making sexual advances while she's under?"

"Always a possibility, but since I don't— make advances—I don't think about it. But Mesmer had his problems, though."

"Who?"

"Franz Anton Mesmer, the German physician who ended up in Paris in the late 1700s practicing what he called animal magnetism. It was hypnosis, actually, only Mesmer didn't know it. It took until sixty years later before a Scotsman, James Braid, identified hypnosis as a medical

specialty. Whatever Mesmer did, he became the darling of Paris, treating lots of
wealthy patients, all of them women. He
traveled in lofty circles, held musical evenings at his home and was actually one of
Mozart's patrons, used to sponsor recitals
by him. Anyway, King Louis something or
other decided that Mesmer was too popular, especially with the ladies, and convened a commission to investigate whether
he was using this so-called animal magnetism to seduce unsuspecting young
women. The king appointed a whole slew
of doctors and scientists to the panel,
including—and get this—Ben Franklin,
ambassador to France. Imagine that, Ben
Franklin, a devoted womanizer, deciding
whether Mesmer was a lecher. Anyway,
the committee ruled against Mesmer and
he faded into obscurity. What's left is the
term 'mesmerism.'"

"Benjamin Franklin was a womanizer?"
Cindy asked.

"According to the historians. Look, when
we see Sheila, I'll just introduce you as a
friend, okay?"

"Whatever you say. Do you think this
other personality of hers, this . . ."

"Carla Rasmussen."

"Carla Rasmussen. Do you think she'll make an appearance?"

"I hope so. At least you'll know I'm not crazy."

When they pulled up in front of the house, Tatum turned off the ignition and they looked for any sign of Sheila. They went to the front door and Tatum rang the bell. The last time he'd been there, the door had been open, with only the screen door in place, and he was surprised that it wasn't that way again on this beautiful, mild, sunny day.

"Let's check the back," he said. "She spends a lot of time there tending her garden."

They circumvented the house and looked in the yard. No sign of her. They returned to the front, where Tatum picked up one of two newspapers wrapped in protective plastic. He removed it and saw that it was yesterday's paper. The second package contained that day's edition.

"She's obviously not here," Cindy said.

"And it looks like she hasn't been for two days," Tatum said.

"She probably got away for a few days. She's been through an ordeal."

"Possible, but I had the feeling that she was so happy to be home and in her garden that she wouldn't be going anywhere."

They drove back to Cindy's apartment.

"Coming up?" she asked.

"No, I have some errands to run. Want to grab an early bite?"

"I'm in the mood for Chinese."

"I'll pick some up and be by around five."

Instead of returning home, he drove to police headquarters on Indiana Street and dropped in on Detective Joe Owens.

"Nic, my man," Owens said. "What brings my favorite shrink here today?"

"I need a favor."

"I always get uptight when I hear that. Before you tell me this favor, you should know that at the urging of your buddy, Mackensie Smith, we ran down financials for Ms. Klaus. Seems she's in pretty good shape, owns the house free and clear."

"How'd she manage that? She left her job with a disability. I can't imagine that pays a hell of a lot."

"No, it doesn't, but she paid off her mortgage in one shot. I sent a detective to the bank that held the mortgage. Seems Ms. Klaus came in with a check to cover what was left on it and told the bank that a relative had died in Bermuda and left her the money. We ran the check before the case was dropped."

"Lucky lady."

"I'd say so. Okay, Nic, what's the favor?"

"It's not a big deal. I need to know if someone has flown from D.C. to San Francisco in the last couple of days."

"Who?"

"Who else? Sheila Klaus."

"Shut the door."

"Look, Nic," Owens said after Tatum had resumed his seat, "that's old news, history."

"Why?"

"Why what?"

"Why is it old news? You know as well as I do that she was released because somebody up top, way up top, put in the word."

Owens was mum.

"All I want to know is whether she's gone to San Francisco. My girlfriend and I stopped by her house earlier today, and there were newspapers sitting on the step."

Owens shrugged.

"I just need to know, Joe. All it takes is a phone call. She always flew United when she traveled with Sedgwick and on her own. One call to the airline to see whether Sheila Klaus or Carla Rasmussen took a flight to the West Coast over the past two days."

Tatum waited.

Owens said through a deep sigh, "All right, Nic. But forget that MPD had anything to do with this. I'll be back."

Tatum knew that Owens had gone to the intelligence section from which official calls to airlines and other transportation entities were made, using a code agreed upon between the carriers and MPD. He returned ten minutes later carrying a slip of paper.

"Well?" Tatum asked after Owens had settled behind his desk.

"No Sheila Klaus on any flights to San Francisco for the past two days."

Tatum's sigh rang of frustration.

"But a Ms. Carla Rasmussen was on a flight."

"She was? That's good to know."

Owens handed Tatum the slip of paper

on which he'd jotted down the details of the flight. "What are you going to do with this, Nic?" he asked.

"I don't know," Tatum replied. "Thanks for this, Joe, I appreciate it."

Tatum had been honest when he said that he didn't know what he would do with the knowledge that Sheila (and Carla) had flown to San Francisco. But by the time he got in his car and started driving home, he had an idea. The minute he entered his apartment, he went online and booked a flight to San Francisco leaving that evening.

Presidential candidate George Mortinson and his staff and reporters flew back to Washington from San Francisco. It had been a successful appearance for the popular Democrat. As he quipped to Meg Whitson on the plane, "Maybe I should run for mayor of San Francisco. They love me there."

"They love you everywhere, Senator. Your poll numbers have jumped another two points."

"Swayze's getting desperate," Mortinson said. "Did you hear what he said in Wyoming yesterday, that if the voters go for me, they'd better get ready for another nine eleven?"

"It plays to his dwindling core," said Whitson. "Swayze knows he's losing and doesn't know what to do."

"Couldn't happen to a better guy," Mortinson said. "What's on tap for tomorrow?"

"A full day."

He moaned.

"I left two hours day after tomorrow for tennis with Mac Smith. Thought you'd appreciate that."

"Thanks. How is the rally at the Reagan Building shaping up?"

"Good. The Secret Service isn't thrilled at how many people you'll be greeting at the rope line, especially stopping to have pictures taken with them."

"Sorry to make their jobs harder," he said. "They're a good bunch. Wake me in an hour."

Jake Gibbons returned to the house, where Peter Puhlman and Iskander Itani were playing cards in the living room.

"Hello, Jake," Puhlman said. "How did it go?"

"How did it . . . oh, yeah, Iskander will

be licensed in a few days, a lot of paperwork to wade through."

"Who am I fighting?" Itani asked.

"I'm, ah, working on that, kid. Should
know in a coupla days."

Itani threw his cards on the table and
went to his bedroom.

"What's with him?" Gibbons asked.

"He's uptight, that's all. Had a headache. He used that imaginary helmet the
doc taught him. Seemed to work. He talked
on the phone today with Borger."

"That's supposed to calm him down."

"It did, but he's gotten antsy again. It's
only a few more days, Jake. Where did
you go today?"

"Around. I went to a museum."

Puhlman chuckled. "I'm impressed," he
said.

"That airplane museum. Interesting."

"I'm sure it was. I spoke with Borger,
too. He says all we have to do is keep Itani
cool and collected, play along with him.
Like I said, just a couple of more days."

"What happens then?"

"Nothing. We leave him here and go
back to Frisco."

Gibbons got himself a beer from the

kitchen and rejoined Puhlman in the living room. "I've been thinking today about that girl Elena," he said.

"What about her?"

"Jesus, Peter, the kid murdered her and we got rid a the body. That makes us accessories, right?"

"Forget about it, Jake. It's over and done with. Doc Borger knows what he's doing." He lowered his voice and became conspiratorial. "Borger has connections you can't even imagine, way up high in the government. He's one of those geniuses that the government pays a fortune to. We never have to worry about anything as long as he's behind it."

"Yeah, yeah, I know, but what's the deal with the kid in there? He moves into the doc's house and they hole up three, four times a day in the doc's office. Now we bring him here to D.C. and we sit in this house with him. For what? You say we're leaving him here and we go back home? What's he here for? What's goin' on?"

Puhlman said, "I know that the kid gets on your nerves, Jake, but you're starting to get on mine. You aren't paid to ask

questions. Just do what I tell you and everything will be fine."

Gibbons drank from his beer bottle, a
scowl on his broad, lumpy face. "I just keep
thinking about that girl, that's all," he said.

"It's a shame it happened," Puhlman
said, "but bad things happen to people.
Forget about it. Let's make some dinner.
I'm hungry."

Nic Tatum grabbed a Nathan's hot dog
and a soda at the airport before boarding
his flight to San Francisco. When he'd
called Cindy to tell her that he was leaving,
she reacted as might be expected. "Just
like that?" she said.

"Yeah. I know it's strange, but I have to
do it. I found out that Sheila has flown to
San Francisco. She would never have
done that if Borger wasn't pulling her strings
like a goddamn marionette. I need to . . .
well, I just need to convince myself that I'm
right."

"You're going to confront this Dr.
Borger?"

"I don't know. Maybe, maybe not. I'll
play it by ear."

"How long will you be gone?"

"A day or two."

"Mac Smith called."

"What did he want?"

"He's invited us to a rally for Senator Mortinson three days from now. It's at the Ronald Reagan Building, in the afternoon. He says he has an extra set of passes and wondered if we wanted to use them."

"I don't know, I—"

"I'd love to go, Nic."

"That's right, I forgot, you have a crush on Mortinson."

"I do not and you know it."

"It's okay with me provided I'm back in time."

"Please try to be. And Nic?"

"Huh?"

"Be careful. If everything you say about this Dr. Borger and the people he's involved with is true, they won't stop at anything to keep it a secret."

Tatum loved flying, any sort of flying, whether in his aerobatic aircraft or as a passenger on a jumbo jet. He considered sitting in a jetliner to be the ultimate getaway—no phones, no TV, just hours of solitude to think things out. It wasn't that he enjoyed the process of boarding a commercial plane, or the lack of amenities once aboard. Like most air travelers, he gritted his teeth each time he had to suffer the indignities and hassle of navigating airports, and the disregard for passenger comfort that prevailed with most airlines. But he was able to cast all that aside once airborne, strapped in his seat in an aluminum cigar tube traveling six hundred miles an hour to his destination, and this trip was no exception.

He didn't consider himself an impetuous person. His life was structured, and he liked to think of himself as someone who gave careful consideration to his options before making a decision. For him life came down to a series of decisions. You made good ones and things went fairly well barring a natural calamity or an air conditioner falling on you while you walked down a street. Make bad decisions and, well . . .

But here he was hopping on a plane to San Francisco two hours after he'd learned that Sheila Klaus had gone there, and he hadn't the foggiest notion of what to do once he arrived. He hadn't bothered to change clothes before the trip and had shoved an overnight's amount of clothing, along with some reading material, into a small backpack.

Once settled in his coach seat—and thankful that he was at the window with no one in the middle seat next to him— he tried to bring order to his thoughts about what he believed was Sheila's programmed murder of Mark Sedgwick and the control that Dr. Sheldon Borger exerted over her.

One of the things he'd stuffed into his backpack was his laptop, which contained, among other things, a file he'd gathered over the years on the CIA's mind-control experimentation. He hadn't collected the material with any purpose in mind. It was more a matter of intellectual curiosity and to remind him to not become ensnared in any government projects that he might be offered.

The reports in the file documented not only mind-control experiments since the 1950s but also described other government medical experimentation on innocent victims as early as the 1930s.

One of the most infamous occurred when the Public Health Service, with the blessing of the surgeon general and the

American Heart Association, launched a project in which 399 poor rural black men from Tuskegee, Alabama, who had syphilis were recruited as subjects along with 201 control subjects who did not have the sexually transmitted disease. The 399 infected men never received treatment, nor were they or their families ever informed that they had the disease. "You have bad blood," was the explanation given them. Although the cure for syphilis, penicillin, was introduced in the early 1940s, it was withheld from these men for thirty years. Lord knew how many wives were infected with the disease, and how many children were born with syphilis.

He scrolled through other reports. Radiation experiments were conducted on six hundred American subjects in the 1940s and continued through the 1970s. People were injected with plutonium and exposed to other forms of radiation without their informed consent. Prisoners received $5 a month in return for having their testicles irradiated. Children weren't spared these vile experiments. In 1961, scientists at Harvard Medical School and the Boston University School of Medicine gave radioactive iodine to retarded kids at a state school, and at another state school MIT added radioactive materials to food fed to children. Their parents signed consent forms in which the stated purpose of the experiments was "helping improve the nutrition of our children."

Although Nic was familiar with the file's contents, his anger level rose as he continued to read. Until his involvement with Sheila Klaus, he hadn't bothered to review what he'd collected in his files on the government's use of physicians, scientists, and many of the nation's leading hospitals to carry out such experimentation. For him the reports had been nothing more than abstract reminders of what he knew to be true, pieces of sordid history that had little or no direct bearing on his life.

But it was different now that he'd witnessed firsthand the damage to Sheila Klaus.

According to a 1954 MK-ULTRA document, a female subject was placed into a deep trance. A second female was handed an unloaded gun and, under hypnosis, was told that she must awaken the first woman using every means possible. If she failed, she was told to shoot the sleeping subject. She carried out the instructions, including aiming the weapon at the sleeping woman's head and pulling the trigger. When both were brought out of trance, they had total amnesia of everything having to do with the event.

Another subject, a Canadian woman, was so destroyed by experiments on her that she was completely disoriented, and didn't know her name, age, or her husband, and was unable to read, write, cook, or use the toilet. She eventually joined in a class action lawsuit against the CIA. But because the Canadian physician who had experimented on her had stopped taking CIA money before using her as a subject (the Canadian government began funding the doctor after the CIA money dried up), she sued the Canadian government and won $100,000 plus legal fees.

"Damn them!" Tatum said loud enough to cause the passenger in the aisle seat to glance in his direction.

Tatum read one final report from his file, a synopsis of the work G. H. Estabrooks had done in creating multiple personalities in order to create the perfect spy, courier, or assassin. The writer of the synopsis ended by quoting Estabrooks about the ethical aspect of his work: "The hand of the military must not be tied by any silly prejudices in the minds of the general public. War is the end of all law. In the last analysis any device is justifiable which enables us to protect ourselves from defeat."

This time Tatum seethed quietly in order to not disturb his seatmate. But he boiled inside. His anger wasn't pointed so much at the government as at the medical world, its doctors and psychologists, scientists and nurses, and administrators of leading hospitals and other health facilities whose stated purpose was to alleviate suffering and cure disease, to make life better for mankind. Yet they'd willingly, even enthusiastically, involved themselves in projects that violated the oath they'd taken as physicians and protectors of public health.

Sheldon Borger.

Tatum recalled the one time he'd met him at a psychiatric conference and tried to envision what he would look like years later. What could cause a physician to abandon all sense of decency and commitment and inflict harm on unsuspecting men and women? Money? For some that would be a motivating factor. Patriotism? That was no excuse any more than it was for former House speaker Newt Gingrich who'd blamed his heightened sense of patriotism for his marital infidelities.

It had to be ego, Tatum decided, massive ego, and he silently cursed that human failing. He also thought of his friend Dave Considine, which reminded him that not all physicians fell into the Sheldon Borger category. He gave a thumbs-up to Considine as he turned off the overhead light and dozed off.

CHAPTER
35

SAN FRANCISCO

When he awoke, the plane was in its land-
ing pattern. He hadn't reserved a car and
was relieved that Hertz had some vehicles
available. It was night; the Lightpath Clinic
would be closed. Going there would have
to wait until morning. He had Borger's
home address. Should he knock on the
door and hope that Borger would answer
and invite him in? Unlikely. Still, he felt he
had to do something to justify his decision
to get on a plane and travel across the
country.

He took 101 into the city and proceeded
up steep Van Ness Avenue until reaching

the fabled Nob Hill where Borger's home was situated. He had trouble finding it and was disappointed that a gate spanned the driveway. He turned off his lights and looked past the gates to the house. Lights were on, and he caught a fleeting glimpse of a figure passing a window. While he sat debating whether to ring the bell on the gate, a car, its lights blinding Tatum in his rear-view mirror, came up behind. It was a patrol car. An even brighter floodlight came on, washing Tatum's rental in harsh white light. An officer got out and approached. Tatum rolled down the window.

"Got a problem?" the officer, a tall black man, asked.

"Problem? No. I was just driving around and pulled over here."

"You from here?"

"Nob Hill? No. Actually, I'm from Washington, D.C. I just arrived in San Francisco and wanted to see the city."

"This your car?"

"No. I mean, it's a rental."

"Can I see your license and the papers for the car?"

Tatum obliged. The officer carefully, slowly perused them before handing them back. "You're staying in San Francisco?" he asked.

"Just for a night or two. I—"

"Where are you staying?"

"I don't have a hotel yet. I have to find one."

"You don't have drugs with you, do you?"

"Drugs?" Tatum forced a laugh. "No, no drugs. I'm a psychologist. Ph.D."

"Uh-huh. I suggest you find that hotel and not be parked in front of a private residence."

"Okay," Tatum said.

He watched the officer walk back to his car.

"Dummy!" he told himself as he started the engine and left the area. What did he think he could accomplish sitting outside Borger's home in the middle of the night? "You'd make one pathetic private detective," he said as he drove until finding a Holiday Inn Express in nearby Fisherman's Wharf, where he checked into a room, then walked to a small restaurant that was open late. He returned to the hotel and fell into a fitful sleep that left the bedding a tangled mess when he awoke at five the following morning.

After showering and checking out, he found a place for breakfast, which he lingered over while skimming a copy of a newspaper provided by the restaurant. He read it from cover to cover while biding his time before heading across the Bay Bridge to the Lightpath Clinic. Tatum always enjoyed reading papers from other cities. It gave him a sense of the place, its pace and the things that were important to its citizens. One small item was a report of an unidentified female body washing up near the airport. A police spokesman was quoted as saying, "We're treating this as a homicide. The victim's body must have been secured to something heavy to cause it to sink, but the weight used wasn't sufficient to keep it underwater." An autopsy was to be performed, according to the police; the investigation was ongoing and no further details were available.

Tatum paid his bill, got in his car, and headed for Berkeley and the Lightpath Psychiatric Clinic, where he hoped he might find Borger. Traffic was particularly heavy that morning, compounded by an accident that closed one lane on the bridge. He eventually reached the address and pulled up in front of the drab one-story gray building on Shattuck Avenue. It was strange, he thought, that there was no sign indicating the existence of a clinic, but then he rationalized that if it was a CIA front, announcing its existence couldn't be expected.

He went to the front door and tried it. Locked. He pushed a button and heard a buzzer sound from inside. He was about to push it again when the door opened.

"Yes?" a short, chubby young man asked.

"I was hoping to see Dr. Borger," Tatum said.

"What's it in reference to?"

"A professional matter." Tatum handed the young man his business card, which he slowly, too slowly, scrutinized.

"I'm afraid that Dr. Borger isn't here."

"Just my luck. Do you expect him?"

"He's away."

"Out of town?"

"Away. When I'm in touch with him I'll let him know you were here. Will he know what it's about?"

Tatum hesitated before saying, "It's about Sheila Klaus."

The young man nodded and started to close the door. Tatum placed his hand against it and said, "You say that Dr. Borger is away. Is he at his home on Nob Hill?"

"I'll tell him that you were here."

The door closed and Tatum heard it being locked.

He drove back to Nob Hill and peered through the gates at Borger's mansion where two Hispanic workmen tended a garden. Other than the gardeners there was no sign of life. A yellow Subaru Outback was parked off to the side of the house and Tatum wondered whether it belonged to Borger. Should I ring the bell on the gate? he mused. Instead, he pulled out his cell phone and dialed the number he had for Borger's residence. It rang four times before an answering machine picked up: "This is Dr. Sheldon Borger. I'm unable to take your call at the moment. If you are a patient seeking an appointment, please call my scheduling office." He gave the phone number. "You may leave a message following the beep."

"Dr. Borger," Tatum said into his phone, "my name is Nicholas Tatum. I'm a psychologist who worked with Sheila Klaus when she was incarcerated for the murder of Dr. Mark Sedgwick. I'd like very much to speak with you." He left his cell number.

Tatum killed time by walking around Fisherman's Wharf, his cell phone in his shirt pocket so that he'd be sure to hear it ring and feel its vibration. At two he called Borger's number again and received the same recorded message. It had been a fool's errand, he decided, and he regretted that he'd succumbed to such an impetuous act. He called United Airlines and secured a seat on its red-eye flight back to D.C. that night. He had no way of knowing, of course, that Borger had been at home and had heard both of his messages.

Borger had been in his study when Tatum's call played on the machine. He wasn't surprised. He'd received a call that morning from the young man at Lightpath who'd met Tatum.

"What did he want?" Borger asked.

"He said that it was a professional matter concerning Sheila Klaus."

"I see," Borger had said. "Thank you for the call."

Borger turned to where Sheila rested on the couch.

"Get up, Sheila," Borger said. When she didn't respond he said, "The red sage Lantana are blooming."

She got up and approached him.

"Sit here," Borger said, indicating the black leather recliner across from the one in which he sat. Once she had, he said, "It's a beautiful day for a cruise."

He waited until Carla emerged.

"What do *you* want?" she snarled.

"It's good to see you again, Carla," he said. "We have work to do."

CHAPTER
36

The medical examiner assigned to autopsy the body of the woman found in the water near San Francisco International Airport had reviewed notes and photos taken at the scene of the deceased's discovery. In addition to these notes and photographs, the lead detective who'd managed the crime scene was present for the autopsy, a routine established years ago by the SFPD. The ME and her staff had determined that the victim had been in the water no more than a few days based upon the condition of her body. She was dressed in black silk baby doll pajamas with a label indicating that the clothing had come from Victoria's Secret. One piece of jewelry was found on her, a simple thin gold ring on the middle finger of her left hand.

A criminalist who'd been called to the scene reported that there was an absence of white leathery foam in the mouth, the most indicative characteristic of drowning. The body had been wrapped in a rug, but the bindings had come apart. An officer who claimed some knowledge pegged it as being an expensive Oriental. Rope marks from where the victim had been secured to a weight were observed on her wrists.

After steeping herself in what the officers and the crime scene specialists had observed and documented, and with the lead detective on hand to answer questions, the pathologist went to work. She carefully washed down the body and did an external examination beginning with the feet and working up to the head. She said into a microphone hanging over the table, "There's a large bruise on the left side of the head, possibly the result of blunt force trauma." She measured and photographed it before proceeding with her external exam. She opened the deceased's mouth and examined her teeth. "Dental work was performed," she said into the microphone. "Refer to an odontologist for ID." She said to the detective, "She had nice teeth, took good care of them."

"How old do you figure?" the detective asked.

"Late twenties."

"What about prints?"

"Shouldn't be a problem," she said. "She wasn't in the water that long. Her fingers are shriveled, but the skin is still intact. A tech should be able to lift prints from her. He can inject water into the fingers to bring them back to their normal contour. There was no ID on her?"

"Nothing. Just the pj's and that one ring."

The pathologist laughed. "Victoria's Secret, huh? Sexy lady. No missing person report to link to her?"

"Not that I'm aware of."

Following the external exam, the pathologist began the process of opening the body, starting with the head and moving downward. "Whew!" she said after having examined the brain. "Whoever did this really whacked her. It broke her skull. Massive bleeding."

"Can you tell her race?"

"Mixed, I'd say."

The pathologist stepped back, removed her gloves, and finished what was left of a scone on a paper plate sitting on a stainless-steel cabinet near her and downed the last few sips of coffee that had grown cold. She put on new gloves and proceeded with her examination. When she was finished, she said to the detective, "I hope you find the guy who did this. She was too young and pretty to die."

The detective, Duane Woodhouse, left the autopsy room and joined up with his partner, who'd been with him when the body had washed up. "Okay," he said, "let's pay a visit to local Victoria's Secret shops."

"There's four of them," his partner said and rattled off the addresses.

Armed with photographs of the pajamas the victim had been wearing, and with a general description of her, they started hitting the stores famous for their lingerie. The first three on the list didn't provide any help in identifying the victim, although the managers were extremely cooperative and went through their records of people who'd purchased the item. It was at the fourth location, on Powell Street, that some headway was made. The manager there told them that while there had been recent purchases of that particular set of pajamas, none of the buyers as far as she could recall matched the description of the victim. "Oh, wait," she said. "There's one." She pulled out a sales receipt. "Her name's Elena Marciano. She's a regular customer. She's bought three or four pairs of this particular item. It's her favorite."

"Have an address for her?" Detective Woodhouse asked.

"Yes. She always paid with a credit card, American Express Platinum, but we had things delivered to her a few times. I have it right here."

"She had some money."

"I wouldn't know," the manager said, "but she was always beautifully dressed. Very nice, pretty, too, never without a big smile."

"Do you know where she worked?"

"I have no idea."

After establishing their identities and the official reason for their inquiry, they were given the address and phone number of the Platinum card holder, Elena Marciano, and went to the address. There was no response from her apartment, so they sought out the building's superintendent, an older Asian man who wore a black patch over one eye. They identified themselves as police officers and asked about the tenant named Marciano.

He shrugged. "Nice enough young woman," he said, "never gives me any problems."

"You know where she works, what she does for a living?"

The question brought a smile to his face. "I really can't say officers, only . . ."

"Only what?"

"Well, she does have a lot of boyfriends, that's for sure."

"What's wrong with that?"

"Oh, nothing wrong with it, only there are, like I said, a hell of a lot of them."

The detectives looked at each other and were thinking the same thing: a hooker?

"Anybody else in the building friendly with her?" Woodhouse asked. "Anybody who might know more about her?"

"She keeps pretty much to herself, never bothers nobody. Maybe Mrs. Crowley might be able to tell you something. She lives next door to Ms. Marciano."

The super led them to the apartment and knocked on the door. The voice of an old woman asked who it was. "Harvey, the super," he replied. "I have two police officers with me who need to talk to you."

"Police officers? Just a minute."

A series of inside bolts and locks were disengaged before she opened the door a crack, its security chain still attached. "Yes?" she said.

Woodhouse showed her his ID and said, "Could we have a few minutes of your time, ma'am?"

"What is it in reference to?" Her voice was like chalk on a blackboard.

"About your neighbor, Ms. Marciano."

"Her?"

"Yes, ma'am. May we come in for a few minutes?"

"I don't know, I—"

"I promise we'll stay only a few minutes," he repeated.

"Well, I suppose so," she said, unlatching the chain and stepping back to allow them to enter.

"Nice place you have here," Woodhouse's partner commented.

"I try to keep it neat and clean," she said.

Woodhouse turned and said to the super, "It's okay. You can go now."

He grunted and closed the door behind him.

"We'd like to talk with you about your neighbor, Ms. Marciano," Woodhouse said.

Mrs. Crowley straightened pillows on her couch as though to avoid answering the question. The detectives waited until she'd finished her unnecessary chore and had said something to a canary in a cage by the window.

"Have you seen Ms. Marciano lately?" Woodhouse asked.

"No, I can't say that I have, never have seen a lot of her since she moved in a year ago. Keeps to herself for the most part. Nothing wrong with that, of course, but I like to be neighborly, get along with people."

"Yes, ma'am, I'm sure you do. Do you know what Ms. Marciano does for a living?"

"I have my suspicions."

"And?"

She's . . . well, she's that sort of woman."

The detectives waited for her to amplify her comment.

"I don't like to make judgments about another person," she said. "My deceased husband, Martin, never liked it when I made judgments, but sometimes you have to be honest with yourself."

"I take it that Ms. Marciano is self-employed," Woodhouse offered, hoping he'd found a less jarring metaphor for what he and his partner had already surmised.

"I wouldn't know," said the older woman, who now was busy rearranging knick-knacks on a coffee table.

Woodhouse decided there was nothing to be learned by continuing the conversation. He thanked Mrs. Crowley for her time, complimented her on her neat apartment, and they left.

"We see if the super will open Marciano's apartment?" Woodhouse's partner suggested.

"No. We don't even know if this Marciano woman is the same one who was pulled out of the bay. We'd need a warrant. Let's see what the print guys come up with, and maybe the dental records. If she was a hooker, it's possible she's been pulled in before. Maybe one of her johns did her in."

"Or a pimp."

Woodhouse looked up at the apartment building from where they stood on the sidewalk. "I doubt if there's a pimp involved. If she *was* a hooker—and we don't even know if it's the same woman—she was high-class, more in the call girl category. All we know is that this Ms. Marciano liked black silk pj's. No crime in that."

Sheldon Borger hadn't read the newspaper that day and didn't know about Elena's body having emerged from the bay. He was too busy interacting with Sheila Klaus.

With Puhlman and Gibbons in Washington, he had to pick her up at the airport himself. He didn't look forward to it. Although he'd successfully manipulated Sheila to the extent that she would do his bidding, and was able to summon Carla without difficulty, Carla often emerged of her own volition and could be difficult.

At first Sheila balked at getting into Borger's silver Jaguar. "I don't want any vitamin shots," she'd said.

"Of course not," Borger had replied. "I didn't plan to give you any, Sheila."

"You always do."

"But not this time. Come on, get in the car."

Carla's sudden appearance startled Borger. He recognized her by her deep, harsh voice and the sneer on Sheila's face.

"Hello, Carla," he said.

"Leave her alone," Carla said.

"Why do you say that? I've always been good to Sheila."

"I'm the only one who's been good to Sheila." She laughed.

"Why don't we get in the car where we can talk about it?" he suggested.

"You and your fancy cars," Carla said as she slid into the passenger seat.

"Don't you like fancy cars?" Borger asked as he got behind the wheel.

"They don't mean anything to me," she said. "Go on, drive. Let's go to your big house, only leave Sheila alone. Don't hurt her."

Borger was well aware that Carla's protective stance of Sheila went back to Sheila's childhood. He'd had her revisit her growing-up years during some of their hypnotic sessions together, regressing her until she became a small child again, speaking in a little girl's singsong voice except when her "playmate" Carla emerged to help fight her battles. It wasn't a matter of Sheila recalling those early years. In her hypnotic trance she was there, reliving them in real time.

Sheila had grown up in a household characterized by hostility and conflict, which is typical of men and women who suffer from multiple personality disorder. The annals of psychiatric research document a direct link between the disorder and childhood abuse of all kinds, physical, emotional, and sexual. Her mother had been a strict, puritanical matriarch with a short temper who constantly berated her daughter for what she considered her sloppy, undisciplined habits, and inflicted a series of punishments far beyond what was reasonable. Her father, who left the family when Sheila was in her early teens, had become addicted to prescription pain medications and alcohol following lower back surgery and was himself someone with seemingly two personalities, violently erupting at times but capable of gentle love for his daughter at others.

Like all multiple personalities, Sheila had tried to cope with the irrational atmosphere in her home by bending over backward to be "a good little girl." But while that was effective at times, it seldom protected her from the harshest of punishments. That's when her imaginary playmate, Carla, began coming to the fore. When Sheila was locked in a dark room for hours on end, it was Carla who took over and suffered for both of them, taking the blows. She increasingly began to emerge, standing up to Sheila's mother, which resulted in only further infuriating her. The punishments, which became more physical over time, kept Carla busy, and Sheila came to depend upon her more frequently. When Sheila attended secretarial school and moved away from home, Carla went with her and continued to fight her battles.

When Sheila fell in love with and married a young man in Washington, D.C., Carla went along for the ride, although she cautioned Sheila against the marriage. Living with two people, Sheila and Carla, was too much for Sheila's husband to deal with, and the marriage quickly ended, much to Carla's delight. As the husband told his mother, "I never know who I'm dealing with. One minute Sheila is loving and pleasant, the next she's cold as ice and angry, always angry. She's like a Jekyll and Hyde. I can't take it anymore."

While Sheila's unpleasant childhood was typical of those with multiple personality disorder, there was a second, less psychological and more physical element—her capacity to enter trance. That ability is innate in each person and remains throughout one's life. Those with a lower trance capacity often prove to be good hypnotic subjects through necessity (a medical situation) or determination, or when in the hands of an especially skilled hypnotist, but the basic inborn capacity never varies. Dr. Herbert Spiegel's eye-roll test validates this physical reality.

Borger knew much about Sheila's childhood travails and her difficulties through their hypnotic sessions and made good use of the knowledge when reinforcing his control over her. He could bring her to instant tears simply by slipping into the role of her mother until Carla stepped in and chastised Sheila for being so weak. From Borger's perspective, Carla was a lot more difficult to deal with than Sheila. Carla would become argumentative at the drop of a hat and was openly scornful of the doctor. But for Borger's purposes, it was Carla who was capable of following his instructions, especially when it meant committing a crime, something that Sheila would never dream of doing.

Borger brought Sheila something to eat and drink. The phone calls from Nicholas Tatum had unnerved him. It was one thing to know that a psychologist in Washington, D.C., was prying into his affairs by virtue of having hypnotized Sheila when she was in jail. It was another, distinctly more threatening situation now that this man had traveled to San Francisco and attempted to make contact.

Something had to be done, and done fast.

With Carla having emerged and sitting across from him in the black leather recliner, he said, "There's someone who wants to hurt Sheila."

"Oh, so what? I'm tired."

"Yes, I'm sure you're tired after the long flight, but you must listen to me."

She yawned loudly and then smiled at him. "What's the matter, the great Dr. Borger can't handle things?"

"I'm perfectly capable of handling things, as you put it, Carla, but this is something that you must do—for Sheila's sake."

Another yawn preceded, "Go ahead and tell me. We can't let little Miss Goody Two-shoes be hurt, can we?"

Borger deepened her trance before picking up the envelope that rested on the floor beside his chair. He opened it and handed Carla a photograph of Nic Tatum.

"I know him," Carla said, giggling. "He thinks he's a great doctor, too."

"How do you know him, Carla?"

"He came and talked to Sheila when she was in jail, that's how."

"Did you like him?"

"He was all right. At least he didn't try to give her shots like you used to do."

"Do you know his name?"

"No, I don't care who he is. Tatum something."

"That's right, Nicholas Tatum. He's a psychologist."

She giggled. "Another damn shrink."

"And a dangerous one, Carla, very dangerous like Dr. Sedgwick was."

"He's gone."

"I know he's gone, because you got rid of him just the way I told you to."

"Do I get a ribbon for it?"

"You get the satisfaction of knowing that you did something good for Sheila. She needs you now, Carla. She needs you very badly."

He handed her a second photo of Tatum.

"Remember when I sent you and Sheila on a cruise?"

She nodded.

"I want you to go on another cruise, a very pleasant one. Now, I want you to go deeper into trance, deeper, deeper, deeper . . ."

CHAPTER

37

Mortinson's chief of staff Meg Whitson arrived back in Washington with a splitting migraine, a head cold, and what she was sure was a terminal case of acid indigestion. As successful as the San Francisco event had been, the pressure and pace of the campaign had finally gotten to her, and she sometimes daydreamed of seeking another line of work. Not that she would have acted upon that fantasy. She firmly believed in George Mortinson and what he stood for, and she looked forward to serving him in some capacity once he was ensconced in the White House. She didn't have any illusions about what sort of job might be offered her in the new administration. Running a campaign was one thing; working for a president of the United States was another. In fanciful moments she envisioned herself as chief of staff to the president, or his top political adviser. None of that was possible, of course. The direction of his campaign was masterminded by others; her job was to see that the candidate showed up on time, was fully prepped about whomever he was meeting or speaking with, and in general keep Mortinson on course, which wasn't always easy considering his easygoing temperament and enjoyment of leisure time. Mortinson had the annoying habit of running late to most appointments, and Meg had learned to lie to him on occasion about what time an event was scheduled to start. Other than his tardiness, which Meg considered his only character flaw, she had nothing but admiration for him. Or was it more? Did she have a crush on him and work as hard as she did on his behalf in order to stay close? She'd never admitted that, even to herself, but there were times when fatigue weakened her defenses and she allowed that possibility to surface.

She'd been involved in politics since graduating with a degree in foreign relations from Penn State, starting with a Wisconsin congressman for whom she'd handled the unenviable task of answering his constituent mail—and making excuses for his absences while he slept off frequent hangovers. He'd lasted only two two-year terms, and she'd wondered if her career as an aide to a politician was over. But then George Mortinson came to her rescue and found her a slot working with a Senate subcommittee. When Mortinson was elected to the Senate, he reached out for her, and she'd been at his side ever since. Meg Whitson lived and breathed politics; a classmate at Penn State had written in her yearbook, "My favorite political junkie." But that fascination—no, call it obsession—had its price. Her love life, what there had ever been of it, was in shambles. There simply never seemed to be time to develop and nurture a relationship. But she knew that that was as much an excuse as it was a reality. The fact was that she found the eligible young men in

Washington whom she'd dated to be self-indulgent and impressed with their proximity to power, bantam cocks strutting around the nation's center of influence with an attitude that was at once all-consuming and at times comical to her. To her mother's occasional question, "Have you met a nice young man yet?" Meg usually replied, "Not yet, Mom, but you'll be the first to know."

Back from this latest campaign trip to San Francisco, she managed some time at her apartment to wash clothes, bundle up some for the dry cleaner, and catch a blessed six hours of sleep before being back at headquarters for a meeting with the Secret Service agent in charge of the rally at the Ronald Reagan Building. He wasn't a happy agent.

"The physical setup concerns us," he said, "and the amount of time Big Easy will spend on the rope line shaking hands and posing for pictures." Big Easy was the code name the Secret Service had assigned to George Mortinson. "We've surveyed the venue and are formulating plans for coverage."

"I know it's tough on you and your

people," Meg said, "but I take orders just as you do. The senator has been looking forward to this event, which he's named 'a coming-together rally,' and he isn't about to have the program modified for security reasons. We have a complete list of individuals and organizations that'll be attending. We've gone over the list with you twice already and—"

"It's not a complete list," the agent countered. "People and groups keep getting added, which makes it difficult to clear them all in time. You're also aware of the chatter on the Internet regarding threats against him by terrorist groups."

"Al-Qaeda," Whitson said.

"And others. His support for Israel doesn't make those groups happy. We'll have CIA and FBI agents at the event."

"Is that really necessary?" Meg asked.

"We think so, and so do those agencies. They'll stay in the background."

"It sounds like you'd like us to cancel the event," she said.

"We're not suggesting that," said the agent, "but we have to respond to the intelligence we receive."

Whitson blew a stray wisp of hair from

her forehead and laughed. "Al-Qaeda and others like them don't have to actually plan any attacks," she said. "All they have to do is chatter away on the net and we raise the threat level and spend another couple of million for security. They can bankrupt us with nothing more than talk."

The agent smiled and rubbed his bald head. "That doesn't mean that they aren't planning attacks," he said. "Look, all I'm doing is pointing out the security problems with this rally. Your candidate calls the shots and it's our job to protect him, which, of course, we will. But do what you can to make our job easier, okay?"

"You know we will. Thanks."

Meg and her staff spent the next hour going over the extensive list of those invited to attend the rally, and some who hadn't been invited but managed to join the crowd anyway through various government contacts, their local congressman or senator, friends of Mortinson's, and others recommended by local politicians whose support for him was unwavering. There were three women from a garden club in New Jersey; a four-man contingent from an Ohio club whose hobby was restoring World War II aircraft; Girl Scout and Boy Scout troops from various states; a Connecticut cancer survivors' club; a New Mexico theatrical group known for re-creating famous scenes from the nation's history; representatives from the American Library Association; the Westside Boxing Club of San Mateo, California; a Demo-cratic women's club contingent from Massachusetts; members of Congress who backed Mortinson's candidacy and in some cases their families; and dozens of other associations, groups, social, frater-nal, political, and athletic clubs. It was Mortinson's goal to put on the sort of grassroots rally one might find in a typical Midwestern town or city, a cross section of America gathered to celebrate the dawn of a new and progressive era in national politics.

A staffer laughed when he came to the Westside Boxing Club of San Mateo. "Prizefighters for Mortinson," he said. "KO Swayze. Send Swayze down for the count."

"Don't laugh," Whitson said. "We don't talk about it publicly, but the senator hap-pens to enjoy boxing, watches it on TV whenever he gets a chance."

"Maybe the senator could go four rounds with Mike Tyson, you know, an exhibition to raise funds."

"Very funny," Whitson said in the most distressed voice that she could muster. "Let's move. It's going to be a long day."

Itani saw Mortinson arrive home from San Francisco on the TV in the house he shared with Puhlman and Gibbons. Anger welled up in him, and he came forward on the love seat as though to attack the television. Puhlman put a hand on his shoulder.

"Bastard," Itano mumbled.

"Yes, that's exactly what he is," Puhlman said. "Don't ever forget it."

The waiting had put everyone's nerves on edge. Of course Itani didn't know that within a few days he would be set loose to kill the man who could be the next president of the United States. As far as he was concerned, he was there to resume his boxing career. But why was it taking so long to become licensed and to pick an opponent? It struck him that he should be in a gym working out in preparation for a bout, and he expressed this numerous times to Puhlman and Gibbons, who were dealing with their own anxieties.

Gibbons was as much in the dark as Itani was. When he'd signed on to work for Borger, he'd never dreamed that he'd be called upon to get rid of the body of a young woman who'd been murdered. He'd done some lousy jobs in his life, but this took the cake, and he'd decided that once back in San Francisco, he'd tell Borger that he would no longer take part in such things. Maybe he should have refused when Puhlman called him, woke him from a deep sleep, and told him they had to get to Borger's house on the double, and once he was there, he should have told Borger to get someone else. He hadn't, of course. He wasn't about to lose the best job he'd ever had. But you reach a point . . .

He also constantly questioned the secrecy surrounding Itani and this trip to Washington. He knew that promising Itani that they would help resurrect his boxing career was a sham, but he didn't know why they were going through this charade. Each time he raised it with Puhlman, he was told to stop asking questions and to follow through with what Borger had ordered. The problem was that he'd begun to doubt just how great a man Dr. Sheldon Borger really was.

Puhlman, too, was growing anxious as the hours passed. Although he knew every detail of what was about to happen, a series of recent doubts had butted heads with what had been a firm and total belief in what they were doing. Up until then he'd been content to work at Borger's side in what Puhlman considered to be a monumentally important experiment in mind control. That people had died, and would continue to die, was irrelevant. What mattered was that Borger, with Puhlman's help, had created a foolproof way to rid the world of its vermin. All the work leading up to recruiting Itani for this particular assignment had been blessed and fully funded by the government, particularly the Central Intelligence Agency and its Medical and Psychological Analysis Center. Creating the perfect spy, the perfect assassin, had been a goal of the agency for decades, and now Borger had proved it possible. His work would give the United States an important advantage in this increasingly volatile and dangerous world, and anyone who questioned it was a traitor. Yes, some would suffer for this greater good. Sedgwick had been a valuable ally in providing good candidates for the experiments, but he'd lost his focus and belief in the program and had to be eliminated. The left-wing columnist who'd constantly attacked the work of the current administration was also a threat, and Borger had swiftly and effectively manipulated him into committing suicide. And now there was George Mortinson, a spineless apologist for America and its precious way of life whose existence threatened everything that Borger and Puhlman stood for. Getting rid of Mortinson would be the capstone of Borger's groundbreaking work, and he, Peter Puhlman, was proud to stand at his side.

So it wasn't that Puhlman now had less belief in the project and his involvement in it that caused him concern. What nagged at him was the fact that too many people knew about it. He wasn't worried about the CIA. After all, this rogue use of Borger's techniques was blessed by Colin Landow, who held an important position in the agency. Should Itani be successful in assassinating Mortinson, the agency had the means to cover up their involvement at every level.

Borger, Puhlman knew, wasn't at all concerned about having Itani traced back to his house. He'd treated him for headaches, pure and simple, and would express shock that this nice young man had turned out to be a killer. Itani's amnesia would remain solid. No, it was the money men bankrolling the assassination who worried Puhlman. How many were there? Could they all be trusted to keep their mouths shut? Perhaps the biggest cause of Puhlman's recent sleeplessness was Itani's murder of Elena. Borger was confident that her body would never be found, and that even if it were, she couldn't be traced back to him. Was he right? Having the CIA back you was one thing; covering up the murder of a young woman at your house was another. If her body was discovered, it would become a matter for local law enforcement, whose mission was solving crimes, especially murder.

He could only hope that everything would go as planned. He and Gibbons had traveled to Washington under false names and would return to San Francisco without anyone even knowing that they'd been there. Borger had said that he intended to shut down the experiments and that he would compensate Puhlman handsomely. "Just a few more days," Puhlman told himself over and over. "Just a few more days."

A tired Nic Tatum got off the red-eye from San Francisco and went directly home, where he called Cindy.

"How did it go?" she asked.

"It didn't go at all," he replied. "I don't know why I even bothered making the trip. I never made contact with Borger, and got the brush-off at the clinic he runs. On top of that I almost got arrested for parking at night outside Borger's mansion. I left messages for him at his clinic and on his answering machine. He was either away—although I saw someone in the house—or decided not to answer the calls. Either way, the trip was a bust."

"But at least you tried."

"A for effort, huh? I feel like a jerk."

"Don't. I'm glad you're back. I really want to go with Mr. and Mrs. Smith to the Mortinson rally."

"Sure. Whatever you say. Mortinson's a shoo-in huh?"

"Looks that way. Welcome back. Dinner tonight?"

"Sounds good to me after I get in a nap. Love you."

She smiled as she ended the call. It was only recently that he said that he loved her.

Things were progressing.

Colin Landow's office suite at CIA head-quarters at Langley was small and tucked in a remote corner of the sprawling build-ing. Only the superior to whom he reported and a select few in the upper echelon were aware of precisely what sort of operation Landow ran. All that was known was that it involved top secret psychological testing and experimental projects, all of it con-ducted away from the agency and em-ploying nonagency medical and scientific personnel. There were many such low-profile offices and operations within the CIA about which only those directly in-volved had any knowledge. Added to the CIA's seemingly unmanageable web of intelligence-gathering apparatus were sixteen federal agencies, each a fiefdom with its own culture, objectives, and funding. It had become too large and unwieldy, its operations wildly diverse and beyond congressional scrutiny and oversight.

Which was fine with Colin Landow.

He'd spent the morning reviewing the results of a pain-management experiment that had been conducted in Seattle, which had gone well according to the report. At noon he left the building and drove to a mall in suburban Virginia, where he met with one of two assistants, Bret Lancaster, who'd been recruited by Landow fresh out of Harvard. Landow had been Lancaster's mentor and protector throughout Lancaster's eleven years with the agency, and he appreciated what Landow had done for him to the extent that his loyalty to Landow was total. Lancaster was a short, slightly built man with a narrow face pitted from a severe case of teenage acne. His interests aside from working for Landow were limited. Some thought that he was homosexual. In truth he was asexual; his disdain for women was almost pathological. Very much a loner, his life revolved around Colin Landow and the CIA.

"How did it go?" Landow asked after he and Lancaster had gotten soft drinks from a concession stand and found a picnic table away from others.

"Fine. I spent time at the building. Koontz from the bureau was there, and we spent time with the Secret Service agent in charge of the event. He'd been made aware that we'd be sending someone, and I told him I'd be there for the event. I and a few bureau agents will be admitted through a separate entrance that doesn't have scanning equipment. There shouldn't be any problem. We've been cleared."

"The location we've picked for the drop?"

"That should work well," Lancaster said.

"And you have the weapon."

"Yes. It was at the safe house as planned. I'm sure that everything will go smoothly."

"Good work, Bret. Our friend has been cleared by the senator's staff and the Secret Service, and he has the necessary ID tag to be allowed entry. I suggest that after you conceal the weapon, you stay for a portion of the festivities but leave before the main event."

"That's my plan."

Landow handed Lancaster an envelope.

"I'm sure you'll find that it's what we agreed upon."

Lancaster thanked him and walked away. Landow left the mall fifteen minutes later and returned to his office, where he considered calling Borger in San Francisco. He decided not to; the less contact with him the better at this late stage of the project. From this point forward, Dr. Sheldon Borger was on his own.

CHAPTER

38

SAN FRANCISCO

The identity of the body that had floated up in the bay off the airport became known to the authorities not through forensic science but by the deceased's mother, Mrs. Caroline Marciano of Portland, Oregon.

"My daughter Elena is always so good about staying in contact with me," she told the officer who took her call, "but I haven't heard from her in days. I'm so worried that something has happened to her."

The officer put the call through to Detective Duane Woodhouse, whose involvement in the case of the unidentified woman in the bay was common knowledge in the department. When he was told that the woman's name was Marciano, he immediately came on the line and asked her to describe her daughter. The general description she gave matched that of the body in the morgue. He asked a few more questions, including what her daughter did for a living.

"She's a model," the mother replied. "She's very beautiful."

Woodhouse gave her the address he had for Elena Marciano and asked whether it was the address she had for her daughter.

Mrs. Marciano immediately sensed that something was wrong. "Why do you know her address?" she asked. "Has something happened to Elena?"

"It's possible, ma'am, that your daughter has died."

The woman's gasp caused Woodhouse to wince.

"We can't be certain," he said, "but I would appreciate it if you would come here to San Francisco. That's the only way we can be sure."

"Oh, my God," she said through gulps of air, "what happened to my baby?"

"Please, ma'am, we really don't even

know if it *is* your daughter. The only way we can be sure is if you are willing to . . . well, if you'll come here and identify the body."

"The body?"

It was the same response that he'd gotten when he asked Elena's next-door neighbor, Mrs. Crowley, to come to the morgue. "To look at the body?" she'd wailed. "No, I will not do that."

And they had no way of forcing her to perform that grisly task. The building superintendent, too, had begged off.

"Yes, ma'am," Woodhouse said to Mrs. Marciano. "It's very important that you do this. Do you have a husband who could accompany you?"

"I did. I mean my husband passed away a little over a year ago. Cancer. His prostate."

After hearing more about her deceased husband's bout with cancer, and a description of the sort of childhood Elena had enjoyed—"a good solid Catholic upbringing"—he convinced her to come to San Francisco and made an appointment to meet with her the following afternoon, possibly with her brother if he could take the time off from his job. He owned and managed a construction company, Wood-house learned before they ended the call.

He reported the conversation to his superior. "If it is her daughter," Woodhouse said, "we'll need a warrant to enter her apartment."

"Not a problem," his boss said. "So the mother thinks her kid was a model, huh?"

"Hookers always tell their parents that they're models," Woodhouse said. "Kind of sad."

"Hopefully she kept a list of her johns."

"Hopefully."

"And hopefully she wasn't too success-ful as a hooker. I'd hate to have to inter-view a hundred satisfied customers. If she was good at her job and as beautiful as her mother claims, it'll probably involve some of our better-known upstanding citi-zens." He laughed.

Woodhouse was out of sorts when he awoke the next morning, a feeling he usu-ally experienced when having to face the parent of a dead son or daughter. He had two daughters of his own, ages eleven and thirteen, and wondered what it would be like to have a cop waltz you into a morgue and pull back the sheet to reveal your own flesh and blood. That contemplation gave him the creeps, and he worked hard to dismiss it as he went through his day at the Thomas J. Cahill Hall of Justice on Bryant Street until Mrs. Marciano and her brother showed up. The mother was a nice-looking lady, he observed, trim and energetic, plainly but appropriately dressed in a blue skirt and white blouse, and carrying a tan raincoat over her arm. Her brother was a big, rough-looking sort of guy who wore an ill-fitting gray suit, white shirt with a too-tight collar, and a thin red tie; he obviously had dressed for the occasion.

Mrs. Marciano started crying the moment Woodhouse introduced himself, which prompted the brother, whose name was Anthony, to put his arm around her.

"I know this is tough," Woodhouse said, "but it's necessary."

"Before we go and look at the body," Anthony said, "can you tell us what happened to the person we're going to see?"

Woodhouse spared them the grim details, saying only that a young woman approximately the age of the daughter had been found dead out near the airport. But knowing how the days in the water had bloated and disfigured the body, he made reference to it to spare them the shock.

"Maybe you'd better go alone," the mother told Anthony through her tears.

"An ID from either of you will suffice," Woodhouse assured. "Shall we get it over with?"

The morgue was located in the same building as Woodhouse's office. He led them to it, where he informed the medical examiner on duty that they were there to identify the body of the Jane Doe taken from the water. The medical examiner consulted a sheet: "Number six forty-two," he said and led them to a window overlooking the morgue.

Woodhouse looked at Mrs. Marciano and her brother.

"You go, Anthony," she said.

He drew a series of deep breaths and announced that he was ready. After giving his sister a reassuring hug, he accompanied Woodhouse and the ME inside to the bay that coincided with the number assigned to the body.

"Ready?" he asked.

Woodhouse observed Anthony Marciano

and wondered whether he'd have to prop him up. The bigger they are, the harder they fall, the detective was thinking.

The ME opened the bay and slid out Elena Marciano's remains. She pulled back the sheet to reveal her face.

"Jesus!" Anthony said. "It's her. Elena."

"You're positive?" Woodhouse asked.

"Yeah, I'm positive," Anthony said, turning away quickly and heading for the door.

"Thanks, Doc," Woodhouse said, following him from the room.

Anthony simply nodded at his sister, who slumped into a red plastic chair, wept, and muttered prayers.

They returned to Woodhouse's office, where his offer of coffee or a cold drink was declined. He elicited from them where they were staying and said that he'd arrange a car to return them to their hotel, adding that he'd need to speak with them the next morning. He also asked the mother whether she had a photograph of her daughter, which she did and handed it to him.

When they were gone, he informed his boss, who'd already arranged for a warrant to enter and search Elena Marciano's apartment.

The superintendent scrutinized the warrant before allowing them access. Woodhouse was accompanied by another detective and two crime scene investigators, who took both still photos and videos of the place. Woodhouse noticed that Elena Marciano was a good housekeeper. The apartment was immaculate, not a piece of paper or a dish out of place. The furnishings were expensive, mostly white leather in the living room and deep white carpeting throughout, except for the bedroom, which differed in its color scheme, the carpet bloodred, the furniture sleek black, and an assortment of pin spots recessed in the ceiling on a series of dimmers. The bed was king-sized and covered in red-and-gold bedding that Woodhouse thought might be Egyptian inspired.

After a walk-through, Woodhouse settled at a desk in the living room and read entries on a monthly desk calendar. Elena's penmanship was as neat and precise as her surroundings. Items noted on the calendar consisted mostly of last names, with a time next to them, and in some instances a comment or two. Some names appeared more than once, some even more frequently than that. After handing the calendar to his colleague, Woodhouse went through the desk's drawers, pulling out anything that might be of use in establishing leads. They included a green leather-bound phone book, envelopes containing sales receipts, a file of paid bills, and a second file that held bills to be paid. There was also a photo album containing color pictures of Elena with various people, including shots of her with her mother and Uncle Anthony. No doubt about it. She was gorgeous.

Everything from the desk went into evidence bags, along with a digital answering machine whose memory was filled to capacity with incoming messages.

"There's no computer," Woodhouse's partner commented.

"Check with the super whether she had a car," Woodhouse suggested.

His partner returned a few minutes later. "He says she did have one but sold it six months ago. She rents, according to him, and takes taxis and car services."

"All right," Woodhouse said. He instructed the crime scene techs to dust for prints, especially in the bedroom, bathroom, and any glasses in the dishwasher. He and his

partner returned to their offices at 850 Bryant, commonly known as "the hall," and
wrote up their report.

"If she was a call girl," his partner commented, "those names on the desk calendar are a good place to start."

Woodhouse agreed and checked his
watch. "I have to get home, a family thing.
See you in the morning."

As he reached the door, his partner
said, "I'd like to nail the son of a bitch who
did this."

"With any luck we will."

And he hoped that they'd be lucky
enough to not *need* luck.

CHAPTER
39

Sheldon Borger had not been aware that Elena's body had washed ashore and was now on a slab at the city morgue. But that changed when he opened the paper the following day and read that the original Jane Doe now had a name, Elena Marciano, and that she'd been identified by a family member. The article carried the headline MYSTERY VICTIM NO LONGER A MYSTERY. The writer reported that according to anonymous police sources, the victim, originally from Portland, Oregon, was thought to have been a high-priced call girl. There were no suspects, but the investigation was ongoing. A photo of the victim taken from the Internet in which Elena appeared to be working at a trade show accompanied the piece. Evidently she *had* done some modeling at one point in her life.

Borger had read the newspaper after returning from the airport where he'd driven Sheila Klaus for her return trip to Washington. The sessions with her, and with Carla, had gone smoothly; he was confident that the control he exerted over her was complete and that she would carry out his instructions to the letter.

"Damn," he muttered as he slammed the paper down on the desk in his study. He cursed again, this time his invective directed at Puhlman and Gibbons. They'd assured him that the body would remain submerged. *I never should have trusted them,* he thought. If her body had been properly disposed of, no one would have missed her. After all, she was just a prostitute, he reasoned, probably from a broken home. Who would worry about her disappearance? No one. And if someone did come forward, the police would dismiss his or her concerns. They had bigger, more important things to worry about.

Borger read the article again.

Now his wrath turned on Itani. He never should have left him alone with Elena. But how could he have anticipated that the young man would turn on her and do such a thing? He was obviously mentally unbalanced. If Itani was capable of turning his inner anger on someone outside of Borger's influence, he might do it again before he was turned loose as an assassin.

He picked up the phone. "Peter, it's Sheldon."

Puhlman had been dozing in a chair when his special cell phone rang in the Virginia safe house.

"Hello, Sheldon, how are you?"

"Not good. There's a complication."

Puhlman had been half awake when he answered the phone. Now he snapped to attention. "What complication?" he asked. "Something with the plan here?"

"That young woman has been found."

Puhlman's face creased with confusion. "Young woman?" The answer came to him during the silence on the other end of the connection.

"How?" Puhlman asked.

"It doesn't matter. They've found her and she's been identified."

"Oh?" He didn't know what else to say.

"Are you there, Peter?"

"Yes, I'm here. Jake assured me that—"

"Jake's assurances are worthless."

"What do you want me to do?" Puhlman asked, realizing that he'd begun to sweat.

"There's nothing you can do at the moment," Borger replied. "But I wanted you to be aware of it."

"Yes, I appreciate the call."

"How is Iskander?"

"He's . . . he's fine. He's right here."

"Put him on."

"Hello," Iskander said after Puhlman had handed him the phone.

"Hello, Iskander, it's Dr. Borger."

"Hello, Doctor."

"How are you feeling? Have your headaches returned?"

"No, they have not. I want to come home."

Borger forced a laugh that was meant to be reassuring. "You'll be home soon, I promise you."

"I want to fight. When will I fight? I want to see my mother and brothers."

"Yes, of course you do, and you will see them very shortly, only another day or two."

Borger realized that he'd said the wrong thing, and Itani picked up on it. "You mean I will be coming back to San Francisco in a few days?"

"What I mean, Iskander, is that you'll be coming back after your fight there in Washington."

"When will that be?"

"As soon as Jake makes the final arrangements." When Itani didn't respond, Borger said, "Revenge is sweet, Iskander."

Puhlman watched Itani slip into a deep trance.

"You must listen to me, Iskander," Borger said into the phone. "You know that you can trust me—and *only* me. I will always do what is best for you."

"Yes, I know."

"I want you to hand the phone to Peter, then go to the kitchen, get a glass of water, and bring it to him."

Puhlman continued to observe as Itani did as instructed and was surprised when

Itani handed him the glass filled with water and took back the phone.

"Did you do as I told you, Iskander?"

"Yes."

"Good. Now, you are to go to your bedroom and lie down on the bed. In a half hour you'll come out of the pleasant trance state you're in and feel refreshed and happy."

"How is Elena?" Itani asked.

"Elena is fine. She asks for you often and is looking forward to seeing you again. Now give Peter the phone and go lie down."

Itani handed Puhlman the phone and disappeared into his room.

"You gave him those instructions?" Puhlman asked.

"Yes. My control is still complete."

"What about the other situation, the one you called about?"

"I'll take care of it. It will be necessary for you and Jake to leave San Francisco immediately after returning. I'll make all the arrangements, including the money. Our friends have been generous."

"And you?"

"I'll need to leave, too. Is everything ready there?"

"I believe so. Colin's deputy called with final instructions."

"Good. Keep a close watch on Iskander until it's done. Do you understand?"

"Yes, of course."

"And I suggest that you not tell Jake about this turn of events."

Puhlman readily agreed. Gibbons had become obsessed with the potential ramifications of having gotten rid of Elena's body. Knowing that she'd been discovered might put him over the edge.

The call completed, Puhlman paced the room. Gibbons had gone for a walk and would be back in an hour. The news about Elena being found hit Puhlman in the gut like a sledgehammer. The assassination of Senator Mortinson did not unduly worry him. Borger had the backing of powerful people, including elements of the CIA. But the murder of Elena was another matter, one that Puhlman was afraid was beyond Borger's ability to control. He didn't need Borger's advice to leave San Francisco immediately upon returning. He'd been planning to do so ever since that morning when he and Gibbons disposed of her body. The need to leave the city hadn't been particularly urgent as long as she remained in her watery grave in San Francisco Bay. But now . . .

While Borger had put on a confident façade during his conversation with Puhlman, his true state approached panic. Like Puhlman, his fears didn't revolve around the assassination of Mortinson. But Elena's murder was beyond his scope of influence.

He forced himself to get his emotions under control and to think clearly.

Much depended upon what the police would find in her apartment. Had she kept a diary, or a so-called little black book with the names and addresses of her clients? He could only hope not. But he had to plan as though she had.

Assuming that his name was found in her possessions, and further assuming that the police would follow up, he had to have his story straight. The housekeeper and cook certainly knew that Elena been at the house on a number of occasions, and had even stayed over a few nights, especially when the young prizefighter, Iskander Itani, had been there. But there was nothing beyond that to link him to her death. "Yes," he said aloud as an idea struck him. He would say that he'd been counseling her to leave prostitution before something nasty happened to her. What would he say if they asked whether he'd availed himself of her sexual services? He'd make light of it and say that it was only after he'd been a client that he began working with her as a patient. He might even say he'd fallen in love with her. No, that was too over the top. His story would be that she'd become a patient and . . . and he would also say that she'd confided in him that she'd recently been stalked by a client who'd threatened to kill her. He'd urged her to go to the police, but she was afraid because of her illegal occupation.

Satisfied with that story line, he proceeded to ponder who else might link him to her. He thought back to what Itani had told Mica Sphere when she'd spent time with him at the house, that he had a girlfriend named Elena. But why would the police question Mica? They didn't even know that she existed. Elena was not such an uncommon name that Mica would remember it. Elena had been identified as

Elena Marciano, but she used the name Jones when working. If Itani had told Mica Elena's last name it would have been Jones, not Marciano.

What about Puhlman and Gibbons?

He had no choice but to trust them and get them out of San Francisco as quickly as possible. Their work with him was strictly off the books, cash provided by the CIA in most cases, augmented by funds from his backers in the assassination plot.

Of course, there was Itani, who'd actually killed her. But his induced amnesia was rock-solid as far as Borger was concerned, both of having killed Elena and for having been programmed to assassinate George Mortinson. And if things went as planned in Washington, Itani wouldn't live to tell anyone anything.

As Borger formulated his story, Detective Duane Woodhouse and two colleagues were sifting through Elena's calendar and address book.

"This name 'Borger' appears on four days on the calendar," a detective said, "and there's an address and phone number for Dr. Sheldon Borger on Nob Hill in her book. Must be the same guy. And look at the last date. It coincides with the approximate time the ME said she died."

"Let's pay the good doctor a visit," Woodhouse said.

Borger saw the unmarked car pull up at the gates and a man in a suit get out and press the intercom button.

"Yes?" Borger said into a unit in the kitchen.

"Dr. Borger?"

"Yes."

"Detective Woodhouse, San Francisco PD. We'd like to have a word with you."

"May I ask what this is in reference to?"

"It'd be easier to explain in person, sir."

"All right," Borger said, pushing a button that electronically opened the gates.

Woodhouse and his partner got out of their car and approached the front door. Borger opened it before they reached it and said, a wide smile on his face, "I'm not used to being visited by members of the city's finest."

"We appreciate your time, sir," said Woodhouse.

"Come in, come in."

He led them to his study and asked if they wished something to drink.

"No thank you, sir. We're here regarding a young woman named Elena Marciano."

"Elena?" Borger said, feigning surprise. "What about her?"

"She's been the victim of a murder."

"Oh, no. Murdered? When? Where?"

Woodhouse ignored the questions and said, "We have reason to believe that you and the deceased had some sort of a relationship."

"Relationship? Yes, I suppose you could call it that. I was her psychiatrist."

Woodhouse and his partner looked at each other. Borger's response was unexpected.

"She was a patient of yours?"

"Yes. I can't believe what I've just heard. Good Lord, who could have done this horrible thing to her?"

"That's what we're trying to find out, sir. Were you aware of how Ms. Marciano made her living?"

Borger paused before saying, "I'm not sure just how much I should reveal about her. After all, she was my patient and there's the doctor-patient privilege to consider."

"That really doesn't hold water, Dr. Borger," Woodhouse said, "not when a homicide is involved."

"Please don't misunderstand," Borger quickly added. "I want to be of as much help as possible. You ask about what Elena did for a living. She was a prostitute."

"Yes, we've pretty much established that," Woodhouse said. "Did she talk about her customers with you?"

"Customers? She referred to them as clients."

"Did she name any of them?"

Borger displayed his widest smile and raised his hand. "I think we're veering into a touchy area," he said.

Woodhouse's partner said, "In other murders involving a prostitute, it's often one of her johns, her clients, who did it."

"That makes sense," said Borger, "but no, she never mentioned anyone by name. That would have been terribly indiscreet of her. But she did—"

Woodhouse's cocked head invited him to continue.

"She did mention one client, not his

name, but said that she was afraid of him. She said that he'd threatened to kill her."

"But no name."

"No name."

"Did you suggest that she notify the police?"

"Of course I did, but I understood her reluctance to do that. She was, after all, a prostitute, which means she was breaking the law. She was concerned about how you, the police, would respond to her."

Their interview with Borger lasted another half hour. It was toward the end of it that Woodhouse said, "We've established that she was with you the day of her murder."

"Why day was that?" Borger asked. Woodhouse told him. Borger excused himself to check his appointment book. When he returned he said, "That's right, we did have a session on that day."

"What time?"

"I don't have it noted in my book, but I remember distinctly that it was four o'clock."

"Why do you remember it so distinctly?" asked Woodhouse.

"I recall it because she was quite upset

about this client's threats, so much so that I suggested that she spend the night here."

"You usually have patients spend the night at your house?"

"Not routinely, but I have done it with certain patients. Sometimes prolonging the time spent with a patient can be therapeutic. Frankly, I was concerned for her safety." He shrugged. "But she refused my offer and said that she'd be all right, that she could take care of herself."

The detectives thanked Borger for his time and cooperation and left. When they were in the car, Woodhouse's partner said, "He's slick, isn't he?"

"Too slick for my blood," Woodhouse replied. "You notice that he had the newspaper on his desk?"

"No."

"He acted as though being told of the murder was a big surprise. I don't believe him."

"Want to go back?"

"Later. Let's follow up on some of the other names we have from her calendar and address book, then we'll pay the doctor another visit."

Senator George Mortinson lobbed a ball over Mac Smith's head and watched his tennis opponent scramble to reach and return it. He failed.

"Nice shot," Smith said as he prepared to serve.

Smith eventually won the abbreviated match, which was cut short when Meg Whitson came to the court and told the senator that he was behind schedule for a noontime speech he was slated to deliver. Mortinson had been running late all morning, much to the chagrin of his staff. Flanked by Secret Service, he walked with

Smith to where their cars were parked, with Meg encouraging them to move faster.

"If we'd played it out, I would have beaten you," Mortinson said.

"Maybe," Smith said.

"You know, Mac, it would be good form to let the next president of the United States win."

"What would I get for throwing the match?"

"A night in—"

"The Lincoln Bedroom?"

"The maids' quarters," Mortinson said through a laugh. "Coming to the event tomorrow?"

"Wouldn't miss it, Senator. Annabel's looking forward to it, too. We're bringing friends, Nicholas Tatum and his gal friend Cindy Simmons. I told you about them. She's a big fan, was thrilled to get a signed photo of you at a restaurant the other night."

"Look forward to seeing them, and you and Annabel."

Smith watched Mortinson be driven away to a shower and to his next appointment on the campaign trail. He and Annabel were staunch supporters of the Mortinson candidacy and the policies that he espoused. But neither was disillusioned about what running for so lofty a position as the leader of the free world demanded. It took an immense ego and sense of self-confidence that few other people possessed. It also helped to have a fatalistic view of one's mortality.

There were always some deranged individuals out there determined to impose their will on the nation by ridding it of someone they considered dangerous and a threat to what they believed in. Four sitting presidents had been assassinated: Lincoln, Garfield, McKinley, and Kennedy. Others, like Truman, Nixon, Ford, and Reagan, had survived attacks. Potential president Robert Kennedy had been gunned down while campaigning, and every president lived with death threats—the Bushes, Clinton, Teddy and Franklin Roosevelt, and Barack Obama. It went with the territory was the way they all dismissed that grim reality when questioned about it in public. But were they always that cavalier in their private moments?

Mortinson and Tricia had discussed the danger to candidates for high political office on more than a few occasions. She agreed with him that protection for presidential candidates was top-notch, the men and women of the Secret Service consummate professionals who would give their lives to protect their wards. But she was also aware that her husband was of the opinion that the best protection in the world couldn't guarantee that someone, sometime, couldn't find a way to inflict injury, especially on someone as gregarious as George Mortinson. She'd urged him to curb his need to press into crowds, seeking every outstretched hand, too often deviating from the scheduled route, to the dismay of the agents assigned to him. She also tensed when he took part in parades, opting for a convertible that afforded the crowds a better view of him than a covered vehicle like that used by the pope and other world leaders. Visions of Jack Kennedy in Dallas always came to mind, and she would breathe a sigh of relief when her husband had passed safely along the parade route.

Yes, it went with the territory, but that didn't make it more palatable.

Mortinson's speech was at the venerable Woman's National Democratic Club, which had been enticing the biggest names in politics to speak at their twice-weekly luncheons since the club's founding in 1922. Housed in an imposing 1894 Beaux Arts mansion near Dupont Circle, its membership, which had included men since 1988, was a friendly crowd to address for any Democrat running for office. Tricia Mortinson not only accompanied her husband on this day, she introduced him. She kept it short; he spoke for twenty minutes and left time for questions. Some were directed at Tricia, including one from an older woman who asked what it was like to be married to not only the next president of the United States but to such a handsome man as well.

Tricia laughed at the question, thought for a moment, and said, "You know how some men consider beautiful women as not having brains? Well, that's not true of my—dare I say it?—beautiful husband. He'll bring to the office a thoughtful, reasoned approach to the multitude of problems we face as a nation. In other words, the United States of America will be in very capable hands."

The men and women in the audience stood and applauded, although some of the more conservative attendees remained seated. The Mortinsons, accompanied by Secret Service agents, left the head table and personally greeted everyone, shaking hands, smiling broadly, and stopping for those who'd brought a camera. Meg Whitson had sat in the rear of the room during the event. She looked at her watch and scowled. They were already a half hour behind schedule, and she mentally grappled with how they could make up the time for the rest of the day.

The Mortinsons eventually reached the street, where their limo waited, along with a black sedan for the agents. A small crowd had gathered on the sidewalk and pressed forward to say hello to the next president of the United States. Two of the agents subtly used their bodies to keep Mortinson from straying from a direct path to the limo, but their efforts failed. He broke from them and started shaking hands with the crowd. A young man wearing a hooded gray sweatshirt and torn jeans, and needing a shave, stood at the rear of the knot of people. As Mortinson reached past others to offer his hand, one of the agents brusquely stepped in front and shielded him from the scruffy onlooker. Mortinson looked quizzically at the agent, who said, "Didn't like his looks, Senator."

Mortinson shrugged at the young man as he turned his back and walked away. The candidate shook a few more hands on his way to the limo, climbed in the back where his wife and Meg Whitson waited, and asked Tricia, "Did you see that?"

"What?"

"The agent didn't like the looks of a kid wanting to greet me. He damn near knocked me over getting between us."

"That's his job, George," she said.

"Maybe he takes it too seriously," was Mortinson's reply.

"I don't think that any of them can take the job too seriously," Meg said. "Relax, Senator. You've got another appearance and we're already late."

As much as Nic Tatum needed a nap, he found it difficult to fall asleep for more than a few minutes at a time. He finally gave up the attempt and got on his treadmill for twenty minutes, then lifted weights for another fifteen before heading for the shower. He and Cindy had decided to go out for dinner at six. At four, he got in his car and drove to Rockville, where Sheila Klaus lived. He didn't know why he decided to do that; it was as though someone was pulling strings and guiding him there. He didn't intend to confront her again. He just had this unstated need to see whether she had returned.

He parked across the street from the house and looked for signs of life. Another unopened newspaper sat on the front step, a signal that Sheila wasn't back from San Francisco. He got out of the car and went to the front door, where he saw something else on the step, a box. He picked it up and read the label: Tangelos from a farm in California. The return address was a post office box in San Mateo. A shame, he thought as he put the box down. If she wasn't back soon, the fruit would go to waste.

Convinced that he'd made yet another useless trip, he returned to his car, but instead of driving off, he sat, the motor off, and gazed at the house as though he could make her appear through sheer will-power. After ten minutes of this, he started the car and was about to pull away when a taxi pulled up in front of the house and Sheila got out. Tatum watched as the driver opened the trunk and removed a small carry-on suitcase. Sheila fished in her purse for the fare, paid him, picked up the suitcase, and went to the door, where she used her key to enter. A few seconds later, she reappeared to fetch the newspaper and box, went inside again, and closed the door.

Tatum considered changing his mind and going to the house. But after fierce internal debate, he fought the urge, pulled away from the curb, and headed back to the District and his dinner date with Cindy, his departure observed through a partially open drape by Carla Rasmussen.

When he was out of view, Carla used a kitchen knife to open the box. Inside were two rows of the orange fruit. She removed the top layer. Beneath it, wrapped in the same crinkly paper used to protect each individual piece of fruit, was a Smith & Wesson 639 Airweight revolver with a matte black finish. Wrapped next to it was a box of .38 special ammunition.

CHAPTER

41

When the mood for crêpes struck Nic and Cindy, they favored the Napoleon Bistro in the vibrant Adams Morgan section of the city. They ate on the patio, and over the restaurant's signature dish, Montmarte Crêpes, Nic told Cindy about his trip to Rockville and that he'd seen Sheila return from San Francisco.

"Did you speak with her?" Cindy asked.

"No. I was tempted to but asked myself what was to be gained. There's nothing I can do to get the truth out because the authorities have stonewalled any inquiries into the Sedgwick murder and Sheila's role in it. It's like the government is covering up her involvement, and *she* sure as hell doesn't want to have the truth come out—if she even knows what the truth is. I've been chasing my tail, and for what? As long as she's under Borger's control, there's not a damn thing I or anyone else can do about it."

"Do you know why she went to San Francisco under that other name?"

"Carla Rasmussen."

"Why did *they* go in the first place?" Cindy asked.

"Who knows? Maybe Borger needs to reinforce the control he has over her." A shrug accompanied that supposition.

"This Dr. Borger is an evil man," she said.

"Evil incarnate," said Tatum. "But he's beyond any chance of having to pay for what he's done to her, and undoubtedly to others. "The government backs him, and the government will cover for him. I don't know what I was thinking, Cindy, trying to get to the bottom of it and bring it to light. Like you said, I'm not somebody wearing a cape out to save mankind."

She giggled. "I think you'd look sexy in a cape."

"Just a cape?"

"Uh-huh."

"I'll give it a try when we get home."

She was well aware how frustrated he was and wanted him to put the Sheila Klaus matter to rest. But was that possible? Would it ever be? What he knew, and what he believed, weren't likely to fade over time. Were she able, she would have wielded a magic wand and made it all go away, dismissed this Sheila Klaus and her strange second personality to some never-never land far away from him—and from her. The truth was that she'd fallen in love with Nicholas Tatum and didn't like competing for his attention with another woman—*two* other women, Sheila and Carla.

He helped assuage her concerns when he said as they entered her apartment, "The hell with Sheila Klaus, Sheldon Borger, and the rest of them. If I never see or hear of Sheila Klaus again, it will be too soon." He kissed her and asked, "Have you seen my cape?"

If there was a cape, it was soon lost in the tangle of their clothing as they quickly disrobed and fell into bed.

* * *

There must have been something in the air that evening in Washington, because Mac and Annabel Smith were feeling romantic, too. After an Italian dinner at Tosca, they returned to their apartment, changed into pajamas and robes, and Mac poured them snifters of cognac, which they enjoyed on the terrace. It was a crystal-clear night in the nation's capital, and surprisingly calm judging from what was on the news that day, no controversial pending legislation in Congress, no escalation of military operations or loss of a serviceman or -woman's life in some far-flung place, no drug-induced drive-by shooting to provide a gory front-page photo.

It had been a good day for the Smiths. Annabel had sold a valuable piece of pre-Columbian earthenware, and Mac had successfully settled a lawsuit brought against a colleague at the university. They toasted their respective successes.

"Looking forward to tomorrow?" Annabel asked.

"George Mortinson's big event? I am. That band they've booked is terrific."

"The music? What about hearing a stirring political speech?"

Mac laughed. "I love George," he said, "but I've heard enough stirring political speeches and seen enough nasty TV commercials. It'll be nice when the campaign is over."

"It will be soon," she said. "Let's make it an early night."

Forty-five minutes after going to bed, they fell into a peaceful sleep, smiles on their faces.

Mackensie Smith wasn't the only person who was eager for the campaign to end. George and Tricia Mortinson returned to their rented home after having attended a fund-raiser at the Hay-Adams hotel.

"I hate having to raise money," he commented as they undressed for bed.

"That won't stop once you're the president," she said from where she brushed her hair in front of a mirror on a makeup table.

"I know," he said. "The fat cats and corporations own the country, and they own Swayze lock, stock, and barrel."

"It'll be over soon," she said.

"And you'll be the first lady," he said, coming up behind and kneading her shoulders, "unless Swayze decides to invade Canada or Mexico and becomes what he'd really like to be, a war president."

She laughed. "Ready for the rally tomorrow?" she asked.

"I'm looking forward to it. You?"

"I'll be glad when it's over," she said, not adding that large public rallies made her especially nervous for his safety. She laid down her hairbrush, stood, and embraced him. "You know, George, that I would love you as much whether you became president of the United States or not."

"I know," he said, kissing her softly. "I never would have considered running if I didn't have you at my side. You'll be a great first lady."

"I'd rather be a great wife," she said.

All thoughts of being first lady vanished as they headed for bed, where they celebrated their love for each other.

And so all was well that night in Washington, D.C., and the weather report for the next day was clear skies, mild temperatures, and a gentle breeze.

A perfect day for a political rally.

CHAPTER 42

Meg Whitson arrived at the Ronald Reagan Building at five the following morning, where preparations were already under way for the rally. Workmen unloaded trucks of construction material that would be used to build the platform on which Mortinson and those closest to him would sit and from which he would give his speech. There were also the booths to house the soft drink and snack concessions, manned by Mortinson volunteers. A second, lower platform was constructed for the six-piece band; a state-of-the-art public address system was provided by a sound company that had worked with the campaign since its inception. Another group of workers established a rope line using stanchions and coils of thick yellow rope, while a group of volunteers prepared to hang banners containing large photos of Mortinson and his running mate, New Mexico governor Raymond Thomas, and hundreds of red, white, and blue balloons.

Meg greeted the lead Secret Service agent, whose fellow agents, supplemented by representatives from the FBI and CIA, scoured the premises for potential dangers and formulated plans for where security would be stationed throughout the event. She looked up at rooftops. If Mortinson were a sitting president, snipers would be positioned on them during the rally. A separate entrance to the sprawling Woodrow Wilson Plaza had been established the night before, through which all security personnel would pass, their identification established by ID badges, as well as a thumb scanner that verified who they were based upon fingerprints provided earlier.

"Looks like we lucked out with the weather," Meg said to the lead agent.

"Looks like it," the agent replied. He

turned from her as he heard a squawk on his small earbud and responded into a tiny microphone on the lapel of his suit jacket. Meg watched him with admiration. The Secret Service was an exemplary agency, their senses highly attuned to the potential of any trouble, eyes never straying from those who would shake their candidate's hand, their keen hearing alert to any sound that might indicate a looming danger.

After two hours, and pleased with the progress she saw, Meg left the area and went to a coffee shop to feed her growling stomach with eggs, bacon, toast, and two cups of coffee. She was exhausted. Knowing that she had to be up at four that morning, she'd tossed and turned in bed and was out of it long before the alarm went off. It always seemed to work that way.

At eight fifteen, she was at headquarters, where she went over a final to-do list. Meg Whitson lived for lists—she often joked that she had lists of lists—and was sure she'd be totally lost without them. At eleven, she returned to the Reagan Building and saw that everything was progressing as planned. The crowd would be admitted to the plaza beginning at one, the speeches kicking off at two. With any luck it would be over by three thirty, but that depended on how quickly Mortinson could personally greet each guest and how fast the two professional photographers could finish snapping candid shots of the candidate with his supporters.

She took the opportunity to admire some of the statuary in the plaza. *Bearing Witness,* a striking forty-foot-tall bronze work by the renowned sculptor Martin Puryear, jutted into the air at the western edge of the plaza, and a cast-aluminum sculpture, the *Federal Triangle Flowers* by Washington artist Stephen Robin—a single-stem rose and a lily, each ten feet high, twenty-four feet long, and seven feet wide, set atop limestone pedestals—dominated the large open space. She was especially fond of this piece and had stopped to admire it from different angles each time she'd been in the plaza.

She checked her watch. A half hour before the crowd would begin passing through the security checkpoints.

George and Tricia Mortinson had enjoyed a leisurely breakfast together. The only campaign event planned for that day was the rally at the Reagan Building, and the senator basked in not having to be somewhere at the crack of dawn. They read that morning's paper and discussed items in it, including a piece about the rally that would begin in a few hours.

"Your speech ready?" Tricia asked.

"A rehash of previous ones, with an added emphasis on initiating policies to benefit the middle class instead of the millionaires."

"Some of those millionaires have funded part of your campaign."

"And I shall be eternally grateful as long as they don't think they've bought me."

He went to a window overlooking the street and saw that his Secret Service contingent was in place and awaiting his departure from the house.

"They work hard," he commented.

"They certainly do. Think I'll hit the shower," she said, placing her hand on his neck as she passed.

A few hours later, their serene morning would end when they climbed into the back of the limo and headed for the Reagan Building.

* * *

The pace at the Virginia safe house was decidedly less leisurely than at the Mortinson home.

Puhlman and Gibbons had quietly packed their bags outside of Itani's presence. The young Arab American had slept until he was summoned to the phone by Puhlman to take a call from Sheldon Borger.

"Good morning, Iskander," Borger said. "Did you have a good night's sleep?"

"Yes. I have asked Mr. Gibbons when I would fight, but he says nothing. He tells me to be patient. I need to work out, to be ready."

"Of course you do, Iskander," Borger said in his silky-smooth, nicely modulated voice. "It will happen soon. Revenge is sweet, Iskander."

Puhlman, who stood close by, witnessed the change in Itani's face. Until that moment he'd been angry; his expression testified to that. Now, sheer serenity replaced the anger, his eyes focused across the room, his body's previous tension eased. Borger's use of the trance-inducing code *Revenge is sweet* had snapped Itani out of the present. He was now firmly under the doctor's control.

"It's time to right a wrong, Iskander," Borger said. "The golden chalice will soon be yours. Are you ready?"

"Yes."

"Good. Now do what you've been trained to do."

Itani handed the phone to Puhlman and walked into his bedroom, where Puhlman had laid out clothing for the day, a new pair of jeans, white sneakers, a royal blue T-shirt on which WESTSIDE BOXING CLUB, SAN MATEO, CA was emblazoned in white across the front, and a lightweight tan jacket with deep pockets at the sides. Affixed to the jacket was a large metal campaign button with Mortinson's smiling face on it, and the words "Mortinson for President." His personalized invitation to the rally was in one of the jacket's pockets. He dressed, slipped the plastic-encased ID card around his neck, checked himself in the mirror, and rejoined Puhlman and Gibbons.

"You look great, kid," Gibbons said.

Itani said nothing.

"Time to go," said Puhlman.

Gibbons stayed behind as Puhlman and

Itani left and walked four blocks before hailing a taxi. "The Ronald Reagan Building," Puhlman told the driver, who wore an earpiece and talked into a hands-free phone. He didn't bother to turn to look at his fares and pulled sharply away from the curb, a defective muffler breaking the morning's stillness.

Puhlman paid the fare and stood with Itani, observing the crowd that had now swelled at one of two entrances to the plaza. The sound of a jazz band playing "Sweet Georgia Brown" mixed with the noise from the gathered. As Puhlman looked into Itani's dark, doe-like eyes, he suffered a sudden twinge of regret. But it was soon replaced by a rush of adrenaline. He slapped Itani on the back and walked away.

As he distanced himself from the scene, he thought of the many months that had passed before he'd found the perfect subject for Borger, a young former prizefighter named Iskander Itani with a built-in hatred of Jews, Israel, and anyone who supported the Israeli state. So much had gone into preparing Itani to assassinate George Mortinson—the weeks of hypnotic sessions conducted by Borger, the lies about resurrecting Itani's boxing career, keeping him under wraps at the house, turning him into a pawn, a cat's paw as the French fable termed it—and finally this day had come, proof that with the right subject, and in the hands of a master hypnotist like Borger, the perfect assassin could be created.

It had gone smoothly except for the incident with Elena. Fortunately, that had happened near the end of the process, too late to interfere with the plans. It was all up to Itani now. He'd been thoroughly indoctrinated, including hours spent practicing using the small Smith & Wesson handgun. Puhlman had suggested taking him to a firing range, but Borger had rejected the idea because of the possibility of it being traced back and because he was confident that Itani didn't need to practice actually shooting the weapon. It would be loaded with five bullets when he picked it up from where it would be left inside the plaza. All he had to do was point it at Mortinson and pull the trigger. You didn't need marksmanship practice to kill someone from a foot away.

Puhlman had a taxi drop him two blocks from the house and walked the rest of the way.

Gibbons paced the room. "Where's the kid?" he asked.

"I dropped him off."

"Where?"

"It doesn't matter. Come on, let's get out of here."

They toted their luggage back to where Puhlman had gotten out of the taxi and hailed another.

"Reagan National Airport," Puhlman told the driver.

As they drove, Puhlman asked whether Gibbons had his false driver's license to show to security.

"Yeah, it's right here." He pulled his wallet from his pants pocket, retrieved the license, and showed it to Puhlman.

"That's your real license," Puhlman said. "What the hell are you carrying that for?"

"I got the phony one here, too," Gibbons grumbled and flashed it in front of Puhlman's face.

"Just don't get them mixed up at the airport," Puhlman said. "Let's not screw up now."

*   *   *

Itani joined the line of people waiting to be granted access to the mall as he'd been instructed by Borger, his invitation in hand. People in front and behind chatted about many things, including the potential benefits to the nation of a Mortinson presidency. Itani heard them, but the words meant nothing. He was in his own hypnotic-induced world, his mind filled only with what he'd been told to do by Sheldon Borger.

"I love that music," Mac Smith said. He, Annabel, Nic Tatum, and Cindy Simmons stood in line a few people behind Itani. Smith was a devoted jazz lover and lately had been transferring his extensive collection of vinyl records to compact discs.

"If Mac is ever reincarnated, he wants to come back as Thelonious Monk," Annabel quipped.

"Who's he?" Cindy asked.

The line moved forward before Mac could respond.

Itani reached the Secret Service agent and handed him the invitation. The agent looked him up and down and leaned closer to read his ID tag. "Driver's license?" he asked.

Itani stared at the agent.

"Driver's license, please."

Itani fumbled for his wallet and found his license, which he hadn't used in a long time. Fortunately, it hadn't expired. The agent looked up from the license at Itani's face, then down at the photo. Satisfied, he checked off Itani's name from a long list of invitees, handed it back, and waved him through.

The crowd in the plaza was in a festive mood, buoyed by the fair weather and the toe-tapping music. The Smiths and Nic and Cindy made their way to a concession stand, where they took cups of soda and bags of popcorn from the enthusiastic young volunteers, some of millions who'd supported this candidate who had promised a change to the way business was done in Washington. Those who'd been around the nation's capital longer knew that changing Washington was an idealistic fantasy, but it played well on the campaign trail.

They stood talking when Meg Whitson approached. "Mr. and Mrs. Smith," she said. "Great to see you."

Smith introduced Nic and Cindy.

"Looks like you've got a success on your hands," Tatum said.

Meg looked to the sky and pressed her hands together in a prayerful symbol. "So far," she said, laughing.

"The senator's rarin' to go?" Smith asked.

"Oh, sure, he always is. I spoke with him a few times this morning. He's enjoying a leisurely morning with his wife."

"Hard to find leisure moments when you're running for president," Annabel said.

"Or when you're chief of staff," Meg said. "Oops, got to run. Looks like they're having a problem with the steps leading up to the speaker's platform."

Nic and Cindy drifted away from the Smiths, who'd gotten into a conversation with a professor and his wife from GW.

"Think he'll recognize me?" Cindy asked.

"Mortinson? Of course he will," Tatum said. "How could he forget the most beautiful woman he's ever signed a picture to?"

She punched his arm.

As the crowd milled about, Colin Landow's deputy, Bret Lancaster, who'd come into the plaza through the entrance reserved for security personnel, casually moved in the direction of the Stephen

Robin sculpture. When he was certain that no one was paying attention, he slipped the Smith & Wesson 638 Airweight revolver nestled in a sand-colored sack from his pocket and secreted it in a crevice in the sculpture of swirling cast-aluminum flowers on the limestone pedestal. Satisfied that his action had gone unseen, he strolled away, a satisfied smile on his lips.

The county fair atmosphere was interrupted when Meg Whitson took the microphone to announce that Senator Mortinson would be arriving any minute and suggested that everyone move closer to the speaker's platform. The more than four hundred people heeded her advice and stood shoulder to shoulder in anticipation of Mortinson's entrance, which occurred five minutes later to the band's spirited rendition of "Happy Days Are Here Again." He was met with thunderous applause mingled with shouts of support. He took the stage accompanied by his stunning wife, his running mate and his spouse, and a handful of staffers including Meg. Secret Service agents assigned to him stood in front of the platform, their eyes scanning the crowd.

Mortinson waved energetically, his familiar wide smile very much in evidence, and did nothing to settle people down. The crowd eventually quieted on its own, and Governor Raymond Thomas, candidate for vice president of the United States, stepped to the microphone and welcomed the faithful. After some remarks and a few well-aimed barbs at President Swayze, Thomas introduced Mortinson, who sprang to his feet, embraced his running mate, took the microphone, and launched into his prepared speech, carefully crafted to elicit applause every few lines. He spoke longer than planned and ended with, "I'm looking forward to personally thanking each of you for your support. Because of you, this long and arduous campaign will be successful and the American people will have back their voice."

He stepped away from the microphone to allow Meg Whitson to direct the crowd to form a single line to the side of the platform to shake the candidate's hand and to have a picture taken. Volunteers stood ready to coordinate the photo numbers with the subject's name and address on the master list of those in attendance.

Signed prints would be mailed to them at a later date.

The band kicked off "When the Saints Go Marching In."

Mac and Annabel found themselves among the first in line. Smith looked for Nic and Cindy, and spotted them at the opposite side of the plaza.

"I don't know why we're bothering to get in line," Mac commented to Annabel. "It's not like we don't know him."

"Go with the flow," she retorted. "I feel good being a part of this."

A number of people shared Mac's reluctance to wait in line and had begun to vacate the area. Nic and Cindy were now positioned in the middle of those who inched forward. Directly in front of them was Iskander Itani. Nic had noticed him and had read his T-shirt, which made him smile. George Mortinson often expressed pride in his speeches that his supporters represented a true cross section of America. If a prizefighter from a boxing club had come all the way from California to express his support, Mortinson's claim certainly had validity.

Itani stood silently, taking small steps

forward as the line moved. The revolver that Bret Lancaster had hidden on the metal sculpture, now free of its cloth bag, sat in Itani's right-hand jacket pocket. Borger had instructed him to keep his hand out of the pocket until he was about to shake Mortinson's hand. Then he was to pull out the palm-sized weapon and fire four shots into the candidate at point-blank range.

Things moved surprisingly quickly and smoothly. Tricia Mortinson beamed as Mac and Annabel wished Mortinson well, thanked him for having invited them, and posed for their photo. Mortinson said to Mac just before the picture was snapped, "Remember that when I'm president you have to let me win when we play."

Mac laughed and said, "I'll think about it, Mr. President," as the photographer's strobe went off.

They retreated to a relatively abandoned area of the plaza and watched others go through the ritual they'd just experienced.

"There's Nic and Cindy," Annabel commented, pointing to the young couple only two persons removed from Mortinson. A middle-aged woman wearing a broad-brimmed red, white, and blue straw hat with Mortinson campaign buttons surrounding the crown shook Mortinson's hand and posed with him for the photo. Her smile lit up the plaza, which caused Mac and Annabel to grin, too.

Next to shake hands was Itani. Mortinson leaned closer to read what was on Itani's T-shirt, bringing him only a foot or two from the young man. As Mac and Annabel watched, Mortinson said something to Itani. Then, in an instant, there was the sound of shots being fired—one, two, three, four sharp reports that sounded like the proverbial firecrackers—*snap, crackle, pop*—barely heard above the crowd noise until . . .

Until screams erupted from the receiving line.

Nic Tatum and a Secret Service agent reacted in concert. Tatum flung himself into Itani, knocking him to the ground. As Itani raised the revolver to his temple and was about to squeeze off the remaining bullet, the agent struck his arm, causing the weapon to be pointed upward. The final shot flew harmlessly into the air. Two other agents pounced on Itani, ripping the revolver from his hand and securing him.

Pandemonium broke out. Some people ran for the exits, others converged on where Mortinson lay on the ground, a swelling of blood seeping through what had been a pristine white shirt. His wife, Tricia, on her knees, ran her hand over his face. Tears cascaded down her cheeks as she said over and over, "George, George, oh, my God, George."

"Get back! Give us room," an agent implored. "Get the medics."

Two EMTs manning an ambulance that had been assigned to stand by at the event rushed to the scene and knelt over the fallen candidate. After checking vital signs, one looked up at Meg Whitson and shook his head.

Itani, pinned to the ground by two agents, didn't struggle.

Nor did George Mortinson.

There was no life left in him.

"He's been shot!"

Borger's cook, who had been watching initial televised reports of the assassination on a small TV in the kitchen, ran into his study.

"I know," Borger said "I—"

"They showed his picture," the cook said through tears. "It was Iskander."

"Yes," Borger said with exaggerated sadness. "I can't believe it. To think that he was here, that I treated him for his headaches and tried to get his life back on track. It's devastating."

"What shall we do?"

"Nothing at the moment," he replied. "I'll notify the authorities, of course. Why don't you go home now? It's best that you be with your family at a tragic time like this."

She left the room, and Borger continued to watch the reports, vacillating between pleasure that the deed had been done and dismay that Itani hadn't successfully killed himself as he'd been programmed to do. Building his suicide into the plan was a fail-safe measure. Borger was confident that Itani's induced global amnesia would hold, hopefully forever, but his death would have ensured that no one could ever break through the control he had over him.

He had no intention of contacting the authorities, at least not yet. Instead he dialed Mica Sphere's number.

"Have you heard?" was the first thing she said. "Senator Mortinson has been assassinated."

"Yes, I've heard. That's why I'm calling. It was the young man I'd been treating, Iskander. You met him here at the house. Remember?"

"Of course I remember. Sheldon, this is terrible. What will it mean for you?"

"Oh, I suppose I'll become involved simply because he was a patient of mine."

"He seemed to be more than that," she said. "He told me that you were going to help him start boxing again."

"Which was part of the treatment. He was a terribly confused young man, riddled with anxieties. But how could I possibly have known that he harbored such hatred? It never came out in our sessions."

"Did you know that he'd gone to Washington?"

"No. All I knew was that he was gone. It didn't overly concern me. Patients like him are terribly impetuous. I assumed he'd gone back to his family, or had decided to leave the city."

"I have to call the police and tell them that I met him," she said. "They'll want to know."

"Yes, you must do that, Mica, but you sound terribly upset. I suggest that you have yourself under control before contacting anyone. You'll want to give a cogent, factual accounting. Why don't you come here first? I'm alone—the cook and housekeeper are gone—and we can talk about it. Neither of us should be alone at a time like this."

"Maybe you're right. I'll close the shop and—"

"I'll be waiting," he said.

He hung up, sat back, and rubbed his eyes. That Mica had met Itani at the house meant little. Authorities would soon learn that Itani had been there without her help. That was all built into the plan. He, Dr. Sheldon Borger, had treated this confused young man just as he'd provided help to others throughout his distinguished career. No, he wasn't overly concerned about his connection with the assassin. Itani's family knew that he'd been staying with him, as did the cook and housekeeper. But there was nothing to indicate that anything had occurred aside from having treated him. Just a doctor and his patient.

There was, however, the matter of Elena Marciano. Itani had told Mica that he had a girlfriend named Elena. Had Mica read about Elena's murder and subsequent discovery in the bay? Maybe, maybe not. Even if she had, it was unlikely that she'd link the dead Elena to Itani based upon only a first name. But that possibility couldn't be disregarded.

He went to the kitchen, prepared a tray

of crackers and an assortment of cheeses, opened a bottle of his best red wine, and returned to his study to await Mica's arrival.

After Mica had hung up, she went into the small office at the rear of the shop where her accountant was preparing the monthly financial statement. His attention at that moment, however, was on a TV set tuned to CNN. "I can't believe this," he muttered as nonstop coverage of the Mortinson assassination played on the screen.

"I met him," Mica blurted out.

"Met who?"

"The man who shot Mortinson. I spent time with him only a few days ago at Sheldon Borger's house."

"Whoa," the accountant said. "You actually met this nut?"

"Yes." She told him of the circumstances that had brought them together.

"You'd better let someone know," he said. "Call the police."

The anchor on TV broke into the report: "We have new details about the man who shot and killed Senator George Mortinson. His name, according to sources within the

Washington police department, is Iskander Itani. His driver's license indicates that he's from San Francisco and gained entry to the Mortinson rally as a member of a boxing club in San Mateo, California. Statements from individuals present at the rally say that after killing the senator, he attempted to kill himself, but a Secret Service agent deflected the shot." The anchor was handed a piece of paper. "The alleged killer is twenty-six years of age. According to our sources, he has refused to say anything to authorities. We've also been told that the authorities are trying to determine how he managed to bring a gun into the rally where security was tight. We'll bring you more details as they become available."

"I'm closing up," Mica told the accountant. "I just got off the phone with Sheldon . . . Sheldon Borger, the psychiatrist. I'm going to his house."

"Call the police first, Mica," the accountant said.

She dialed 911, told the operator that she had important information regarding the Mortinson killing, and was put through to the SFPD, where a detective took the call. After telling him that she'd known the shooter, she mentioned that she'd met him at the home of Dr. Sheldon Borger. "Dr. Borger is a friend," she said. "He's a psychiatrist who'd been treating the young man who shot the senator."

"Where are you?" the detective asked.

She told him.

"Don't leave," Mica was told. "We'll have someone there shortly."

The detective hung up and told others in the office about the call.

"Wait a minute," Detective Duane Woodhouse said. "What's this about Dr. Borger?"

After Woodhouse had been filled in on the gist of the call, he told a colleague, "Get hold of the FBI. Tell them to send someone to the caller's address. I'm heading there now."

While Mica awaited the arrival of the police, she called Borger and told him why she wouldn't be coming, at least not right away.

"Oh, Mica, I thought you agreed to not contact the police until we've had a chance to talk."

"I wasn't sure what to do, Sheldon. It doesn't matter. I would have had to contact them at some point. I'll come after I've spoken with them."

Word that Itani was from San Francisco sent the FBI's headquarters on Golden Gate Avenue into high gear. Using information transmitted from the bureau in Washington, the special agent in charge of the San Francisco office sent special agents scurrying across the city and neighboring counties. A team was dispatched to San Mateo to interview people at the boxing club. Another went to the home address taken from Itani's driver's license. When the call from Mica came in from SFPD, two special agents were told to meet Detective Woodhouse at Mica Sphere's shop.

Woodhouse, a second detective, and two agents sat with Mica in her office after her accountant, whose name and address were taken, had been told to leave.

"Tell us about your meeting with Mr. Itani," an agent said as he placed a small tape recorder on her desk.

Mica gave them a succinct accounting of how she'd ended up having a drink with Itani at Borger's house. When she'd finished, an agent asked if she could remember any further details of what they'd talked about.

"He was a nice young man," she said, "very polite but not very talkative. He seemed to be in his own world at times."

"What did he tell you about his relationship with Dr. Borger?"

"Just that Dr. Borger was helping him with headaches, and that he was also helping him resume his boxing career." She smiled. "He was very sweet. He told me that he had a girlfriend. Her name was Elena, I think."

Woodhouse jumped into the questioning. "You're sure the girl's name was Elena?" he asked, unable to keep enthusiasm from his voice.

She nodded. "Yes," she said, "that was the name."

The agents, unaware of why Woodhouse had injected this line of questioning, followed up. "Can you tell us more about this Elena?" one asked. "Where she lives, a last name?"

"He did mention her last name," she said, her face twisted as she tried to remember. "It was a common name. Jones!

Yes, I think it was Jones. That's all I know. Sorry."

"You say that Mr. Itani was living with Dr. Borger?" an agent asked. "Isn't it unusual for a psychiatrist to have a patient living with him?"

"I suppose so," she said, "but Dr. Borger is a very compassionate physician. He's treated some big celebrity names, and patients have stayed with him before. It gives him a chance to do more in-depth, sustained treatment."

One of the agents said, "We'd like you to come with us, Ms. Sphere."

"Where? Why?"

"Our headquarters. We'll want a detailed statement from you."

"I've already given you one," she said. "You have it on tape."

"Yes, ma'am, but we're dealing with the assassination of a leading political figure. We can take you in as a material witness, but we'd rather not."

"I have to close the shop."

"Just make it quick."

"Can I make a phone call first?"

"All right, but we have to move."

Woodhouse and one of the agents went to the sidewalk. "Let me bring you up to date on something," the detective said. He recounted his interest in Borger because of the Elena Marciano case.

"This dead prostitute might have been involved with the shooter?"

"Seems so, doesn't it?" Woodhouse responded.

"And this psychiatrist, Borger, was involved with both of them?"

"Right again."

Peter Puhlman and Jake Gibbons arrived back in San Francisco early that evening and went directly from the airport to Borger's house. Gibbons was in an agitated state. He and Puhlman had heard coverage of the assassination on the taxi's radio, including that the alleged assassin was a twenty-six-year-old male named Iskander Itani.

"What the hell is going on?" Gibbons demanded the minute he walked through the door. "The kid shot the next president, for Christ's sake. Jesus!"

"Calm down," Borger said, although internally he was anything but calm.

"You knew that this was goin' to happen all along, didn't you?" Gibbons yelled.

"I had no idea that he would do what he did," Borger said. "It doesn't matter. It's done. I have money for you to leave the city and—"

A buzz indicated that someone was at the gate. Borger looked out the window. A half dozen cars were at the foot of the driveway. A voice came through the speaker: "Dr. Borger, FBI special agents Carlson and Morel. We're with detectives from the San Francisco Police Department. We wish to speak with you."

Borger looked at Puhlman and Gibbons. The timing was atrocious.

"What are you going to do?" Puhlman asked.

"Let them in," Borger said, forcing a smile. "Go into my study. I'll speak with them out here. If they realize that you're here, I'll say that you work for me and that we've been having a meeting. Say nothing about having been in Washington. Understand?"

"I want out of this," Gibbons said.

Puhlman grabbed Gibbons's arm and yanked him in the direction of the study.

Once they were behind its closed door, Borger said into the speaker, "I'll open the gates." He pushed a button and watched as the cars piled into the driveway, led by two marked SFPD vehicles.

He opened the door and greeted the two agents, and a familiar face, Detective Duane Woodhouse. "I've been expecting you," Borger said. "I've just heard about the dreadful event that's taken place in Washington this afternoon and that a patient of mine was involved. Come in, come in. I'm eager to cooperate in any way I can."

They went to the living room. Borger sat, the agents and Woodhouse remained standing.

"I suppose you want to know anything and everything about Iskander, about Mr. Itani. Let me begin by saying that in more than thirty years of practice, I have never had anything even approaching this happen. Where do I begin? He became my patient because of debilitating headaches, the result of having been badly beaten in two previous boxing matches. He was confused, in pain, frightened, almost suicidal.

I took him on as a patient without compensation and—"

Five minutes into the questioning, Gibbons's loud voice was heard from behind the door to the study.

"Someone else is here?" an agent asked.

"Yes," Borger said. "Colleagues of mine. We were having a meeting when you arrived."

Woodhouse had noticed two suitcases in the foyer when they'd entered and asked, "Going on a trip, Dr. Borger?"

"Oh, those suitcases. No, no trips planned."

"We'd like to speak with the others," said an agent.

"Of course, although I'm sure they have nothing to offer."

He opened the door to the study and said, "We have visitors from the FBI and police. They're here regarding the terrible thing that happened in Washington today. Come, they'd like to meet you."

Gibbons followed Puhlman from the room and greeted the agents. Woodhouse took note of Gibbons's nervousness;

he sweated profusely. He also wondered what possible business connection the rough-hewn man might have with the smooth-talking psychiatrist.

"In previous conversations I've had with Dr. Borger," Woodhouse said, "he's admitted that he was friendly with a Ms. Elena Marciano who, according to Dr. Borger, was also a patient. Did either of you gentlemen know Mr. Itani or Ms. Marciano?"

Gibbons shook his head. Borger jumped in and said, "I believe they might have met her once or twice."

"That's right," said Puhlman. "I met her a couple of times. Itani, too."

"You?" Woodhouse asked Gibbons.

He shrugged and said, "Yeah, maybe, once or twice."

"We have a witness who says that Mr. Itani told her that Ms. Marciano, or the other name she used, Jones, was his girlfriend," Woodhouse said.

Borger laughed. "Oh, my, how pathetic. It was all part of his fantasies. I did introduce them once, and I remember how smitten he was with her, his eyes following her every time she crossed the room. He lived in a dreamworld, gentlemen. It was one of the things I tried to work on with him, to give him a healthier sense of reality."

"Ms. Marciano is dead," Woodhouse said flatly.

"I'm well aware of that," Borger said.

"Not a great track record, Doctor," Woodhouse said. "One patient assassinates the next president of the United States, the other is murdered and dumped in the bay."

"I resent that," Borger said.

Woodhouse said nothing as the agents asked more questions of Puhlman and Gibbons. When they were finished, Puhlman said, "We were just leaving. Those are our suitcases in the hallway. Are we finished?"

"You both live in San Francisco?"

"Yes."

"How can we contact you?"

They gave their names and addresses and left.

"Obviously, Dr. Borger, your close knowledge of Mr. Itani will be valuable as we try and put together the pieces of Senator Mortinson's assassination. You aren't planning any trips."

"No, as I told you, no trips planned."

"The press will get hold of your connection and want statements from you. You're not to give any while the investigation continues."

"I have no intention of talking with the press. You have my word."

"We'll leave uniformed officers outside your house."

Borger started to protest, but the agent added, "For your protection."

"All right," Borger said. "I suppose I don't have a choice."

The agents were polite as they said good-bye to Borger, but Woodhouse, who was the last through the door, fixed Borger in a laser stare and said, "We'll be talking again, Doctor."

CHAPTER

44

WASHINGTON, D.C.

In Washington, Mortinson's assassination had sent an emotional tsunami washing over the city. The Woodrow Wilson Plaza had been locked down following the shooting, but by that time most people had fled. The FBI, CIA, and Department of Homeland Security had gone into high-alert status. Had the shooter, this Arab American named Iskander Itani, acted alone, or was he part of a larger plot? The official rulings on the killings of John and Robert Kennedy and Martin Luther King were that Lee Harvey Oswald, Sirhan Sirhan, and James Earl Ray werc "lone nuts," demented, evil people who'd violently acted out their warped grievances.

Conspiracy theorists immediately went into action, blogging that another white-wash was in the making à la the Warren Commission, which had concluded that JFK's assassin, Lee Harvey Oswald, had not been part of a conspiracy, nor had Os-wald's killer, Jack Ruby, acted out of any-thing but a need to personally avenge the fallen president.

President Swayze held a press confer-ence in which he praised Mortinson as a formidable opponent, a man of integrity and vision, and assured the nation that the investigation would be thorough and ongoing. But he urged all Americans not to jump to conclusions about whether some sort of cabal was behind the shoot-ing. "From what we know at this early date the assassin"—he consulted his notes—"Mr. Iskander Itani, was not a part of any organized plot, and I repeat *not*. My prayers go out to the Mortinson family."

The Smiths navigated those left in the plaza and found Cindy Simmons, who wept openly, her arms wrapped tightly about herself.

"Where's Nic?" Mac asked.

"With agents," she replied, pointing to where he was being interviewed. "He knocked the bastard down," she said between sobs. "It can't be," she said. "It just cannot be."

Smith gave her a hug and said, "You were right behind him."

"I know," she said. "It all happened so fast."

"Did you or Nic have any hint that something was about to occur?"

"No. Nic had noticed him earlier and commented about his T-shirt. He's from some boxing club in California. Nic said that he looked a little odd, sort of a vacant expression on his face, but it didn't mean anything then. He joked about it. 'Too many punches,' he said. Oh, my God, this can't be true."

They waited until Tatum was able to join them.

"You knocked him down," Annabel said.

"Not soon enough. He tried to kill himself. He put the gun to his head, but an agent hit him and his arm went straight up. They wanted to know what I saw."

"Let's get out of here," Mac said. "I could use a stiff drink. We'll go back to the apartment."

The streets were now choked with people who'd heard the news and needed to leave their homes and stores and to join others in shock. Official vehicles, their sirens blaring, converged on the scene from every direction as Smith managed to find a cab.

Once at the apartment, Annabel turned on the TV and Mac made everyone a scotch and soda. They sat transfixed in front of the set, the words and images on Channel 5, the Washington CNN affiliate, jarring yet unreal. The reporters tried to keep up with information being fed from various sources, switching to correspondents around the country. Much of what was being reported was speculation based upon rumors culled from unsubstantiated sources.

Mac ordered in Chinese food. As he paid the delivery man, the TV coverage shifted to a press conference from FBI headquarters in the J. Edgar Hoover Building on

Pennsylvania Avenue. At the podium was the bureau's director.

"First of all," he said, "I urge you to report responsibly and not react to rumors that naturally circulate in events like this. That said, former Wisconsin senator George Mortinson, candidate for the presidency of the United States, was killed this afternoon by an alleged assailant identified as Iskander Itani, twenty-six years old, a resident of San Francisco. Senator Mortinson was pronounced dead at the scene. He'd been greeting visitors to a campaign rally at the Ronald Reagan Building at the time of the shooting. The alleged assailant was immediately taken into custody by the Secret Service and other agencies, including the Federal Bureau of Investigation. He is being held in a secure facility, the location of which I am not at liberty to disclose."

Tatum, who'd been sitting with his elbows on his knees, face cupped in his hands, sat up and said, "San Francisco." Mac, Annabel, and Cindy looked at him but kept their attention riveted on the screen.

The director continued. "I know that it is not unusual for some to suspect that a plot of some sort, a terrorist plot, is behind such assassinations, but I assure you that we have absolutely no information at this time to indicate that anyone was involved besides the alleged assassin.

"Your FBI has agents investigating the alleged assassin's background and is attempting to ascertain the motive for this senseless killing. I'll now take a few questions, but bear in mind that I am not able to discuss any aspect of the investigation."

A chorus of voices erupted in the room, reporters trying to outshout each other to gain his attention. The director dismissed the first three questions but answered the fourth, which was posed by a reporter from the *Washington Post.* "How can you say that you've ruled out a conspiracy? From the little we've learned so far, the shooter is an Arab."

"Mr. Itani is an Arab American, but let's not jump to premature conclusions," the director said sternly. "We'll schedule regular updates as further information becomes known to us."

With that, he left the podium, a cacophony of questions following him from the room.

Mac turned down the sound as Annabel served the Chinese dishes. They had little to say, nor did they eat with any relish. Nic and Cindy left at nine and went to her apartment, where they watched television until falling asleep on the couch. Mac and Annabel also stayed up taking in the steady stream of information, real and imagined, from the CNN studios, and they, too, made it to bed after dozing off. Unlike the previous romantic night for the Mortinsons, the Smiths, and Nic and Cindy, this one was somber for everyone involved.

Mac and Annabel had just gotten up the following morning and hadn't yet turned on the TV or read the newspaper, whose front page carried the sort of huge, bold-faced headline used only for meaningful, usually grim, events. Annabel answered the phone.

"It's Nic," Tatum said breathlessly. "Do you have the TV on?"

"We just got up."

"Turn it on quick!"

She did as the anchor was saying, "Let's go back to our correspondent in San Francisco."

A young familiar female face filled the

screen. "As I reported a few minutes ago, we've learned that the alleged killer of Senator George Mortinson, Iskander Itani, had been treated by a local psychiatrist here in San Francisco, Dr. Sheldon Borger. According to our sources, Mr. Itani was a patient of Dr. Borger's for a number of weeks and actually lived in the doctor's Nob Hill residence during that time. Dr. Borger is a well-known, well-respected physician whose patient roster includes a number of famous people from show business and industry. Attempts to reach the doctor have failed, but we will continue to try."

Annabel handed the phone to her husband.

"You heard it, Mac?" Tatum asked excitedly.

"Yes."

"I knew it yesterday when I heard that he was from San Francisco. I just knew it, damn it!"

"Hold on, Nic. That's a pretty big leap."

"What is it, Mac, a coincidence? Can't be. Sheila Klaus is a patient of Borger, who just happens to be a CIA-funded shrink doing mind-control experiments on unsuspecting men and women. She returns from seeing him and runs down Mark Sedgwick. Now another 'patient' of Dr. Borger, who stayed in his house, travels to D.C. and guns down the next president of the United States. *Coincidence?* Give me a break."

Smith's legal instincts told him to poke holes in Nic's conclusion, but he couldn't. As circumstantial as Tatum's evidence was—and it didn't even meet that standard—something told Mac that what the young psychologist was saying rang true.

"Let's say what you say is valid, Nic. What do you intend to do about it?"

"Tell the story to anybody who'll listen. Just before I called you, I got a call from the FBI. They want me at headquarters this morning to go over again what I saw yesterday. I'll start by telling them. If they won't listen, won't give it any credence, I'll go to the media."

"The press will run with it even though there's no proof of what you're claiming."

"That's not my problem. What's important is that Borger and others like him be stopped, that the CIA's insane experiments stop."

It occurred to Smith that accusing Borger of having manipulated George

Mortinson's killer could put Tatum on the receiving end of a slander suit. But judging from the zeal he exhibited on the phone, that possibility wouldn't deter him. But a much larger issue came to the attorney. If Borger was what Tatum claimed he was, a man capable of masterminding two murders including the leading candidate for president of the United States, he wouldn't hesitate to eliminate someone accusing him of those crimes, nor would his backers, that element presumably from the CIA that supported Borger in his efforts.

"Do what you think you have to do, Nic," Smith said, "but be careful how you go about it."

Smith ended the conversation with Tatum and told Annabel what Nic intended to do.

"He's walking into a hornets' nest," she said.

"A hornets' nest would be a walk on the Mall compared with what he's about to get into."

CHAPTER
45

SAN FRANCISCO/WASHINGTON, D.C.

Detective Duane Woodhouse had been involved in numerous cases over the years in which jurisdiction had become a thorny issue, with both the FBI and the SFPD withholding information, even evidence from each other. But the barriers seemed to have come down now that the next president had been gunned down in cold blood. This wasn't your run-of-the-mill local turf war; Woodhouse and the San Francisco FBI director shared everything they knew.

* * *

In Washington, investigators into the assassination went down every possible avenue in search of information.

An attempt was made to locate a taxi driver who might have taken Itani to the rally. It resulted in two dozen cabbies whose logs indicated that they'd dropped passengers off at the Ronald Reagan Building early that afternoon. They were shown a photo of Itani, but no one remembered having had such a fare, or in one case would not admit it. The driver who'd picked up Itani and a second man remembered them but opted to not tell the authorities because his resident status in the country was shaky. He didn't need trouble with Immigration.

Other agents questioned the flight attendant who'd worked the flight Itani had taken to Washington from San Francisco. She remembered him well, even knew the drinks she'd served him.

"Was he traveling alone? she was asked.

"There were two other men with him. I mean, they sat on either side of him in coach, but I can't say that they were traveling together. I mean, I don't know if they were friends before the flight."

"Can you describe them?"

"Oh, wow, I think so." She laughed. "One of them kept complaining about the size of the seats in coach. They were big guys. I know that they talked to each other, although the one in the middle, the one who shot the senator, didn't say much. He asked me for a drink, a Tom Collins or something like that. We don't carry that drink on board so one of the big men told me how to make it." She welled up. "Is he really the man who shot the senator? It's scary that he was that close to me." She broke into tears and hugged herself.

Itani was held in isolation and under twenty-four-hour guard in a cell at Fort McNair, the two-hundred-year-old army base at 4th and P streets, on land where the Potomac and Anacostia rivers merge. Teams of FBI special agents took turns around the clock interrogating him.

"When did you decide to kill the senator?" they asked.

Itani's answer: "I want to see my mother and brothers."

"You have to answer our questions before you can see them."

Itani hadn't been told that his family had

been taken into protective custody in San Francisco and flown on a government aircraft to Washington, where they were being held in secured quarters at the Washington Naval Yard, not far from where Itani was sequestered and where the Washington Nationals baseball team played its home games.

"Why did you kill Senator Mortinson?"

Itani: "He had to die."

"Where did you get the weapon?"

Itani: "I want to see Elena."

"Who's Elena?"

Itani: "I want to see my family."

"Did anyone help you plan killing Senator Mortinson?"

"No. He was a bastard. He had to die. I want to see my family."

Armed with information gathered from the flight attendant, the agents pressed Itani to admit that he'd traveled from San Francisco with two other men, which he vehemently denied. Because they didn't have tangible information about his alleged traveling companions, they were unable to resolve that lead, at least until some corroborating evidence surfaced.

And so it went, interrogation after interrogation, the agents' efforts stonewalled at every turn. Some leading attorneys called for Itani to have the benefit of legal counsel and to be properly arraigned, their protests countered by FBI and other government agency claims that Itani represented a threat to national security and was being held as an enemy combatant.

And conspiracy buffs ratcheted up their theories that Itani was part of a larger plot.

In San Francisco, Detective Duane Woodhouse had another meeting with the FBI's regional director, who outlined for him the result of the questioning of the flight attendant.

Woodhouse laughed. "I complain about those small coach seats all the time," he said. "You have names of the other men, the big guys as she described them?"

"Yes, based upon their seat assignments." The director named them.

"Frankly, that's disappointing," Woodhouse said. "I thought the names you came up with might have been different."

"Sorry to disappoint you."

"You'll follow up on their identities."

"We already have. The names on their

tickets, and the IDs used at Security, don't match up with anyone. False names."

"Which means they *were* traveling with him. Why else go to the bother of using phony identities?"

The director ended the meeting by asking how Woodhouse's investigation of Elena Marciano's murder was progressing.

"We're making progress," he said. "We sent officers to boatyards in the area where her body surfaced to see whether anyone had rented a boat on the day that the ME determined she'd died. It would have been a wasted exercise if the killer owned his or her own boat, but it was worth a stab. And it paid off. The owner of a boat rental company says that he rented a boat to two men early on the morning in question. One of them signed the rental agreement and gave his name and address: Jacob Gibbons, the same guy who was at Borger's house, Borger's so-called business associate. The boatyard owner provided sketchy descriptions of the men, one big and 'tough looking,' as he put it, the other also big but 'sort of puffy.' He didn't have a name for the man with Gibbons, but we're assuming that it was Peter Puhlman, the other guy at Borger's house."

"Another connection between Dr. Borger and the murder," the FBI director mused. "Anything else come out of it?"

"Yeah. We ran the names of Gibbons and Puhlman through the FBI's national database, and the results came back just before I came here. Gibbons is a former prizefighter who'd had run-ins with the law in San Francisco over the years, mostly connected with loan sharks and minor-league hoodlums. His name also surfaced as the result of what was described by Washington cops as having been involved in a minor bar fracas there. No arrests were made, but names of the participants were noted and entered into the daily report. This is what you'll find interesting. The dustup in the bar occurred just a few days before the assassination."

"Then Gibbons was in D.C. at that time."

"Right. And if what we suspect is correct, he was one of the two men the flight attendant said were with Itani on the plane."

The director scribbled notes as Woodhouse talked. "What have you found out about Mr. Puhlman?"

Woodhouse sighed and said, "Puhlman is a psychiatrist who's been charged with Medicare fraud on two occasions. Charges were dropped both times. He's been sued twice, once by a landlord claiming back rent was owed, and once by a woman who claimed he'd made unwanted sexual advances to her during a therapy session. Both suits were settled out of court. By the way, did the flight attendant describe the second man as 'puffy'?"

"No."

"That's how the boatyard owner described him. You've never had the pleasure of meeting Mr. Puhlman, but 'puffy' would be an apt description."

They ended their meeting and pledged to stay in close touch as new information developed.

Woodhouse returned to his office and met with colleagues to report on what had come out of the meeting.

"Catch this," a junior detective said as he handed Woodhouse a report that had just come in from the FBI after the bureau, at the urging of the SFPD, had run a check on the tax status of Borger, Puhlman, and Gibbons. Borger's record as a taxpayer was clean, everything paid up to date, but neither Gibbons nor Puhlman had filed tax returns for the past two years.

"They got paid off the books," the detective offered.

"Right," Woodhouse said, "but for what? Borger says that these two guys are in business with him. What kind of business? Dumping murdered hookers' bodies in the bay?"

Woodhouse and his wife had planned dinner out at Waterbar at the Embarcadero. She'd already secured the table when he walked in a half hour late. "Sorry," he said, kissing her cheek and taking the chair across from her. "I got tied up."

"The Marciano case?" she asked, knowing the answer. It was all her husband had talked about for the past few days.

Woodhouse's obsession with the Marciano murder and the possible role Sheldon Borger had played in it wasn't hard to miss. His wife had seen it too often before, cases that were particularly grim and involving victims with whom her husband had bonded in a way. She was never comfortable when he worked on such cases but understood that it went with the territory of being a detective. Like all cops, he spent his days, and too many nights, dealing with the sort of carnage and evil people that most of society only read about in novels and see in movies.

After twenty-two years on the force, Woodhouse was well aware that turning a case into a personal vendetta was futile at best. But this one was different. Very different. There was a beautiful young woman whose life had been snuffed out prematurely. Sure, she'd been a prostitute, a lawbreaker in her own right. But she didn't deserve to die by a vicious blow to the head and dumped into San Francisco Bay. The vision of her mother coming to San Francisco to identify her daughter's body had stayed with him.

Now there was the assassination of a man who was poised to become president. Woodhouse liked George Mortinson and had intended to vote for him.

But that wasn't the driving force behind his obsession.

It was Dr. Sheldon Borger.

The detective had no idea how Borger might have been involved in the assassination, nor did he have any evidence that he'd played a direct part in Elena Marciano's murder. But he knew one thing for certain. He'd formed an immediate dislike and distrust of the man and was committed to pulling out all the stops to nail him for something—anything.

Dinner at Waterbar was delicious as usual. Woodhouse successfully compartmentalized his constant obsession with Borger in order to be a pleasant, involved dinner companion to his wife of more than twenty years.

But once they were home and she'd gone to bed, he sat up late, nursing a drink and writing down what was known so far.

Elena Marciano had been a patient of Dr. Sheldon Borger. (Or was she more than a patient?)

Two men, Jacob Gibbons and Peter Puhlman, claimed to work for Borger. One of them, Gibbons, had rented a boat the morning that she was killed from a boatyard near where her body had been dragged from San Francisco Bay.

Both Gibbons and Puhlman fit the description given by the flight attendant

as possibly having accompanied Itani, the assassin, on the trip to Washington from San Francisco, and Gibbons had been in D.C. just days prior to Mortinson's murder, according to the local police. Yet if it was Gibbons with Itani, he'd booked his flight and gone through airport security using false identification. If it was Puhlman on that flight, he, too, had concealed his true identity. Why?

Senator Mortinson's killer, Iskander Itani, had been a patient of Dr. Borger's just as the slain prostitute had been. (Hell of a coincidence!)

According to a witness (Mica Sphere), Itani had claimed to her that he had a girlfriend named Elena. (The same Elena? Must be.)

When the detectives had visited Borger's house, there had been two suitcases in the foyer. (Gibbons and Puhlman just returning from Washington? Good bet.)

Itani had gained entrance to the rally using a forged pass from the Westside Boxing Club in San Mateo. Detectives had interviewed everyone there and reported on the anger the owners and managers expressed that their organization had been misused by someone in order to kill the next president. It was clear from the report that no one there had ever heard of Iskander Itani and that his credential was phony. (Question: Who arranged for Itani to be on the invite list, and who provided the false ID?)

Senator Mortinson was killed with four bullets from a Smith & Wesson 638 Airweight revolver. (How did he get the weapon past security? Everything points to his having had help.)

Woodhouse had also checked out Borger's history. The physician had a clean criminal record, not even a speeding ticket. The only blot on his professional record was an ethics charge brought against him by the girlfriend of a prominent West Coast columnist who'd shot himself after spending a night at Borger's house as a patient. The girlfriend claimed professional negligence. The charges were summarily dropped by Borger's professional peers.

Borger was in hibernation and being repeatedly questioned by the FBI about what he knew of Itani. According to the bureau, the psychiatrist had nothing to offer aside from having treated Itani as a patient.

Woodhouse knew in his bones that there was a link between Borger and both the Marciano murder and the assassination of Senator George Mortinson.

But feelings in one's bones didn't make a case in court.

After an abbreviated night's sleep, he went into the office the following morning and, after receiving approval from his superior, sent detectives to bring Jacob Gibbons and Peter Puhlman in for questioning in the Elena Marciano murder. His timing was perfection. They arrived at Gibbons's apartment hours before he was about to leave San Francisco, and it was obvious to the officers that Puhlman was poised to do the same.

CHAPTER
46

WASHINGTON, D.C.

Nic Tatum was twice interviewed by the FBI and found the experiences frustrating. They made it plain from the outset that their interest was in what he'd witnessed during the shooting, which took him only a few minutes to cover. It was then that he'd expressed his belief that Dr. Sheldon Borger may have played a role in the assassination. His thesis was summarily dismissed by the special agents. As one of them said, "We don't need idle speculation about CIA conspiracies, Dr. Tatum."

His second meeting with special agents from the bureau was even more dismaying.

There was a new face at the table. He was introduced as Bret Lancaster. "Mr. Lancaster is CIA, Dr. Tatum. He'll be sitting in on our meeting."

At first Lancaster's presence in the room dampened Tatum's enthusiasm for outlining his beliefs that Borger, using mind-control techniques developed and funded by the CIA, programmed Sheila Klaus and Iskander Itani. But he soon overcame his reluctance and laid out every aspect of his "case." The two special agents said little; Lancaster uttered not a word, nor did he take notes, leading Tatum to believe that he was being taped. At eleven that morning, when the allotted time was up, one of the agents thanked Tatum for his assistance, and an angry Nicholas Tatum left the room.

He had a lunch date with Mac Smith scheduled for twelve thirty, but before going to the restaurant he called his friend Dave Considine.

"Hi, Dave, it's Nic Tatum. Got a second?"

"Got two of them," Considine said. "A patient just left. What's up?"

"I was wondering if you ever ran across

someone at the Company named Lancaster. Bret Lancaster."

Considine paused before answering. "Yeah, I do remember him. Strange-looking guy."

"What's he do there?"

Another pause, longer this time. "He worked in the Medical and Psychological Analysis Center at Langley, reported to Colin Landow. Why are you interested in him?"

"He was at a meeting I just got out of."

"At the Company?"

"No, FBI. They've been interviewing me about the assassination. Lancaster works for Landow, huh? No surprise."

"I meant to call you. Not often that I have a hero for a friend. I read about what you did."

"Nothing heroic about it, Dave. You'll be reading more."

"Oh?"

"I've been trying to get someone in government to listen to me about Borger and his role in the assassination."

"*His role in it*? Hey, pal, are you going off the deep end?"

"Maybe so, but I'm not going to let the official stonewalling shut me up. I've avoided press interviews, but I think it's time that I start agreeing to them."

"I'd walk easy, Nic."

"Why? So that bastard Borger can keep on destroying people? Can't do that, Dave."

"I think we need to get together again, have a few drinks, maybe more than a few."

"Love to, but not for a few days. I'm sort of busy right now. Thanks for the info. I'll call."

Tatum asked Smith over lunch at a restaurant in the Watergate complex if he knew a good investigative reporter who would listen to his charge.

"I know a few of them," Smith replied, "but the good ones will question you the way a lawyer would, looking for evidence to corroborate what you're claiming. Your word won't be good enough, I'm afraid. Sandra Harding's column in today's *Post* questions the lone assassin theory. She wrote that chalking up the assassinations of the Kennedys, King, and now Mortinson strains the imagination. She doesn't cite anything to support her feelings, but maybe she'll listen to what you have to say."

"Maybe a book," Tatum mused.

"That's a possibility," Smith agreed. "I know a good literary agent in town and a couple of publishers in New York. Want me to run interference for you?"

"I'd really appreciate it, Mac. I'm not asking for anything for nothing. I'll be happy to pay whatever—"

Smith's raised palm stopped Tatum. "Let's not talk about money, Nic. But can I make a suggestion?"

"Sure."

"Take a few weeks to think this over. See how things fall in the investigation, what new information surfaces, whether others looking into George Mortinson's assassination will produce findings that back up your story. This isn't going to go away for a very long time."

They continued to discuss what Tatum intended to do over soup and salad. During the meal, Smith was aware of how tightly wound Tatum was. His eye twitched and his hand trembled when he passed the salt and pepper. "You look like you haven't slept in days," he commented.

"I look that way because I haven't," Tatum said. "So Governor Thomas is taking Senator Mortinson's place on the ballot."

"The party's national committee voted for Governor Thomas, same number of votes as each state had delegates to the convention. Their choice of Congresswoman LeClaire from Massachusetts as a running mate was a good one, I think, balances the geography and genders."

"Think they'll win?"

"Hard to say. President Swayze is now putting a national security spin on Mortinson's murder, claiming it *could* be the work of foreign terrorists, a prelude to worse things. If they still used the colored threat level meter, he'd have it up at red. His narrative will play with some people, but hopefully not enough to sway the election."

Tatum moved his hand and knocked over his water glass.

"Mind another suggestion?" Smith asked.

"No, of course not."

"Go home, get some sleep, maybe take that plane of yours for a spin, and enjoy a quiet dinner at some fancy restaurant with Cindy. You're a mess."

CHAPTER
47

SAN FRANCISCO

Woodhouse's petition to a San Francisco court to authorize a wiretap on Sheldon Borger's phone was denied. In turning down the request, the judge said, "You want me to tap the phone of one of the city's leading citizens on your unsubstantiated suspicion that he had something to do with the murder of a prostitute? Forget it, Detective."

"It's possible, sir, that he also played a role in the assassination of Senator George Mortinson," Woodhouse argued.

"Is that so?" said the judge behind a cynical smile. "Maybe our mayor and members of the city council did, too. What do you want me to do, tap the phones of every upstanding citizen in San Francisco? Nice try, Detective, but no cigar."

Had Woodhouse been successful in obtaining a tap, he might have heard Borger on the phone with Puhlman and Gibbons, going over their story, which had been concocted early on and was reinforced during the call as well as modified to suit the changing circumstances, namely, that Gibbons had gotten involved in the bar fracas in D.C. Had he not, no one would have known that they'd been there.

Without having been privy to the call, Woodhouse's interrogation of the two men amounted to a wasted exercise. Interviewed separately, they spouted the same story, so much so that it was evident to the detective that their responses had been rehearsed.

Faced with evidence that they'd flown to Washington on the same flight as the assassin, using bogus identifications, both Puhlman and Gibbons said, "We went there to try and set up a business deal. We used phony IDs so that our competitors wouldn't know what we were up to."

"What sort of business deal?"

"It didn't work out."

"But what sort of business are you involved in?"

"Consulting."

Woodhouse looked skeptically at Gibbons. "What sort of consulting do you do, Mr. Gibbons?"

Gibbons shrugged. Puhlman answered: "Mr. Gibbons has been involved with boxing, sir. We thought the government might be willing to put up money to sponsor a youth tourney, you know, help young people."

"But you're a psychiatrist," said Woodhouse. "What do you know about boxing?"

"Not much, sir, but I do know how having a sport can be good for young people, help get their heads straight, avoid drugs, that sort of thing."

"The man who shot Senator Mortinson was a boxer."

"I know," said Puhlman. "When Dr. Borger started working with him to cure his headaches so he could go back into the ring, it gave us the idea of looking for government money."

"Who did you meet with in Washington?"

"We didn't," replied Puhlman. "We decided after we got there that the project we'd come up with wasn't ready to be presented to anybody. You know, it needed more work, so we hung around a few days, took in the sights like the Air and Space Museum, and flew back."

"Where did you stay in Washington?"

"The Allen Lee Hotel, small and cheap. It was okay."

A check of the hotel records would confirm that they'd registered as guests there.

"You knew Mr. Itani from Dr. Borger's house and traveled with him to Washington where he intended to assassinate the senator."

"That's right. We just ended up on the same plane as him. We weren't traveling together. He said he was going to D.C. to arrange a boxing match. We got off the plane and he went his way and we went ours. He said he was staying downtown someplace, the Marriott, I think."

That would check out, too.

"Who could ever imagine that he was going there to kill the next president of the

United States?" Puhlman said. "You should hang the bastard."

The interrogation lasted for hours.

Woodhouse thought that Gibbons might crack, especially when the murder of Elena Marciano was raised. He pointed out that because it was Gibbons who'd rented the boat, he was the prime suspect in her killing. But the big former pugilist stuck with his story that they went fishing, and Woodhouse had nothing tangible to refute it.

The FBI was also brought in and tried to establish a connection between Puhlman and Gibbons's trip to Washington and the assassination, but the agents were no more successful than Woodhouse had been.

A representative of the prosecutor's office observed the interrogation through a one-way mirror. When it was obvious that little was to be accomplished, he told Woodhouse, "Let them go. You don't have anything to hold them on unless you want to charge them with using false identification to breach airport security." The FBI special agent in charge of the San Francisco investigation of the Mortinson assassination conferred with Woodhouse, and she and the prosecutor agreed to dismiss Puhlman and Gibbons with the admonition that they were to remain in the city and were subject to recall.

And so Puhlman and Gibbons were released, with the vague, empty threat that the authorities weren't finished with them yet.

While all this was going on, Borger was busy burning papers in his fireplace. He'd shunned all media requests for an interview, as had been requested by the police and FBI, and had repeated the story of his connection with Itani to a steady stream of FBI special agents. The street in front of his house was a media circus; shifts of SFPD officers tried to maintain order and to keep the driveway from being blocked. At one point Borger told the agents, "This has to stop. I'm a prisoner in my own home. I have done everything possible to cooperate with you and to give you my professional insight into the mind of Senator Mortinson's killer. There is nothing more I can offer, and I would like to be able to leave here and go to my home in Bermuda. If you needed me for anything else, you would have no trouble contacting me there."

At one point, the FBI's San Francisco director told Woodhouse that Itani was repeatedly asking for Elena. "Looks like he doesn't know that she's dead," she commented.

"Maybe if he'd been around, she wouldn't be," was Woodhouse's ironic reply.

Itani was assigned an attorney and was formally charged with the murder of Senator George Mortinson. He pleaded not guilty. No matter how often he was questioned, no matter how aggressive the interrogations were, he continued to deny any memory of having traveled to Washington and shooting the senator. When asked about his relationship with Dr. Sheldon Borger, he would say only that the doctor had helped him overcome his headaches and that he had stayed at Borger's house during his time as a patient. His only nod to reality was when he stated that Mortinson had to die because he was a "Jew lover" and "an Israel lover."

And so it went during that days following the assassination. It was toward the end of the week that President Swayze announced that he was convening a blue-ribbon panel of distinguished Americans to examine all the facts as they surfaced and to determine whether Iskander Itani acted alone or was part of a cabal. The president concluded his televised speech with, "There have been irresponsible parties, including certain members of the media, that have fanned the flames of conspiracy, which accomplishes nothing more than setting an already anxious nation on edge. I ask every American to withhold judgment until this panel has been able to ascertain the facts."

Nic Tatum and Cindy Simmons watched President Swayze's announcement on TV at his apartment.

"I can see it coming," Tatum said. "Another whitewash like the Warren Commission Report. You read that piece in the *Post* today about how Itani claims he doesn't remember anything. Of course he doesn't. He's been *programmed* not to remember. Those two clowns who say they worked for Borger and flew with Itani to D.C. What a joke. What's wrong with these people? According to what I've read, they've been cleared by the bureau, released, just like

that, coming up with some phony statements that were probably concocted by
Borger himself." He punched his left palm
with his right fist. "How did Itani get the
gun into the rally, Cindy? He had to have
had help. This guy is a down-and-out former prizefighter who spends a week or so
with Borger and then has the wherewithal
to fly to D.C. and stay in a high-priced hotel like the downtown Marriott. Come on, I
may not be the smartest guy in the world,
but this is ludicrous. Sheila Klaus pays off
her mortgage with money allegedly from
some relative who died. Interesting that
the money came from Bermuda. Guess
who has a house in Bermuda? Dr. Sheldon Borger.

"Everybody's a lone nut, Oswald, James
Earl Ray, Sirhan Sirhan, and now Itani.
None of them had any help, none of them
were involved with anyone else. Crazy,
right?"

"I don't know," she said. "I just don't know.
Nobody knows."

"And this so-called blue-ribbon panel
will get to the bottom of it, tell the truth. Ha!
They'll claim that Itani acted on his own
because they don't want the nation to think

that we have cells right here in the good ol' U S of A that spawn political assassins, and by the way, sponsored by our own government."

"Did that journalist you spoke with this morning offer any suggestions?"

"Yeah, that I try and get more facts before I start accusing anyone. How do I do that? Did you read that statement from the CIA about Borger and his connection with them when they were asked about it? I loved that one line: 'Dr. Sheldon Borger has been instrumental in advancing science that has been extremely useful in our national defense.' Next they'll be giving the son of a bitch the Medal of Honor."

She wanted desperately to calm and comfort him, to say the magic words that would ease his frustration, but the words weren't there.

He also vented his frustration and anger to Mac and Annabel Smith, neither of whom had better luck calming him than Cindy had, nor did an afternoon putting his Micco SP26 aerobatic through its paces ease his upset.

The day after he'd gone flying, he called Cindy at work.

"I'm going out to see Sheila Klaus," he told her.

"Why?"

"Because if I can break through the control Borger has over her, I'll at least have something tangible to offer."

"Don't, Nic. Let it go. You're tilting at windmills."

"I have to."

"No, you don't. At some point someone will come forward and reveal something that you can work with. Until then—"

"Nobody has ever come forward about the other assassinations, Cindy, no one. Sheila Klaus knows what happened with Borger. If I can get her to shake him loose from her life, the truth can come out."

Her supervisor at Walter Reed stood in the doorway and indicated he needed to speak with her.

"Nic, I have to go," she said. "When are you planning on seeing her?"

"Today. I have patients until four and then I'll head there."

"I get off at five," she said. "I'll go with you."

"You're sure?"

"Yes, I'm sure. I'll be home by five thirty. Pick me up."

He was waiting at her apartment when she arrived from work. Fifteen minutes later they were on their way to Rockville.

"Maybe you'd better stay in the car," he suggested when they pulled up in front of Sheila's house. "She might be reticent to talk with a second person present."

She didn't argue. She'd hadn't come with him to be privy to what transpired between him and Sheila. She wanted no part of that. But she *did* want to be there to offer moral support, to be with him when his attempt to break through Sheila's barrier failed again, to hold his hand and tell him it was okay.

He exited the car and slowly approached the house. Cindy watched as he went to the front door and rang the bell. Moments later Sheila appeared. Cindy held her breath. Would he be summarily dismissed?

He wasn't. Sheila opened the door and Tatum followed her inside.

Sheila's willingness to invite him in took Tatum by surprise. He'd mentally prepared what he would say, how he would try to convince her to at least hear him out. But he didn't need to present those arguments. After he'd reminded her who he was, she'd simply said, "Come in," and walked into the living room.

"I'm here, Sheila," he said, "because . . . well, because you know about Senator Mortinson being shot and the part Dr. Borger played in it."

"Sit down," she said. "Would you like something to drink, a cocktail, coffee or tea?"

"No, thank you," he said and sat on a hassock in front of the couch. The ease with which he'd gained entry had thrown him and he had to regroup.

Sheila went into the kitchen. When she returned, she carried a glass of cola and sat on the couch. She was dressed in baggy tan cargo pants, a teal T-shirt, and red sneakers.

"I appreciate your seeing me like this," he said. "How have you been?"

"I've been fine," she answered. "You?"

"Me?" He laughed. "Thanks for asking. I've been fine, too. Well, that's not quite true. Sheila, I know what Dr. Borger has done to you, and it's important that the world know it, too. We can work together to expose him and rid you of the control he has over you. I'm sure you'd like that."

She fixed him in a stony stare.

He waited for a protest from her. Instead she said, "I'm listening."

Again he was taken aback by her lack of defensiveness. Buoyed by this turn of events, he said, "Will you let me hypnotize you, Sheila, the way I did when you were in police custody? It's the only way I can break the hold Borger has over you. He's an evil man, Sheila. He has to be stopped. Together we can—"

The change in her expression, the sudden cruel smile and the narrowing of her eyes, sent a chill up his spine. And then the change in her voice followed. "What makes you think she wants to do anything with you?"

"Carla?"

"Who do you think it is?"

"I *know* who it is. You're Carla."

"Aren't you smart."

"You're here to help Sheila. Right?"

"I always help Sheila. She always needs help." The laugh that came from her was demonic.

"Then work with me, Carla. Let's work together and—"

Carla reached into a pocket on her cargo pants and came out holding a small Smith & Wesson 638 Airweight revolver. She pointed it at Tatum.

"You don't need that, Carla," Tatum said, his pulse now racing, beads of sweat suddenly appearing on his forehead. "Put the gun away and let's talk about how we can both help Sheila."

In the car, Cindy Simmons looked at her watch. Nic had been inside for almost fifteen minutes. She could only assume that things were going well, which pleased her. There was a moment when she'd considered going to the door and seeing if she could join him. But she didn't want to do anything that might get in the way of his succeeding. She leaned her head against the back of the seat and closed her eyes. She'd wait forever as long as he was making progress. His obsession with Sheila Klaus, Sheldon Borger, and the assassination of George Mortinson threatened to derail their relationship. All she wanted was for Nic Tatum to find at least a modicum of peace and to return to what he'd always been, a contented, clear-thinking, loving man with whom she wanted to spend the rest of her days.

The sound that came from inside the house snapped her out of her reverie and caused her to sit up. It sounded like fire-crackers. Or could it be . . . ? Gunshots were always described as sounding like firecrackers. Four reports came in rapid succession.

She threw open the door and scrambled from the car, slipping as she did and falling to one knee on the pavement. She got up and ran to the house. Before she had gone up the front steps, a single report, the fifth, was heard from inside.

She pushed open the door. What she saw horrified her. Her mouth opened but no sound came from it. She felt faint and braced herself against the doorframe. Nic was on the floor, half his body on the has-sock, the other half sprawled in a grotesque, twisted position. Blood flowed freely from his chest and neck.

Sheila Klaus was slumped on the couch, a revolver in her hand. Blood from a single shot to her temple ran down her cheek and onto her neck.

EPILOGUE

In the years that followed, the assassination of Senator George Mortinson was added to the annals of political assassinations in the United States. Dozens of books would be written, none of them putting to rest the question of whether Iskander Itani acted alone or was part of a larger plot. A few movies would be made based upon the most sensational of the books, and a cottage industry of blogs and websites claiming that there had been a larger conspiracy were launched, each taking issue with the commission convened by President Swayze. That august body concluded after more than a year of interviews and examining the evidence that Iskander Itani, a demented young man whose rage was fueled by a hatred of Israel and all things Jewish, had acted alone. He was found guilty at his trial and would spend the rest of his days behind bars, his memory of what had transpired unavailable. His family was urged to return to Beirut for their safety, and Itani's mother and brothers heeded that advice.

Sheila Klaus's murder of Dr. Nicholas Tatum, and her suicide, would eventually be deemed exactly that, a murder-suicide. Cindy Simmons told the police why Tatum had gone to Sheila's house and how he was convinced that she'd been programmed by a physician connected with the CIA to run down Dr. Mark Sedgwick and had also apparently been manipulated into killing Tatum. Her claims were, of course, dismissed by the investigating authorities as representing a fantasy-infused imagination. The final report concluded that Tatum had forged an unhealthy relationship with Sheila Klaus during the time that she was held by the police for the Sedgwick murder, and he had harassed her into a fragile emotional state leading to the death of both. In other words, Tatum had brought about his own demise because of his unprofessional actions involving Ms. Klaus.

Mac and Annabel Smith were, of course, devastated by what had happened at the house in Rockville. Mac offered testimony to authorities that he hoped would bolster Cindy's explanation of what had happened and what was behind it. But all he could do was reiterate what Nic Tatum had told him. As an attorney, he knew that all it represented was hearsay, hardly capable of making a case for anything. Because of his excellent reputation in the legal community, he was treated with great respect, but his recounting of everything leading up to the murder-suicide in Rockville was politely dismissed.

The Smiths lost track of Cindy Simmons after a year. She'd quit her job at Walter Reed and left Washington for her hometown of Davenport, Iowa, where she went to work at a local hospital. She and the Smiths promised to stay in touch, but as often happens, action doesn't always match well-meaning promises. For weeks after Nic Tatum's funeral, Mac and Annabel lamented his passing and tried to make sense of it and everything surrounding it. They finally agreed not to torture themselves and to hope that someone, someday, would step forward and tell the truth about the Mortinson assassination and Tatum's death. They would never enjoy that satisfaction.

San Francisco Detective Duane Woodhouse retired from the SFPD without ever having brought Elena Marciano's killer to justice. It would haunt him throughout his retirement years.

Peter Puhlman would die of cancer eighteen months after leaving San Francisco.

Jake Gibbons moved to Los Angeles, where he landed a few bit parts in B movies until his alcoholism turned him into a stumbling drunk, who died when he rammed his car into a bridge abutment.

CIA psychiatrist Colin Landow enjoyed his retirement on his ranch in Oklahoma, where he raised quarter horses.

David Considine attended the funeral of his friend Nic Tatum and told Mac Smith immediately following it that Nic had possibly gone off the deep end in trying to link the CIA to illegal psychological experiments. When questioned by Smith about what Tatum had told him of the conversations he'd had with Considine, Considine dismissed it as Tatum hearing only what he wanted to hear. Smith took an immediate dislike to Considine and decided that Tatum's so-called friend was hardly that. But he also knew that his evaluation of him was irrelevant. Who knew what the truth was anymore except that it was a rare, precious commodity in Washington, D.C.

George Mortinson's running mate, Raymond Thomas, won what turned into a closer election than had Mortinson been the candidate. He was urged occasionally to reopen the investigation into the assassination, but he declined to do so until new, hard evidence was unearthed. It never was during his eight years in the White House.

And Dr. Sheldon Borger sold his Nob Hill mansion and Washington condo and moved permanently to Bermuda, where he was quickly absorbed into the island's upper stratum of society. That he'd been an assassin's psychiatrist made him a popular guest at dinner parties, where he fascinated the other guests with his profes-sional profile of and analysis into the mind of a killer.